BLOOD NUMBERS

C. F. KREITZER

Immortal Works LLC
1505 Glenrose Drive
Salt Lake City, Utah 84104
Tel: (385) 202-0116

Cover Art by Ashley Literski
http://strangedevotion.wixsite.com/strangedesigns

This book is a work of fiction. Names, characters, businesses, organizations, places, events and incidents either are the product of the author's imagination or are used fictitiously. Any resemblance to actual persons, living or dead, events, or locales is entirely coincidental.

ISBN 978-1-7349046-0-4 (Paperback)
ASIN B086Z5TNXC (Kindle Edition)

For Josh
The first donor.
The love of my life.

And to Linda, who loved books but never got to read mine.

I've had nightmares about my Blood Test Day before. But none of them started like this. None of them prepared me for the nightmare of reality.

The technician stands on my porch in his white lab coat with his black bag in hand. My mind goes blank. I blink over and over, willing myself to wake up, yet there he is, standing before me with unnatural precision and a purposeful stare.

Stitched over the pocket of his white coat are the giant red letters "DMR," like blood seeping from a wound. My sweaty palm slides against the wobbly door handle.

Why is he here? It's June. I'm not sixteen yet. My birthday isn't for another month. Surely this technician is mistaken, or lost, but the Division of Medical Resources doesn't make mistakes.

"Aston Vazeto?"

His pronunciation of my Hungarian name is close enough, so I nod. He eyes my body in a way that makes me shiver, and I cross an arm over my chest. My hair falls forward; I hide behind it hoping to mask my shock and fear.

This technician is older than I expected, and surely too old to be donating. His hair is graying on the sides and worry lines linger on his brow. The eerie donor smile that flashes across his face makes my heart quicken. All citizens like me are Donors to some degree, but he looks too healthy to still be donating at his age. Why, when I'm home alone, and weeks away from my Blood Test Day, is he here—without notification or preamble?

"I hope you don't mind." He puts his bag through the door and shimmies his way inside. "But I had another Donor to test today in your town, and thought I'd kill two birds with one stone."

The reference to killing anything has my stomach twisting, and I stand stupidly at the door with my mouth agape. All I can do is stare as he sets his bag on our scratched-up coffee table in the living room, throws back the buckle, and opens the bag's wide mouth.

"New Livonia is lovely, I must say. Most of my visits have been in Dearborn as of late, and I do miss the bustle of your enchanting market." He retrieves several small items and lines them up on the table: fluffy cotton balls, a tiny device resembling our miniport screens, and white bandage tape. "There's something about being this close to the Recipient walls that feels almost magical, especially New Detroit's wall. So close to the royal family."

Yes, he is much older if he still refers to our leaders as royalty. The decrepit Recipient leader, Adakin Malloy, lives with his son, grandson, and all other Recipients over the wall. The way our Donor population worships them sickens me.

The technician cuts his eyes to me and clasps his hands anxiously, as if to keep them from trembling. Why is *he* nervous? *I'm* the prey. It's *my* blood they want. I knew this day would come, but I thought there was still time to perfect my plan of escape.

Blood Test Day is meant to be spent with family, a celebration, bonding over the number of antibodies discovered in my blood to offer the sick Recipients. Lazuli and I had a foolproof plan that depended entirely on the chaos of that day, but now...?

I grip the door handle tighter, trying to make sense of why this day finds me so soon, so alone and vulnerable. Then again, perhaps it's better this way. Alone, maybe I can find a way to cheat the system without any witnesses. I finally release my grip on the handle, sweep my long hair up into a quick bun, and close the door behind me.

"Have a seat here, Donor." He points to our rocking chair.

I move stiffly across the floor and ball my fists to keep them from shaking. The nerve of calling me Donor already. I am *not* a Donor quite yet, and if I can help it, I never will be.

"Don't worry, it's just a tiny finger prick." He wipes at his shining brow. The last thing he retrieves is a black pen-like device. He stretches it apart with a click, like he's cocking a handgun. His breathing is wheezy, making my own panicked breathing increase.

I can't concentrate on how to get myself out of this. All I can do is stare as his trained hands move swiftly about, readying the bandage. He sits on the coffee table, wipes his brow again, and eyes the door. With an extended hand, he waits for my finger.

Think, Aston, think. Lazuli's voice is in my head, listing the possibilities we gave up on. All too risky. All too complicated. Her dramatic, dark eyebrows, pinched in worry, appear across my vision, and she seems to tell me, *Just run.* But how?

I wipe my hands on my jeans and hold out my finger. His clammy grip on my palm makes my stomach flip again. Maybe I can somehow alter the reading of my blood. Knock the device out of his hand or spill something on it. I look across the room to where my glass of water sits on the kitchen table. It should at least give me time to come up with a better plan.

"I'm thirsty," I say frantically, as if I've spent days in a desert prison begging my captor for water.

He already has the flat pen pushed up against the side of my middle finger. Blood pounds in my head as if it could get away from him. Not only does he ignore me, but he squeezes my hand tighter and pushes a button. Click! The sound vibrates in my ears. A sharp pinch shoots up my finger, and I yelp.

He grunts something that sounds like oops.

I look at him again. The balls of sweat on his temples protrude off his skin like scars. Is it supposed to hurt this bad? I grab at my forearm.

When he removes the device, I see it. Darker than I ever

imagined, my blood bulges bigger and bigger until it drips a warm sticky river down my finger. Just a tiny finger prick, huh? How much blood does he need?

As it sneaks into the webbing between my fingers, the smell of rust floats up to me and my stomach churns. I've been indoctrinated to believe this is what matters most: my mutant blood, the cure for Recipients still fighting an ancient virus from biological warfare. My whole life I've been jealous of it, angry at the attention my blood gets, determined to be something more. But here in this rare moment, all alone with my blood spilling before me, I find it remarkable. That something so simple, so ordinarily beautiful, can hold so much power.

The technician fumbles with the handheld miniport and drops it. The crashing sound brings me to my senses. I must act fast. When he bends to retrieve it, I try to pull my hand from his grasp, but he tightens his grip even further. It hurts where his thumb nail digs deeper into my palm. He doesn't speak, only moves faster as if he's racing someone.

My head feels disconnected from my body for a moment as my blood now pools around his thumb. "That's a lot of blood, technician." My voice sounds funny—quiet and distant. Too much blood. This isn't right. Something splashes against my bare legs and I notice my blood is dripping, forming a small, dark puddle on our newly polished floorboards.

Gurgling sounds echo through the room. The miniport device is pushed up against my messy finger and sucking the blood off my skin like a mechanical vampire.

"No," I say faintly, realizing it's too late to do anything. The nauseating scents are too much. The sounds tunnel away from me. All I can think to do is run, but when I stand, my head swirls and the floor rushes to greet me. Everything goes black. The black is even darker than my blood.

THE SOUND of a zipper wakes me. My eyes flutter open, I'm stretched out on my sofa with both hands folded neatly over my chest like I'm lying in a coffin. I turn my head to see the technician picking up his black bag.

"Ah, there you are, Donor," he says with a carefree sigh. "Took quite a spill."

When I sit up, pain fills my head, pushing against my skull, threatening to explode. I lean my forehead into my hands and wince.

"Careful. You hit your head pretty hard."

I remember trying to get away. I bring my hand down in front of me. My palm is clean, and a thin white piece of tape is wrapped around my middle finger. I stare at it as I fall back into the sofa, then look to the floor where the puddle of blood was. The floor is pristine, glistening even. Did I imagine the puddle? The pain in my finger, throbbing against the tight bandage, says otherwise.

"I think it was all worth it, though." He grins broadly as he hands over a small slip of paper.

I numbly take it from him.

"Just take this note to your nearest donation facility and they will assign you your place in line. And good luck at the auctions. I'm excited to see what they bring for you." He steps to the door, seeming anxious to get away, then turns back to me with a quick wink. "Congratulations, Donor. That's a number worth celebrating."

With a loud thud, he shuts the door. The word "celebrating" lingers in the air like a mean joke. There's no one to celebrate with; I'm alone. And there's nothing to celebrate; I'm defeated. The numbers printed in red on the little white slip of paper seem to shout at me. Traitor. Failure. Donor. What will Lazuli say? She'll be furious. In all our scheming, we never thought of an escape out of the donations *with* test results. We were never supposed to make it this far in the first place, never have a number to tempt our families. How am I to convince my family now since they know what I could offer them?

I scan the room that seems emptier and lonelier than before. So still. It's as if no one ever came and nothing ever happened. Staring at the closed door with its chipped paint and dents, it dawns on me that no one knows the technician came. No one knows my numbers but me. Is there still a chance to escape donating?

I let out a slow breath, thinking of the possibilities, considering the risks. Of course Papa will understand, but Mam will want the money. Maybe Papa will help me. He says my paintings are good—perhaps I could open a booth on the market street. If I could change New World history, be the first Donor to never donate and still make money, maybe even Mam will be ok with the news. I cringe at the thought and ball up the paper in my fist. Mam will never accept such negotiations.

Someone pounds up the stairs of the porch, and I rip the white tape from my finger, stuffing it, plus the note, into my back pocket. My eyes narrow when I look at my bare finger where a chunk of flesh is missing out of the side. Just a finger prick. Right. The sight makes my head throb, and when I grab at it, I discover a giant goose-egg near my temple.

The door handle wobbles and clunks in place. Quickly I tug at my ponytail, letting my wild, yellow hair spill across my face. I jump to my feet, teetering in place as Mam enters the house.

"Good gracious, child, you startled me. What are you just standing there for?" She grabs at her chest for emphasis, her brown hair pulled up too tightly in a bun, making her eyes slanted and angry looking. Mam is always angry. She balances brown paper bags in one arm, and her blue, floral skirt spins out behind her as she turns to shut the door. "Well, don't just stare at me like you've got nothing better to do. Help your mammy with these groceries."

I stare into Mam's cold gray eyes as I approach her, and though keeping a secret from Mam is never an easy feat, I feel it in my bones —in my blood—that she can never know about my numbers. She will never understand why I hate the system so much. But Papa will. Papa, who taught me the truth about what goes on at the facility, about the drugs that keep Donors happy and complacent. Papa, who taught me the ways of an old economy not separated by illness and the cure.

I take the bags from Mam and tip my head down to shade my face. Papa will know what to do. My blood is still mine. For now.

I fell asleep last night with contraband in my hands. An approved history book, *New America: A Geographical Timeline of the Last Biological Warfare*, lies heavily against my chest. I've had all the schooling available to a Donor, and our history books are mostly rubbish according to Papa, but the crumbling paperback novel hidden in the cut-out pages is why I treasure the large textbooks. The novel is missing the cover and first few pages, and from the worn spine, all I can make out is the name "Austen." It's my favorite, though, and I often try to guess what Austen's title would have been. *First Impressions* maybe or *The Daughter's Bennet*. The descriptions of outrage and passion intrigue me in a world of emotionless Donors and repressive Recipients.

The smell of bacon filters through my door, followed by an eerie cloud of smoke, and an unpleasant flip in my stomach. It brings back memories of my older sisters' Blood Test Days. Days that only meant good food and visits from Grandma Bolgi. Now it means something else. It means I'm officially sixteen, an adult in the eyes of the law. It means I can no longer hide the fact that my Blood Test Day already happened, and that I don't plan to donate.

My sisters arrive downstairs, already reprimanding their children. Torrin's door swings open, hitting my wall, and his feet thump down the hallway. He stops by my door first, poking his head in.

"You asleep?" my younger brother whispers, struggling to contain his excitement. His dusty brown hair sticks up in the back like a fish fin, and his sleepy face has imprints of wrinkled sheets across it.

"With you in the house?"

"I can't believe you're just lying there. I mean, I know donations aren't your favorite thing but...Aston, the food. Can't you smell that?" He closes his eyes and takes a deep breath. The smell summons him, and he closes my door without another word.

Lying to him has been the hardest. My stomach lurches with the thought of finally revealing my secret.

I pull back the covers, unveiling my legs, and look down at them. Ugly, scabbed knees and calloused feet stare back at me. How will Mam dress up these tom-boyish features in ball gowns and heels for blood auction parties? More importantly, how will I convince her I don't want any part of them? How will I assure her that I will not parade myself around at pre-auction balls or in front of the camera droids just to boost my ranking in the country's catalog?

I pull out the technician's note from that strange day and run my fingers over the numbers on the soft, worn paper. I've kept it safe and hidden from Mam for weeks now, always with the promise to tell Papa, but never the nerve. Secrets have nasty ways of ripping us of courage over time.

I scoot to the edge of the bed, grab the jeans from yesterday, and slide my legs through. Throwing on a black T-shirt, I flip my hair out of the collar as I hear Mam greet Lazuli at the front door. Heat rises up my neck at the sound of her voice. We said we'd never donate, but I knew the moment she did. The goofy Donor grin was hard to miss. Recipients drug the Donors somehow. It's the only way to keep them going back and make them so eternally happy.

"Aston, Lazuli's here," Mam yells up the stairs.

Leaving my room, I roll the doctor's note up and stuff it in my back pocket, telling myself it's the last time I'll do so. I grip the rickety railing to the stairs, trying to level my breathing before I go down.

Letting the splintered wood dig into my palm distracts me and clears my mind. I can do this.

Scanning over the family photos on the wall as I descend the stairs, I catch my sisters' Auction Day photos staring back at me. I stop when I am eye level with the portrait of my eldest sister, Sybil. Her hair is beautiful, nothing like my straw-colored hair that sticks out in all the wrong places. Sybil's brown curls frame her high cheekbones and pointed chin. Her makeup is perfect, with dark eyeliner that accentuates her almond eyes, the only part of her lovely face that resembles me. Her blood made history in our small New Detroit town several years ago. She was tenth in the nation in the catalog and gained a high bid and contract of twenty thousand a year for only two donations a week. She didn't get all the vacation days she wanted, though her lawyer fought the Recipient Ambassador for them.

I don't understand how anyone with that much money can complain, but Sybil always finds a way. When she married Derek a year after auctions, she entered a new marriage contract, which Mam was nervous would affect us, but with twenty thousand a year, there is still plenty to make its way to our family. Too much in Sybil's opinion.

I take another step, looking at Ari's Auction Day portrait, and smile, remembering how she threw up on Mam right before the photo was taken.

Next is poor Shannon smiling back at me with the same wild hair as mine though a darker blonde. Her low numbers didn't bring much to begin with, and they bring even less now that she's married to a facility maintenance worker.

Marriage is the only way for low-numbered Donors to make it. It's the reason I love the books I manage to find in rubble and smuggle into the house. They speak of a world where matches and marriages had less to do with the sum of two Donors' numbers and more to do with something these reticent Donor hearts know nothing about. Love.

My heart sinks when the last step creaks beneath my feet. The old wood, a loose board that for some reason Papa never fixed, sags and protests. Maybe it has something to do with Mary's portrait that stares back at me through the long crack in the glass. In the photo, her eyes were already sunken with dehydration, and at the sight of them, ghost memories play across my mind. She donated like it was a religion yet refused to have the glory. Insisting on never attending the balls, where high-numbered Donor families watch the televised auction, and never entering the auctions is what kept Mary dependent on the daily pay of the regular donations. The strain of such little pay kept her returning so often, and everyone knows death is the imminent risk of donating that much without a contract. Thanks to Mary, who lost Mam a fifth paycheck with her radical views, it'll be especially hard to convince Mam she doesn't need my blood money.

I brush my hand over the note in my pocket and convince myself there is nothing to feel guilty or scared about. These photos prove it. Thanks to my other sisters, the family is doing fine. We've never been better. We don't need my blood to live on. Sure, there's no market for artwork anymore, but I'm going to change that somehow. They'll see.

Taking the last step into the living room, Lazuli's giant smile lights up the room. It's not a pleasant sort of light, but the kind that hurts and draws your hand to your face to shield your eyes. Our plans are ruined now that it's clear she is a Donor and going to auctions. I'm alone. She wears the smile of a traitor.

"Aston, aren't you just so excited for today?" Lazuli bounces in place by our brown sofa. "Do you know what time they're coming?"

Coming? I try not to grimace as I recall the technician's surprise visit.

"Yeah. Exciting," I say, trying to smile.

"Don't be nervous." She misreads my worry. "It's not much blood, you know, just a little finger prick."

She steps closer to me, drawing together her dark eyebrows that match her black hair.

"I know," I say. Believe me, I know. My stomach rolls at the memory of the "small prick" of blood. I'm glad no one was there for my Blood Test Day. A Donor who's afraid of blood? I can almost hear Mam's laugh at the irony.

"Okay, well, I just wanted to wish you good luck." Lazuli puts her hands behind her back. A sadness grips my chest. The old Lazuli would have given my arm a squeeze or a genuine hug. Donors try to avoid touch. I have spent my life analyzing the changes in friends and family, yet this one feels more cruel. What kind of relationship exists with no human contact?

"And I wanted to give you this." She pulls her hands from behind her back, producing an envelope. The recycled Donor paper is bumpy and speckled, making it look like it's celebrating my special day with confetti.

"Thanks, Laz." I open the small envelope and look up at her pale, angelic face. Her brown eyes dance with something sparkling in them that wasn't there before. My real friend is under there somewhere. I pull out a small, purple card.

Inside is a fingerprint on top of a dot of blood and a small written message: *To Aston on her Blood Test Day.*

I narrow my eyes to keep them from rolling. How long did it take her little, drugged heart to come up with that touching note? I may have failed at escaping the initial blood test, but I didn't rush off to the facility the first chance I got. And to think I was worried about her being angry at me if she found out. Lazuli couldn't be angry now if she wanted to be. I recall the smile that crept over her face weeks ago when I visited her: eerie like the technician and frozen in place like all Donors. It was the first sign that something was wrong, the first hint that her fight was over—she was a Donor on the fast track to auctions.

"It's a gift card," she says. "I convinced my mom to let me give you a little of my donation money. I thought maybe we could go to the mall this week. There's a new drink there I heard about."

I stare at the blot of blood that, if scanned, can access her blood bank. I will myself not to argue with her. Drinks? Blood cards and donation money that we can't really access without permission? These were things we made fun of before. What a difference one short month can make. Does she not remember those days at all? I can't seem to move my eyes away from the red dot, so I slap the card shut to break the trance.

"Thanks," I say stiffly.

After a small, familiar knock on the front door, Grandma Bolgi steps through it and a sigh escapes me. I say a quick goodbye to Lazuli to greet the woman most like myself. With her own straw hair that has morphed to a silvery white, she smiles and puts her arms out toward me. Just the sight of her brings to mind stories of barefoot days, happier times, and blood-free years before the Germ Wars. She hugs me so tight I think she may squeeze all the nerves right out of me. Sinking into her warm, peppermint scent, I sigh again at the gravel of her laugh that vibrates in her chest.

"Are we a bit nervous about today, Little Ash Tree?" she says with her familiar thick accent and strokes the length of my hair.

"A little," I confess. If only she knew it was Mam who I am most afraid of.

Mam shouts, and we all gather around the table obediently. For every Blood Test Day and Auction Day party, Mam brings out the same red tablecloth. Sitting at the breakfast table, I fidget with the hem of it and listen to the guesses that move around the room of what my numbers will be. Ari and Derek guess one hundred and one, the same as Sybil, and she rolls her eyes at them. Sybil may be the only person I wish was still donating more often and getting more of whatever makes them happy. With each child Sybil bore, her contract was amended, returning her to her old sour self.

Torrin guesses close to my actual numbers, and my cheeks are on fire when everyone laughs. From middle grade health classes to brochures to my sisters flaunting contracts, I have been prepared to be a Donor my whole life. My parents were both Donors and theirs before them, except for Grandma Bolgi, my Papa's mother. I look across the table at her. Deep wrinkles etch her face from years of smiling. Having survived so long with a useless blood number of only fifteen, Grandma Bolgi's wink gives me hope. She told me once about a day when her blood type of O negative was a universal Donor, rare and valued. Since the Germ Wars, the type of ones' blood matters less than the quality of the plasma. Grandma never donated but married a high-numbered Donor. I will show there's a way out of donating other than marriage. I won't let someone else bleed for me anymore than I will bleed for a stranger.

The bacon smoke still floats in the air, making this scene feel like a dream. Or maybe another nightmare. The chatter dips and waves with intensity. When is the right moment to explain that this party is in vain?

Soon, my plate is full of foods that most of our community never sees in their life. I stare at it with guilt for having so much when others have so little, yet comforted since it will only make my news easier to bear. We don't need my blood to survive.

"Don't worry, Aston," Papa reaches out and gives my shoulder a squeeze. "We are all here for you. It won't be so bad." I see him give Grandma Bolgi a smile.

Staring into Papa's blue eyes that match my own, I search for a way out of this ordeal. Maybe I should wait. Pull Papa off to the side and tell him. Let him break the news to everyone. He and Grandma Bolgi will understand, but not this table of bloodletting sisters and an auction-loving Mam.

"Did you drink plenty of water, Aston?" Mam says with a mouth full of strawberries.

I look away from her just before she wipes at the red juice sneaking out of the corners of her mouth.

"No," I say.

"Patar, put some water on the table. She must have water before the test. I'm sure she has stingy veins like all the other girls."

Papa's wooden chair scraping against the wooden floor makes my heart race.

"I don't need water," I squeak, barely heard over the commotion. The talking dies down from my back talk. Papa freezes in place, looking down at me. The only sounds are the news reporter on the screen behind us and my nieces and nephews who haven't learned to fear Mam quite yet.

"Of course you do," Mam says with a laugh. "That poor technician today will be poking and squeezing that finger of yours forever if you're dehydrated. Patar..." She waves her hand at Papa.

He steps away, and I take a deep breath to speak quickly before Papa leaves the room. I need him here.

"I don't," I insist. Papa stops in his tracks. I take another breath, hoping to somehow speak up through the strangling lump in my throat. "I don't need any water because there won't be any technician."

"Aston, you—" Papa says.

"Not today at least." I look at Grandma. Her old eyelids sag slantways over her eyes. There's more than just wisdom in her eyes. There's confusion now and concern.

I stare at her as I speak. "There won't be a technician today because he already came. I already have my blood numbers."

The room has entered a sort of time warp and everyone is stuck in an unknown world. No one knows what to say or do or who to look at. The sound of the news playing over the screen in the background bounces through the room and the news anchor's flamboyant voice seems to mock our dramatic scene.

"How long?" Papa finally says.

"A few weeks." I look down at my hands, unable to make eye contact.

Time finally catches up with everyone in the room, and a flood wall of questions descends.

"Have you started donating?"

"What are your numbers?"

"What were you thinking?"

"Why didn't you tell anyone?"

I don't answer any of them, only twist my head back and forth between each family member. When Mam speaks, the whole room shushes.

"What are your numbers, child?"

Mam will be happy with my numbers, but it's the news that I will never donate that will be hard for her to bear. This is all happening out of order, but time's rushing by without my control. I look around at the wide eyes before I answer.

"A hundred and fifty-seven."

A tickling silence hushes over the room. Torrin lets out a whoop first, ushering in the hollering and whistling and clapping. Derek looks to his wife, as if Sybil will need consoling after such news. Mam shouts and is close to tears when she puts both hands to her mouth like she is praying. Grandma Bolgi's face turns bright red, and I see a look pass between her and Papa again.

"How could you keep something like this from us?" Papa roars. My head shoots up to his outraged face. I have never heard him so angry, even at Mam. The cheers around the table dim.

"I—"

Grandma Bolgi takes a turn yelling next. "You should have told someone when that technician came, Aston."

The way she shouts my name carves a hole in my chest. She has never spoken to me like this. Her already shaky, old voice now quivers with anger. Or is it fear? My shoulders slump as she continues.

"Technicians are *not* supposed to come before you're SIXTEEN!" Her voice rises with each word, and only a small part of me can make sense of what she is saying. Of course I knew technicians weren't supposed to come before then, and it did seem odd to come unannounced, but I was a bit preoccupied with my blood pooling on the floor. I look back and forth between Papa's creased brow and Grandma's frightened face. Why do they seem so worried? These two are supposed to be the understanding ones.

What are they afraid is going to happen? They just need to hear my plans. Then they will calm down.

"Who cares with numbers like that!" Mam shouts, and the room cheers in agreeance.

I yell overtop of them, frantic for Papa and Grandma Bolgi to hear me.

"I don't plan to donate!"

Sybil, the only one not marveling over my numbers, laughs out loud.

"What?" Mam shrieks.

"I don't plan to donate." I lift my head confidently. "Not today. Not ever."

"Oh, you'll donate." Mam stands so fast her chair shoots out behind her and teeters on its legs like a seesaw.

"Evelyn..." Papa steps toward her but stops when Mam puts a hand in the air.

"Just what do *you plan* to do then, Aston?" Mam sneers.

"Well, we don't really need my donations now, and I hope to sell some of my paintings in the trade store and—"

"Your paintings? Ha." Mam steps away from the table.

"Are you crazy?" Sybil shouts, but I don't take my eyes off Mam.

She marches toward me, and Papa lunges for her.

"Evelyn..." Papa tries again.

"Don't you 'Evelyn' me! I knew I was wrong to let you encourage this childish obsession with drawing! It's *your* fault these ideas are in her head. It's *your* fault she thinks she can waltz through this town better than any Donor and hating Recipients!"

"I do hate Recipients!" I shout at her and stand, feeling the weeks and years of secrets charging through my legs like rocket fuel shooting a jet in the air. "All of you should! They take our blood and our money and our freedom—"

"How can you say that, you ungrateful child? They put that food on your plate, that you're evidently too good to eat. Recipients are sick. They need us, and we need them!"

"They blackmail us, Mam! Into sympathy, into poverty. They do it so we feel there's some mutual need for each other! But I've never even seen a Recipient! Have you?" When Mam's mouth opens, I don't give her a chance to interrupt. "No, 'cause we're separated under penalty of death. They're like mythical creatures who exist only on our port screens during auction season. How do we even know what they're doing with our blood when they take it over that wall?"

"You watch your mouth, child," Mam whispers. "You'll put us all in jail with this talk of treason!"

Before Mam finishes the word "treason," a ring trills through the room, letting us know a call is coming in. We all grow silent and turn to see the news on the screen in the living room shift into an image of Greg, one of Papa's head electricians. He is holding his ears and screaming into the receiver.

"Patar, we need you! There's been an accident. I've—"

The sound cuts out and the screen flickers, distorting his picture, and sometimes doubling his image. There's nothing but red and orange lights behind him. His face is back again, and we hear bits of his sentences, "—A stranger—a Recipient—"

The screen flickers again, and the room falls silent. After another secretive look passes between Grandma and Papa, he scowls at me and points to the screen. "*This* is why *you* should have told us, Aston." His whisper is gruff with anger.

Me? How is whatever's happening at the plant my fault? I open my mouth to protest, but the screen flickers to life again. The room glows red and orange. Greg's next words "—slag tank—" though disjointed and fleeting don't make sense to anyone else in the room except the girl who spent her days at her Papa's power plant. A cold terror races up from my toes as I realize what the red and orange in the background finally mean: molten slag, iron lava. A slag tank must have exploded somehow, making the plant more like an active volcano.

Papa rushes out of the room without speaking to anyone,

including Greg on the screen, and Mam shouts after him. The door slams, and we all watch the flickering images in horror: a silent film of destruction.

When a clear image of Greg appears again, I run toward the screen and shout to him. "He's on his way!" I say, gripping the rocking chair in front of me. I want to yell again. How is this my fault? What do my blood numbers have to do with this? Recipients aren't allowed anywhere near the Donors, or vice versa. It's too dangerous. They could infect us, jeopardizing the cure, or we could weaken their already pathetic immune systems killing them with one measly cold. Why were they at the plant? Why would they risk their lives to do this? I yell at Greg louder this time. "He's coming!"

The image on the screen shrinks to a small orange line before it darkens completely. A low rumble cracks in the distance like thunder, and the ground trembles, making the floorboards creak as if Papa was stomping across them. Papa! I run past the pictures on the wall that rattle and the plates on the table that tinkle like wind chimes. Papa is my only thought as I swing open the door. I jump down the porch steps and dodge the memorized piles of broken road by our house.

Our streets fill with people as neighbors gather to find the source of the explosion and gawk at the black tail of smoke trailing from the plant. I'm frozen, staring at it as well.

My head spins, and my legs feel weak. I grab at a streetlamp to steady myself. Why were Grandma Bolgi and Papa so frightened and angry instead of supportive about my news? Did they know this would happen? And Recipients at the plant—what does it mean? I let my heavy head fall sideways on the cold metal of the green streetlamp. The coolness makes the spinning in my head more bearable. I shut my eyes, remembering the way Papa looked at me. What have I done?

THREE

When another explosion pulses through the air and makes the lamp I hold vibrate, I'm suddenly very aware of everything happening around me. I push off and run. Swerving through murmuring neighbors, I look up at the new cloud they point at. The billowing black smoke grows upward, and I can't take my eyes off it. As I draw closer to it, I can smell the pungent burning iron. People are running in the opposite direction, and I collide with someone. My head bangs against their hard chest, and I feel myself falling backwards as if in slow motion.

"Don't you people know what 'orderly fashion' means?" the stranger's voice calls out as his warm, bony hands grab at my arms. "More people die from stampedes than fires every year."

When I regain my balance, he yanks his hands away as if my skin's the one burning hot. We stand so close I can smell his laundry soap floating off his clothes, and the growing morning sun makes his golden hair almost glow. His hair shades his face so I can't make any features out other than a hard, square chin.

"Thanks," I say, turning my attention to the fire. The people coming our way are coughing and covered in soot. I step towards the fire when the stranger grabs at me again.

"What, are you crazy?"

There's something familiar about his voice, but when I look over my shoulder at him, he drops my arm and turns away. He's afraid. Of the fire? Or of me? I watch his retreating back for only a moment before facing the flames again.

Officers have arrived now with their black droids floating over their shoulders. A red laser beam shoots out from the bobbing disks and creates one long red line along the ground in front of the officers. The line moves forward with each of their steps.

"Move back," an officer yells and makes eye contact with me. "Let them do their job. Return to your homes; we'll keep you updated on any evacuations."

The red line dances close to me, and I step back. I want to shout out that my papa's down there somewhere, that they need to get him, they need to save him, but when the light comes only inches away from my feet, I sense the electric heat coming off the lasers and have no choice but to turn back home.

It's the middle of the night when Papa comes up the stairs. My chest heaves with relief when I hear those giant boots shuffle heavily past my door. Down the hallway, my parents argue in whispered yells, but our walls are too thin. I hear everything they're saying. Papa's voice trails toward me and my ears tingle with strain. He pushes through choking emotion as he blames the Recipients for the "accident." Mam discredits everything he says with the same lies the news reported earlier this evening: reports that the plant ignored safety regulations and failed to pass New Detroit's safety inspection. The plant is now under investigation as to why Detroit Electric failed to comply when warnings were given.

"I'm the head electrician, Evelyn! I'm the one they're saying ignored the warnings. But those failed safety inspections don't even exist. No one ever comes to check our plant."

"Watch your voice, you'll wake the kids," Mam hisses.

"It was the Recipients, Evelyn. They sent a technician to our house early to test Aston without notification; they knew her blood numbers, and when she didn't donate they—"

"Hush."

Mam's voice sounds weird to me—like I'm in a foggy tunnel trying to make sense of Papa's words. Of course Recipients would want my numbers once they knew how high they were. Hadn't I yelled the very answer to my question at breakfast so long ago? "The Recipients blackmail us." Someone sent Recipient spies to the plant to punish us for my not donating. My neck aches from lying tense in bed and my head starts to pound as I strain to hear more.

"Listen to yourself, Patar, you're worse than the gossips at the market. You know no such thing."

"You heard Greg yourself."

"You never did get to speak to him, did you?" Her words sting and punch through the air. We all know the answer. Greg is dead. "You don't know what he saw. What we *do* know is this accident has made national news, and it will not be quickly forgotten."

There is a long pause as this news settles in.

"How much money will we lose? How many workers were lost today?" Mam's formality and unmerciful focus seems to sober Papa. His voice is so low I shift in the bed, leaning closer to the wall to try and make out his answer.

"Fifteen."

Mam's gasp echoes through my head.

Papa continues, "Fifteen men not with their families tonight."

"And the—" Mam doesn't care about the families, she cares about the money, and Papa obliges.

"The fine will be massive, Evelyn. The whole company will be docked harshly. I've already lost my entire paycheck."

There's nothing else said. After a long silence, a door shuts, and I picture Mam locking herself in the bathroom.

I roll over in bed staring out my window. The smoke from the power plant fire that has been out for hours lingers in the bright moonlit sky. My day started in smoke and ends in smoke. Nothing happened how I thought it would. Fifteen deaths? Because of me. Because of my blood. My blood that is boiling now at what the Recipients have done. I shut my eyes tight and bring my knees up close to my chest. When my door creaks open, I keep my eyes closed and don't move.

"Aston?" Papa's voice is scratchy from the fire.

I saw him on the news being the hero that he is. Pulling men out of the plant and helping douse the flames. He probably feels guilty for not being there today. I am what kept him from going. I killed people with my naive misconception of what my life could be, but I also kept him alive.

His hand is in my hair, and he sniffles. Has he been crying? Or perhaps more irritation from the fire.

"What were you thinking?" he whispers, believing me asleep.

Gee, I don't know, Papa. Maybe I was thinking about the time you told me the power to choose is a human's greatest distinction, what makes us separate from the animals. Maybe I was thinking you meant something more when you told me my paintings were masterpieces and explained how the old-world economy used to work. You raised me to think for myself without warning me of the consequences.

"I don't want to donate," I whisper back.

The springs of the old hand-me-down mattress squeak as he sits on it behind me.

"So, the rebel is awake then?"

I don't face him, only grip the pillow underneath my cheek. "I'm sorry. I—"

"Shh. You won't have to donate if you don't want to, Aston." His exaggerated sigh makes the bed jostle and squeak again. "I just wish you would've come to me first. It's going to be harder now that you have your real numbers already. Grams and I could have..."

I roll over to finally hear what was transpiring silently between those two all morning, but he stops.

"It's just going to be harder now, but we'll help you." He cups my cheek, and it's that brief weary emotion wavering on the end of his words that keeps me from drilling him with questions.

The bright moon casts a gray glow around the room. Through the darkness, I can see Papa's worn face. Moonlight shines through his thinning blond hair, making his scalp glisten and his cheekbones shimmer from fading tears. The smoke smell cascading off of him burns my nose and eyes. "You don't have to donate," he says again. He kisses my forehead before staggering, drunk from exhaustion, out of the room.

I stare at the door after he leaves only to see a shadow cast along the thin line of light underneath. The door cracks open.

"Aston?" Torrin whispers.

The arguing must have kept him up too. I scoot over on the bed and pat the brown linen blanket beside me for him to come in. He doesn't hesitate and shuts the door behind him. Twelve is too old to let me snuggle him like I used to, so I keep my distance when he curls up beside me and puts a hand under his face.

"Why didn't you tell anyone?" he says.

I know he's really asking why I didn't tell him. I was the son Papa never had until Torrin came along, making us more like brothers. I tousle his hair, knowing how much he hates it, and think of what to tell him. His questioning blue eyes, like Papa's, like mine, like Grams', they all seem to stare back at me through this young boy's gaze.

"I was scared," I say, "that no one would understand."

"Understand that you don't want to donate? Was it because of your numbers? You thought Mam would want them too much?"

"Mam wouldn't understand no matter what my numbers were." I can't help but growl the words. Looking back at Torrin, I feel the need to teach him what Papa taught me. "But it's more than just the numbers, Torrin." I put my own hand under my cheek so we are face to face on my pillow. "It's about being more than just my blood. It's about choosing my own life."

"You mean choosing your paintings."

I hear the words *instead of helping us* at the end of his sentence, but that's what Mam would say. There's still time to help Torrin see that he could do more with his love of architecture and mathematics than the Recipients would have him believe.

"Yes. I want to be recognized for something more than what runs under my skin without my control. I want to make my own choices with my body no matter how much someone says it's worth. I want to be my own master."

"What about the Recipients?"

"What about them, Torrin?" I roll onto my back, look up to the ceiling, and sigh. "They're sick, I get it. There are so many more Donors than Recipients though, they should be fine. They have their pick of blood. There's no reason they need to monopolize Donor blood in a way that keeps us so poor. It's all an economical game they play with us. Did you know that before the wars donating used to be something people volunteered to do?"

"Yeah, and lots of people died."

"Donors die," I say defensively.

"Because they donate too much."

I hoist myself up onto my elbow and look down at him. "And why do you think they donate so much, huh? Because they need the money. If every Donor got paid the same amount for donating maybe they wouldn't donate so much. But it's Recipients' plan, it seems, to weed out the low-numbered Donors by paying so much at auctions for high-numbered ones. Maybe they should be the ones plucked off the planet."

"Aston—"

"No. They're the weak ones, Torrin. They're the ones that still have the virus in them from the wars and depend on this poor band of refugees to survive. They depend on us, yet they're in control. How does that make any sense? They may have the technology, money and officers that give them power, but let something as simple as natural selection take over on *them* and see how they survive it. See? They force this life on Donors but can't swallow the same treatment. What makes them better than a Donor, Torrin? Or why not at least allow a normal market and Donors to own land and build upon their dreams? We can't even have our own bank accounts without Recipients monitoring and their approval."

A small squeak escapes him. I hadn't realized I sat up in my bed.

"I just wanted to know why you didn't tell." His voice is tiny, like he's lost in my blankets, and on the verge of tears.

I lay down again next to him and put a hand on his cold arm. "I'm sorry," I say. What a rotten, insensitive big sister I've been. It's like I'm a drugged Donor already. The excitement, the arguing, the traumatic accident at the plant—this day has been long for all of us. "I should have told you all sooner. It's going to be okay though, Torrin. You'll see." I don't think he sees at all, but I feel him relax under my hand anyway. "Hey, remember when we broke Shannon's bed trying to build a fort?"

His giggle soothes my worries.

"I really thought you put the bed back together right," I say.

"The way she screamed when it fell apart on her..." he says through another round of laughter before he sobers. "Mam was so mad she almost—"

"But she didn't. See? I got us out of that mess of trouble, and somehow I'll get us through this."

"The Recipients are worse than Mam, Aston."

"I don't know about that."

Torrin gives one last little laugh before he rolls over and out of the bed.

Just before he shuts my door, he turns back to me. "I hope you know what you're doing, Aston." He says it like he's years older than me, and in some ways, I suppose he is. It happens to all Donors. Expected to mature years ahead of schedule for the sake of being a savior of Recipients.

It's several more hours before I'm able to cease my worried thoughts and rid my body of tension. Right before the smoke of dreams creeps its way into my mind, I recall my Papa's words as he sat on my bed. What did he mean by "real numbers"?

The muffling screeches of Mam's angry voice have me standing by my door, unwilling to go down to breakfast. It's surprising she hasn't lost her voice from yelling now for four weeks straight. Not a single one of my paintings has sold in the market, and the funny stares of passersby are draining my hopes. As silence hushes over the house, a heavy sigh gets me moving, and I clomp down the stairs.

The tension in the air is so thick and taut I bet it would bleed if stabbed with a needle. Bleed like my finger that is now healed, whole and no longer needs to hide in my pocket. There's no bacon anymore. The only smells floating on the air are the chemicals from Mam's cleaning that sting my nose. Bangs and clanks sound from the kitchen. Papa and Torrin sit silently at the table. Torrin's hair is combed neatly, and he holds his spoon in the air over his bowl, letting the lumpy mush drop back in with loud slaps. Papa, with his elbows on the table, is hunched over his bowl as if he's protecting it, but I know he's on guard for different reasons.

The screen blares in the background a recapping of last years televised Auction Day. Clips of the most famous Donors walking down the blood-red carpet shoot across the screen, and I roll my eyes. Those readying themselves for the upcoming auctions started their donations a month ago. I ball my fists as I turn toward the kitchen table.

Papa's docked pay was immediate, but Mam covered her ears and closed her eyes when he tried to show her that the change was dated before the incident even happened.

I think Mam burns the oatmeal on purpose. She's complained every day this week about the absence of sugar. Burnt oatmeal without sugar is unbearable, but if you eat it quickly, when it's still hot, you can't tell. We have it every meal now, and it's not the only change. At least with September blowing in, the absence of expensive air conditioning is no longer noticeable. However, the open windows allow the whole neighborhood to be a part of our heated debates and Mam's wild fits.

The news switches topics. It's still obsessed with the incident at Papa's factory. Mam enters, making a beeline for the screen. With a loud, unnecessary hand slap, she turns it off. I flinch as I sit at the table.

"Eat your breakfast, Torri," Mam snaps. She glares at me next, and I brace myself. "If you don't like it, Torri dear, then I suggest you take it up with your sister here. Maybe you can convince her to donate."

Torrin doesn't make eye contact with me, and my heart aches for the trap he is caught in—between a growing hunger and his love for me.

"That's enough, Evelyn," Papa says wearily.

"Oh is it now, Mr. Vazeto? Is it enough that we lost your paycheck at the plant? Is it enough that the other girls' contracts were mysteriously changed to give us nothing? Is it?" Her head turns to me again. "Is it enough yet to make you see? Or will you wait until your parents are starving beggars, donating their old blood to death just to feed you?"

Heat rises up my neck at Mam's words, but there's a portion of truth to her words that sickens me just as much.

Papa's chair scrapes against the floor as he stands, and he doesn't need to say anything more. Mam and Papa stare each other down before she leaves the room to clear her plate. I stare back down at my mush and squeeze my spoon in hand.

"It's not so bad," Torrin says through a mucky bite.

Awkward silence stretches on until Torrin makes an audible gulp and mumbles, "Bet you could start a fourth Germ War with this stuff." He drops his spoon into his bowl and leans back in his chair, more relaxed with Mam out of the room.

"Torrin," Papa chides wearily. He sighs and towering over the table looks down at his own bowl as if he is thinking the same thing and hasn't the energy to correct his son. "You mustn't joke about the wars that way. We should be grateful to have any food at all."

Torri gives a quick apology, and after a pause long and reverent enough to be penitent, he takes a deep breath. "Why was the third Germ War so much worse than all the others? My teacher wouldn't answer any of my questions." Torrin's sapphire eyes twinkle with curiosity. He lifts his face to Papa.

"People forgot what they were fighting for by that point," Papa says, lowering back into his seat. "The virus was no longer a controlled thing but a vehicle for revenge."

"But what made it different than the other Germ Wars? Why did she say it was the one that changed history? Were the others not as bad?"

"The first wars were simple oil disputes. Scientists became the new war generals, inventing and introducing new genetically-modified diseases as weapons. A little disease here in this country when an oil ban was placed, or a village wiped out in another country when prices went up. All the germs were contained at first, they were tested viruses that ended with a vaccine just in time for another country to retaliate. The age of the third Germ War, however, brought the discovery of vertical transfer disease." Papa squirms uncomfortably in his seat.

Torrin leans forward, wanting more, sitting on his hands probably to keep his questions in. The freckles on his nose and cheeks move as he bites his lips together.

Papa pauses and his eyes gloss over seeing something we cannot.

"The disease in the Recipients," Torrin says urging Papa on.

"Yes, a disease like no other. Do you know why it was so different? Do you know why they call it vertical?"

When Torrin doesn't answer, Papa looks to me.

"Because it transfers genetically as well as virally," I say. "There is no cure, no way to keep it from passing from generation to generation—unless you kill off the line of hosts, but even then, it might not be fully eradicated."

Papa's eyebrows bunch together. He leans forward as if he is going to counsel me before he thinks better of it and leans back never looking away from my face. Did he hear me speaking to Torrin that night? Does he know I wish the Recipients *would* die off and let us just keep our blood to ourselves and die from natural causes instead of the risks of donating?

"Right," Papa says slowly. He turns his attention back to his plate and then continues to answer Torrin. "The vertical transfer virus never went through a trial period. Countries were in a frenzy of revenge. Once it was released there was no controlling it. It spread through each country faster than people could flee. By the end of the third Germ War, Old America was the only land left habitable, and the vaccine was discovered in refugee blood."

"But how did it get there?" Torrin looks down at his arm, tracing the blue lines of his own blood.

"That—" Papa smiles at Torrin, trying to hide the sadness of our world from his view— "Is a question not even I can answer."

"And why doesn't our blood just kill the virus? Like once and for all? Just one donation? Or why don't the scientists just use our blood to recreate a vaccine instead of using us over and over again? Why are they still sick?"

Papa chuckles, and it makes my chest tingle. I haven't heard him laugh in so long, and even this one isn't as genuine or carefree as they used to be. It's the arguments that have changed that. I have changed him.

"Torrential Torrin, so many questions. I'm no scientist, but it seems whoever created these viruses or vaccines didn't want it solved that easily."

Papa's words leave me unsettled as he stands and walks across the room to the kitchen. It was always the assumption that our blood just mutated and evolved to survive, but it makes sense. I've never given much thought to the creator of the virus or the possible inventor of our new blood. I wonder if they're the same person or connected or enemies. Did the person want the separation to gain power over refugee people, or did a plan backfire leaving each band of people struggling for something? One for money and the other for their very life?

Once the swinging kitchen door is closed behind Papa, the arguing strikes up again.

"Where?" Mam's voice trembles expertly. "Where will it come from, Patar? The pantry is bare! Our food storage is used up!"

My face burns. Papa's muffled words are undecipherable and are cut off by Mam who rings loud and clear through the house.

"Oh, you fool, you don't care a wit about any of us, do you? The answer is sitting right there at the table, Patar. That little brat would rather see us starve than do the honorable thing."

Torrin's stomach chooses that very moment to growl loudly across the table. He grabs at his waist as if he could shield me from the sound of it.

Leaving my untouched bowl on the table, I run to my room to escape Mam's conniving tears that are sure to be next. Once I'm dressed and my hair is pulled into a loose bun, I sift through the canvases that lean against the wall in the corner of my closet. I choose my favorite ones this time. The orange sunset from the roof of the mall one night, Shannon rocking baby Pip, and a close up of Papa's hands with oil and dirt from the machines hidden in the cracks of his skin and under his nails.

I just need to sell one. Just one to prove it's possible. I squeeze the paintings into my bag and sling it awkwardly over my shoulder.

The arguing is in full force when I race down the stairs. Papa is yelling, and Mam is shouting right over him. I pause by the sofa, staring at Torrin still sitting at the table listening to the mind-numbing sound of our parents. His head bowed so low he looks headless. Papa's booming voice finally silences screeching Mam.

"You led our other daughters right into this life with the promise that it would be worth it, but what did it get us, Evelyn? Where's your promise now? Where are your mansions? Can't you see? No Donor will ever be rich."

"Well, we didn't know your precious little girl was going to pull this stunt, did we?"

"She should have a right to choose, and I support her in it."

"Of course you do!"

I grab a jacket from the hook by the door and run before I hear any more. Something's going to happen today, I can feel it. I'm going to sell a painting. I'm going to bring art back to a dying world and become famous for something more than blood.

On the tram ride I think about Papa's words. He believes in me, but his trust eats at me instead of empowering me. Are we right to try and stump the system?

Getting off the tram, people look at me as my bag bumps and pokes them. The market is crowded today. Donations for auctions started a month ago, and the streets swarm with young blood setting out to make their place in this world. Even if I were to donate now, I wouldn't have donated enough blood to compete against other Donors across the country. I would get paid for regular donations, yes, but nothing like what the auctions could bring. It would be something, though. Something right now would fill our pantry.

I pick up my pace at my disheartening thoughts. What foolishness. Papa believes in me. I can do this. My paintings will sell.

I stop when someone grunts in the wet gutter and the smell of sewage pulls my hand to my face like a gas mask. There, in the crumbling curb, a heap of rags moves with each shuddering cough. A man, with skin so dark his features are lost, moves the rags like a bad puppeteer. His graying stubble shows a face amongst the pile and the scars of so many donations shine on his forearms. Beside him rests a guitar with a splintered hole in the side, and the strings shoot out in different directions at the top. I'm not sure if it's the stench or the injustice that turns my stomach and sends heat rising up my neck.

I hook my shirt collar over the tip of my nose and pull a bottle of water from my bag. Stepping forward, I reach out with the bottle and a hand to support the back of his head. When the rim touches his lips, his groans stop. My heart stops. Time stops.

There was a day people supported themselves by their occupation alone—doctors, teachers, musicians like him. We need them still, but none of those positions hold enough importance in the New World. Blood matters most now, making my art worthless and my blood priceless. It's difficult to swallow while I stare at the guitar. Do my paintings carry the same fate?

My hand is wet, and I notice water dribble down the man's face, wetting his neck and shoulders. His eyes twitch slowly behind his black eyelids. I lean back on my heels as I screw on the lid.

The sounds around me of wooden wheels pulled across a broken road draw my attention. The shouting over prices and the condition of vegetables never ceases. No one acknowledges this stranger. No one cares. They are a village of Mams never seeing truth or caring enough to do anything about it. How will my art survive in a world where no one sees what I see or feels what I feel? The man's movement slows and soon he doesn't move at all as the Donor body loses all life. His face wears the Donor smile, but his blood is finally resting.

I can't take my eyes off his frozen smile. His death is probably as lonely as his life was. This Donor probably died because his numbers were too low, and he had no other way out but to donate to survive even though it's also what killed him. Why can't people see the trap these donations put them in? Anger is pushed aside, however, by the truth this dead Donor awakens me to. I have the highest numbers I've ever heard of, and I'm refusing to donate, for what? To prove a point? A point that no longer feels worth the cost. So much has changed since that day I set out to tell my family. That day, my blood was not needed. Now, until the investigation is through at the plant, we have no source of income. Unless my sisters' contracts change back as suddenly as they disappeared, which is as likely as a swift report on the incident.

Now Torrin goes to sleep with a stomach half full of oatmeal and no promise of anything better. What if I *chose* to donate? Not to help the Recipients, but to help me and my family. Would that be so much like Mam and my sisters doing it for dresses and parties and recognition? A dull ache starts in my stomach.

I stand with a jerk and throw the bottle across the street. A black cylinder droid appears, bobbing in the air by the Donor's head. Of course the street cleaner would notice him. I'm too angry to be scared of the robot. I clench my fists. A red beam shoots out from the droid and expands around every inch of the Donor. Black skin glows red, and the lifeless body is caught in the droid's grasp as it flickers, then disappears from the street all together. The soil has recovered since the wars now, but still we do not bury the dead. Instead, they are disintegrated through molecular dynamics and evaporated into the air like drying hand sanitizer. Our past is the very air we breathe.

Acid burns up my throat and my fingernails dig into my palms. What else could this man have offered us if he was allowed to truly live? I don't want this life the Recipients are forcing upon us, but maybe Mam is right, will I wait until my family is starved and dying before I donate?

The eye of the droid faces away from me as it whirs and beeps. Austen's words spring up in my mind, "It isn't what we say or think that defines us but what we do." Without another thought, I swing my bag of paintings up over my head and come down hard on top of the Recipients' droid. The red beam vanishes and the black hunk of metal crashes to the ground. Sparks fly in the air as it skids along the pavement and bumps into Mr. Winter's grocery. The street is still. *Now* the market looks this direction.

My heart stops, but it also feels as if a weight were lifted. It felt good to do something.

"Ha," I laugh out loud, and the stares turn on me in full. I step backward as a woman points at me, and then I run. I zip between the frozen crowd and turn down a thin, damp alleyway that smells like the dead Donor, but I don't stop to cover my nose this time.

My mind is racing with me. Donors die every day. Lots of them. Most of them are old and unwed, unable to stay away from the facility long enough to replenish their plasma. But I had never actually witnessed death until today. At least not in person. I squeeze my eyes shut for a split second, as the image of Greg on the screen flashes across my memory. When I shake my head, it's only replaced by the dark Donor smile. How could any parent consent to send their child to the facility? The smile on his face is stuck in my vision, like a freeze shot Torrin makes on the screen. Forever and endlessly smiling.

When I exit between the two brick buildings, I instantly collide with something, knocking it over. It feels so hard it surprises me. I look down and see a person. I rub at my head where it hit his evidently bony chest.

"Ah, New Detroit market, the best place to buy anything."

The voice sounds familiar, and I'm relieved he sounds more amused than angry. Until I see his face. Relief is not what I would call the feeling that washes over me when I see the young man lying on the ground before me. I recognize his hair, even though there's no sun today to shine on it, and that square chin with barely any meat on it. It's the guy I ran into on the day of the accident.

"What do I owe you for the bruise you have no doubt accosted me?" He rubs his backside as he straightens taller and taller, and his corn-colored hair, more straw-like than mine, shades his eyes again. It's his face that has me speechless. No wonder he hid it from me that day. It's sunken and hollow like the skin is nothing but makeup on a skeleton. His lanky body looks like an under-stuffed scarecrow, and his clothes dangle off his shoulders. From under his matted hair, he peeks at me.

I resist the urge to gasp at the sight of his eyes. They are haunting and somehow stunning at the same time. Maybe it's the dark circles above his bony cheeks that make them stand out, like the donations dug trenches under his sunken eyes. The more I look at this boy, the more I hate the system. Hate Mam. Hate the droid. Hate the Recipients.

"I'm sorry. I didn't see you," I say.

He grunts and smacks the dust from his worn jeans. He can't be much older than me, yet here he is with numbers probably so low he's on the fast track to the deadly gutter.

My cheeks burn when I realize how long I've stood there staring at him. I peel my eyes off his sad face only to be drawn back again.

This poor, dirty Donor is sucked dry. Probably not a single immunoglobulin in him. Nothing left to fight for his body. No life left at all. It's all given to the Recipients. I repeat the question I asked Torrin that night. What makes his life less important?

"Excuse me." I step around him, resisting the urge to look back over my shoulder. I can't think about him right now. Nor can I think about the Donor dead in the gutter, nor the many others like him that walk zombie-like through the town. I have to sell my paintings. I have to succeed.

I move through the memorized streets with urgency. When I peek over my shoulder, he isn't standing by the alley where I ran into him like I pictured. Instead, he's only a few steps behind me. His long strides keep up with me easily.

"Did you want something?" I wish I could keep my cheeks from flaming. "I said I was sorry."

Why won't he leave me alone? I'm on a mission today, and I don't need Donors draining their lives away at the facility getting in my way.

His laugh is full and pulls my eyes back to him.

"Well, aren't you a little ray of sunshine," he says.

I harden my brow and walk faster. He may be resigned to this life, but I am not.

"Let me get this straight," he continues. "You run into me, knock me over, and *you're* the one who's angry?"

"I'm sorry! I didn't see you."

"You said that already." His smile sinks his eyes deeper as his cheeks point up over them. They look darker gray than blue.

Why can't I stop looking at him? He isn't attractive, too dirty to see anything to appreciate. Though the way he carries himself, with squared shoulders and purposeful steps instead of a drooping head like most Donors, is admirable.

"What do you want me to say?" I wind my way around the carts and tables in the market, hugging my paintings close to me.

"Asking after my well-being is a good place to start," he says with another smile.

"Are you ok?" I say, failing to keep the sarcasm from my voice.

"I'm fine. Thank you very much for asking. A little wounded pride maybe, but overall I'd say this is a good day."

I roll my eyes when I see him step next to me and look at my face. His laugh sounds like a waterfall, but it makes my chest tighten. How can a man I barely know irritate me so?

"What have you got there?" he says pointing to my bag.

I hug my paintings closer to my side with both hands. "Nothing."

"Are you an illegal trader? You know I must report you if that—"

I spin to my side and hold out a hand to stop him reaching over. "It's nothing illegal."

He pulls back from my hand to keep it from touching him and looks at it before he smiles up at me again. His smile is intoxicating. The way his eyes gleam behind the shadows of his skull looks almost genuine. It's not the ghostly counterfeit smiles I see from every Donor. It's as if the very smile is the poison and I'm the victim. How can someone that sick smile like that?

"That's good to hear. Then what is it?"

I turn away from him before I answer. "My paintings," I whisper.

"An artist. Well, that is a surprise. Can I—"

"No." I start walking again, and he jumps in place by my side.

"You really think they'll sell?"

"I was taught not to talk to strangers." I see him smile again out of the corner of my eye.

"Then tell me who you are so we are no longer strangers."

"Look, just because you're sick doesn't mean you can badger people." I regret the words as soon as they leave my mouth. Unable to look at his sad face, I stare out into the crowd, trying to ignore this stray following my every move. I spot Lazuli. Her long dark hair sways over her pale face as she weaves through the street.

"Lazuli!" I call out hoping she will save me from this stalker. I don't exactly feel afraid of this strange man. I pity him too much to see him as a threat. But I won't retract the truth either.

As soon as Lazuli smiles at me and heads my way, the stranger bows in front of me.

"It was a pleasure walking with you, miss. Good luck on your endeavors to sell those paintings."

He disappears into the walls of shifting people before I can apologize, which is probably for the best. Lazuli bounces in front of me.

"Hey. Are you going to the facility? I just finished. My technician thinks I will do really well at the auctions."

"That's so great," I say through clenched teeth. "No, I'm going to the trade store." I don't dare tell her why. She wouldn't understand now. Besides, Lazuli has already accomplished what I wanted her to. She helped me get rid of the stray.

"I'm going to the mall this Friday," she says cheerily. "We should go together. You know, like old times."

How can she say that? Does she even remember old times? Does whatever she's drugged with affect her memories as well because I'm pretty sure it would be nothing like old times? "Uh... I'll let you know."

She beams as if I've agreed to a whole lot more and then we go our separate ways.

The market store stocked by Recipients is full of new technology and ridiculous prices. It stands right next to Mr. Burke's Trade store making it look dull and dusty in comparison. When I pass the large glass window of the Recipient store and stop right in front of the trade store's old wooden door, I see something move across all the new Recipient screens that are for sale. Footage of a girl with a blonde bun swinging her arms over her head like an ape and attacking a droid. Footage of me.

I race into the trade store making the bell atop the door ring. Safe inside, I lean against the back of the door before I move forward and picture again the televised footage of the back of my head. What was filming me from behind? Was there another droid? Is there a fine for attacking one? Punishment? I've never heard of anyone doing it. Maybe they're not protected in the way officers are. Attacking an officer, now that—

"Aston," Mr Burke says from behind his desk.

I sigh deep and long, pushing away concerns I can do nothing about now. Besides, it's just an image not my blood. No way to identify me.

He removes his glasses, exposing his bushy white eyebrows. "I don't have any new art supplies today."

"I'm actually here to see if I can sell something in your store."

His eyebrows lift, creasing his forehead, and he follows my gaze as I pull my bag (now evidence in a crime) onto his old glass counter. My fingers shake against the coarse fabric of the bag wondering how long it'll be until they catch me. Maybe droids have some recognition programs I'm unaware of. I take a deep breath and hand over my work. My babies.

His face is unreadable as he surveys them. "These are beautiful. I've always been curious about your work." He looks at me, then a familiar glance, the look I tried not to give the sick Donor in the street. Pity. His mouth doesn't move. His eyes say it all.

"It's ok." I fail to conceal the panic in my voice. The pressure in my chin warns me that I may cry at any moment. "I don't know what I was thinking."

"Art just doesn't sell, dear. I don't have money for things that don't sell."

"Of course not. I understand."

"I'm sorry, Aston," he finally murmurs.

His sad eyes burrow into me, gut me, and then dispose of my remains. The sunken eyes of the sick Donor carve an image across my vision. My future. The lifeless eyelids of the dead Donor make my chin quiver. My fate. And then I hear Mam in my head as if she were here reprimanding me herself in place of Mr. Burke, who's too afraid to do it. "Stop worrying about people you can't save," she seems to scream at me. "Just donate, you ungrateful child."

"If you want, I can put them up in the store? Sell them as consignment?"

I heave a purifying sigh and smile as best I can. "That would be nice." If nothing else, it will help me get rid of evidence.

Mr. Burke gives me another sympathetic smile and takes the paintings behind the counter.

"I'll let you know if they sell. Would you be ok if I priced them? Or did you have an amount in mind?"

I don't trust my voice, so I shake my head with a grateful smile and walk away. The bell at the door feels torturously loud now, and I tug at my bun, letting my hair fall over my face. The blanket of hair ironically reminds me of another day, a day I wanted to hide my numbers from my own flesh and blood. Now I want to hide from everyone, from everything.

I trudge back home with lead feet and fallen hopes.

Mam is in the kitchen banging away when I step into the living room. There's an odd smell that makes my face twist but at least it's not oatmeal. It smells like onions and something sour.

Mam steps out of the kitchen with a steaming pot in her oven-mitted hands, and when she sees me, she stops and glares. "Torrin!" she yells as she puts the pot on the table. "Your dinner's ready. Come set the table."

The bang of his door is followed by his pounding steps.

"How many times do I have to tell you not to swing that door so hard?"

"Sorry, Mam."

Papa comes silently into the room, and I can tell we're all walking on eggshells—because of me, because I won't donate.

When we each lean over a bowl of onion broth and old cabbage, Torrin speaks first.

"I never thought I would wish for oatmeal."

"Shush," Mam says with pursed lips and a scowl for me. "Cabbage is very nutritious. And like every meal, if you have a problem with it you should—"

"I'll donate," I say without looking up. My eyes sting from the hot onion steam filling my view. The room is so silent everyone must, like me, be holding their breath.

Papa speaks first. "Aston—"

"Patar, don't you talk her out of this. It's her decision," Mam says frantically.

"Now it's her decision? As long as it meets your demands, it can be her decision?"

"It just took her longer to see through the error of your fanciful stories, that's all." Mam turns to me sweetly. "You're making the right choice, dear. We will all be very grateful."

Papa is now the one giving me glares, and I don't know how to tell him. Tell him that I saw a man die today, that my plans are immature and naive, that I don't have a choice when I can hear Torrin's grumbling stomach each and every day. And how do I tell Papa that I can hear him each night? That the sound of a grown man, my powerful Papa, sobbing in the dark when he thinks no one can hear will never leave my memory? I'm doing this for you, Papa. For everyone. I hope you can see that.

Papa shoves his blue bowl out in front of him as he stands. The soup sloshes when it stops, and wilted chunks of cabbage with tiny black dots of mold on them land in a heap on the table. He stomps out the door.

I stare at that puddle on the table for what feels like forever, also unable to eat. My head swirls again, remembering another puddle. My eyes dart across the room where my blood once dripped. The soup suddenly smells like copper, and I rub my head. What did I just agree to do?

The squeal of the tramcar brakes makes my bones shiver. The waking market street comes into view. Stepping off the yellow and gray tram, I pause for a moment, letting the burnt wood smell of the brakes morph into the scents of burnt sugar wafting through the air from Mr. Winter's bakery. People bump past me, hurrying on their way, as I let memories of sweet rolls eaten at my Papa's knee root me in place. I look back over my shoulder and squint at the rising sun beaming through the cables that feed electricity to the rickety tramcar. The market looks, sounds, and smells the same, but I feel like I'm an intruder.

I march across the new white pavement surrounding the tracks and approach the line where the smooth concrete ends and the old war-ravaged streets of New Detroit begin. The physical line feels symbolic as I cross it. I've walked these streets a million times before, but the crumbled remnants of another world, an old world, feel different under my feet this morning. Or maybe I'm different.

I walk numbly through the crowded market with my head down. The crowds thin and soon are nonexistent as I move closer to the donation facility. The paved road turns to crumbled remnants before disappearing altogether. I kick up dust as I walk, and soon I see the building in the distance. The only white one on the street, it seems to glow. This is not a repurposed building like the rest of them. Its three-stories tower above the others, matched in height only by the lawyer's offices behind.

All too fast, I'm standing in front of the sacred building: the donation facility. I stare at the clear, clean doors and perfectly manicured bushes lined against the white outer wall. They are the only plants on the street. Every other building is covered in dirt and dust and looks like death. I should know now that I've seen it.

I'm surprised to notice the donation facility is actually lit up, as though the wall is made of bright screens. It does funny things to my eyes, like I can see the sick Donor's sunken face on the outer wall as if it's a bad omen staring me down. I try to transform them into my brother's clear blue, innocent eyes. Focus on Torrin. Instantly, I can hear his questions about this building.

My heart hammers. This is it. I will actually step foot into the very place I said I never would. I stuff my hands into my jacket pockets to keep them from shaking.

If our situation wasn't already so desperate, I would consider only offering daily donations. With one hundred fifty-seven percent of the antibody, my daily pay would still be a good amount. It's what most Donors would do. Those with birthdays too close to the auctions to get the full three months' worth of offerings would wait until next year's catalog to increase their chances. But at this point I don't think I have a choice. Somehow, with high numbers but a month behind the other Donors, I *have* to make it to auctions. I *have* to find a way to make up for my sisters' lost contracts and Papa's docked pay. I have to feed the family and make up for what I have cost them.

Stepping off the dirt road, my feet strike new pavement again. I have changed. I'm an adult now. It's time to do adult things. It's time to give up on the idea of supporting myself with silly paintings and save the lives that matter. I just hope someone saves mine as well.

I will myself to move.

"Hello," a deep voice says from behind me.

The sound makes me jump. Without needing to turn around, my eyes focus on the reflection in the doors of a guy standing behind me.

Everyone in town my age is a Donor to some degree. This one behind me is clearly not as dependent on the donations as the scarecrow I ran into on the streets yesterday. This boy's shoulders are full and rounded. His clothes fit him nicely.

We are alone on the perfect sidewalk, and I step aside to let him in. Looking into his face confirms my suspicions—he is young and healthy, wealthy enough to not need the donations often. He either has high numbers and a wonderful contract or low numbers and a dependable paycheck. This guy doesn't follow his heart after silly things like music or art, but plays the system well instead.

His eyes are kind though and not haughty like my high-numbered sisters and their self-important friends. My guess is he's numbered low and works for the system somehow, although he doesn't hold his chin in the air like my brother-in-law the lawyer. Maintenance maybe, but definitely low-numbered. Cute, but very low. I bet this guy didn't even make it into the catalog.

The guy steps up onto the curb of the white pavement. My face hardens at my own thoughts. How quickly I'm changing. First agreeing to donate and now already judging a person's ability to make the catalog. It's hard enough to see my sisters and Mam crouched around the red-covered brochure every year, waiting to see their numbers. Now the thought of Recipients shopping through it, looking at my own blood numbers, makes my stomach shift with anger.

I can picture the Recipients in their secluded little towns, separated from our New Detroit city, always separate, sitting and drinking their tea while they chat about which numbers they will bid on. I'm sure every other Recipient town all across the northern states is just like ours, huddled greedily around the great lakes, the only untainted water. All Recipients are the same. Sick, greedy, rich.

I focus on the face before me to calm my anger as he steps closer. His brown hair is perfectly curved in a wave parted to the side. His cheeks are flush and plump, not sunken and ashen.

"Are you going in?" He stops right in front of me, studying me as much as I am studying him. The only difference is the Donor grin he wears.

"Eventually," I finally say to his sickeningly joyful face. My comment only seems to encourage his happiness, and his round cheeks push up against his eyes.

"It's not that bad you know. They don't bite."

"So I've been told." My hand automatically grabs at my finger that proves his statement wrong.

If crickets had survived the Germ Wars, you probably would have heard them now. I read about them once. I try to imagine their chirping as we stand staring at each other and waiting for the other to move—me and my scrutinizing raised eyebrow and him with his happy super-glued perfect face.

"Well, good luck," he nods to me, and his warm hazel eyes glisten as he passes. The doors slide effortlessly out of his way, and the facility engulfs him.

I step and don't think, not about the needles or the blood or the drugs that make Donors happy. I just move, as if his motion has created a vortex pulling me toward the doors without my consent.

The smooth hiss of the gliding doors feels as sterile as the smell that engulfs me when I step into the donation facility. It stings my nose like Mam's chemicals. My hair swooshes forward as the doors quickly shut behind me. I'm in.

Voices are muffled, shoes covered in little booties whisper across the floor, even the air seems to carry a hushing hint. Everything is too clean. Too white. Too bright.

A giant flashing poster screen is hung to the side where I read "Division of Medical Resources — Where you help dreams come true." The information desk stands before me with frosted glass rounding the front, glowing bright with back lighting. The overly cheerful woman behind it has a red disk bobbing over her shoulder—a security droid, with the same all-seeing eye in the center. I squeeze the doctor's note rolled up in my palm. There will be no more hiding the smooth, worn paper or its numbers after today. My family knows, and soon, so will the whole New World.

Screens line the wall to my left, some of which are occupied by people on white metal stools. They press their fingers against the screens. Small earbuds glow in their ears, making even their information that flashes across the screens silent. What is the obsession with being so quiet? It's as if they have a secret hidden in silent white walls and quiet glass doors.

The sound of my panicking heart and loud wheeze echo through the entryway. The looks aimed in my direction make me think even breathing is against the rules here.

Adakin Malloy, our faithful leader, flashes across the screen now. His wrinkled, withered face stares directly at me. He led the people out of death. He found hope in a world covered in destruction. At least that's what our history books say.

"Can I help you?" the desk receptionist says, with her cheery eyes and plastered smile.

"I'm here to donate," I say.

The receptionist's smile widens, which I didn't think possible, digging further into her wrinkles.

"Yes, dear. Do you have your papers?" Her voice is too sweet. Her posture too perfect. She feels as antiseptic as the facility.

I stand frozen again, staring at her perfect lipstick—searching for at least one flaw, one trait that would make her more real.

The papers, rolled up in my hand, are sticky from being held so long. My heart drums against my ribs, and I don't move.

I'm being ridiculous. People don't die their first week of donating, Aston.

"I can scan your finger if you forgot them? It would take a little longer but—"

I step forward briskly and thrust my hand over the desk.

Smiling sweetly, unconcerned by my stiff reaction, the desk lady places her hand underneath mine, and I let the sweaty roll drop.

Wiping my hand on my jeans, I try not to think about poor

uncontracted Mary who entered these rooms one day and never left. I try not to think about the needles that are somewhere behind these walls as the woman unrolls my little papers and reads them.

Her eyebrows raise. "These are high numbers." She looks at me differently now. Tilting her chin up to see over the edge of the desk, she sizes me up and down, her smile finally faltering. It is her first sign of being authentic, of slipping from behind the control of whatever makes them so happy. The look of hunger, as though she may drain my blood right here and now to sell for her own gain, sends a chill up my spine. She brings back her smile in such full force it squeezes her eyes shut.

"What a lucky family to have a daughter with such high prospects. I'm sure they're very proud."

I roll my eyes. Proud?

"Now before we go any further, we need you to go through a presentation and answer a few questions. There is the option to read the information, but most people just use these headphones instead."

She holds out the tiny earbuds. They look like two metal peas rolling in her palm. I stare at them, willing myself to not take as long as I did to enter or hand over the paper. I look her in the eye.

"No, thank you. I'll just read."

Her arm lowers slowly as she scrutinizes me. Must not get many readers.

"Suit yourself, sweetie." Her sugary smile returns. "Here's your code to enter into the screen."

She hands me a new slip of paper with four numbers on it. I take it, and she rattles on.

"Try to memorize it because it will also be your number for each of your visits. Just take your time to listen...er...read the information and answer the questions while I get your file ready. When you're done, you can have a seat over there," she points over my shoulder to a corner waiting room beside the sliding doors I had entered through, "until your number is called."

"My number?"

She points down to the slip of paper in my hands that looks like a little fortune from a fortune cookie. She leans over the counter to peer at the slip. "Yes, dear. You are now number thirteen forty-two." She smiles into my dumbfounded face.

Things I've always known but never processed. I don't even remember my sisters' auction numbers. I was too focused on my own little world. My own fantastical dreams. Dreams that are quickly being broken apart with each step I take. Auctions are supposed to protect the identity of the Donor. I will forever and always be a number. I stare down at the paper—thirteen forty-two.

They might call this voluntary, but it never felt more forced upon me than when Mam urged me to save the family business. They might tell us that donating doesn't change us, but I have never felt so different. They have taken everything. I am no longer Aston Vazeto. I am a high-blood rate. I am a series of faceless, characterless, meaningless numbers.

I study the woman's features more intensely. Does she have a name or a number? Is that what makes her less human—more robotic? Is this how they make society care so little about the bribing of donations? Remove our identity and our emotions, give us numbers and drugs, and we'll do whatever they want us to?

I see something in her eyes that is faded and hidden and overtop is a shimmering curtain making them look like glass eyes. Will I be like her too someday? Nameless? Fake? Drugged to submission?

I almost gasp as something dawns on me. That's what was different about that sick Donor in the market street. He might have been sick, but, somehow, he was real. I picture that broad smile as I piece it all together. Somehow this sparkling glaze over the eyes, that hides the real person, wasn't placed over that sick man's face. He didn't seem drugged into complacency. I want to know how he did it. I want it as much as this woman wants my blood. I want to be me forever.

SEVEN

I'm glad I chose to read. It's nice to go at my own pace. I can speed through the consent and About My Health pages and slow down on the odd personality quiz.

> ***As a child, when my friend was in trouble, I was:***
>
> *a. Concerned, empathetic, and loyal - regardless of the problem*
>
> *b. Supportive, patient, and a good listener*
>
> *c. Nonjudgmental, optimistic, and downplaying of the seriousness of the*
>
> *situation*
>
> *d. Protective, resourceful, and recommending of solutions*

What does any of this have to do with my blood? And how do I choose an answer? I am all of these things.

I recall instances in my past that help me answer the questions. When I caught my friend Ryan trying to sneak sausages from the shipment of food for the local officers that kept the peace, I felt protective of him, responsible even, since it was my father's machine malfunction that caused his father's injury and lack of pay. I found a way to keep the cameras from reporting his actions. I scaled the side drainpipe and made a tile shingle "fall" off over the camera. The building was falling apart already, so it wasn't hard to believe. In fact, it led to a renovation of the building. I did the town a service.

Clicking away at my own screen, the metal stool beside me screeches across the floor. With a room this silent, everyone turns to look, even the Donors with headphones. When I turn my head, I see next to me a boy with red hair and freckle-covered arms, and my throat feels dry.

"Oliver," I hiss at him as the faces around us turn away. "What in Scar's sake are you doing here?"

He is trembling and doing his best to ignore me. I stare at his shaking hand as he lifts it to the screen. "Leave me alone, Aston. Just mind your own business."

His voice is lower than my brother's and is a common sound around our house. Everyone always thinks Oliver is older than he is. I scan the room again. The secretary is smiling away at her desk. There are no officers in sight.

"Oliver, you know tampering with blood numbers is against the law. You could get into big trouble." I try to put as much warning into my whisper as I possibly can as my mind races with ideas of how to get my brother's best friend out of this predicament.

"Some rules are enforced more than others," he says. "It's like littering, everyone knows there's a blood fine, but people still throw their trash on the ground anyway. No one cares if someone wants to donate early. The more blood the merrier."

His lip curls on the words, and he taps harder at the screen. I see the resemblance of Greg, his father, in the way he holds his chin. His father who yelled through our living room that awful day. His father who is now dead because I didn't want to donate. I swallow hard before I speak.

"Look, I know it's gotta be hard with the twins at home to feed, but this isn't going to help them if you get caught."

"I won't get caught," he grumbles.

"Just come by the house, I'm sure Mam would share some of our cans with—"

"We don't want your charity."

He probably sees through my lie. Mam wouldn't share with a

neighbor or friend if they were at death's door. We don't really have anything to share right now, either. Oh, how selfish I've been. Look at all the pain and hardship I caused on more than just one family. I lean in urgently closer to him.

"Papa will come over. Surely he can help—"

"Look, Aston, I know lots of Donors that sneak in and donate early. I know all the precautions to take: stay hydrated, don't lift after donating all that great stuff. It's never really been proven it's dangerous to donate before sixteen anyway."

"I'm not worried about your health, Oliver. I'm nervous the—"

"Thirteen forty-three."

I fall off my stool at the sound of the officer. It's not until I find my balance that I realize the officer didn't call my number. Oliver is statue still and staring into the expressionless face of the officer.

"Y-yes?"

"Come with me." The officer turns, expecting Oliver to follow, and I panic.

"Officer, this boy is with me."

I continue to face Oliver and see out of the corner of my eye the shadow of the dark uniformed figure turn. Oliver's terrified, confused face burrows into me.

"And you are?"

"Asto—thirteen forty-two." I turn to the officer and lift my chin to keep it from quivering. The officer's smooth bald head and shiny face looks bored with the conversation. They all wear the same eyebrow-less expressions. Taking away the soldier's emotions wasn't enough for the system, they needed to rid the face of even the hint of sentiment. They were the only people in the town not happy all the time. They were instead an endless stream of stoic.

"This boy," the officer starts in a monotone yet commanding voice, "has tampered with the donations, in an attempt to donate before the age of requirement."

"No."

Small gasps burst around the room, and suddenly my heart is

beating, kicking me, for being so stupid. This is not knocking off cameras behind their back or hitting robots in the market; this is dangerous; this is face to face defiance. I speak to release the tension that fear is building in my chest. "I asked him to come with me. He was curious about the process. I was nervous to come alone."

The officer's face never changes. In my mind, I picture him giving an evil condescending grin before commenting—if he ever could have such control over his face.

"Nice try, Donor. But this boy turned in false papers.'"

He grabs at Oliver's thin, ripped jacked, and without thinking, I grab for his other arm. The officer gives me an eye. The most emotion I've seen on one yet. It's a warning, and now when I look at Oliver, I see Torrin. I hear my own words to Oliver in my mind. What use would I be to my family from prison?

"I'll watch after your family," I whisper to horrified, defeated Oliver. I relax my fingers but can't seem to let go of the cold, damp windbreaker. When my gaze falls, the officer yanks on Oliver, making him yelp, and his jacket rip from my hands. I turn to my screen numbly as the scuffle echoes behind me in the silent facility.

I can't focus on the questions that reel across the screen because my mind is full of my own. Where will they take Oliver? What will they do with him?

After the questionnaire is over, I sit in the waiting room corner. I bounce my right knee as I sit in the leather chair, trying not to picture Oliver, or the boy in the market street. Instead, I think of the meals we will eat with my paycheck. The chocolate pudding that will cover Torrin's face when he grins after eating it. Papa will help Oliver's family. It will be ok.

The girl next to me is reclined with crossed legs and a Cheshire Cat grin. Slowly, she flips through her magazine. She could be the poster child for the facility billboards. I can't help but stare at her, wondering what is so wonderful in that magazine that could make her smile like that?

I hear my Papa's words from years ago. *"There's gotta be*

something they poison high Donors with that makes them so happy, so complacent and giving!"

"Clearly they aren't poisoning you with any complacent juice. Maybe you could use a little bit of happiness potion." Mam had teased. *"You're just as stubborn and bullheaded as ever."*

My father smiled then. I picture it now in my head and compare it to the clown face next to me. His smile was warm, free, and welcoming.

My father hasn't smiled like that in months. He hates that I gave in, hates that he can't donate in place of me. To donate at their age would kill them, but it doesn't keep the old and childless from doing it. Lazuli's aunt never had children and died at the age of thirty-four. People have children to take over donations for them, but I often thought Papa had children because he genuinely enjoyed being a father.

Cheshire Cat girl nudges me with her elbow. "I think they're calling you."

"Thirteen forty-two?" a slender woman in a white lab coat calls. She looks up from her clipboard, of course smiling around the room. I roll my eyes as I lean forward to stand up. The happiness here is making me sick.

But it won't be long. Soon I will be as happy to be here as the rest of them—unless I can learn that sick Donor's secret somehow.

I follow the technician to a room of desks. She gestures for me to sit on one side as she circles around the desk to her little black leather chair on wheels.

"First, we just need to take a drop of blood to make sure you're healthy."

What? Blood before the blood? I wring my hands.

"Why not just a scan?" I say. My stomach flops. It's just blood. No one dies their first week. Just make it to auctions.

"A scan is enough to identify you and access your blood bank but not enough to show us the information we need."

After snapping on red rubber gloves, she prepares the white desk between us with a half-opened bandage and the evil pen-like device. My blood starts to pound in my ears again like an animal that can smell danger. They are lined up perfectly, and the sight of the cotton ball in the middle makes my stomach buckle. I close my eyes and make an "O" with my exhaled breath.

"We'll do this every visit, and if your immunoglobulin is ever down, we'll send you home and try again another day."

I peek at her. She's done with her prepping, and her hand is extended over the desk, waiting for mine. I only stare at hers.

"Middle finger of your less dominant hand is usually best."

Middle finger. Every visit? Can I do this? I close my eyes again as my hand slowly lifts.

"Clarissa," a man's voice breaks through the air behind me, and the wave in my belly calms at the sound of it.

"Mrs. Fewks says to trade Donors. My Donor is number thirteen twenty-nine in room 12b."

I recognize the voice. My breathing settles even though I keep my eyes closed. There are some protests by Clarissa before an exasperated sigh, and I can tell from how the chair hits the wall that her retreat is not happy. The familiar voice sits at the desk of prepared cotton and needle, and I finally open my eyes. It's the guy that witnessed my hesitation at the entrance.

"You made it in," he says with a joking grin. It's so easy to smile back at him now for some reason. I completely forget that he is fake.

"Did anyone bite?"

"You're about to."

I don't think twice about placing my hand in his cold, soft palm. It's as if our own hands are speaking to each other. My hand naturally answers his outstretched arm, moving against my will, like I had followed him into the facility. His smile is so captivating. It's much more convincing than the front desk lady, and the shock of it distracts me for a moment from what his hand is about to do.

"You have really high numbers," he says as he works.

"Is that why you traded?" I ask. "To work with a high-rated Donor?""

"Was I that obvious?" His mock concern makes me laugh.

"You're a bad actor." Is it just me or did his smile falter? Have I offended him? "Do you get paid more to be a high Donor's technician?" I ask.

"I wish!"

"Then why?"

His nice round cheeks redden, and his smile deepens with his obvious discomfort. It makes me notice him for more than just the technician he is. All of a sudden, there is no blood status or numbers. I'm just a girl and he's just a boy blushing because he doesn't want to admit why he wanted to be my technician.

" 'Cause you looked like you needed some help. All done." He turns my hand over and pats the top of it. The small gesture makes my hand tingle. Finally registering what he said, I look down at my hand. I study the finger now covered in a neon pink bandage. I felt nothing. No pain, no dizziness or nausea. He's a miracle worker. I don't have time to consider the astounding differences between this and my first experience with "a tiny finger prick" because a machine beeps, and he retrieves a little tiny cartridge with a red dot, my blood, on it.

"All healthy."

He grins at me, and then I see it. He's not just a boy, he's a technician, a technician drugged and manipulated to do what he's supposed to do. And I'm not just a girl, I'm a Donor, a high-rated Donor, idolized by my peers and sacrificed no matter the cost. Something from this place makes him appear kind. Something here forces him into a mask of happiness. None of it is real. It's the drug. It's all a charade to lure me into the wonderful life of donating.

"Ok, now for the good stuff," he says.

I follow him down the hall past posters of Recipients: images of wives and husbands, parents and children—all people our blood helps. Their healthy faces stare me down, meant to encourage me to do good. Instead, it makes me want to punch the screens their grateful faces shine on.

"Here we are."

We turn a corner at the end of the hallway. A row of cubicles is stationed on both sides of the room we've entered. Though I can hear the soft hum of conversations, I see no one. The small partitions offer a sense of privacy. Just as fake as everything else here.

"We're going to go in the last one on the right," he says, looking at me over his shoulder as he takes off down the aisle. "Each day that you come in, you'll check in at the desk and then wait for your number to be called. After the immunoglobulin test, you will come back here for the hour of retrieval."

His tone makes it sound like it's the most exciting thing on New Earth, like I'm receiving instructions on how to find a puppy or solve the mysteries of the universe instead of how to have my blood taken out of me against my will.

At the end of the hallway is a door with an emergency door handle reading "Warning, Alarm Will Sound." I stand at the opening of our little cubicle, staring at the lounge chair and giant machines and tubes. Too clean. Too bright. I start the list again. Too different. Too big. Too much.

My technician gently grabs my arm. His cold fingers pierce my skin again.

"It's going to be ok," he whispers.

He does a good job making me believe him. My chest relaxes as I look into his warm hazel eyes. I lied. He's an amazing actor when he needs to be, I guess. The next second, a wax coat goes over his eyes, reminding me that he is owned by the Recipients. Like I will be.

"Just get comfortable in the chair, and I'll set everything up."

I climb onto the reclined leather chair. The white protective paper wrinkles and tears as I move across it.

I twiddle my thumbs and avoid looking at the needles.

He claps his hands then rubs them together. "Alrighty. Now I'm going to ask you to squeeze this ball over and over again. Good."

He wiggles his hands into rubber gloves, and my eye catches sight of the needle. It's bigger than any I've ever seen. No wonder we're divided off from everyone; I wouldn't have followed him in here if I had seen this needle in everyone else. It's more tube like with a slanted, pointed end and a dark hole in the center resembling a tiny monster's jaws ready to devour me.

"I'm going to wrap this heat pack on your arm around the site."

The site? *The site* is a term you use when going camping or even construction sites, but my arm is not some land to be claimed or worked on.

His hands are on my elbow as he places a warm plastic pack in the crook of my arm. His touch calms me again. With the heat pack on top and his ice fingers beneath, my arm is sandwiched in warm and cold. I wonder if having cold hands is a side effect of donating. My stomach twists at the possibilities of my new future. Think of Torrin. Think of Oliver. I'll donate to save them. I close my eyes and breathe.

"How often do technicians donate?" I ask without opening my eyes. I'm somewhat grateful to this good-looking technician to distract me from my worries. "Do you get paid well enough to not have to often?"

"We get decent pay, more than my father, the train conductor, that's for sure. But not enough to keep me from donating three times a week."

I can't keep from bugging my eyes. He seems too healthy to be donating that often.

"Did you get high numbers? Did you enter...the auctions?" I hate even saying the words.

"Nah, I got ok numbers. I was a forty-four immunoglobulin, but none of them were good enough to try my chances at the catalog."

My face pinches, and I flinch at the term. Catalog. Like we are merchandise. I attempt to relax my face as his words sink in. An antibody count of forty-four is pretty average, and he could have got an average contract but probably not better than what he makes here.

I size him up and down again as I respect his logical analysis of his situation. How sensible to look at his options instead of running to auctions with muddled hopes.

"I was pretty fascinated with the process though," he continues, "and they were hiring the month of my first donations. Now you on the other hand, your hundred fifty-seven is unheard of. I don't think there has ever been a higher immunoglobulin number in history."

He beams at me with admiration. That glassy effect covers his eyes. If I was affected like everyone else on this happy juice, I might marry someone like him someday. Perhaps after this donation I would. Perhaps after they do whatever exactly they do here, I will wear these glass expressions and be self-satisfied and follow the path of my sisters. My parents would be thrilled to have a technician in the family; his family would boast of the good number match; the whole neighborhood would speak of our chances of prosperity with high-numbered children to bring in the wealth and end the donations for ourselves so soon. This is why there's so much pressure to marry so young. No matter how happy everyone is about donating, there is still a part of them that is driven to end it. Some call it love, but I know better. No joy juice could take away a person's desire to feel free. Marriage and children made you free. A quick young family meant early retirement.

I don't want to be unattached from the world around me, unable to see what really goes on. I want to really feel, even the bad, even the rough rocky parts of life. I want to cry whenever I want to. My Mam cried last night. I would be able to cry again someday. Perhaps waiting until my future children are sixteen wasn't so long. Maybe living in a fake, fulfilled world for a time won't be so bad.

I look away, staring at the white partition wall beside me.

"I'm sorry. I thought you would be happy with your numbers."

"I'm sure I will be soon," I say.

He gives me a look of *I'm sure I have no idea what you're talking about*, and he probably doesn't.

Without a word, he removes the pack from my arm and places a glowing green sticker over my inner elbow. It makes my arm a neon green with shining white snake-like lines. My blood. The prize.

His face pinches together in concentration. He's more handsome when contemplative. He looks like a distinguished royal, instead of a low-class worker. Yes, I can totally see my satisfied, uncaring self marrying him.

"Once I have the needle in the injection site, the machine will do the rest. It will take about thirty minutes to retrieve, a five-minute separation process where it collects the needed antibody in your blood, and then another twenty-five to thirty minutes to return the blood to your body. When returning the blood to you, it will be mixed with chemicals that help your blood not clot. It will feel cold as it returns."

Cold blood.

It makes the term cold-blooded murder take a different meaning in my mind. It feels like something is lodged in my throat making it difficult to breathe. Chemicals? Is this the joy juice? The drug that is going to make me indifferent? I see he has removed something from the machine, and it sits on the floor in the corner: a blue liquid in a clear plastic bag. I stare at the sparkling mixture instead.

"Have you always been this scared of blood?"

"I'm not scared," I argue. He laughs, and then for the first time, I can't wait to be happy and enjoy making boys like him laugh instead of caring about my freedom. "I'm just...I'm..." A stab in my arm like he's using a dull knife instead of a sharp needle shoots up my arm, and I close my eyes. I squeeze the side of the chair with my other hand and clench my teeth to keep from yelling. My head spins.

"I'm dizzy," I whisper.

"Breathe, Aston. Take nice deep slow breaths and relax. I think you're hyperventilating."

The use of my name and not my number pulls me back to the room, and I do as he says. I fill my nostrils and lungs with the stale mediciney air.

"Thatta girl," he says cheering me on. His cold hand rests on my wrist. The ache in my arm dulls and is more like a bruise than a stab. I open my eyes and give him a deprecating smile.

"Thanks."

He pats my wrist like he patted the top of my hand earlier.

"Now we're all set. For the next hour or so the machine will do everything else."

I look down for the first time. First at the red tube exiting my arm, then at the tape so expertly holding it there and then at the hand that still rests on my wrist. For a second, I think I must have taken the drug, the happy juice perhaps, because I like his hand there and how it makes me feel warm inside. But then anger crashes through again at my freedom taken from me. Freedom to choose when I marry, or to never marry, to devote my life to art instead of the craft of staying alive. This tube is still only retrieving my blood, nothing is entering me yet. Reality sets in. I can't feel this way about him because none of what he is doing is sincere. None of it's real. His touch is an act. Until the juice takes over my emotions, I can't see it as anything else. I cling to my last moments as a free thinker.

"Did you want something to read? Or watch a show?"

"Do you have books here?"

He shrugs his shoulders. "Magazines."

"No thanks."

"I have to step out real quick."

He stands and retrieves the bag of blue fluid before leaving. While he's gone, I follow the red tube up to a computer screen by my head and stare at the little spinning wheel showing the progression of retrieval.

He returns with a small paper cup and several boxes under his arm. One is a dark cherry-colored wooden box. He flashes me a proud grin as he comes and sets the cup by the table.

"I thought maybe you would want to play some games."

My family has never owned any games. I doubt he would know any of the games my sisters and I made up as bored children. Embarrassed to admit it, I blush and look the other way.

"I don't know any games."

"Then I'll teach you," he replies swiftly. "Pick one."

"But I don't know anything about any of them."

"Then it won't matter which you pick. There's no wrong answer."

I bite my lip looking over the pile of boxes in his arms. None of them have words on them. The only one standing out is the wooden box. I point to it wordlessly.

"Ahh, great! You've actually chosen one that has lots of games. There's chess, checkers, Chinese checkers—"

"Chinese?"

"Just the name of the game. Let's start with checkers; it's easiest, I think."

He places a lap tray over me and sets up the game on it. I'm evidently red, and he's black. How appropriate. Looking at my red tube winding on my lap like a red snake, it is nothing like the color of the little red disks that I line up on the board like he does. It is dark and thick.

After explaining the game to me, we play for several minutes in silence. My technician keeps cutting his eyes over to the little cup sitting on the desk beside the computer screen. His mind is clearly elsewhere because it seems as if I'm winning the game even though I don't know what I'm doing half the time. He chews on his left thumb nail and stares at the cup again. Would distracting him from whatever's making him nervous be a service or an annoyance? I decide to take my chances.

"Thank you for helping me calm down today," I say, taking another one of his black checkers. "And thank you for calling me by my name and not a number."

His face answers with understanding "You're very welcome, Aston. I like the name. It's very original."

"I wish I knew your name. I don't even know your number."

"I'm ten ninety-seven."

A moment passes, as if he is questioning if he can trust me with his name.

"I'm Gannet," he finally says.

I can't help but raise my eyebrows and smile. "Like the bird?"

He gives me a questioning look like, *how did you know?*

"My Papa's a birder," I explain. "He finds them, and I paint them. My best friend is also named Lazuli after the la—"

"Ahh, the lazuli bunting, that's a beautiful bird. You know I've seen them before. I think they're just about as blue as your eyes."

I lower my face to the game board to hide my blushing cheeks. It's not flirting, how could it be? It's fake dull kindness. He isn't capable of anything else. He and Lazuli are both named after birds, perhaps *they* should be matched. It takes little to make a couple fall in love here. The slightest commonality it seems has cause for nuptials: "You like pickles? Me too! What are your numbers? We should get married!" More proof that marriage has nothing to do with love and everything to do with ending their donations as soon as possible. But it's not this commonality with my best friend, or his talk of my blue eyes that has me confused and calculating. Moving my red circle checker chip, I ask him a question without looking up.

"All the way in New Detroit? I didn't think they came this far."

I look at him then with his shifty eyes and squirming body. Why is he lying about knowing birds?

"They're a West Coast bird," I push further, studying his discomfort. "They don't come this far east, and no one ever goes west of Minnesota."

His eyes nervously shoot over to the cup on the desk again. A timer goes off, and he slaps his knees before standing. "Well, it's done coming out. Now it's gotta go back in." He steps to the computer screens, pushing buttons even though he already told me it did everything else on its own.

"Ok, where were we?"

Finally, his mind seems to be in the game, and the conversation is over. He proceeds to kick my butt at checkers. The game is over in only a few minutes.

"Ready for another round?" he asks.

I shake my head. "It's too hard to move the pieces while being strung up to a machine."

He doesn't look like he wants to talk to me anymore though, and I wonder what we will do. I feel guilty and uncomfortable at forcing him to be here for me, even though it's his job. Catching him on his lie must have deflated his self-confidence. I need to think of something to bolster him again, though I wonder why I even care. I don't, I'm just being nice.

"Thank you for rescuing me from...Clarissa...today."

"It's nothing. She's a good technician too. You looked as if you were going to faint though, and Clarissa isn't as...attentive to those things."

"Well, you were great. I didn't even know what was happening, I was so distracted."

He smiles.

It had seemed like a good idea to compliment him but now it's just awkward. My admission at him distracting me seemed innocent in my head, but now replaying the words, I can see that they could be taken a different way. My cheeks burn again in the silence. His occasional grimaces towards the cup are exchanged for staring it down as if at any moment the cup is going to do a song and dance number. His brow is knit tightly together, and several minutes pass.

"You didn't want to donate today, did you?" he breaks the silence.

It isn't like I tried to hide it, but still his question catches me off guard.

"No, of course not."

"What do you mean, of course not? You have the highest numbers I've ever seen. With the auctions, your family could become very wealthy, and you could have any match you wanted instead of marrying for numbers."

"Wealth," a scoff escapes me involuntarily. "That's only

something the Recipients want us to crave and chase. We're Donors. We always give. None of us ever receives. They dangle money and prosperity out in front of us like a carrot in front of a donkey."

He mulls over my words. I must be breaking through the film over his eyes or whatever fog is over his brain. This is something my Papa would be proud of. The thought bolsters my courage. I will at least enlighten one person before I perhaps forget it all and turn into one of them.

"Even the infamous Richard Fenway," I continue, "with his high auction contract, can't keep from starving now and then. Wealth pours in for a time, yes, but when Recipients own everything, the money is just going right back to them." Richard Fenway is the wealthiest, oldest Donor, and he is always paraded about at auction parties and televised interviews. His seventy-four-year-old self never has inspired me though, with his dripping skin and hollow frame. His ten children added to his wealth, and his long life was placed on a pedestal for us all to admire. Out of those ten children, four died from making him wealthier. I don't say wealthy, just wealthier. "They keep a string of old elite Donors to display on television, just enough to make us think it's possible. No matter how much they donate, though, they're always just as dependent on the system. How is that? How are even the wealthiest Donors still poor?" I'm leaning forward now in my seat, resting my warm arm on my knees. I feel self-conscious with how he is studying me and slowly lean back making the paper covering the chair rustle. "I have seen too many coincidences to believe that the Recipients truly want the Donors to prosper," I say, wishing I could wipe the images of the slag tank fire from my mind. "And no Donor wealth is making them live any sort of good quality life either. They're all just a sack of bones. And for what? To eat well for a few years and spend money on flashy clothes and furniture? Recipients have a way of always keeping us down. They depend on us too much to ever let us stand." I lower my head as I think about my masterpiece painting that I tried to sell at the trade store.

"What about a match?" He ignores my long outburst. "Why not

find a young man and have your children overtake donations soon, so you will only have but a handful of years to do it? You wouldn't have any trouble finding one I'm sure. That perhaps would make them easier for a short while."

I want to put my hands over my cheeks to hide their redness again. He isn't asking me to marry him, he's asking me about getting married in general. How can I tell him that my books have ruined my life as a Donor, that I don't hope for a high number match to save myself, but to love someone no matter their station or label in society, that I long to be recognized as a talented, gifted artist and not known by a math equation to only be recognized as a sum of some man's numbers with mine.

"I want to be free on my own terms, not when the Recipients say I can be. I don't want their watered-down version of freedom."

Irritation leaks into my voice, but I don't care. He needs to hear this. I think of Oliver and the boy from the market and the Donor in the gutter and Mary, and I'm determined to help at least one person see reason, even but for a moment. "How is raising the next generation of Donors really freedom anyway? Every tear I wipe off their cheeks, everything I'd teach my daughter or son would be numbered, just another number. Number of days, number of years, everything pointing and leading them to the life I ran away from, the life of identity being wiped out by numbers, the life I threw on them just so I wouldn't have to live it again?" My eyebrows are raised, and the hint of a headache pulses behind my eyes. I lower my head and bite my lip. My words move me more than him. Why am I here? Hands in my lap, I rub at the cold entering my arm as if I can make the blood coming back into my body warm again through layers of skin.

"Yeah," he almost whispers.

I'm embarrassed by my outburst.

"You get what you get, right?" he says. "If only we could choose our lives." He shrugs his shoulders. Turning serious again, he continues quietly, "I know plenty who would choose your numbers though, Aston. Make the best of it."

His advice makes my stomach twist, and all the anger comes rushing back. The best of it? Which part is the best? The one where I will be forced to marry to escape? Or the part where I will donate to death just to feed my family? Or how about the part where I will sell my inner space for money, like a modern-day wench.

I look at him, firmly setting my gaze on his smooth handsome face. I square my shoulders and lift my chin.

"This," I place my hand over my heart, "is *my* body. This is *my* blood." I hold up my hand, dangling the tube of blood in the air. "I should have a say in where it goes and what it does."

"No one is—"

"Forcing us, I know. But the sound of my brother Torrin's stomach *forces* me. The sobs of my tired mother *forces* me. The sad eyes of my beaten father *forces* me. The blank faces all across my town like shadows of the people they used to be *forces me*, forces all of us to fall into the system the Recipients have created."

I lower my eyes and play with one of my fingernails. I can barely get the next words out as my throat closes with impending emotion. "I tried to choose my life for a whole three months. Told myself what you just said. That no one is forcing us. That might be the truth the Recipients want us to believe, but no one can stay away from donations for long. Believe me, the Recipients make sure of it. People are hurt because of my choices. Donors aren't forced, but they're far from free."

I look up into his face. His brown pleading eyes above his red healthy cheeks. He offers no more advice. No more trying to convince me to "make the best of it." He is no longer anxiously looking at the cup either. It looks as if he is content with my answers instead of riled up or aghast. I didn't get through to him. His mask lowers over his eyes before I can say another thing, and then the timer goes off. I slump against the leather chair. My breath was wasted though I don't know what I expected.

After removing the tape and needle, he has me hold a cotton ball over the hole before he places a bandage. I swing my legs over the reclined chair about to hop down when he puts that cup of blue substance in front of me.

"Here," he stares at the cup instead of my face. "This is the juice."

He says it as if he knows my suspicion of the happy juice that affects the Donors. Is he trying to tell me something? That this is it? That it's not in the IV but in this little cup?

"You will probably feel lightheaded and woozy for the next few hours, especially after your first time. Drink this, and it will help."

I stare at the cup in his hands now too. It's blue like the little sack of liquid he removed from the machine earlier.

"But it is your choice."

Now he is looking into my eyes. I wish I could read what he is trying to tell me there. Is he making a mockery of what I had shared with him? Maybe I had said too much.

"I'll leave it here on the desk while I go turn these forms in. Do you know the way out?"

The last question seems to be emphasized as if there's a message I'm supposed to be getting. I feel like he is asking more than the way down the halls of this building but a way out of the system, out of the trap set forth by the Recipients, out of a half-life with hazy memories and fake smiles, out of a young marriage and life tainted with illness. I nod my head slowly while looking at him.

"Good. It was nice meeting you, Aston." And then he leaves.

I hear his footsteps trailing down the shiny white tiled floor.

I pick up the cup and hold it in my shaking hand. Could he really have been telling me what I think he was telling me? Is this the complacent juice my father was so certain about? It seems too simple and awfully ridiculous all of a sudden. A drink that makes you happy. When you put it like that, it doesn't sound so bad. Who wouldn't want to be happy?

I shut my eyes and see Oliver being carried away. Officers always have a way of finding out. What if I get caught?

Then my own words echo from only moments before. I want to be happy on my own terms, not the Recipients' version of happiness.

I see a small metal drain in my room. I wonder if they all have them or if this is why Gannet chose this cubicle. Did he know all along I needed this way out? I kneel over the drain and dump the cup before I can change my mind. The blue sparkly drink takes its time, and the smell of honey drifts up towards me. It bends back on itself on top of the drain before it slides through the cracks.

My breath is stuck in my chest, and I belatedly check around the ceiling for possible cameras or droids. The cup begins to drip, and I throw it in the trash can as I stand. When the drain shows no signs of blue, I exit my cubicle. Walking down the hallway, I smile in victory. I don't feel dizzy or woozy. Not one bit.

EIGHT

I survived my first week of donations. But the sight of the needles still makes my breath catch. Mam insisted I catch up with the other Donors, so I'll be donating three times a week, but Gannet assures me he will keep me safe. Gannet is my technician every time. They must assign technicians for one's stay in the facility similarly to how a Donor is contracted to a Recipient or assigned a lawyer. I'm confident in our routine and almost certain Gannet is only following procedure—that there was no hidden message in his words meant for me to decipher. He is a dutiful employee of the facility. His glossy eyes prove he is owned and controlled by the Recipients, and their magic potions are the same as everyone else's. Still, he leaves at the same time each visit and heads out to turn in my papers and my baggie of blood, never waiting to watch me drink the cup he leaves on the counter, and I leave the facility undeterred. I enjoy watching the sparkles in the turquoise-blue liquid swirl down to the pipes under the building.

As I walk down the hallway of the facility, my right arm bandaged and cradled by my other arm since it aches when it hangs, my heart trips and skips again worried someone will know I am not like them. But as I pass the test of health cubicles, it looks as if I may slip through these doors as uneventfully as I entered.

I trace my hand across the bright wall, wishing Torrin could see it. When I told him how the facility building glistened like a giant screen, he ran to his translucent miniport that glowed at his touch. With his skill in angles, math, and technology (mostly used to rig his school assignments into games), he quickly recreated a miniature model of the building while theories on what it was made of poured from his mouth.

The sting of proud tears threatens again as I recall how his fingers flew. He would make an excellent architect if not for his status of Donor to someday overshadow all his talent.

Entering the waiting room, the metal benches in front of me are occupied by several new Donors filling out their questionnaire. The empty bench at the end has me frozen in place and thinking of Oliver.

Papa sent me with a basket of canned goods to Oliver's family like I knew he would. The house was rushing into ruin already when I went; its door falling off its hinges and leaning in place. The round eyes of Oliver's twin brothers burn into my memory. Like another pair of sunken eyes that haunt me, they were as hollow as their stomachs when I heard their bloated bellies churn and grumble.

Their mother grabbed at my arms as if I was a life preserver thrown to her. She didn't cry when I told her about Oliver, and her words are etched into my skull.

"Recipients are entitled to whatever life they want," she said. "We cannot even earn ours."

I shake my head to rid myself of the image of Greg's last scream across the screen. It hurts to admit to myself, even if begrudgingly, that donating isn't as bad as I originally thought. It means lives could have been saved if I had just told Papa or started donating right away. Leaving the building, I momentarily question my triumph over fake happiness. Am I justifying the visits because I have already been subjected to their poison? Was it not the blue cup like I thought but something else mixed in with my returning blood? Perhaps Gannet was playing a trick on me to make me think I tricked the system. That thought seems more ludicrous than the idea of blue antidepressant fed to the Donors. I wash the conspiracy theories away with thoughts of it being Friday. Maybe I will go to the mall with Lazuli after all.

"Thirteen forty-two?" the receptionist says right before the doors close.

I've slowly gotten used to my number. I step back through the doors hesitantly. She motions me over sternly. I begin my march back to the front desk. They know. They know I've been dumping the drugs. I don't know how, but Recipients always find out. Recipients always have control. My heart wants to leap out of my chest and run away, which is exactly what I want to do, too.

I finally reach the bright desk.

"You almost left without your first paycheck."

My shoulders collapse with a sigh of relief. "My paycheck?" I forgot even auction Donors are given a small amount until the bidding begins.

"Yes, dear. Here you go." She hands over a white envelope with my number written across it. "This first one is a paper copy, but from now on, they'll be automatically transferred into your blood bank. You'll receive similar notices through your B-mail account each payday. You do have a screen at home, yes?"

My smile soars, as if it's full of blue serum, from the release of fear. The joy of realizing I'm not actually caught ceases when the envelope is in my hands. I should be happy for this money. It's what I worked hard for all week. I can feed Torrin. I am providing for the family. But no matter how many justifications I give myself, I can't make my chest relax. Hard work? I just sat and bled. Did I forget who I am so quickly? A number is written across the front, not my name. I nod finally to her question. "Thanks."

Maybe if I hadn't been thinking about Oliver's family this would have been easier to receive. Guilt is still fresh in my bones. Deflated, I walk through the sliding doors again. The knot in my throat is the first sign that I truly beat them. As I stumble down the dusty road, tears slip silently down my cheeks. I've got another block before I hit the crowd of the market, so I don't wipe at the tears. I feel them. I let them seep into my skin like paint drying on a canvas. A tear for Greg again. A tear for his son Oliver and his family I couldn't save. Why am I so lucky with a paycheck in hand when others are struggling so harshly? Just because of something born within my veins.

The tram whines against its track in the distance, and I start to jog as I wipe at my face. The doors open with the same swoosh of the facility doors, and I jump on, placing my finger over the metal box by the door. It scans my finger with a red light paying my transport fee. The red light can access my blood through the skin knowing everything about me. Now, I'll have my own blood bank account for it to access instead of my parents'. Still a joint account that Mam won't let me touch without permission but my own nonetheless. The red glow of my finger makes me think of my first painting of the red sunset with bright red watercolors. I haven't painted all week. I've been absorbed in the process of giving away my blood for profit. I should feel happy. I'm bringing in money. It's what I wanted to do, feed Torrin, help the family. The shame that fills me is refreshing in a way. I'm still real. I'm still free. I can still feel. I cajole myself on with half-truths.

By the time I make it home, my face is dry. I enter the house, careful to hold the knob in the particular way that keeps it from falling off and smell the reheated onion and cabbage soup. Perhaps now with the paycheck burning in my hand, we can afford fresh vegetables. Maybe even cheese like that Auction Day celebration when Sybil scored well in the catalog, tenth in the nation. I picture the strings of orange grated cheese, remembering how it melted on the creamy potato soup forming one solid gleaming mass. I miss cheese. It was days like those that made me never feel poor.

Today, however, I know there will be no bread or cheese with this soup. I should feel happy to share my first check with them. Instead, I am scared of Papa. I frantically scan the front room for him as I contemplate how he will handle my first payday. The brown patched sofa is empty, but the Donor newspaper spread across the brown knobby coffee table suggests he will return soon. I stare at the table, remembering the day that started this all. How different things may have been if I wouldn't have hidden the test result from Papa but had taken them to him like I'd planned. My fingers fidget with the corner of the envelope. I haven't learned my lesson though. How could I show this to Papa?

I should wait and hand it over to Mam when he isn't around. Then she may gloat and gush all she wants without Papa being subjected to it. As I move my arm to slip the paper into my pocket, I hear the creak of the floorboards.

"Whatcha got there?"

So much for that plan. Each of my Papa's steps toward me makes new sounds on the shifty wooden floor. Thirty years ago, this home was probably beautiful. But with a world ravaged by war and a society of poor Donors unable to rebuild, everyone moved in where they could. Some neighborhoods are separated by gaps of destroyed uninhabitable houses. The piles of rubble make playing grounds for the neighborhood children. Mam had ripped out the mold-infested carpets when they confiscated the place ten years ago when an old couple was away. Since Donors can't own property, leaving a home empty is always a risk. Mam was happy to find the wooden floors underneath.

It's too late to hide what's in my hand. The bright white envelope stands out in our dingy brown home.

I can't find the words to say it. Instead, I hand it to him and go to the kitchen to help Mam. The news on the kitchen screen shouts through the small room announcing the Donor deaths of the day. It starts with local Donor deaths and then reports the Recipient deaths throughout the country.

There are always fewer Donor deaths than Recipient deaths, but as my father likes to point out, Donor death announcements only cover local reports, dealing with a population of only a few thousand. The Recipient deaths cover every Recipient city across the new country, dealing with several hundred thousand. It's always a biased, advantageous report. The Recipient deaths have sad violin music playing and footage of their lives that ended too soon. I stand frozen in the doorway as the familiar statement at the closing of every news piece comes. "Help these innocent Recipients. Please visit your local facility today to learn how you can help. Make more than one dream come true, and enter the auctions."

"Aston!"

My Mam cheerfully greets me and turns down the news show. The squeeze of each hand on my shoulders as she kisses my cheek feels reassuring, even from Mam.

"Get the bowls from the cupboard, will you?" I can't tell her about the check, either. I can't bear to hear her delight. But I can't enter the other room just yet because I don't want to see Papa's face just now.

"What's wrong with you, child? Get the bowls and put them on the table."

Holding a stack of blue bowls, I enter the dining area that is only a table set in the corner of the front room. I stop as my feet wobble on the creaky boards and scan the empty room. My gaze lands on the torn envelope and blue rectangular piece of paper that lies on top of it, positioned directly over my mother's tan placemat. I carefully place Mam's bowl by the papers, seeing my name out of the corner of my eye. I can't make myself look at it directly. I make every effort to not touch it. I have seen too much of what money can do to Donors. Greed sends them into a rampant status war. When Donors get money, it's as if their history has taught them nothing. This money is my family's to deal with, not mine to ogle at.

Mam brings out the spoons to hand over and sees the papers.

"What's this?" She looks at me with hope in her red plump face.

I shrug my shoulders and set down the last bowl.

"Your first check?" She snatches the blue paper, letting the torn white envelope fall to the ground.

"Oh, Aston!" She places her hand on her chest as if she can't catch her breath. "Two hundred sixty-two dollars? For one week? That's more than any of your sisters made! See? What did I tell you?"

Mam makes the check dance in her hands as she gives a giggle that barely leaves her throat. I can't look at her face. The way she so easily falls into the Recipients' trap, into submission so easily, excited over a small sum while ignoring the signs that the Recipients were responsible for her husband's lack of paycheck in the first place. It makes my stomach twist. Maybe if Papa had left me out of the loop, I could be as easily convinced to be happy with this money, to be relieved at the help it will provide. Perhaps if Greg had never called, if we never knew about the Recipient, I could giggle with Mam. Yet even without all this knowledge, there would always be a pang reserved for how Mam rejoices over my blood money and never cares about any of my paintings. I am only good for one thing in her eyes. I'm happy to have helped; I know deep under this wounded little girl I am happy. *Just use it wisely Mam*, I wish I could say to her. *I bled for this money, please feed Torrin.*

"Has your father seen this? He's got to see this! Surely he will have no qualms about you entering the auctions now."

Torrin comes bounding in, letting the front door whack against the wall and rattle the mirror on it before bouncing back for him to swing shut behind him. My mother is evidently too happy to give him her usual reprimand.

"Torri, dear, come look." Another half-suppressed throat giggle. "No more watered onion soup next week! Oh, we'll go shopping first thing in the morning."

Torrin swoops in and snatches the check from Mam's hand, only to have it swiped back with a small smack on the hand from Mam. She doesn't skip a beat as I begin to place the spoons around the table that she forgot about.

"Oh, but first I will stop by the flower shop for Susan to see." A wicked, gleeful laugh escapes now, and swooping her old beige dress out dramatically, she turns. "She will be so jealous. Two hundred sixty-two!" she hollers as she re-enters the kitchen.

I stand there looking at my warped reflection in the curved spoon, making my pointy nose swoop up and my high cheek bones balloon out round and wide, when Mam pokes her head back through the swinging door.

"Aston, put three more bowls on the table. Shannon is coming to dinner to celebrate with us."

I silently do as I'm told. When Sybil married, she quickly moved two towns over, and now raises her three children in Canton. Ari married a decent-numbered boy who worked for the local lawyers and even met the New Michigan ambassador once. Ambassadors and lawyers live at the edge of town as the dividing line between Donors and Recipients. They are by far the richest of all Donors, richer even than Richard Fenway, but they are chosen, not something to aspire to. Ari and her husband used to only donate twice a month before their contracts amended and they had their first little boy Roylance. Now they can afford to only donate once a month, and their new contracts are very accommodating. They have only ten more years until their contracts end, and they are done with them forever.

Shannon only contracted for six thousand a year, which was low, even for our town. Thankfully, she caught the eye of the mechanic who works on the facility machines. They were married only two years ago and live three blocks over.

I move the bowls closer together to make room for them and their little baby girl, Pip.

Papa returns just as I sit at the table. The sound of his chair scraping against the floor reminds me of that awful Blood Test Day and makes the hair on my arms stand up. I hate that it's like this. I miss the Papa who would share newspaper articles with me or tell me about new hires at the plant.

Whether I was born melancholy and skeptical like him, or it was all a product of being his substitute son, it didn't matter. Either way, I am who I am because of him.

Sitting here now, I feel the guilt settle in; the silence is full of it. I betrayed him. I chose them over him. I chose Mam's radical persistence. I chose my sisters' masochistic frivolity. I chose the system. And with it, I took his pride. Even though I know it's the

Recipients' fault, I feel the blame as my father's silence at the table beats and slaps at me.

"I'm sorry, Aston," his gruff, emotion-filled voice slices through the still air.

"For what, Papa?"

"For letting you down. For not being able to keep you from the facility. For—"

"Papa—"

"For sharing my crazy ideas about the system." I smile at the confirmation of my own thoughts. We are so alike. "If I had kept them to myself, perhaps you would be happy about this day like your Mam and sisters. They say ignorance is bliss, and I took that from you. Try to—"

"Don't you dare say enjoy this. You might have taken my innocence of this world we live in, but you gave me an understanding I will forever be grateful for. I wouldn't have it any other way, Papa." I can tell he is not convinced. "Besides, I'm too much like you to have been ignorant for long. Our system sucks. And they are horrible at hiding it."

He smiles, and I can tell I have him back.

"Did it hurt?" he turns solemn again.

It feels so wonderful to have him talking to me again. "No. And I even got to learn a new game."

He leans over the table with obvious interest.

"It's called checkers." I hear my sister Shannon and her family enter through the back, but keep talking. "My technician is named Gannet," I say with a smile.

"Ha!" My father's surprised laugh makes me smile. "A seabird."

"Yes, and he's so nice. Nicer than I thought technicians would be. He brought out checkers every day, and today, I actually beat him."

"Playing board games with your technician?" Shannon enters the room. "Is he good looking? You know, they have made all the blood numbers available on the public record now. We should look him up." She gushes excitedly as she brings in the highchair for Pip who's perched on her hip.

Torrin enters and makes funny faces at Pip.

"I am not going to date my technician." I can't keep my face from burning. Of course, I would date Gannet if I didn't know how ignorant he is or how absurd and unfair this process is.

"I see those cheeks, Aston dear." My sister smiles and giggles. "You shouldn't wait too long, but I see your point. With numbers like yours why stop with the technicians? You could probably get anyone."

I open my mouth to protest, but it's Papa who ends it.

"That's enough talk about ensnaring boys. Save this girly, ridiculous prattle for when the men leave the room." He gives a playful grin towards Torrin who beams at being called a man as he sits at the table.

I want to add *and when I leave the room*, but Mam enters with the soup.

The dinner is full of Shannon trying to control the mess of Pip learning to eat. The sounds and smells of the ordeal leave me unable to finish my soup. They remind me of the need to rush into marriage to hurry along into motherhood. My contraband books with lessons of choice are warring with our world and what I have been taught. Couples falling in love as late as thirty, some never having kids at all, unpressured by the idea of saving their lives. A time when children were had for the joy they would provide instead of for ending a prison sentence.

There's a knock on the front room window that stops the conversation, and I see Lazuli through the glass, waving and grinning.

After being excused, I flee from the expectations of my parents and from my sister, who represents what I have to look forward to. Spending time with Lazuli is not my idea of fun anymore but definitely trumps a night with my family right now.

I jump over the porch steps and catch my balance when the dusty gravel shifts beneath my feet. "Where are we going?" I ask Lazuli as we head down the rocky street, bypassing the broken-up sidewalk as best we can.

"We're getting Brandon first and then heading for the mall. You know when I was reading the paper the other day about the history of malls, it said that the New Wisconsin Recipient village has restored their mall to its original state. Can you imagine? A building filled with trade stores and shops with everything you need in one long strip?"

"Recipients *would* do that," I groan.

"Huh?"

"Nothing." How do I keep forgetting that the day of being able to joke with Lazuli about those things has passed?

After getting Brandon, Lazuli's boyfriend, we walk along the sidewalk since it is smoother and flatter. In only a few more weeks he may be her husband. Perhaps I wasn't escaping marriage lessons after all. I watch my feet kick out in front of me as we walk.

"Did you see the news?" Brandon asks with a pretense of pity.

"No, what?" Lazuli says.

I lift my head to Brandon's pock-marked face.

"They reported the Donor deaths today, and one was a newbie from our town. He was from our facility even. This was his *first week* donating."

His words send a chill through my spine. A Donor died on his first week? I re-analyze myself. Am I hurt? I feel fine. Yet someone in the very facility I entered for the first time isn't. They're dead. The very thing I chanted to comfort myself, that urged me forward, is now proven false. A Donor died on their first week of donating. My dead sister Mary's face flashes across my mind. I could die at any time. We all could.

"Oh my scars! What happened?" Lazuli looks half concerned but mostly enthralled to hear the details. Her dark eyebrows are inched up her milky white forehead, and the corners of her mouth are slightly upturned like she's anticipating the details of a new screen show. Only the way she fidgets with her hands, wringing them nervously, proves that the old her is trying to be present. Lazuli always was the worrywart with questions, and I was usually the one with answers. But now the new Laz is too strong. The serum overpowers her desire for concern.

"They said he had a citrate reaction. The coagulant they put in the blood after donating reacted to the loss of potassium. Said he had complained to the facility all week, but they didn't recognize the signs because it's so rare. He went into cardiac arrest today."

"Oh, how awful."

I hear my friend's words, but it's so hard to not notice the difference. Her happy serum is in full effect, and even this awful news can't bring back her sincere emotion. Lazuli would have been outraged by this. Laz was my co-conspirator in the hate crime of bad mouthing the system. Now her words are monotone and careless.

"I hope his family still gets his paycheck."

Her uncharacteristically stuck-up, whiney voice is too much for me. I stop mid stride. The two of them notice once they're a few steps away from me and turn back. They both stare at me questioningly.

"I..." I suddenly don't want to go anywhere with Lazuli. "I'm not feeling well." I used to look forward to Friday nights when we went to abandoned warehouses where teen bands were playing, or a basement of someone's house where we found a movie hidden in rubble that wasn't too scratched to watch. But now... "I think I'm going to head back."

"Ok," Lazuli says quickly. "The first week is rough. Make sure you get some rest. Do you need me to walk you back?" Her words seem planned, as if she sits at home making up statements that sound caring to keep herself from actually having to be. There is no inflection whatsoever. Her words are borrowed from the thoughtful friend the facility took from me. I can't even bare to look at her fake face right now.

"No, I'll be fine." The words are for me more than them.

They turn as soon as I say this, without another thought for me. I walk through the same market I did on my donation day. The street is emptying as the sun falls. I pass the road to the facility and wonder about Gannet. I wonder if he knew the Donor that died or knew the technician that was assigned to the Donor. I think about what this Donor's family must be feeling right now. Would they still be as ready to hand over any children they may have? What a horrible way to die, and so soon, a Donor on their first week.

I picture the lanky boy that ran into me on this very road and momentarily reflect on the possibility of it being him. That boy had been donating for much longer than a week though. His face was sunken from dehydration, and I feel a sudden surge of anger towards the facility—*our* facility, the place that was overlooking the signs of death and dehydration. This was probably why Gannet always left the room before I drank the serum—he was just as negligent as the rest of their staff.

The trams were closed this late at night, and so I walk over the metal rails that are flush with the new pavement. I scuffle through the neighborhood streets that grid in opposite directions of the market to my home. Passing the kinder school I attended, I wonder if I possibly ever sat next to the boy that died, or shared a swing set with him. I wonder where he lived.

They killed that boy. I repeat it over and over before the statement forms into a direct internal warning. *They will kill you. They will kill you.* My panic is unavoidable. My life is uncontrollable. Tears run down my cheeks again today. I don't want to die. I don't want to donate.

NINE

"Scars, that's a lot of money," I mumble under my breath to no one. Standing in the trade store, the new blank white canvas is by far the largest one I've seen. It stares at me like the giant white facility building, screaming for color, or dirt, or something to make it come to life in this dead town.

The canvas is one hundred dollars. It's more than anything I've ever purchased. I proceed to the next aisle, trying to distract myself from the blank canvas and from the two paintings of mine in the store. No one has money for art. I know exactly where they hang. They haven't moved in weeks.

Running my fingers along the shelves, the numbers and prices zoom by me. Twenty dollars for a used lamp with no lamp shade. Ten dollars for a picture frame with no glass. Funny term, *dollars*. I don't know why we still use it when I have never in my life seen any actual money. Paper is a precious thing. I have heard that Canada still uses paper currency. New Detroit, the capital of New America, has used electronic blood devices since the dawn of our new society. It's how we pay for tram rides, purchase food, and pay our bills over port screens. Our blood is our key to everything.

A dramatic sigh escapes me, making my shoulders heave as I spot the item Mam sent me for. Who cares that we still can barely afford food to put in these new mixing bowls, with the new sofa and other items. Mam says she *needs* new blue ones to go with her plates, for some small dinner party tonight.

The only blue bowl is lopsided around the top. I bite my lip as I study the others on the shelf. She will be mad to not have blue, yet she could be just as livid to have a bowl that looks like a kinder art project. Perhaps I could trade the returned bowl for the canvas. I smile as I cradle the lopsided bowl under my arm.

The clunk of the bowl against the counter makes me flinch and earns a habitual warning scowl from the store owner behind the desk.

"Sorry, Mr. Burke." I shrug my shoulders.

His face relaxes when he spots me, his leathery wrinkles shifting into a familiar smile.

"Aston! Did you see what I got in for you today?"

"Yes, but you priced it for the Recipients," I tease.

His laugh sounds as rough as his skin looks. Without permission, my eyes flip to the corner above his head where my paintings collect dust. I haven't asked about them since I left them in his care. We are both too nervous, I suppose, to revisit that awkward, difficult moment, too consigned to the realities of our world where we are not free to enjoy beautiful things that hold no value.

"Though from what I hear, you've entered the auctions now and have high numbers to boot. You could afford that with one donation I bet."

My mouth twists into an answering smile, but my eyes are tight with annoyance. Coming from someone who feeds my art addiction and knows how much I want to be known for my work, it cuts a little deeper. He can't help it though. Everyone's sick with greed from watching the news. Watching a number, an unknown person, be the next famous blood idol. Watching lists of numbers and salaries scroll across the screen while being fed with the lie that they could be next. That their town could be important, their people could be valued. Everyone wants their moment of fame. To put their town, their home, their trade store on the map. A high contract can draw the attention of out of state bidders. My face is a full grimace now, and I'm thankful he is tapping away at the white handheld port screen.

"That'll be ten dollars." He points to the small device sitting on the counter sending a wireless message to his screen.

My heart pounds as my mind turns to my precious paintings again. I have to say something. I have to ask now. "How are my paintings?" I mechanically place my pointer finger over the hole at the top of the machine. I stare at it to help hide the pain that I'm sure is evident on my expectant face. My fingernail turns red from the scan of my blood through my skin. This payment method is a foolproof plan. No more identity theft or stolen purses. It's all in our blood. It is calculating my identity and worth. Before now, it never bothered me. This small scan is how they can tell who I am, what my numbers are, who my parents are, their numbers, and access my blood bank. But now it is a semblance and a reminder of *what* I am: the glowing red finger of a Donor.

Mam balances the account and approves transactions. I have no clue how much is really available, but for a moment, I want to dash to the canvas and buy it without thinking, without permission. For a moment, I want to try again to prove that I could do it. Maybe if I painted something different. Maybe now that my number is known. Maybe...

When he doesn't answer, I look up into his tan face and see the same look in his eyes. They're slanted, and his lips are pulled into a straight line as he shakes his head at me.

I have to sign on his screen with the same finger to confirm the transfer of funds. I take my time signing as silence stings through the room. As I do, I imagine myself sitting in a lawyer's office signing a contract, signing my blood away. With each wave and dip of my blood signature, I vow I never will ask Mr. Burke about my paintings again. I finish with a head held high and dry face. I leave the store without looking back at the paintings and before I change my mind. Besides, if I go home with a hundred-dollar canvas, this lumpy bowl doesn't stand a chance at impressing Mam. She would be too angry to see straight.

I skirt along the edge of the street, avoiding the carts and rickety tables that crowd the market. Mam's bowl clanks against a street worker's wooden pushcart, and the woman pushing it gives me a menacing glare. I go flat against a brick building and give her an apologetic grimace.

Her cart moves along with the flow of the busy donor traffic just in time to reveal a familiar sickly donor. His hair is twisted into dirty dreads that hang around his eyes, and even across the chaotic motion of the market street, he sees me. His wicked smile makes my stomach twist. Out of pity, of course. He may not have died like I feared, but his skeleton face looks not far from it.

Shouting up ahead catches my attention. I follow those around me as if we are sheep being herded along, drawn to the sound of distress, but that mop headed donor retreats into the shadows. I wonder what makes him run instead of follow like I feel so compelled to do. I wonder how he fades away just as quickly as he appears. The yelling makes a hush wave through the crowd toward me, and, forgetting all about the sick, annoying donor, I push through people like a child drawn to the pied piper.

"Officers!" the voice yells.

Above the heads of the pushing and peering crowd is the brown canopy of Mr. Winter's market store. My stomach twists remembering the droid that slid into the side of this store when I hit it.

"Officers!" he yells again.

I wonder if he yelled for officers that day, too. No one likes Mr. Winters or his high-priced goods, although there are spices and wares we are forced to purchase from his hot house in the winter. Other than that, most people do their best to avoid him.

The whir of the droids answers his call, and soon, I'm shoved into the crowd by a marching black-suited officer. Another follows, shoving off me to gain momentum towards the yelling. I rub my chest where his elbow dug into me.

As the crowd reforms their circle around the scene, I now have a perfect front row view. Old Mr. Winters, with his missing teeth and waspy hair, trying to cover the brown spots on his wrinkled head, looks as if he's dancing. He is crouched over and shifting across the ground sporadically. Finally, I see why. Tightly gripped in his hand is the arm of a girl who's thrashing wildly. Mr. Winters looks like he's trying to wrangle a wild horse or reel in a fish as he is jerked about.

The officers approach, and I clutch the ceramic bowl in my hand. The muscles in my cheeks tense as my teeth clench together. The girl goes still as she sees the tidal wave of black approaching, maybe ten officers and each with a droid humming over their shoulder. It seems a bit extreme for a street disturbance.

"Officers," Mr. Winters says through his labored breathing. His voice is strained because no one is ever quite comfortable around the bald officers, even crabby Mr. Winters. "This, *creature*," he sneers towards the girl who lunges, making her brown matted hair fling across her dirty face, "stole from me a whole bag of goods."

"I didn't!" When the girl stands, she looks almost as tall as me, and I wonder about her age.

Mr. Winters staggers and then regains his footing not having to pull on her anymore as she stands her ground. I'm suddenly proud of this stranger, because she lifts her chin courageously in the face of the emotionless soldiers. Proud and scared for her stupidity. My fingers ache from my death grip on the stupid bowl.

"I scanned my finger and paid for these things." She points to a brown crumpled bag on the ground near them.

I have never heard the market so quiet as when the officer turns his head to the store owner for an answer.

"Her scan was rejected. Denied funds," he takes a moment to catch his breath before finishing. "And then she ran."

At the mention of running, the girl lunges from Mr. Winters' slack hands. She deftly swipes the brown bag into her arms without missing a step. The wall of people tries to part to make way for her when red light shoots from one of the droids. The crowd gasps in unison as it watches the red beam expand around the girl, just like it did around the dead Donor. It holds her in place, her feet in mid-stride, dangling in the air. Her face is distorted with pain and fear.

When the droid moves, it carries the girl caught within the red beam with it. I step forward without thinking, but a stranger next to me holds me back. I stare at him. He only shakes his head at me.

A zapping sound stings through the air like an electrical shock, and the hair on my neck prickles as it rises. The red lines around the orb that holds the girl vibrates, and she contorts stiffly as if in pain. Some grab their ears and shade the eyes of younger children as the zapping shoots through the marketplace, and the poor girl convulses and screams again.

I shake off the hand that grabs at me. My mind is racing, trying to be faster than my feet. Soon, I'm before the officers, and I shout the first things that comes to mind. A name, make up a name.

"Sandy!" I shout. "Sandy, what have you done?"

The red lines calm, and the girl frozen in place stares at me through the red orb with terrified eyes.

"You know this girl?" an officer says.

"Yes, I sent Sandy to buy groceries for me while I shopped for a new bowl." I hold up the lopsided dish as proof.

"And you are?"

My heart and throat have caught up to what I'm doing and constrict with fear. I couldn't risk anything trying to save Oliver, but now I'm willing to risk so much more for a stranger. Doubt strangles me, and I wonder if I could just slink back into the crowd behind me. What if someone here recognizes me as the girl who assaulted the droid?

The fear in this girl's eyes blinds me though like the red glow of my red Donor finger, and I know I cannot stand by and do nothing. Instead of answering, I hold out my finger for them to scan, for them to be certain of who I am. The portable device on their belt lights up my finger then beeps, and the officer eyes me skeptically.

"Thirteen forty-two," he says aloud.

Murmurs move across the crowd as I cast my eyes around at them. The reaction is so different from when I tried to save Oliver. I couldn't even remember my number then, but now, this whole market street seems to know me. It seems my number is getting around town quicker than the catalog can be printed. All the officers shift their weight and lean closer to me, and people's heads poke out around them.

"You know this girl?" the officer repeats, pointing to the red orb.

I look again at the frightened, unfamiliar face suspended in the air and nod.

"Pay for her goods then, and be on your way."

Instantly, the other officers break apart from their formation around the droid and begin pushing the crowd along. Another officer escorts me into the shop and to Mr. Winters device. I scan and pay for the food while he taps his foot and grumbles.

Finally able to breathe, I watch the transaction of forty dollars finalize, and my stomach sinks with new fear: Mam. How will I explain this money to her?

When the brown bag is handed to me, I step out of the shop to see two officers holding the wrists of the girl. I don't know why they didn't scan her. I don't know why they let me just pay and walk away with this thief. I have witnessed torturing, or lessons, in the crowded streets before. They never just let thieves say goodbye and skip happily on their way. The market is not silent anymore as feet scratch across the pavement and carts are moving again, but there is no laughter or chatter like there was before. It's as if they're programed to know when to fear the officers above all else.

"Thank you, officers," I say putting in a smile for good measure. "Now let's go, Sandy, we have to hurry if we are to catch the tram."

They release her and walk off. We head towards the tram in silence. I feel the officers' eyes on my back as if they themselves have red laser vision. My legs start to shake and wobble with each step while what I have just done sinks in. I don't understand what just happened, but I'm thankful my limbs move robotically with the brown bag in one hand and my lumpy bowl in the next.

"Follow me onto the tram, and I will hand over the bag," I whisper to the girl next to me. "Ok, *Sandy?*"

"My name's Gloria."

The rest of the walk is in silence. When we board the tram, we sit by each other, and I smell the body odor drifting off of her, and a sour stench lingers on her clothes like she washed them in the river. When she cradles the bag, I see her bare arms and notice the smooth inner part of her elbow. There's no small scab from the donations like on mine.

"Are you a Donor?" I say.

"Next year. My parents both have low numbers though. They've been donating for so long. My mom's pretty sick and—" Her sentence is cut off by a crack of emotion in her voice. The adrenaline fading from her body makes her face as white as the facility.

I peek into the bag and find a chocolate bar. When I retrieve it and hold it out to her, she shakes her head.

"No, I got those for my brothers."

I am this girl. We are all bleeding or waiting to bleed for our families, for a bit of chocolate, a bit of happiness before the fake stuff takes over. The hundred-dollar canvas slips across my mind for a moment. Nothing for us. Always for them.

"You need to eat something. I paid for this," I say. "Your brothers can share. Now eat."

The stubborn streak from the market returns across her face, and she eyes the door between tram cars over my shoulder.

"I'm stronger and faster than an old storekeeper. Now eat," I say.

Defeated, her shoulders droop before she rips open the chocolate-covered granola bar. Her eating makes her breathing loud, and I shift in my seat uncomfortably, smiling at the few onlookers in the car.

"Why did you help me?" she whispers with a full mouth.

"You were in trouble."

"Why did they let us go? Why do they know your number?"

I shrug my shoulders, though I had the same questions. "Catalog leaks information sometimes."

"And you couldn't think of a better name than Sandy?" She snorts as unladylike as a girl raised with a hood of boys would.

I stare out the window at the passing trees whizzing by. "I had a cat named Sandy once. Followed me home from middle grade and stayed when I kept feeding it milk." I picture the little yellow cat with a striped orange tail and how she curled up in my arms like an infant. I close my eyes to stop the images. "She stole my Mam's turkey from her plate, and Mam chopped Sandy's tail right off. Told me with the dangling bloody thing in hand that the system would do worse things to us if we ever stole." I look this girl in the eyes and see the flecks of beauty hidden under layers of grime. "I don't know why they let us go, Gloria, but it's true. They will do worse. So you must find other ways to survive than stealing."

She keeps her eyes on me long after I look away. I try not to picture bloody Sandy and the sounds of her eerie moans.

"What's your name?" Her voice is hushed, perhaps out of respect for her namesake.

"Aston."

The tram slows and some are standing and making their way to the exit.

"Thank you, Aston," Gloria says.

After going down the stairs on the tram she disappears around the corner. Finally, I let out a full, loud, cleansing sigh. I couldn't save Sandy all those years ago, I couldn't save myself, and I couldn't save Oliver, but today, I finally saved someone. Does that make up for the lives lost at the power plant? Does this avenge my actions that ultimately killed Greg? Even if it doesn't, it feels good. This is why I bleed.

TEN

After climbing the stairs to our porch, I pause when I hear unrecognizable voices coming through the window. The window to the right of the door looks over the living room section where our new blue sofa is empty and the screen on the wall is turned off. The other window on the other side of the door that looks into the dining area shows Mam standing with Shannon and speaking with a stranger. Leaning on the cracked tan siding of the house, I study them. Mam is moving and smiling the way she does when she is with her Auction Day parade committee—extravagant hand gestures and tilted head. Why is she acting so funny?

The stranger is short and chubby as if he were purposefully flaunting his high numbers all over his body. The side of his cheek is overtaken with fluffy black sideburns, and the way he wipes at his upper lip looks unsanitary.

"No use avoiding the onslaught, Aston."

My father's voice makes me jump, and I spin around. He inches up the stairs one heavy boot at a time.

"War has begun," he says with a wide grin, "and we must enter bravely to our defeat."

"You're speaking in code, Papa. Who is it Mam has invited to dinner?"

"A powerful weapon. Be on guard." He tweaks my nose like he

used to when I didn't understand the jokes the factory workers would make. Why do I feel like I'm the punchline?

I'm utterly confused as Papa opens the metal screen door that squeals and scratches, announcing us before we even grab for the new handle that is bright and shiny.

"Ah, here she is." Mam doesn't even greet Papa. She only waltzes across the room with outstretched hands for me. Once an arm is around my waist, she takes the lumpy bowl and hands it to Shannon who whisks it away.

"Aston dear, this is Leonard. His mother and I are both a part of the Auction Day parade this year."

Leonard extends his pudgy hand, and I see the top of it glisten from where he swiped his lip. I can't pretend I don't see it. I'm staring right at it. My mother's hand squeezes against my waist, pinching my skin, and I take his hand swiftly.

"He's entering the auctions too this year. An eighty!" she says with raised eyebrows.

"Well, seventy-eight, Mrs. Vazeto, but yes, pretty close to eighty." His voice sounds like he is trying to lower it and sound more mature than he really is.

"Oh, you're so humble. And honest, too!" My mother sounds lovestruck, but it's me she's smiling at.

"I should help Shannon in the kitchen." I attempt to step away, only to have Mam grab at my shirt untucking the back of it in the process.

"Oh I'll do that, Aston dear. Isn't she so thoughtful and helpful? She's always doing everything for us. You take a minute for yourself, sweetie, and sit with dear Leonard for a bit before dinner."

Sweetie? Dear Leonard? What is going on here?

We sit on the blue sofa, and I begin playing with the string from the tag that never was removed.

"Are you ready for the auctions?" he asks.

How could he be so breathless just from the few short steps over here? Or perhaps his forced voice makes him unable to breathe.

"Hmm?" I say, trying to compose myself instead of laughing at this whole ridiculous situation.

"My father has already saved up my donation money for the best lawyer. Do you have your lawyer yet?"

"I thought we were assigned one once the catalog is released," I say as innocently as I can even though I know very well lawyers are bribed early in the game. But I can't rein in the smile that teases my lips.

"Right, Aston, we mustn't spill the beans on our tricks to success."

The silence that ensues seems to have its own sound, not like the hiss of the facility, the absence of nothing, but a hum of creaky boards and settling walls. The smell of a roast dances out towards me. I let the sounds and smells lull me as we sit there, uncaring if the conversation ever picks up again.

"I like you, Aston Vazeto. I know my numbers are not as high as yours, but I would very much like you as my match."

The humming seems to stop, and the smell of the rare meat brings me finally to Papa's meaning: *at war, and this boy is the weapon.*

"Scars!" I hiss as I stand.

"Aston!" He seems to chastise my cursing.

Yes, we are not supposed to swear, and we are taught to accept the best sum of numbers in a match, but I can win this war.

I turn to him with a pitying smile. "I'm sorry, Leonard, but I am considering higher numbers first." I let anger with Mam fuel my remarks.

Poor Leonard can't help his forwardness; he was brought up to run in the wheel of the system; he was drugged to never know anything different. His inner desire to free himself subconsciously makes him blurt out his only route to freedom. The same drug also keeps him from feeling dejected. Surprised at first yes, but then his smile seeps into his round shining face.

"That's fine. It's to be expected." All form and precision. No emotion. No love.

If only Mam could see things this way. After the quiet delicious dinner, and a polite goodbye to Leonard, I answer Mam's prying questions, and she flies off the handle.

"Aston, how could you? Unless you really intend to hold out for higher-numbered offers? Of course you don't, you...you fool of a daughter. I blame you, Patar!" Mam doesn't stop and turns right onto Papa never taking a breath. "You filled her head with inconsequential rubbish! You both will be the death of this family with your better-than-thou attitude and haughty dreams! Oh, you care nothing for my poor health and Torrin's future. How you toy with our lives!"

Her cries echo down the hallway as she runs. Father gives me a wink before he follows her. I won this round of proposals, but I need to be more prepared. The smell of roast will always put me on guard now.

ELEVEN

The next several weeks blur together. I fall into the routine of donating more easily than I ever imagined I would. And like a good Donor, I stay hydrated and go through the motions expected of me. I avoid Mam's attempts to set me up with boys as much as I avoid Fridays with Lazuli. Mam is much more concerned about my avoidance than Lazuli is.

Each facility visit with Gannet is difficult. I often find myself forgetting that he feels nothing, that he is a robot to the system. I almost smile at his corny jokes and almost believe his story about his fun Friday at the mall. It makes me glad I didn't go. How weird it would be to run into Gannet outside of the facility.

My first month of donating flies by, and before I know it, the leaves are changing colors, and the wind hints of more to come. I find myself sleeping a lot, and some days eating right by the pantry door with my hand stuck in a box of food. With the added income I bring in, Mam doesn't complain when I eat a whole box of crackers.

There is only a month left before the catalog will be released, and I will get an entire month off for the festivities. Parades, dances, amazing food, and ending the celebration with the televised Auction itself. For the first time, I am looking forward to the Auction parties even though I will be celebrating for different reasons than the rest of them. An entire month of no donating and lots of food sounds heavenly to me now.

Gannet reminds me of our time left together as he expertly pricks my finger for the test of health.

"Only ten more of these left for the year."

"Ten?"

"We aren't open November twenty sixth and twenty seventh of this month."

"Really?" I can't help but sound enthusiastic. "Why?"

Gannet shrugs his shoulders. He says he doesn't know, but his face seems to say otherwise.

"Don't worry, the small number of donations you have shouldn't hurt your chances with blood numbers like yours."

I practically groan as I rub my bandaged finger. "I'm so sick of hearing about my blood numbers."

Instead of asking me why, he only smiles as if he knows exactly how I feel. How could he? He is happily married to his life of donating. This thought brings my attention, for the first time, to the curious question of his singleness. I check his finger. There isn't even a white line where a ring may have been.

"How old are you, Gannet?" I blurt. I rarely see him so flustered, and I find it cute and endearing.

"Eighteen."

"And still single?"

He blushes as he answers. "Low numbers. Remember?"

"So? You're a technician." It's my turn to blush, and I scold myself for being so forward. If I'm not careful, he will think I'm asking because I'm interested in him. Am I interested in him? What am I wanting to gain from this drill of questions?

"I didn't say I don't date. Just haven't found the right number I guess."

I don't miss the use of "number" instead of "girl." It seems as purposeful as his glance in my direction.

"What about you, Aston? Are you trying to find the right number? Or are boys with numbers to compare with yours too hard to find in our town?"

I correct my posture under his smiling stare for some reason.

"I..." I haven't been on one date. Mam has brought dozens of boys to the house, but I haven't even spoken to one of them since Leonard. I look at my bandaged hand as he speaks.

"I'm going to the mall tonight. You should come," he says.

Is he asking me to go with him? I just nod, looking up at him finally in awe. A strange feeling is building inside of me.

"I'll look for you," he adds.

He's not asking me to go with him. He only wants to see me there. I don't know why this makes my shoulders slump. Why is his acting so hard to disregard? Perhaps his dimpled cheeks and soft eyes have something to do with it. Perhaps I could be happy with a blind Donor if he looks like Gannet. I feel shame as soon as I think it.

When his cold hands move across my skin, my heart hops like it could leap out to greet them, to warm them. This is what I would feel and give in to if I was drugged like all my friends. I have already reluctantly accepted the ways of the system by donating for my family to eat. To accept one of them, and pretend to be a happy couple like all the rest around me, just for the sake of digging myself out of the pit of donating, was more than I could swallow; I had to draw the line somewhere, or at least a new line since I already crossed over the first one.

Gannet takes my blood in silence. He stares at the dark, almost black blood passing silently through the tube as I watch his hazel eyes. I am looking for the glaze of happiness that should coat them, but his eyes look sad as he stares at my voiceless blood. I wonder what he's thinking about to look so forlorn. It is so uncharacteristic of him. But everyone is allowed their slips I suppose. I remember the receptionist that sized me up when seeing my numbers. The facility's serum doesn't make the real person disappear; it only dresses them up in a costume resembling their former self.

"Another Donor died today." His voice is low, perhaps to not be heard over the partitions.

I don't know what to say. I feel the same sadness and shock I did when Brandon and Lazuli told me about the newbie Donor. But Gannet wouldn't understand the anger and revolt this makes me feel. I swallow the worry and fear and attempt to play the part of the dismissive, untroubled Donor that I'm supposed to be.

"Don't several die a day?" I say.

The way he looks at me makes me wonder if my voice wasn't steady enough.

"Yes, but this was another new Donor. Her first week. Another allergy to the coagulant. It's so rare that it doesn't make sense."

He catches me eyeing his furrowed brow and concerned face then straightens his back. I agree with his assessment, something strange is going on. To have two at the same facility die so young of the same rare allergy is suspicious. The reports of Donor deaths are usually of the old, the unmarried, or the Recipients that didn't fare well with their contracted Donors. But new Donors dying in their first week is concerning. I'm not going to tell him that though. It would clue him in to my lack of happy juice and that I notice and acknowledge his slip from the expected robotic behavior.

"I'm sure the facility is handling it," he recovers just as the timer goes off.

◇

AT DINNER I bite my thumb nail as Shannon wrangles Pip into her highchair. I can't concentrate on the table conversations because all I can think about is what it will be like to see Gannet at the mall without his white lab coat. Will his brown hair be in the same perfect swoop, or will he let it be more free outside of his workplace? I shake my knee and push the lumpy mashed potatoes around to free my thoughts of such nonsense. Why should I care if he shaved his whole head?

My plate is full, but I haven't taken a bite. As forks clank against our blue ceramic plates and Pip bangs her plastic cup against her chair, my mind is debating on going. Should I call and see if Lazuli can go? Will I have to apologize for not talking to her in weeks? I don't think she will even care. She's probably engaged already.

"Aston, I've asked you three times to pass the corn! What's the matter with you tonight?" Mam shrieks.

"Deep in thought about a boy, I bet," Shannon says as I hand the corn to Mam. "Who is he, Aston? Come on, spill it! Are his numbers even half of yours?"

I give Shannon a glare and stick my tongue out at her. It makes Pip giggle, and everyone laughs.

"It's no one. I'm just thinking about going to the mall tonight. Is that ok?"

"Are you going with someone?" Mam asks.

"No."

"Because I hear that Trenton fellow down the street, you know Patricia's son. He got good numbers this week. He won't be entering the Auctions until next year of course, but I can give his mother a call if you'd like." She places both of her hands on the arm rests of her chair as she scoots out from the table.

"No. I just want to go with Lazuli."

Mam takes a breath to say more as she stands, and I frantically add, "I'm meeting someone there."

The whole table is looking at me now. They are all waiting for an answer.

"Stop looking at me like that! It's just my technician."

Mam raises her eyebrows at my father who for once seems speechless. It doesn't last long, however.

"A technician?" Mam says in a sing song impressed tone. "No wonder you keep turning down all my dinner guests." Her giggling throat gives her mouth a break. "Did you hear that, Papa? A Technician. Are his numbers high too? A technician's pay and high numbers would—"

"No," I say, cutting her off. "Can I go? Cause if I can—"

"Yes, yes child, go. And wear your blue top with the lace across the front. I tied up the holes in the lace and it looks good as new and truly brings out your eyes. Shannon, give Aston some of your lip color and—"

"No. I'm fine."

◆

I ESCAPE AS QUICKLY as I can though I lost the war on the blue top and make-up. I feel ridiculous in this shirt. It makes my dirty jeans and worn brown shoes stand out more.

I escape outside, waiting for Lazuli since I couldn't take anymore of Mam and my sister poking and prodding at my body. I run my fingers through my blonde hair trying to take out the hasty curls they put in. Next to our house is a pile of bricks where another house once stood. Climbing happily over the mountain of rubble is a boy with a patch of missing hair and boots so big on him they reach his thighs. I see the remnants of the sidewalk Papa removed from in front of our house and remember the argument Mam had with him that day.

"*Don't just throw it over there with those bricks! That looks awful!*"

"*Where would you have me put them, woman? And exactly how would you have me move them?*"

"*Oh, this whole pile needs to go! I hate living by a giant disaster! At least the last house had real neighbors on either side.*"

"*You know very well this is larger than the last house. With no leaky roof, or a fireplace that smokes to boot, and with a nice working stove as well, I think we can handle a pile of bricks for neighbors.*"

"*Oh Mr. Vazeto, how you mock my emotions! Do you not care a wit about how I feel? What I want doesn't matter to you at all, does it!*"

"*I do care about your feelings.*"

Mam had sighed with victory before Papa continued. "*If you do not like how it looks, my dear, simply look the other direction, for we are on a corner lot, and thankfully have no neighbor to the east.*"

Mam stomped her foot and growled more complaints before she

left. Mam complained of the dirt left exposed by the removal of the broken cement for an entire year until the system finally declared the soil safe and Papa planted a garden along the edge of the road. Three stones made a pathway down the center of it to enter by. The burying of the diseased corpses is what spread the disease further. The disease lived on in the dead corpses and spread to our food and water. Ten years of pumping our dirt with chemicals and the ground was now man's to tend to yet again. Papa's garden was thriving for years before others dared to try it.

Mam then complained that to have a garden in the front was foolish for it was only begging to be picked by thieves. Papa's retort was that if people were hungry enough to steal from their kind, hardworking neighbors, then perhaps they needed it more than we did.

Mam gasped. *"Nonsense. We have six children to feed. How could anyone need it more than us right now?"*

I'll never say Mam was right, but since then, the garden's done little to support us. It often makes me wonder if it was Papa's design all along to plant a garden for others. Or perhaps it was just a way to prove we could do something on our own without Recipient control. A way to feel more human, digging closer to the earth we came from, farther from the earth we now live on.

Looking at this dirty boy, with his elbows bulging above skinny forearms, I'm aware of how much more in need he is. I eye the new bench Mam has bought that sits on our front porch under the living room window and the new wreath and door handle. All to show how well we are doing since I began my donations. I shift my eyes down to our measly garden that is scrambled with brown, dead plants; finished for the year. There is nothing there to give. Do I dare risk going in the house again to help feed this stranger?

"Aston!" Lazuli calls out. "My mother sent one of our extra loaves of bread she made from my donation money." I have to remind myself that her broad self-important smile isn't really her fault before I eye the bread.

"Lazuli!" I exclaim triumphantly with her salvation of my problem. I grab at the bread thanking her and then carefully cross the sidewalk piles towards the brick rubble.

"Excuse me," I call out to him.

The skinny boy freezes making the pile of bricks he stands on shift and slide slightly. His weight isn't enough to move them much. His face looks frightened, as if I have caught him making trouble and will report him.

"Don't worry. I just wondered...if you were hungry?"

"Aston..."

I ignore Lazuli behind me.

He eyes the bread in my hands, and I feel like I can see his stomach ripple and rumble from desire through his tattered gray shirt.

"Please, come take it."

"Can I bring it...to my family?" His voice makes him sound older than he looks, and my heart drops at wondering why he looks so much smaller than he should be. All I can do is nod.

Like a Jesus lizard across the water, he quickly skips across the top of the bricks. Dirty hands snatch the bread, and then he's off down the road making a tiny dust path behind him. A faint thank you is thrown over his shoulder.

"Aston, I don't know why you did that! My mother gave me that for your family." I picture the blue sparkly juice going down the drain to help myself recover from Lazuli's comment. It's not her, I remind myself.

Three blocks away, I realize her boyfriend isn't with us.

"Where's Brandon? Is he meeting us there?"

Without making a face, lowering her head, not an ounce of sadness or worry she answers, "He's sick."

"Oh no, Lazuli, is it serious?"

"It's just a cold."

Most of the serious and deadly illnesses that come from the

donations begin with just colds. The effects of the donations on Lazuli are more subtle. She doesn't notice or care or comment.

We turn a corner and head four blocks north where the streets become flatter and nicer as we near the Detroit river. On the other side of the river, I can see the line of lawyers' homes. Behind them, the ambassador's home shines with so many lights in the growing dark night it looks like it is made of gold. Behind it lies the forbidden world of Recipients like a fairy tale, like they are the Gods of our temporal little world. For all I know they could be camera tricks, and the ambassadors are our true leaders using the Recipients as a decoy.

"It's beautiful, isn't it?" Lazuli says.

For one small moment, I forget that she's changed and hear the same Laz I grew up with. A small memory flashes across my mind of the two of us throwing rocks across this same river hoping to hit a window or something to make the foreign mansion a little more like us. Inadequate in even the simplest of ways, it would have made us feel a little equal and not so segregated.

"It would be so awesome to live in a house so big and clean and beautiful. I can't wait for the Auctions so I can see it on the screen. I bet they will have it decorated so pretty!"

Her sigh is what brings me back to reality. She is caught in the dream of being wealthy like all other full-time Donors. It's sickening how easily the donations change them. Even when I know what is making them this way, I can't handle it. I thought I could come here and pretend with her, but how will I be able to handle a whole room full of people like her? A girl who despised the Auctions, who avoided the televised events as best she could with me, who complained and made fun of the Donors who took these events so seriously, was now sighing over the ambassador's house and dreaming about those same parties.

I pick up the pace, stepping away from Lazuli and speed walk against the edge of the riverbank. I hear Lazuli's feet catching up to me completely oblivious to anything going on around her, completely ignorant to anyone's feelings or fears or true joys even. I flick the tear that escapes before it has a chance to run down my cheek.

I should mourn the loss of my friend. It has been a lonely few months without her. But I push it aside like I find myself doing a lot lately. For someone who risks everything to still have feelings I sure do suppress them quite a bit.

I know it's because I haven't painted since I started donating. I'm out of a lot of colors, but I'm too nervous to ask for money for paints.

Soon, Lazuli and I are not alone on the riverbank. Other kids and couples and parents are either out to stroll along the river or headed to friends or the mall like us. The building is in view over the top of the market buildings and even the facility. I can hear the faint sound of drums as we, step by step, draw closer.

"Did you watch the news today?" Lazuli catches up. "I heard another new Donor died today."

"Another one?" I question without thinking. It's the fourth new Donor death this month. I quickly regret encouraging this conversation with Lazuli though as she drones on about how these local deaths will better their chances at the Auctions.

I ignore her as best I can the rest of the trip. Through the closed market, the facility street, the doctors' street and then the lawyers' offices we work our way forward in silence.

I try not to think of the nights we ran through these streets. When we felt rebellious for being out so late and when we snuck into a lawyer's office just to see what it was like. Hating the system years ago feels like a game we played. I never attached the

ramifications of actually not donating. I never thought about anyone but myself.

We finally cut through the last row of buildings. Dark mounds of rubble stand before us like an obstacle course. We have the paths through these war zones memorized. We join the small crowds of people that make their way to the only light in the distance: the mall.

There is never a line waiting to get into the mall because not only did the building have several entrances when it was in use decades ago, but all the windows have been cleaned of jagged glass and are used as new entrances.

I step through to a now empty store. Even many of the shelving units were taken and used for market stores. There was a day when Lazuli and I would step through, linking arms, and giggle, but not today. Lazuli is beaming as cartoon-like as the girl from the waiting room, and I can't bear to look at her.

The music grows louder while we exit the abandoned store and enter the main room. I read once this was a hallway, meant to pass from one store to another. It's possibly as large as my home. At the end of the hallway the makeshift stage stands unchanged. I don't recognize the kids on stage, only that they look younger than I remember band players looking. I'm the one who's changed though. It's crazy what a few months can do to a person.

The band members are tuning their guitars and playing sporadic test beats on their drums. The sound of the crowd happily murmuring to their neighbor makes a hum that starts to give me a headache. I hear Gannet's words in my head, *Breathe,* and I inhale as much as I can of the sweaty crowd aroma.

"I'm going to get a drink," Lazuli says. "My mom gave me some of my paycheck. Want me to get you something?"

Fake kindness or not, I don't turn down a free drink. After I nod my head, she takes off in the opposite direction of the stage just as a band member starts speaking into the mic. The sight of his sad guitar with chipping red paint brings back memories of the dying Donor in the streets. The arts are not valued anymore. Maybe once there was a day when people played music and went to concerts and stepped through art galleries, but not anymore. Today, the books, instruments and supplies found in the rubble are picked up by dumb, untrained kids who want nothing more than to feel something real. The guitar player is introducing his next song and apologizing about the stupid piece of crap guitar that evidently broke a string on him in the last song. He looks young, not much older than Torrin, except for the peach fuzz that shades and mottles his face under the lights.

I automatically start bobbing my head to the song as I try to nonchalantly scan the crowd for Gannet. I tell myself I didn't really come for him, but I know it's a lie. He said he would look for me. With this crowd of people and flashing lights, how in the world are we to find each other?

And that's when I feel it. The cold fingers on my left elbow. My head spins around to see his smiling face.

"Gannet!" I can't help but sound relieved and surprised. My stomach twists in different kinds of knots than the ones from seeing blood, and I wring my hands to try and loosen it.

"Aston... Um, this is Marnie."

I follow the direction of his gaze, looking down to see a girl for the first time. I had been so distracted by his smooth face and combed-over hair that I hadn't noticed her. The girl hanging on his arm is short, barely reaching Gannet's armpit. She has strawberry blonde hair and light blonde eyebrows. She bounces on her toes; she's so happy. I can't keep my lip from curling. Is this girl for real? Does Gannet slip her extra serum or something?

"Hi, I'm Marnie," she says with rapid moving miniature lips. Her grin overtakes her face in a way that looks painful.

I shake her tiny hand carefully so as not to break it.

"Are you here alone?" Gannet asks.

"Oh, no. I'm here with..." I don't know why but I contemplate lying as I look over my right shoulder. Lazuli bumps into my left shoulder with the two sodas, saving me from dishonesty and humiliation. "With Lazuli, my friend. Lazuli, this is Gannet my technician and his friend Marnie."

They all shake hands and exchange pleasantries while I stand with my soda and rock on my heels. I can't help but critique Marnie's size and pale complexion and how sweet she is. It's like nauseatingly sweet, like a rich double chocolate cake. Sure, it's wonderful at first, but you can never eat much of it without getting a stomachache. Looking at her is giving me a stomachache.

"Well, it's good to see you, Aston. Have fun." He actually winks at me before walking away with Marnie. I nod my chin up at him as he goes.

"Your technician, Aston?" Lazuli rounds in front of me. "Scars, but he's hot! Why didn't you tell me you had such a good-looking technician? What's his number? Would you be ok if I requested him next week?"

"What?"

"It's ok if you want to keep him to yourself. I didn't know you were seeing anyone. But it looks like he's dating midget girl... So...just let me have Tuesday with him."

"Don't you like your technician?" I squeeze my cup at the idea of losing Gannet. He has been the only way I've made it through the facility without fainting and, well, I can't think of any other reason why, but she can't have him.

"Well, I have had some nice ones, but the girls always seem to be more rough with the poker. I think they have it on the highest setting, as if I have tough skin or something."

"You don't have the same technician each time?"

Lazuli laughs, and I don't have time to think about how different her laugh is now from the genuine glee she used to express.

"Of course not, Aston. You've been donating enough to know that by now. I mean, I've gotten the same one every now and then, but it's all based on which one's available and which cubicle is free and all of that. You can hand in requests, but it never guarantees that you get them. If I could choose though, I'd pick him every day!"

It's her laugh again that awakens me to my surroundings. I look down at the cup of drink she got me. It's blue.

"What is this?"

"A new drink called 'rage'! It's fruity! You'll love it."

It's too much like the cup Gannet hands me minus the sparkly thickness. Lowering my nose to it, I smell honey. I drop it without thinking and all those around me jump away, forming a circle of space between us. I stare at each of them one at a time. Smiling,

smiling, smiling, they're all smiling at me. Why would you smile at someone who just splashed drink on you?

"Aston, are you ok?" Lazuli says in the flat tone I hate so much.

My eyes land on possibly the only person in the entire dark, run-down mall not smiling. Gannet's face appears in the distance between the heads of the throbbing crowd.

Instead of staring at his concerned face or listing the questions that are forming from Lazuli's news, I run. I push against the back of the person by me and run. I don't wait to tell Lazuli; I just push against another back and another forcing my way through the crowd. Once I reach the dark cool November air, I let my legs really move. They don't have to think about the boulders of cement or piles of brick; the path is memorized, and my mind is free to finally ask questions. Why did Gannet ask to be my technician? Why is he my technician every single visit? Why the same cubicle every single time?

I make it home in no time. As I swing open the door, seven pairs of expectant eyes stare back at me, the white flashing screen reflecting in each of them. Torrin sits on the new woven yellow rug, hugging his knees. Shannon is frozen in the rocking chair by the door, mid-rock, with a sleepy Pip dangling over her shoulder. Their faces are a pale yellow under the light of our cheap bulbs hung by a wire from the ceiling. The new screen that Mam has purchased blares on about the explanation of Citrucel allergies, and how to prevent them.

"You didn't stay long," Mam says.

I don't wait for anyone else to say anything; I walk briskly across the room. One foot on the stairs, my eyes land on Papa's mini port screen on the desk near me. I remember Shannon saying all numbers are on public record now, and I snatch it. I take the stairs two at a time.

I make sure to lock the door before I throw myself on my belly down onto my tan bed. I set the screen in front of me, prop myself up on my elbows and begin tapping away.

Compass is the search engine that leads me to Michigan's DMR site. I click on New Detroit, then on the name of our facility, Livonia. In the top right corner, I see a mark of blood, like it is dripping on the page. When I press on it, a list of options appear: contact info, location, system rules and regulations, blood numbers public record. I remember to breathe again as I tap. Three options then appear: Donors, auction contestants, or contracted. Gannet didn't enter the auctions, so I press over Donors. A large list scrolls before me, and I watch the cursor on the right of the screen zip to the top as the page fills. When it stops, I tap at the numbers on the side trying to narrow in on the thousands. There's a ten ninety-six, and then it jumps to eleven zero four, but there is no ten ninety-seven. Did he lie about not being contracted?

I go back to the options and click on auction contestants. He's not there either, nor under the contracted list of numbers. I roll over onto my back putting my palms against my forehead. What does this mean? Suddenly being so insistent to be my technician and then being my only technician ever seems more than just odd. Do the Donor deaths have something to do with him? My heart is racing, and a weight rests heavily on my chest—not smooth faced, makes-my-skin-tingle Gannet. It has to be wrong. But DMR doesn't make mistakes, right? The weight on my chest drops down to my stomach for an instant when I recall the last time I said those words with a technician standing on my porch. Someone is making mistakes. Or at least making it look like mistakes. But Gannet?

Another idea comes to mind, and I roll over to the screen again. This time I tap on the white search window in the left corner and type in ten ninety-seven. The screen flashes like the battery is dying before it brings up its results. There is Gannet, his soft face, smoothed brown hair and fake twinkling hazel eyes. His numbers are what he told me they were. All the information he gave me is there.

The adrenaline of the search is wearing off, and I wonder why this makes me angry. What was I hoping to find? That he was lying and really was an auction contestant like me. Would I have found comfort knowing someone like him also chose to go to auction? What did "someone like him" mean? Was I hoping he really lied about it all and was a...a...what am I? A traitor? A rebel? I was both, technically, depending on who you asked. A traitor to my father, a rebel according to Mam.

I stare out over my room now. It's so plain and barren. A brown wooden chair, identical to the kitchen chairs, sits in the corner. The dark wooden door to my closet is beside it. The only other furniture in the room is my brown bed and dark wooden nightstand. Everything I ever cared about is outside of these walls, I made no effort to bring them in. This is only where I sleep. The separate garage in the backyard is where I keep everything important to me.

A soft knock at the door lets me know Papa wants to come in. Mam and my sisters don't even bother knocking. After telling him to come in, his head peeks through the small crack he makes before stepping fully through the door. I sit up on the edge of my bed.

"I convinced Mam to give you this."

He hands out a bundle of rolled papers. When I open it, I find a blot of blood and fingerprint with Papa's chicken scratch scrawled across it: one hundred twenty dollars. The tiny paper seems to weigh more once I read it.

"Papa, I'm not doing this to have money for myself, and I didn't come home early because I didn't have any to spend."

"I know. But I thought maybe you could buy some paints with it. It's been awhile since I've seen you out there."

I glance out my window. This would be enough to buy that giant canvas, and paints too. But I can't accept this in front of him now. Why does this feel like he is testing me to see if I will give in to the way of the system and use their money for greedy desires?

"Thank you." I say without looking at him.

"Yes...well. It would be good to see it used on something sensible instead of all the frippery bought in this house."

Mam had been true to her word about going shopping that next morning. But the watery potato soup and lumpy mush only stayed away for a week. Donors don't know what to do with money once they receive it. It's not in their blood, I guess you could say. Papa ducks out of the room.

I clutch the note to my chest and curl up on my bed. Why do I feel so guilty about taking this money? Why can't I just forget about the happy juice theory and drink and eat and be merry like everyone else? Why can't I just trust my technician, trust the facility, trust the system, and live an uneventful life of smiles and bands and dances? I accept my Papa's apology now. He took my ignorance from me. It's because of this that I can't just move on.

It's Thursday, my day off from donating. School for Donors is over at the age of sixteen, but Papa tells me there used to be more to learn. He says that before the wars people had infinite possibilities for schooling. Something called college and master's programs, PHD's and post doctorates. All the possibilities of further education sound frightening and exhilarating at the same time.

Wealth used to be placed on a person's choice profession, not by the status of their blood, or their DNA, or the genetic side of the town they were born in.

Now money is precious even to the wealthiest Donor. We have no choice. I've finally reconciled to spend my money and get paints from the market, but before I can leave, Mam demands that I winterize "father's garden." It's never just the garden. It's always "your father's" nut brain idea.

I set out to the front yard with a small spade. Pulling my hair up into a ponytail, I look across the overgrown mess, trying to decide where to start. In the beginning, I'm frantically pulling at the weeds and chopping at the dying vegetable plants. Soon, however, I'm slowing and tiring of the job. Before long, I too am referring to the garden as "Papa's garden" and grumbling about the need for it at all.

"You?" The surprised accusatory words make my head fall backwards and my chin tilt up toward the sun. When I see the face of the sick boy from the market, my face contorts without permission.

"What do *you* want?" I sneer.

His face makes a similar shape, and I'm at least relieved he's learned a lesson and hopefully saving me from any repeats of the other day's rude remarks or flirtations. I lower my head again to the pesky weed held firmly in my hands. Putting my weight on my heels, I tug hard.

He hesitates, then gathers his lanky arms behind him and stands haughtily and formal. "I came to apologize," he says.

I raise my eyebrows without lifting my head. Wasn't he just surprised to see me? A scoff escapes me. I would do very well to never believe a word out of this sick Donor's mouth. My grip tightens, and the prickly fibers of the weed sting my hands.

"You were right," he says. "I was rude and, well, anyway... It's just not often I come across someone so refreshingly difficult."

The weed doesn't give way. I relax to readjust my grip and look up to see his forced smile and how his skin stretches across his pitiful skull. Refreshingly difficult? What does that even mean? The dark blond hair on that skull is splayed across his brow, messy and straw-like. It looks as if he bathed in the river and let his hair be whipped dry by the wind. Pity again keeps me from saying what I really think. Instead, I take the small spade and chop at the obnoxious weed, trying to loosen the earth around it. Pieces of earth fly up around me. Getting a better grip on the weed, I put all my weight into it now, leaning backwards with stiff shoulders, scowling and ignoring his skeletal smiles.

"I'm looking for an Aston Vazeto."

The root comes free, and I fall backwards, sitting with a bump onto the sidewalk. Instead of moving right away, I look again into this guy's face. Nothing has changed. His eyes are still buried into his skull; his lips and face muscles protrude from under his thin skin. Yet there it is again. Confidence in the way he holds his chin and determination in his stance. It's as if he's had years of correct training and schooling instead of a Donor's ten years of education before they are forced to become an adult. He fears nothing and no one. Suddenly, his eyes intimidate me. How does he know my name?

I stand, brushing my dirt-ridden hands on my jeans before placing them on my hips. "That's me," I say with a sigh.

"Oh."

That confirmation is clearly not what he expected. Or perhaps the one he dreaded.

He steps forward, retrieving something from his pocket. "I've been sent to give you this."

His knobby thumb atop the envelope looks mechanical as if the visible tendons are electrical wires underneath. The thumb is even more ashen than his face.

As soon as my fingers touch the envelope, I know it's by far the nicest paper I've ever held. There are no lumps of the recycled paper fragments. The gold-trimmed edges shimmer under the sunlight, and my fingertips slide over it easily.

"It's an invitation," he says.

I look at him, confused.

"At least, I think so. The last Donor opened it right away in front of me, and that's what it looked like. Not that I was reading over her shoulder; it's just—" he rambles and then clears his throat. "Anyway, there you go."

"Thanks." I slip the paper in my back pocket.

"Aren't you going to open it?" he asks.

"Maybe later." I don't want to share with him how much I treasure this fine paper and want to keep it clean from my dirty laboring hands.

"Aren't you at all interested about who it's from?" he asks incredulously. "What it's for? That paper—" he stops himself.

"Did you have anything else for me...um," I gesture my hand out with airs realizing I don't know his name.

"Marcus," he answers anxiously. He eyes me as if he's waiting to see my reaction to his name. The same look of fear he gave me in the market.

"Marcus, are you quite done? Because as you can see, I have a lot of work to do." I gesture to the dying land that needs to be prepped for the oncoming frost.

Marcus gives me the most genuine smile I've ever witnessed. It takes my breath away. I've never seen a Donor with such straight white teeth. Perhaps they appear whiter next to his gray, dying skin. Perhaps his stretched, thin face makes his smile seem more real.

"Why do I make you so angry?" His shoulders relax as he smiles differently now. "Do you know the angrier you get, the more tempting you become?"

"Excuse me?" I say, bugging my eyes. The nerve of this pitiful thing!

"It's too tempting to just walk away from, the way you egg me on so."

I sigh, roll my eyes, and let my arms drop to my sides. I sit to work over the dirt. "I promise you, *sir*, I do no such thing."

"There you go again. You know when you crinkle your eyebrows like that it makes a little 'v' on your brow." He points to his own fine brow. "It's adorable."

Another weed comes free, and I throw it, barely missing his feet.

He steps aside and laughs without taking his comical gaze from my face. "It looks like a little bird trying to fly away, making it very hard to take you seriously."

"You've delivered your message, now go," I say.

"Are you always this demanding?"

"Are you always this annoying?"

He chuckles, and I contemplate throwing dirt at him without missing this time.

"Only around beautiful girls who catch me off guard."

"Perhaps you need to set higher expectations. Or mingle with prettier women."

He laughs again, and I see the effect it has on his eyes. It doesn't just make him look less sick, it makes him look unaltered by the serum. Is it really possible that he has discovered the truth behind it as well?

"I don't think either would prepare me well enough for your company, Miss Aston Vazeto." He smiles warmly down at me before squatting. His bony knees protrude outward, and he rests his elbows on them. I try not to be too obvious as I study him and continue to remove the bits and pieces of dead plants, only glancing up under my eyelashes occasionally.

"Vazeto. That's a different name. Do you know if it is Italian?"

"Hungarian."

"Ah. Do you know who brought—"

"My grandparents. My grandmother moved to old America after the second Germ War. All the youth were moved first, before...well... before Europe was overtaken."

For the first time, silence settles in. Marcus seems to have run out of ammunition and has nothing to say. I am surprised at how the silence doesn't feel uncomfortable or awkward. It feels...respectful, if that's possible, as if he were purposefully pausing to remember those who were left behind in the wars.

"Do you know my last name?"

I don't even look up.

"How would I know that? I just met you." I flick my eyes up quick enough to catch a smile.

"Actually," he says, "we first met when you plowed into me in the market. Remember?"

"You make it sound like I'm a bulldozer, wrecking anything in its path. You were just as much in my way as I was in yours."

"But you did wreck me, Aston." He puts his hand over his chest dramatically. "You wreaked havoc on my heart in a way that I will never recover from." His voice sounds childish.

Now he's egging me on in his annoying, better than thou attitude he does so well. Making fun of me as if somehow he knows how much I treasure the proper romances of decrepit books. He's the low blood, though, and has no right to mock me. Why, if he only knew who he was talking to…if he knew my numbers…

I stab my spade into the earth and tilt my head up at him with a scowl. His wicked smile is about to send me over the edge when he slaps his knees and sighs as he stands.

"Well, Aston, it has been refreshing to not be pitied or respected with fake airs, and for that, I thank you." He gives a theatrical bow, which makes him miss my glare. "But as you can see," he fans himself with a handful of gold-trimmed envelopes, "I have more invitations to deliver. So, until next time, Miss Aston Vazeto." He puts his hand to his head as if he were tipping an invisible hat. Then smiles at me in a way that makes me adjust the collar of my shirt to make sure I am not revealing myself from this unpleasant lower angle.

"Goodbye!" I say with finality, relief, and agitation. "And good riddance," I mumble as he steps away. I hear his small chuckle from a distance and can't help but smile myself. What a weird man.

By the time I finish the garden, I am too exhausted to walk to the market. I stay home with Mam and then help Torrin with his schoolwork.

At night, I slip into the shower and am never more grateful that we have running water. How could I think we are really so poor when we have such luxuries? It feels like satin running over my skin, and it's as if I am melting into a puddle in the tub. The system tells us we are poor because we are not rich like them. Shouldn't there be an in between? We have too much to be in true poverty. Perhaps it is only perspective. But then I remember we are only doing well now because I gave in to the donations. I recall the boy I gave Lazuli's bread to, Oliver's family and Gloria I met in the street. My blood number makes us live well. Others are not so lucky.

It isn't until I am about to climb in bed that I remember the envelope. It pokes out of the dirty jeans as I move them to the pile of clothes on my closet floor.

I stand in the middle of my dim room holding the soft paper, afraid to rip it or fondle it too much. The small yellow light of my nightstand lamp makes the gold edges dance. On the back of the envelope, a wax press seals it shut with the mark of the New America: a droplet being held up by two curved palms. The two hands are supposed to represent the Donors and Recipients, but the two would never be this close. The arms of the two hands are practically connected underneath the droplet of blood.

I slip my finger under the bright red wax, separating it carefully from the paper. Under the flap, a maroon card is peeking out at me, repeating the color of true blood. My curiosity overtakes any desire to salvage this paper, and I quickly extract the card and open it. I speed over the words stupidly.

*The Ambassador of New Livonia, New Detroit,
invites you, Aston Vazeto, to attend his annual Auction ball.
The ball will commence on Friday the thirteenth
of December at 7:oo pm at his estate on Hempshire Avenue.*

*Please wear your finest attire and prepare for a night of surprise;
for no one knows what the Auctions may bring.*

I scan the invitation over and over again, and still it's as confusing as the first time I stumbled through it. Clearly it is a printed invitation with my name filling in the blank. For the sender to afford a printer, they must be wealthy, and paper like this...well. It can't be a joke though. I wouldn't put it past the sick boy, I mean Marcus, to pull this off. If it is real, then I can't... I just don't know what to think or feel.

Ambassadors are the mediator between the lawyers and the Recipients. No one really knows what they are. Some believe they are a rare breed born without the disease embedded into their body but also without the cure running through their blood. Some believe they are Donors that found favor with the Recipients while others believe they are Recipients that lost their wealth and work for their cure.

No matter what the ambassadors are, they are for the first time inviting auctioned Donors to their parties. These parties were reserved for lawyers and other ambassadors as far as I knew.

I pull the rickety drawer to my nightstand out and stash the invitation in. I shut it as if someone were coming in my room any second and I didn't want them to see it, but when I spin around, I am still alone. Perhaps the idea of being in the ambassador's lavish home is what makes the smell of my dirty laundry bring me to my senses. I go to my closet, but instead of shutting the door, I pull the string that turns on the light and eye my paltry wardrobe. I am in no state to attend a ball. I own nothing decent enough to dance in, especially not while in the presence of lawyers and ambassadors. I am a Donor.

Papa would be ashamed of these girly nonsense thoughts. He would tell me I am as good as any lawyer or ambassador out there no matter what I wear. I turn out the light trying to hold my chin high. Papa will know what to do with the invitation. Papa always knows what to do with the system. This time I must go to him. No dawdling or waiting.

There is still a drop of fear that lingers in my heart, though, as I climb between my scratchy sheets. Laying across my sunken mattress, handed down from Shannon, I can't help but wish I had one decent thing to wear to such a ball, not this ball, of course, for it would only be like that night in the mall, full of fakes and masks. But, oh my scars, did I want to see the inside of the ambassador's mansion. Yes, my Papa would be ashamed to know the things going through my head lately. Enjoying a soft boy's face, and cold technician hands, and dreaming about wealthy homes and dances. I guess Papa and I are not as alike as we thought.

THIRTEEN

The next morning, I stuff the invitation in the back pocket of my jeans before heading down to breakfast. I leave the pretty gold envelope in the safety of my nightstand.

My fingers brush the top of my pocket several times during breakfast, ready for Mam to leave, ready to hand over the invitation to Papa, but Mam never leaves the table. She never even breaks for air as she complains to him about the paint she must have for the front porch.

"The Jensen's painted their house a bright red, and their daughter only makes one hundred and sixty a week! We need to look like the level of numbers that we are, or people will begin to call me a liar!"

"Not the worst thing to call you right now, I dare say," Papa mumbles.

"Ah," Mam shouts as she jumps in her seat at the table and lets her fork clang down out of control. "Mr. Vazeto, how mean you are to me! You will be the first one to spread rumors of my horrid state no doubt! I dare say you'll happily agree with all the accusations of my lying when they spread through the town."

"Torri dear, is that what I say of your Mammy around the factory? That she's a dishonest chit?"

Several more harrumphs from Mam.

"No, Pa."

"See there? Here's my witness. I do not and will not spread any such rumors."

"But," Torrin begins. He doesn't see my bulging eyes and slightly shaking head as he continues. "You do say she will spend a hole in our pockets faster than a hound after a—"

Torrin is cut short, both by Mam's screams and Papa's hand that is now clamped over Torrin's face.

I run around the table grabbing Torrin by the hand and lead him out of the house while Papa chases Mam to the kitchen.

"Torri, what were you thinking?" I hiss once I shut the front door.

"I was trying to help Pa. He's mad that she keeps buying all this stuff, and he works hard! You work hard too."

"Torrin, there are some truths that...well, though we see them and hear them, doesn't mean we repeat them. You got Papa in more trouble instead of helping his situation."

The sound of Mam's wails come through the upstairs window, and I put my arm around Torrin's shoulders leading him down the stairs of our front porch. The gray paint is chipping in places, and I did get a splinter from the railing last week, but I don't think it looks too bad, especially not since we had mushy noodles and watered chicken gravy twice last week because of the new bath towels Mam bought.

"Come on, Torrin. I'll walk you to school."

After dropping him off at the middle grade playground, I watch the children swinging carefree from the metal swing sets for a moment. What I wouldn't give to be with them again. Feet up in the clouds. Cares far beneath me.

When I'm done dreaming, I have to race for the tram. The walk with Torrin took up my chance to buy paints from the market. I eye them as I pass quickly by the trade store trying to see what stock they have without stopping. I crane my neck behind me, stretching to make out what looks like a new box of pastels. I haven't painted with them in over a year. I see the large white canvas is still there, and my stomach leaps with excitement before I plow again into something flat and hard. The smell of soap and something sweet washes over me. Warm hands grab at my arms easily, putting me in an upright position. The contrast to Gannet's cold fingers is the first thing running through my mind instead of my war with gravity. Their warm heat presses into my upper arms where I hadn't realized how cold my skin was.

"Run into me once, I say an accident." The sound of Marcus's voice makes my eyes roll as I find my balance. "Run into me twice, and I say you're planning these meetings. And right into my arms this time..." He leans in close and squints his eyes with a smile. "Do you have a secret crush on me, Miss Aston Vazeto?"

I hadn't before realized how tall he is. Being this close to him, I barely see the top of his shoulders.

"Yes," I say. "Because having a crush on you *would* be something I would want to keep a secret. From *everyone!*"

His undeterred chuckle somehow comforts me. Looking at his face, it seems somehow less gray than before. I am glad to see he is cutting back on the donations. With a bit more weight on his cheeks, I could picture this face somewhat good looking, not the striking features of Gannet, but pleasant in a grow-on-you sort of way. I would say that the personality helps the features, but that is not the case with sick Marcus. Poor guy, would he ever be without the title of "sick" in my mind?

"Studying my handsome features I see, Miss Aston. And how do I compare to your many suitors?"

My face is on fire, and I swat at his hands as I lower my face and step around him. "I have never met someone so...so annoyingly full of himself," I grumble.

"You are too kind." He steps in rhythm with me easily. "I dare say I have never met someone quite like you either."

"Case in point."

Marcus only smiles as we walk, and I study his eyes, waiting for the sheen of poison to fall over them. When it never comes, I wonder how he escapes the serum as well? Perhaps Gannet is his technician too, or, as I suspected, all technicians just leave the room with the cup. No one else would think to question a technician. But how do I bring this up? How do I ask Marcus about the serum without also exposing my own criminal action? This does at least explain why he irritates me so. I smile back at him with this thought. The only two people on the whole New Earth not drugged up on antidepressants find each other and drive each other mad.

He looks up briefly, and then I feel his hands on me again, one on my arm the other around my waist. Before I can protest, he is pulling me towards him away from a trading cart speeding by. I look up at him wordlessly, and we stand for a moment like this. Cradled into his thin side, I feel his ribs move up and down against my arm.

I push off of him with my elbow. "Thank you," I say as I wring my hands.

"Miss Aston, I do believe I make you feel flustered. A little case of butterflies?"

"You make me feel a lot of things, but I wouldn't call any of them pleasant or enjoyable I assure you."

He clasps his hands behind his back as we continue walking through the market.

"I saw you eyeing something in the trade store. What captured your attention so, that you fell into my arms?"

"If you saw me, then how is it you did not step out of my way?"

"Believe me when I say you are a hard one to dodge."

I let out an annoyed sigh in response to his playful grin.

"Is there something in the store that your thousand a month can't afford? Tell me so I may get it for you and change your poor impression of me."

My brow bunches together. "I don't want your money." The very idea makes me feel more like a traitor than I already do. It's confirmed now what I had worried before when thinking about Gannet. I could never marry another Donor knowing what I know. Putting another through the donations and taking their blood money to support myself on. However, something else bothers me from his statement. "And how do you know my blood amount?"

It is the first time he actually seems ruffled. He puts his hands in his pockets and looks down at the ground.

"Ehhh..." His head pops up again with the same rueful happiness. "Numbers are public record now."

"So, you're looking me up on Compass and stalking me?"

"Don't you feel flattered?"

I keep walking. I can't tell what I feel. Skeptical maybe. Defensive for some reason. Slightly frightened that this strange man seems to be following me in town and on Compass. But how could I be afraid of someone so ill and weak? I cut my eyes over at him. His cheek wrinkles with another smile.

"Pastels," I say to avoid the question of feelings. We round the corner nearing the facility.

"Excuse me?"

"I was wanting to buy pastel paints from the store. I haven't seen some in quite some time. But I can afford them. I don't need you buying anything for me. I'm the top blood number at our facility, you know."

Why do I feel this sudden desire to prove myself to him? It is the first time I ever feel the need to show off my blood numbers, to feel more powerful than someone else. It sickens me, who I have become. I am turning into a regular high Donor, finding others to stand on like the system would have us do.

"I'm sure you don't."

His smile only infuriates me. It builds the growing impulse to be better than him. I squint more than smile for I know I'm already better than him. He is sick Marcus fighting for his life, and I will marry quick and well and am invited to the ambassador's home. I am turning into a sick competitive brat. Why does he do this to me? Why does he taunt me to see him as competition? I search within myself earnestly now for the pity to come. I should pity him. Then perhaps I could be nicer to him.

"I am sorry I ran into you again," I say. "I will be more careful."

He grabs my hand, startling me again with the foreign warmness of his grasp.

"For my sake, I hope you will be." He kisses the top of my hand, a gesture I have only read about. His lips are warmer than his fingers and they seem to transport the heat to my cheeks. "But for my heart's sake..."

I pull my hand from his grasp at the mention of his heart. We are stopped at the corner of the street to the facility. It is void of all people because shifts at the facility have already begun, and the other buildings are full of lawyers, busy preparing for the Auctions. I rub my hand gently where his lips wetted my skin. My eyes dart to the ground, to the facility where I should be, and occasionally under my eyelashes up at him. His smile seems to grow with my uneasiness.

"Until next time, Miss Aston."

Calling me "Miss" again seems to break whatever spell he has me under.

"Well for my sake, I hope there's never a next time."

I lift my chin and spin in the dirt. It is the only time I have wished I wore work dresses like my sisters and Mam. My skirts hitting his shins would have been much more dramatic. Look what he makes me think. Marcus is a horrible influence on me, and I truly do hope there is never a next time. I nod my head silently as I fume down the street agreeing with myself. My mind is a logical thing, and I would do well to listen to it. If only my skin was as wise, for it is already missing his warm touch. I rub at my arms where his hands had been. How does he have such warm hands? How does he infuriate me so?

M am has invited a boy down the street, with high numbers and a crooked smile, to dinner. Shannon says all the girls swoon over that half-smile, but to me, I find the distortion of his face unnerving. The fact that it's really the comparison to Marcus's genuine smile that has me flustered is not something I am willing to admit to myself.

With this dinner guest, there is still no good time to bring up the invitation to Papa. After Mam shuts the door behind our guest, she turns on me. I haven't a moment to think or even blink. All I see is the fire in Mam's eyes as she stomps towards me, retrieving something from the pocket of her blue floral dress.

"What is *this*, Aston?"

My heart is already jumping anxiously up into my throat before I see the empty gold-trimmed envelope in her hand. The room is silent. Even Pip seems to know not to make a sound as the room seems to tunnel away from me. Maybe if I took the blue serum, I wouldn't feel this woozy. Maybe then I would be able to spout out some monotone reaction. But I refused the serum, and all I can feel right now is rage at Mam for going through my drawers. If I argue with her, they will all suspect something is amiss with my donations.

I take a breath to push my heart back down into its rib cage and clasp my hands behind my back. I squeeze my wrist and am unsure of what to tell her. When no good idea comes to mind, the truth slips over my lips, and I cringe.

"It's an invitation."

"For what?"

My eyes plead with Papa to save me. I retrieve the invitation still resting in my back pocket. Slowly I stretch it out towards him, but Mam pounces upon the burgundy card and has it open in a flash. Her head bobbles with concentration, and her lips flutter as she reads.

"Oh!" she yelps. "Oh my, the honor." She looks up at me in perfect awe, stimulated either by pride at having her daughter invited to such an event or wonder at why someone like her daughter would be invited to such an event. Or perhaps why in the world her daughter would keep such news from her. More than likely it was a mixture of all three.

The shrieking and jumping sets in now and she races to Shannon who reads the invitation aloud. Each member in the room begins having audible reactions to the news, even Pip is bouncing and clapping in Shannon's arms. Everyone is excited, except Papa. His stunned face takes on a different sort of mood.

He eyes me with concern on his face. "You don't have to go."

"What do you mean, she doesn't have to go?" Mam chirps and glides over to Papa. "Of course she has to go. It's the ambassador! She might get arrested for not taking up such an invitation."

"Don't be absurd, Evelyn. She doesn't have to go if she doesn't want to. Aston has never cared for these parties and dresses, and you know that. She would make a mockery of our family with her ill—"

"What?" I blurt out, hurt by Papa's words. A mockery of our family? I would never admit to my father my secret desire to have a nice dress, but I won't sit here and let him ridicule me, either, especially when he was the one who put me in this situation in the first place, raising me as his son and exposing me to the truths of the system.

"Aston, you know you don't like these sorts of things. I don't want you to have to do anything you wouldn't want to. It's still your choice."

"But that's not what you said."

"I was only trying to help your case by appealing to your—"

"What if I want to go? What if I want to dress-up?" I see the upset that is exposed on Papa's face, yet I hold his stare. Why should he make me feel guilty for being a girl? I am a girl. I'm not his son. Still my words are as unsettling to me as they are to the entire room.

Mam puts her hand to her mouth and squints her eyes as they fill with tears. A humming squeak starts up like a crying engine as she then puts her arms out to hug me. "I knew you couldn't be his forever. No daughter of mine can have my nose and figure and be so ignorant to the wonders of this life! Oh Aston, you just wait, your Mammy will take care of it all for you."

I hug her dumbly while Papa fumes.

"We will find you the perfect dress, won't we, Shannon? What do you think? Blue like her eyes? Or gold like her hair?"

I'm forgotten now, as Shannon and Mam huddle together eyeing my body and making plans for its showcase. Papa storms out of the room, and I feel my shoulders lower like I am melting through the floorboards.

This was definitely not how I pictured telling Papa about the invitation. Papa was supposed to solve it, and I ruined my chances of getting out of this. Again.

I run unnoticed through the door, skipping the two middle steps of the porch and jump over the crumbling road. Three blocks west and two blocks north, I make my way towards Lazuli's house, running with my arms wild about me while questions run through my head. What did I just get myself into? Why did I speak up when Papa was only trying to defend my right to choose?

Reaching Lazuli's house, I grab at my knees and pant heavily. Her house has a new coat of paint as well, but the place where we carved our names in the side of the porch is still visible from the shadows cast by the setting sun. The new brown paint clashes with the red brick, and the black door stands out like a beetle amongst the dirt.

I hear the screen from inside blasting before I make it to the door and recognize the jingle advertising the new port screens now available for purchase at the system stores. System stores don't hold the discounted trade items but are all completely new technological devices offered to us by the Recipient marketers. You would think the store manager of a Recipient-owned business would do well, but I hear it is a hard position to keep. Mr. Price also depends on his daughter's blood to make a living.

I knock, and Lazuli excitedly greets me as if she was expecting me all afternoon.

"Aston! Great, you're just in time for the news."

I roll my eyes and shut the door behind me as she heads for the sofa. The wallpaper is new; the brown and white stripe with floral print shimmers under the light. The light is clear, nothing like the harsh yellow glow of our bulbs at home. I look at the ceiling and see the brass chandelier with odd-looped light bulbs emanating the clear light. How much is Lazuli making? I realize now I've never asked her what her numbers were. I was so hurt by her secret betrayal I never brought it up.

"What are your numbers, Lazuli? I just realized I never asked you."

The nice thing about being drugged up is nothing seems to phase you. Lazuli doesn't blush or cock her head or give me a questioning look. She only smiles.

"I got one hundred and eight."

My jaw drops and my eyebrows jump.

"One hundred and eight? Are you serious?"

The only thing fake-drugged Donors can do better than smile is smile more. Lazuli beams at my reaction.

"Yeah, and Brandon hopes to be picked as a lawyer like his uncle. He is training with him and says that he saw an email about the catalog. I am going to be the top on the list for Livonia Auctions!"

A few puffing noises escape as I try to think of what to say. "Wa... whoa...well, that's awesome!"

I look around the room now and spot the other new additions brought on by Lazuli's paycheck. The most obvious is the giant screen rolled out and attached to their wall.

The paper-thin screens fill the homes of Donors everywhere. This one has such bright, vivid colors it's as if the screen is a window to another world. The opening music of the news show blares across the room as the camera scans the clapping crowd. Lazuli waves me over to her nice suede reclining sofa. It makes me feel poorer to sit in such a comfortable soft chair. How can she afford these things? My numbers are still higher than hers. Maybe Mam is not being as frivolous as we all tease her for.

The familiar news anchor's dark face, framed by his orange hair, fills the screen. His blue eyeliner and dramatic contour lines make him look like a clown with his painted face instead of the fashionable Donor he is taken for.

"Out with the old." He smiles and places his hand out towards the camera as the audience shouts back, "In with the news!"

"That's right, New America, I'm Griffin Manny, and I just want to know are YOU in with the news?" His perfectly even laugh makes my fingers twitch. If this were my house, I would be turning it off right now. I can't stand the sounds and pictures and footage of the approved news stories. Lazuli used to be the same way. I turn to look at her beaming face and how she sits on the edge of her expensive couch anxiously listening. I know my anger should be aimed at the system for taking away my friend and not her, but she's the only thing before me right now. It's much easier to hate the physical evidence in front of me than find the true source somewhere in the distance.

"Now." The theme music dies as Griffin Manny takes his gray upholstered seat with his downturned face. "For the Donor deaths of the day."

There's never any music because the Donor deaths are only business. He announces our town, and we lean forward in unison.

Griffin Manny sighs with much more counterfeit emotion than what is usually attending the Donor deaths.

"And in Livonia, again another new Donor death. Christina Weiler, number fourteen seventy-five, died on her first week of donations."

"Scars," we both whisper at the television screen together. We look at each other while Griffin Manny continues on about the particulars, and I am half expecting Lazuli to turn the screen off and stand up while waving her hands saying something has to be done. Finally, I remember my mistake in forgetting her transformation before she breaks out in giggles. She grabs my knee as she turns back to the screen like us cursing at the same time is just the sweetest thing in the New World.

The music gears up again as he shares the death of Recipients throughout New America. Three total deaths take up twice as much time as our entire town's long list of dead Donors, with videos, pictures, and stories of these Recipients' lives.

One Recipient death was a mother of three, who was a jewelry designer. Her line of jewelry is holding a sale, all profits going to the family she left behind. She showed improvement with her auction-purchased contract of Donor blood, but within the second year, she took a turn for the worse when she developed a cold she never recovered from. It was thought to be contracted after her son attended a tour through the lawyer's offices, a common practice by Recipient middle stage schools during the lawyers' off season. It is assumed this exposure to the Donor part of town led to the woman's immunity to her own cure.

The other two Recipients were young. Speculation was made of changing the Donor and age to secure more blood for the younger ones. This talk is nothing new. It's been rumored for years with no action actually being taken.

Lazuli's movement catches my attention, and I notice she's wiping away a tear. I breathe deeply and look away from her. A glimpse of her true self is wasted in feelings for the Recipients. Or maybe the serum makes them only feel for Recipients. I don't know exactly how it works.

The news now turns to other current events, and we sit there in silence while I concentrate on keeping my food down. How did I think coming here after the outburst at home would make me feel better?

"And in Livonia news, the ambassador, along with a few ambassadors across the province, has announced he will be inviting a few of the top Donors of their area to his annual auction ball."

Lazuli jumps up at this news and puts her hands to her head.

"We look forward to seeing live footage of these rare blood numbers face to face at these famous Ambassadors' Balls. Check Compass for your Ambassador's Ball date and tune in to see your very own town heroes!"

"What?" Lazuli squeals excitedly. "Aston, did you hear that? Donors! Top Donors are going to get invited to the Ambassador's Ball!"

I stay frozen in my seat as she starts to pace.

"I mean...can you believe it? We were just there a week ago dreaming about what it would look like, and now we might actually get to see it! And not on a screen but in person! Ha!"

"I know," I grumble.

"You know? How did you know already?"

"I mean, I know... I saw the same show as you right here on your sofa...it is...great." I put no effort into sounding excited. She wouldn't notice anyway. I miss the friend I could have confided in about my Papa's words and being tricked into going to the ball. I miss a friend's advice about what to do about going. Right now, however, I feel even more unconnected to her as I realize she was somehow not included in the top Donors. She was not invited to the ball if this is news to her.

Lazuli smiles and jumps across the room, bubbling like she used to just not over the same things. This gives me a thought. If she could care so little about my thoughts and feelings and always stay so even keeled, then what was keeping me from still sharing things with her? She wouldn't care anyways. Right? It was the best sort of listener really, when you thought about it. If nothing could phase or bother her, then I could tell her anything.

"Lazuli...I actually knew already because..."

Her brown eyes are fixated on me with the same waxy sheen over them. Her face is flush with all her excitement from the news.

"Because I already got an invitation to the ball."

I exhale with a loud whoosh once I get the sentence out. It feels good to say it. To not be hiding it anymore or be found out but to confess it.

Her expression changes. Was I wrong? I begin rambling with worry as I see her smile falter.

"I received the invitation the other day, and my Mam found the envelope tonight, and now they're making me go. Or rather, I got upset at the wrong things, really, and made it perfectly impossible for me not to go at this point."

"You got invited already?" How could she sound so disappointed? She is on happy serum! Nothing bothers her. Right? Then why did she sound so deflated?

"You got invited and didn't tell me? And why wouldn't you want to go?"

I only shrug, confused by her lack of smile.

"Well..."

She looks away, still no smile in sight, and I bite my thumb nail now. This was a really stupid experiment.

"Well, if you already got your invitation, then I guess that means I'm not..." She trails off sadly.

Sadly? How can this be? I remember the lady at the front desk on my first day. The slip that happened there, too, with her judgmental stare.

"I'm sure yours is on the way, Laz," I try to reassure her. "Mine only came just the other day. Look, it's not something I want to go to! You can have my invitation if you want!"

"How could you not want to go, Aston? It's the ambassador's mansion! For scars sake, you're such a blood head!" I gasp at her name calling. "So full of yourself and your numbers you can't even go to the mall with us anymore. Is that why you wanted to know my blood numbers? To see if I was invited? Worried I would take your precious place at the top?"

"What? No..." Her face is red and brow furrowed.

A sense of accomplishment steals over me for uprooting the emotions buried deep within my friend. No matter that it's hatred and jealousy toward me that she feels; it is real, it is possible. All my pride vanishes however when the smile overpowers her.

"It's ok, Aston. I know I'm not the top number; I just hope you have a great time! Scars, I'm so jealous, though!" she says it with a wide dummy grin.

I fall back into her sofa in relief. I should feel angry at the system for keeping my friend from feeling what she really feels—mad that I didn't tell her or let her ramble on while I knew. Hurt and rejected that she doesn't get to go to the mansion she dreams about. Instead, I feel like I escaped death. Death By Jealous Friend would be a horrible Donor death announcement.

We watch the rest of the show in silence, unless you count the sound of my twiddling fingers. The image of Lazuli's angered face haunts me all the way home. If that was the real Lazuli coming through, why was she jealous? Wouldn't the old Lazuli be as upset about the ridiculous Donor ball and parade of blood?

Not being invited at all doesn't make sense either. One hundred and eight? And she has the full three months of donating so far. If Brandon is right, and she is going to be number one in the catalog, she should have been first on the invite list. Perhaps there was a mistake. Another one.

THE HOUSE IS dark and still when I arrive home. I zig-zag across the floor knowing all the places that are less creaky and grab the mini port on my way to the stairs. I wonder if there's a list somewhere on Compass of Donors invited to the ball.

When I get to my room, I search on Compass for numbers of attendees to the ball, but nothing shows up. There's never been a ball like this before; of course there wouldn't be a data base already for it.

The miniport takes its time to load the facility site, so I toss it on my bed as I change into my night dress. The first white nightgown I pull on has a hole in the hip, and I slip it off for another one that, though dingier, is whole. With a sigh, I sit on my pillows at the head of my bed and begin tapping away at the mini port again. Maybe there is a new option on the DMR page for ball guests. My searches are in vain, and frankly, I don't know what I'm looking for anyway. Something just doesn't seem right.

A yawn escapes me, and I lean back against the wall, making the bed scoot out. My fingers tap to the list of auction contestants, and I look at my own number. Thirteen forty-two, ranked with a hundred fifty-seven antibody rate. Then I see Lazuli's number, a wonderful one hundred and eight like she said. My eyes trace the eight with disbelief. It's ironic how the two girls who grew up never wanting to donate are now the two highest-rated Donors.

Like uncontrolled machines, my fingers meander, tapping on the drop of blood again but searching out Gannet this time. I stare at his perfect technician stock photo and strangely wish I knew Marcus's number. Perhaps it's better this way. Would it be easier or harder to be nice to him if I knew exactly how beneath me he really is?

Eyes drooping, I look up my own number again under the public record instead of auction contestants, pictureless and as anonymous as possible. Then lazily, I check Lazuli's too. My finger slides up the side of the miniport to turn it off since I'm half asleep already when my eyes glance at Lazuli's numbers. My eyes pop open, and I sit up in bed. Red numbers stare back at me, and my palms start to sweat. I can't take my eyes off of them. One hundred and three? I search over the public page. It's definitely Lazuli, but this is not her blood number. My fingers race back to the auction contestant page, and there it is, one hundred and eight. Back to public record, one hundred and three.

In a normal world it should be reasonable to believe it's an honest mistake, eight and three look similar after all, but not in our world. The DMR doesn't make mistakes. At least it shouldn't. Most simple mistakes such as these stem from tampering with numbers, at least it's what we're told on the screens. A mistake like this would look suspicious. Lazuli and her family wouldn't have tampered with numbers, would they? Why take the risk? Surely this is a mistake, but still, they could be in big trouble even if it wasn't their blunder at all.

Staring at the lower number three, my mind shifts and whirls at the meaning. Would Papa know what it means? What to do? Or is this over his head? After tonight, I'm not sure I want to turn to Papa for help. Or that he would even want to help me.

What about Gannet? I turn the screen off and stare into the complete black space as my eyes slowly adjust. These numbers have to be changed to match and changed quick. It's a risk, but Gannet may know how to make corrections to the system. It's the keeping it secret part that I'm not so sure I can trust him with.

FIFTEEN

I've been roped into shopping for dresses, which makes me wonder why I ever wished to have a pretty dress worthy of the ball. With all the shopping, there isn't a chance to think about what to do about Lazuli's predicament. My fingertips are raw from zipping and buttoning pink satin gowns, emerald green tulle, and black sequined skimpy dresses. Nothing meets Mam's standards. Each one of them makes my face squint with embarrassment. They are all too flashy or bright or revealing.

Stepping into the mirror with a pink sleeveless dress that has a giant droopy bow across my chest, Mam throws her hands in the air. "For scars sake! Is there nothing in this town decent enough for an Ambassador's Ball?"

A mother would have every right to complain about this dress. My figure is nothing to be proud of to be certain—too straight, flat, and plain like a tall and skinny pin needle—but in this dress, I look like a meatless piece of raw sickly chicken.

Mam of course screams for different reasons, scanning the room to see who notices or cares about our dilemma. She likes announcing to everyone we encounter that her daughter is one of the few attending the ball. Her foot beats against the black tile of the elaborate dress shop as she folds her arms.

A worker rushes to her side. "I think she looks lovely." His shirt sleeves are rolled up to his elbows. He holds his suspenders and smiles a wide grin exposing much of his upper gums.

Mam scowls down at the man. "She looks like a package that got left in the rain!"

Everyone in the store is looking at our corner. The worker puts his arm around Mam making his brown straight hair that is long on top and shaved bald on the sides fall over his face, as if creating a cover for the secret he is about to share. "Perhaps it would help to see what others are wearing to the ball."

"They bought their dresses here?" Mam's conspiratorial whispers make her eyes sparkle with delight. She shoos me with her hand and finally releases me from the tortuous dress.

I enter the dressing room, step out of the pink gown, and hang it over the door like I was ordered. It isn't until the pink taffeta is pulled from its place by a worker that I realize this isn't my dressing room. Instead of my jeans and gray shirt I left on the green leather chair, there is a yellow floral sundress and yellow knit sweater. I stare at myself in the mirror at my beige bra and black panties as I panic about what to do.

"Excuse me." I turn to the hallway grabbing the top of the short white dressing room door. I crane my neck to peek over the top.

"Excuse me?" I try again.

I let go with a whoosh of air escaping me. I don't want to wait for the owner of that yellow dress to discover me in her room, and if no one is out there to answer me, then perhaps I am safe to slip over to my room quickly. Though this hallway of dressing rooms is unisex, it's also secluded enough from the store. If I'm quick, I should be fine.

"Ok," I say out loud to myself trying to psyche myself up for this.

I crack open the door to peek and give a final attempt. "Anyone there?" The hallway is clear, and I count in my head. One. Two. As I say three, I whip open the door and turn to shut it inconspicuously. I spin and collide with someone, making me yelp. The warm hands against my cold skin makes me yelp again.

"Marcus!"

He clamps a hot hand over my mouth.

"Shh," he says looking down the hallway.

My eyes widen, and my hands shift across my body. I inch my arm up over my bare cleavage and can feel my erratic heart drumming wildly. I want to shrug off his hands on my shoulder and face him, but something has me frozen. The surprise, no doubt, as these minutes both draw out forever and speed by in no time.

My movement catches his eye as they shift down to my arms holding myself together. Then he swiftly removes his grip on my shoulder and clamps it over his eyes too.

"This isn't exactly redeeming myself is it?"

I grunt frustratedly as I sidestep away and lunge for my dressing room. The sound of voices nearing the corner of the hallway makes him follow me, however, and he is soon in my dressing room with me.

"What are you doing here?" I hiss at him.

"Someone's coming."

"No, I mean back here at all?" I lock the dressing room door behind us.

He holds up a peach-colored blouse with a shrug. "Shopping," he says, as if shopping for women's clothing is the most normal thing for him to do. "I heard someone calling out—" Footsteps draw nearer, and he ducks his head behind the door.

"So you just decided to waltz into the dressing rooms?" I grab my clothes. "How chivalrous of you."

"Well, I wasn't expecting someone to come out, especially not naked." His eyes flip again to my exposed body, and I shove him in the corner where he plants his nose dutifully. "And I definitely wasn't expecting that someone to be you."

The voices are growing louder, and just as my jeans are zipped, I hear Mam. I rush to the corner to guard the man in my dressing room with me, but he is too tall; there's no point in trying to hide him.

"Aston, dear?"

"Mm-hmm?" My breathlessness would betray me if I spoke just now.

"Try this on. It doesn't look like much, but it is for sure the only thing in this whole town not being worn to the ball."

A champagne dress is flung over the door, and the beaded overlay clanks and scratches against it.

"Ok...just wait for me out by the mirrors, and I will come out when it's on."

"Oh, just hurry up, no need to tell me where to go or how to wait for you, just try it on, child."

She's not going anywhere, which means Marcus isn't going anywhere either. I step away from him to pull the dress from the door. It slides off like a loud rattle snake. When I turn, Marcus is grinning at me with his genuine evil self. I point to the corner firmly without a sound, and he pouts dramatically. I can't help but smile. His frank way of expressing himself is so genuine, new, and exciting.

I'm nervous to change with him in the room, but I haven't any other choice. The silence of this dressing room is yet a different one. Different than my house. Different than the facility. This silence is strangling. Every sound of the fabric sliding off my skin is torture. Every zipper and button on my jeans seem to suffocate me. My eyes never leave Marcus, to make sure he doesn't peek. He is statue-still and seems to tense with each sound.

I study his back as I change. There are muscles there around his bones. His black shirt still hangs on him, but his Khaki pants are fitted around his backside. He has gained weight. He seems healthier, I think. My face burns, and my heart gallops. All it would take is one peak in the mirror for him to see me blushing and staring at him. The thought doesn't scare me as much as I would think it should.

I turn to the mirror to examine the dress. It has an overlay completely made of clear jewels somehow strung together. It slides across my skin like the tinkling of a crystal chandelier. With my eyes back on him, I reach and twist but cannot finish the zipper.

"I need help," I whisper through the room.

I place my hand to my heart as if I can make it stop its marathon as he turns, and my breath catches when his clear, untouched eyes reach mine. Silently, I turn my back to him.

The pinch of my dress at the base of my back as he reaches the zipper sends chills down my bare legs. The dress tugs against my waist as he inches it up slowly. Marcus's warm fingers brush against my neck as he buttons the clasp at the top.

We freeze as still as our room is silent. I feel the heat of his breath where his fingers had been on my neck, and when I look sideways into the mirror, I see the way he looks down at me. Like he is wanting something. Wanting something he can never have. It reminds me of the moment I realized I couldn't be an artist, and I feel a sudden odd connection to him.

His eyes are less sunken, and his skin is almost pink. His hair is as straw-like as ever, though. I see him close his mouth and then open it again as if trying to say something. I have the strange urge to lean back into him. Just a small tilt and I would be against his body on purpose, connected to another real person. I turn before he can say anything and before I give in to whatever foolishness has taken over me.

"Thank you," I mouth to him. He retreats back to his corner as I reach for the door.

I crack the door only enough for me to escape through.

"Hmmm." Mam gives me a scrutinizing face pucker. "Let's go to the mirrors, the lighting here makes you look like a dead fish."

I walk humbly down the hall and turn the corner looking over my shoulder. It isn't until I step up onto the pedestal and look into the mirror that my breath is knocked from me in a different sort of way. I take my own breath away. My face is flushed beautifully, and my eyes seem affected by the excitement as well. But the dress is dazzling. A champagne-colored sleeveless satin lies under the jeweled see-through garments. A trim of slightly larger rectangle jewels line the collar and the edge of the jewel-puffed cap sleeves.

"I...I actually like this one," I whisper in awe as I slide my hand over the form fit to my hips. It seems to be made for me. Mam should at least like that there's no need for a tailor. The satin fabric ends at the knees where both layers are fitted like a pencil skirt, but the sheer jewels fall to the ground like a shimmery draping waterfall.

"Hmmm," my mother contemplates. "Can you guarantee she will be the only one in this gown?"

"It will cost extra to close the shop to this dress for a month. This designer is very popular right now."

"What a trifle little thing. Don't you know she has the highest numbers in the state? Possibly the whole New World as well?"

Barely registering Mam's words, I descend the steps of the platform while watching myself move in the mirror. There's a trim of gold around the collar, and the way it shines makes me think of the pretty soft envelope.

I am instantly ashamed at my thoughts. Excited for a ball that celebrates my blood! Dressing up in costume to hide the fact that we couldn't afford eggs just this week. My dress is suddenly a symbol of my life. I am the champagne satin struggling to be seen through imitation jewels that glisten and distract.

I, all of a sudden, run to the dressing room. To the only other person who knows how to escape the system, who knows what it's like to be real amongst a sea of imposters. The way he irritates me makes me feel alive at the same time. His touch makes me feel things that remind me I am real. I can't believe I'm thinking it, but I am wishing to run into him. I'm wanting to run to Marcus.

But when I open the door to the dressing room, my clothes are the only things there. Mam shuffles up behind me in her nicest blue dress that drags against the floor with a warning sound.

"Come, don't be so distraught," she says, looking at my reflection. "I'm sad the shopping is done now too, but we still have shoes to find tomorrow, and we will be very merry again."

On our trek back home, my feet feel the strain of our day. At least the shoe shopping shouldn't require climbing pedestals with each fitting. At least I don't think they do. We stroll past the trade shop and I beg to take a look inside.

Mam makes a face. "I hate going in that store. The dust irritates my lungs. Go ahead then, if you must."

She yells after me as I race ahead. "But don't be long, the last tram leaves in only an hour!"

I race to the isle of art supplies, but I know before I even stop that it is gone. The giant white canvas has been taken as well as the pastels. I make no hurry to catch up with Mam. Who else in Livonia is painting? And what will they possibly paint on such a large white canvas?

SIXTEEN

Shopping for shoes is thankfully less eventful than my escapades in the dressing room. We visit two shops and are done in time for my ten o'clock donation. My mind drifts nervously to the dilemma of Lazuli. I still have no clue what to do, but I know I have to help fix it somehow.

I stroll through the market rubbing my bare arms as the chilly November air sets in. From books I've read, Old Michigan had different weather patterns then. By now, we would all be bundled in jackets or coats and revving up for winter completely. Though our gardens won't grow anymore through these chilly months, a real winter isn't due until after December festivities. Even then, our storms pale in comparison to those of the past.

I find myself dreaming about Old America as I habitually walk towards the facility. What would it have been like before so much land fell into the ocean? We have the same bodies of water and the lands that huddle around it greedily. The same rivers, though more of them and less land. Everything north of New Detroit is under water as well, and I hear there's a place called Toronto down there with it. I have never left New Detroit. I have only seen images on the screen of places past Ohio and Illinois.

I scan my finger at the front desk and sit in the waiting room. On the gray end table next to me sits a magazine with the profile of our leader, Adakin Malloy. The red words in the bottom corner of the front cover are what catch my eye: Death Tolls Rise in Detroit's Town of Livonia. Will Adakin Malloy Have Answers? I pick it up to flip through it.

Finding the page, I see a short article with another headshot of president Malloy. The photo takes up the right half of the magazine with his blond hair towering in a tall swoop above his large brow and completely white on the sides above his ears. It's an unnatural sort of yellow. Too bright and rich. His serious face is covered in a matching blond beard with a large white stripe of hair on his chin. Gray eyes, like dirty ice shoveled off the tram tracks, pierce me with a knowing stare. He is sporting a similar gray suit and silver tie. I peel my eyes off his picture with a shiver, like a scary story you don't want to hear but can't drag yourself away from. After scanning the interview, I realize there's nothing substantial here. It's just a circle of questions being answered by other questions. It leads the reader in a muddled goose chase.

> *"Mr. Malloy, can you tell us the reason first-time Donors are the only ones affected by these allergies? And why do you think it's so concentrated in this small town?"*
>
> *"Do I know how viruses mutate or how the blood evolves from person to person? No, I do not, but I do have a team of the smartest scientists that do."*

I slap the magazine closed as I look up and see Gannet coming. I don't wait for him to make his way to the waiting room, I briskly stride to him. He stops and smiles at me with his perfect smile. I make an effort to return it, considering I should be jacked up on happy juice by this point.

We go about our routine like it's a dance—me in the chair, him with the needle. Everything is practiced and choreographed perfectly. I tap my fingers on the armrest when he steps away. Somehow, I have to bring up the issue about Lazuli's numbers without getting her into trouble. I rub at my arm and look at Gannet as he untwists the tubing. Papa has always called me an open book so how do I close it for once and be stealthy?

"So, how are numbers recorded?"

"Oh…uh—"

Way to go dummy. Just blurt it out; yeah, that's not obvious at all. My fingers fidget with the tape around the needle, and it makes my arm ache as it jostles it in my vein. "I mean, do the technicians that come to our home fill out the forms for our public records? Or maybe a special division in charge…"

"Both actually. Blood test technicians submit their findings to the DMR vital records department, and there, someone enters it into the database."

"And auction contestant records? Are they handled by vital records as well?"

"No, I think that's a different department."

"So it's possible for mistakes to occur from the transfer of the information."

Gannet chuckles, and I know why. DMR doesn't make mistakes. The system is perfect. At least it's supposed to be.

"More likely hacked than a mistake. That happens all the time. You'd be surprised how easy it is to infiltrate the database with just a miniport. It's the doing it without your port ID pinging the wrong people that is difficult. And it's a serious crime. Tampering is punishable by…" He tries to hide a shiver by shifting in his chair. Then he looks at me with his smile that makes me shiver. "Why the sudden interest in records? You know all the record keepers are technical officers. I don't think that's something you want to aspire to."

"What? You can't see me as an officer?" I try to smile, but I want to wring my hands instead.

"No," he says smiling pleasantly at me. "I definitely can't."

I look away. "I was just asking for a friend," I say. "She said there was a mistake on her numbers. Records didn't match." I look up under my eye lashes, afraid that I've said too much. His smile has already vanished, and he looks concerned.

"Don't match?"

"Silly, huh? Maybe her miniport had a glitch. DMR doesn't make mistakes."

He stares at me. We are back to silence. I can't think of anything else to say. My mind is busy with the information he just gave me. Easy to hack? Easy enough that a teenage Donor could do it? I'm sure it's an accident that has nothing to do with Lazuli. She doesn't know how to use her miniport half the time, much less hack into secured facility records, but I doubt the system would see it that way. She could get into so much trouble if, as Gannet said, "the wrong people" discover this mistake. Yet if I try to fix it before anyone else sees it and get caught, then we're both in trouble.

The machine beeps. Soon I'm patched up and on my way, not even making eye contact with Gannet on my way out.

On the short ride home, I stare out the tram window blindly, mind full of the what if's and risks of both decisions.

Torrin is the only one home when I arrive. He jumps up from the sofa with miniport in hand when I open the door and then relaxes when he sees me.

"I need the port, Torrin." I grab it from him with a shaky hand and see him playing a virus game Mam doesn't allow.

"Hey," he shouts and grabs it back. "Just let me sign out first." He taps away and then hands it back.

I pace the living room, squeezing the port in front of me while Torrin climbs the stairs. When I open the miniport, I see the original screen as if Torrin had never played that forbidden game.

"Torrin." I spin around excitedly.

"Yeah?"

"How did you get into that game? Mam blocked your port ID from it."

He descends the stairs halfway and bends over to look at me through the railing. He studies my face, wondering how serious and trustworthy I am. And then a wicked smile spreads slowly across his lips.

"Mam locks you out of something, too?" he asks.

I sigh, and my own smile smears across my face. "Yeah."

He continues down the rest of the stairs. "It's easy. You just need to block the port ID altogether. They're built to have an override feature, mostly for officers to check all details about a house's Compass searches and any information linking them to tampering or other crimes. A way for the system to investigate our lives without anyone ever knowing." He taps away with more than one finger at a time, and none of what he's doing makes any sense. He holds buttons down and counts to three when pressing one button until the screen flickers on and off over and over again, and then a new screen appears in all red. "And you're in. Now it's like you're in a private version of the miniport where no one can track or keep a history of what you do."

He beams up at me, and I stare into his face. His instructions send a chill up my spine. Has he been playing games this whole time? Or has he been up to more we don't know about? His smile is so childlike and innocent.

"What game are you going to play?" he asks.

Game. Yes. I smile back at him. He is still just as carefree and ignorant as he should be. It's a game called hacking into the database, but now I don't feel as sure about my abilities. "Um. I was actually going to correct something on someone else's Compass page. Write them an anonymous note on their page somehow, too." I don't know what I'm saying or if it's even related enough to what I actually need to do. I'm not the brains, I'm the artsy one. But how do I get his help and still keep him innocent?

"Well, that's even easier. You just find the source code on the script and choose your input. I usually use ADMIN or one equals one and a number symbol, or if that doesn't work, then I use one equals one with a slash and a pound symbol. Pull the site up and let me see."

I pull up DMR and go to the public record hoping that's the easiest one to alter. Hopefully with the page scrolled down so only numbers are seen, he won't look at it. I hold it out only slightly and have my hand cover most of it. He taps away at certain bars and places. He seems to be in his own little world and doesn't stop to look at the page.

"There, now you're in. Change what you want on the page, and then just click there when you're done. What is it—"

I jerk the miniport away. "Oh nothing. Just something I saw that I wanted to point out to someone. Something about art."

He shrugs his shoulders, seeming disappointed. "Okay."

I stare at him, waiting for him to leave. "Thanks," I hint.

He sighs and returns to the stairs.

Taking turns wiping my hands on my jeans, I look at the unfamiliar red screen. The same numbers are now white against red instead of the other way around. With trembling hands, I tap the delete button and watch the number three disappear. An eight is put in its place, and my mouth is dry. As I log out the way Torrin told me to, the front door swings open. It startles me so that it feels like an electric shock pulses through my fingers. I twirl and throw the miniport onto the sofa as Mam enters.

"What'd you throw the miniport for?"

"No reason." I take the stairs two at a time, and my breath is strained like I've run a marathon. How many hours or days will it take the system to notice what I've done? How much time must pass before I know I'm in the clear? I hope Lazuli was worth it. My heart sinks at the thought. How cruel of me. Of course she is worth it. She would do the same for me if she were in my position. She can't help it if she doesn't remember who she was. But I remember. No one may ever discover what I accomplished today, but it was worth it. I will feel everything and remember it all.

SEVENTEEN

The loud noises don't belong in the facility. Like the wrong soundtrack dubbed over a movie. I count the droids in the waiting room. Five bobbing black disks. Are there usually this many, and I've just never noticed? I'm probably being paranoid. No one knows what I've done. Yet how can I be sure? They could have discovered the hack last night and are on their way to find me this morning.

Gannet calls my number. I walk stiffly by his side. We go through the test of health silently, then make our way to the cubicle. The needle is in, and the machine is going, yet silence still prevails. My mind is elsewhere, as his is, until it dawns on me: I never figured out the mystery of why I have the same technician every time and why I am in the same cubicle each visit.

He speaks without looking at me. "You left the mall pretty quick that night. I never had a chance to ask you if everything was ok."

"Yeah, I just didn't feel well."

"Are you drinking enough fluids? Did you have any of the new blue drink that night?"

His concern seems more than the trained technician caring about his patient, and I blush under his watchful stare.

"Yes, thank you. I am, and no, I did not."

"Good," he sounds relieved and looks away to the machine instead.

"Been back to the mall much lately?" I say, at least priding myself in a little more tact than last time.

"No, not really. You?"

"No. How's, um, what's-her-face?"

His smile makes my heart dissolve, and my determination to see him as the tainted Donor that he is falters. It sometimes makes me wish I was under the serum's spell, if it meant to be more than friends with him.

"Marnie? She's fine. Getting married this weekend."

"Married...?" My voice cracks on the unfinished question, and my cheeks burn.

"Evidently, she met someone, and they hit it off. They got engaged almost right away."

"Well, I guess when you know you've found, erm, love, there's no use waiting around." I try to give a little chuckle, but it comes out airy from my relief that *he* is not getting married.

"Yeah, something like that."

I'm also relieved that he doesn't sound upset about Marnie's engagement, though I know the serum keeps him from having any emotions. For all I know, Gannet really likes that girl and would be heartbroken over losing her if he wasn't drugged up.

The machine clicks and whines, and soon I feel the cold as my blood is returning. My warm hand absentmindedly rubs my cold hand as I do every time.

"Um...is this your cubicle?" I decide it's better to sound dumb than to accuse him.

"What?"

"I mean, does every technician get their own cubicle to work out of? 'Cause, you know, you could spruce it up a bit, a few posters on the wall or something."

He snickers as he shakes his head.

"No. But I noticed on your first visit you have a rare component to your blood that would react to the mixture of anti-nausea medicine and coagulant. They needed to be separated. This is why I give your anti-nausea medicine in a cup. Having one substance through the blood system and the other taken orally is separate enough to not cause a reaction." He stares into my eyes as he spouts off a speech that seems recited and planned and...fake. "This cubicle has the only machine that will allow the process to be separated manually."

"Oh," I whisper. A thought chills me, and I rub at my cold hand harder. "Is this the same allergy that's killing new Donors?"

"No." He is wheeling over in his little black chair to my side, trying to interrupt me as I speak. But I am suddenly panicking.

"Have you told anyone? Do the other technicians know to look for this component in other's blood too?"

"Aston." He is right by me now, and his eyes have transformed as if the real Gannet is fighting through to show real emotion and real concern. He rubs my cold forearm, careful to avoid the tubes, and our fingers bump. "Aston, those are allergies to the coagulant itself not the combo of these two. Basically, their blood begins to clot before the coagulant can be introduced, and well, there isn't much to do. We are working on new tests to be included in the test of health to screen for this mutation, but... I've already said too much... We are working on it. I am working with you each visit for this reason. There are new discoveries in the blood every day, and I am here to guarantee nothing goes amiss with your donations."

His touch is comforting. His words are comforting. But nothing comforts me quite like what I see in this rare glimpse of a moment in his eyes. I am looking into the eyes of Gannet as he is meant to be seen, as the man he was born to be, free of the system, free to be loved, and oh, how I wish I could be the one to love him. But then he is gone. Gannet straightens his back and removes his hand.

"Thank you," I whisper.

He seems flustered, like he doesn't know what happened, as if he is awakening from a coma and is trying to remember where and who he is.

"Yes, well...you're welcome."

Poor Gannett, lost in his own body, paralyzed by his own mind. I want to reach out to him, but I know there's no use. These glitches in the drug are fleeting. I couldn't bear to get close to someone only for moments of their true self. Living a life with a version of Dr. Jekyll and Mr. Hyde, some days kind and sincere others drugged and robotic, while I am never changing and know the truth of them both would be impossible.

The machine beeps, and we finish our routine in silence. When he hands me the cup of blue liquid, the true Gannett returns for a minute more as if to say goodbye, to say sorry that he can't stay for long, or as if there is more he wants to say to me.

When I grasp the cup, he doesn't move his hand, and his fingers do not feel as cold now that mine match his. If I drink this cup now, I could be like him. Like a modern-day Romeo and Juliet, should I give up my life as a knowing authentic contributor for a blind carefree imaginary life with Gannett? Our minds would be altered, but at least our inner selves who deserve each other would be together. All it would take is a drop of this poison. I could always take some now to see how it feels and then stop taking it at any time. Our hands begin to warm each other by the long touch before he slips away his fingers and the cool juice can be felt through the thin paper cup.

He turns without a word and walks away. Only the soft hiss of his slippered shoes on the tile can be heard above the hum of the other Donors in the other cubicles. This thought awakens me from whatever charm was put on me, and I quickly bend over the drain. These Donors, hundreds of thousands of Donors, all drugged into submission. It's not right. It's worse than slavery, for at least slaves throughout history had their minds to escape to.

I mope slowly through the facility hallways. I mourn the life Gannet and I could have had together, if only I hadn't known the truth. When I get home, I will be done with this foolishness, but for now, I want to be sad a little longer, to feel real a little more, for the both of us, since Gannet can't.

As I step out of the hallway of cubicles and into the giant entryway with the front desk to my right and the screen of advertisements to my left, I see officers at the sliding doors again. Black and red Droids circle around the facility. In my numb mourning march, I think nothing of it until they call me.

"Are you Thirteen forty-two?"

"Yes," my voice quivers as it was already on the verge of tears. I pick at the new bandage over my arm as my eyes jump from one officer to the other. Two, three, seven officers total, drown the white facility with their black uniforms and move loudly across the floor. Their shining bright heads make my stomach clench.

"We need to scan your finger please."

All the things I think I would say in these situations like "Is everything ok, officer?" and "Why, what's wrong?" are all flushed out with nerves and my own speculations of what it all means. I guess when I've been cheating the system by washing expensive mind-controlling drugs down the drain, and hacking their database, it's not so easy to act nonchalant.

I lift my finger, and it feels as if my arm's a lever, squeezing and tightening my chest. I can't breathe. I can't swallow. They don't give any explanation; they only lift the portable electronic blood devices that are attached to their belts.

I examine this officer and realize how young he is. Maybe my age. Men fulfilling their inherited duty, following a line of fathers to the military, or boys running from poverty-stricken homes to have a warm blanket on their cot, whichever background they emerge from they all wear the same shaved shiny head and eyebrow-less expressions. This soldier's lack of eyebrows makes his forehead long, and his blue eyes look pale and pathetic alone on his face. He uncaps the scan hole and gently places my finger over it. The red light appears immediately.

I turn my head and see Gannet turning in a folder at the front desk. He eyes me and then the soldier with a furrowed brow before he stuffs his hands in his pockets and approaches.

"I am this Donor's technician. Is everything ok here?"

Oh, how grateful I actually am that Gannet is unable to have emotions right now to get in the way. His clear head and calm words allow me to finally breathe, and I look at the young soldier for a response.

"Nothing concerning her donations, technician. There has been a breach of system records. A Lazoolie—"

"Lazuli?" I interject. Scars above but I can't breathe. I had been so stupidly wrapped up in dreams about a romance that only exists in another time that I completely forgot about my escapades on the miniport. Why had I wasted all my time reading classic romances? I'm sure there were other contraband books full of espionage or how to succeed in the art of deceit. Scars! What do I do? What do I say? Does my face give it all away? My cheeks are cold, but my face is wet with perspiration. I'm sure it screams "I'm guilty! Arrest me! Torture me now for my crimes against the system!"

Flashing across my mind comes a vision of young Lazuli with dark giant curls. Her pinky is entwined with mine, and we spit on the ground after saying, "Friends forever." Her tiny eight-year-old voice coos through my mind, *"We'll always tell each other everything. Blood doesn't make our friendship."* What have I done? I should have talked to Lazuli. Why didn't I think about just asking her? Because she's a drugged dummy, that's why. The pressure in my head feels like a buoy on the water keeping me afloat, or maybe it is dragging me under. Scars galore, protect my friend from my stupidity.

The young officer is eyeing my face, which only adds to my panic.

"Yes. It seems the Price family has tampered with the numbers."

Stay calm. Breathe normal. Don't pass out. But deep down, I know this is it. I'm done. And I took Lazuli with me.

"A full investigation will be under way, but for now, we are checking all high-numbered Donors, especially those close to the family. You are friends with Miss Lazul...i?" The soldier stumbles over her name again.

I nod my head.

"Did she or anyone in her family say anything to you about her numbers or how she acquired them?"

His machine beeps, and I retrieve my hand as he moves the small screen closer to read.

"No," I answer, hoping I look shocked and not as terrified and guilty as I feel. Speaking does wonders for my stomach, and I shift my weight back and forth on my feet to help clear my head. "The other night she told me her numbers were 108 I believe. I know they have been fixing up their house quite a bit lately with her donations. But..." I think momentarily about his words. *How she acquired them?* What does that mean? Suddenly, it's like the adrenaline has focused my mind, and it's sifting quickly through signs and evidence. Why wasn't she invited to the ball, and why was she so upset about it? Is it possible the glitch wasn't as much of a mistake as I thought it was? Did the Prices tamper with her numbers? Did Lazuli? Or is this my guilty conscience trying to justify my sin? This tampering could very well be me they are referring to. Scars, what do I do now?

"Yes?" the soldier lifts his head to me.

"No, nothing was ever out of the ordinary. She never told me she was donating or when she got her numbers. She just all of a sudden was..." I almost say zombie-like, happy like the rest of town before I catch myself. "All of a sudden, Lazuli was a Donor and getting a check and entering the auctions. I didn't even know."

"And when was this?"

He is typing away now as if adding notes to my file.

"July," I say, instantly recalling the summer night we sat with feet dangling over the edge of the river. The night I told her about Father's factory accident, and she cheerily told me to just donate. That's when I knew my suspicions were correct. That she was donating her soul away.

He taps away at the screen and then looks at me. If he had eyebrows they would possibly be bunched together in question, but instead, small shiny wrinkles form almost unnoticeably.

"It says here that you received your blood numbers in June?"

"Yes," I whisper.

"Yet you didn't start donating until October? How come?"

I fidget with my hands nervously. I look to Gannet for support, but he only eyes me with eyebrows that *do* show curiosity.

"Uh...I was nervous."

"But with numbers like yours..." The skin on the naked brow shifts out of habit, and it is possible his eyebrows would have been raised at the sight of my numbers.

Gannet steps forward. "Number Thirteen forty-two has a rare mutation in her blood that makes it difficult for her to donate. With all the allergies being reported in our facility, I am sure it isn't difficult to understand her hesitancy." His hands are behind his back, and he is staring down the young officer. Gannett smiles and then waves out his arm to me as if I am a display in the trade-sale window he is bringing the officer's attention to. "However, since her first day, over a month ago, she has been more than compliant. Her numbers match every test in the division's records, and I see it very likely that she will be a top catalog number, even with her delay." His smile is eerily frozen in place. Time slows to a crawl.

"I would like to do one more scan."

I lift my finger automatically, but the officer puts out a hand to stop me.

"Not with my scanner, but the droids."

As if the black machine is a mind reader, one whirrs into place by his side. Its giant camera eye in the center of the orb seems to scan my whole body.

Gannet speaks confidently, "Yes, and if you need my scan too, as a witness, I'd be more than happy to—"

"That won't be necessary, technician," the officer says as a little arm with a scan circle on the top slides out from under the droid's eye.

It's a wonder it can scan my blood at all since it seems to be racing through my body pushed out and in by my erratic heart. But a short beep indicates it's done, and the officer checks his screen with the delivered information.

"Everything seems to check out here. Thank you for your time,

Donor. Congratulations on your good numbers, and good luck in the auctions; you never know what they may bring." The rattled speech sounds like a funeral service in the sober tones of the officer. He moves on to find another Donor to question.

I exhale and follow his movement with my eyes before I look to Gannet.

"Thanks," I say.

"No problem," he beams.

Scars but he's hot when he smiles like that. I smile back at him, filled with relief for a moment, and then I'm worried about Lazuli all over again. Am I the reason they discovered the mistake? What a stupid question; of course I am. What will they do to her? How long until they see my connection to it? Or perhaps I fixed the problem, and there will be no evidence against them. Yes. Gannet and Torrin pretty much both told me themselves there's no way to track it without port ID.

"I forgot to remind you," Gannet says.

I take another deep breath to loosen the tension in my chest.

"Tomorrow and Friday are the days off."

"Oh."

"My friend found a movie I haven't seen before. Would you like to come see it with me?"

In books I've read, boys were nervous to ask girls out for the first time. There is no nervousness in his asking. No jittery hesitations waiting for how I would take his question. Only confidence, and he would possibly have the same nonchalant attitude if I turned him down. How can I turn down these bright hazel eyes though?

"He lives in Dearborn," he continues, "so it's a bit of a ride, but if we take the morning tram, we could go see the shore before the movie maybe."

"Dearborn?" That piques my interest. "I've never seen the shore before." The idea of leaving Livonia has me locking my hands together and squeezing them tight to hold in my excitement.

"Great! How about we meet at the Merriman tram stop at ten a.m.?"

"That's my stop."

"I know." His smile deepens. "Ten o'clock, then?"

"Yes," I say.

He's walking backwards and smiling.

All I can think as I exit the facility is I should have taken the poison. The street is abuzz with officers, but all I can think about is what just happened with Gannet. Is this outing a date? Will he think it's a date? Could a relationship still work with a dead Romeo and a Juliet too chicken to die for him? To kill the real me inside?

NINETEEN

I walk home with a buzzing but confusing sensation. I'm not sure if it's joy or fear. Probably both. It's like I'm freefalling, but not sure which way is up or down. Gannet and Lazuli: two extreme situations that make me feel more hopeless than donating ever could. I want to like Gannet, but getting too attached feels wrong. It would be like the ultimate betrayal that I could never pull off. I dash up to my room before dinner, and as I open the door, I am blinded by something white in the corner. In my brown room, the giant white canvas sits in the corner with the paints resting on the floor. I should have known Papa would have snatched them from the store for me before I could.

After changing for dinner, I run down to the table and hug Papa around the neck.

"What is that for?" He laughs a laugh almost like the ones before my donations.

"The art supplies, of course. Thank you for getting them for me. I don't know when I would have had time."

"*I* didn't get them. I thought you had them delivered." He grabs the bowl of peas as I fall into my seat. "They were on the porch when I got home this evening."

I take the bowl of peas from him, dumbfounded, as Shannon snickers.

"Someone's got an admirer," she sings.

I immediately think of Gannet and then chastise myself. He

doesn't even know I paint. The conversation in the market floods my memory. Marcus spent his precious blood money on these things. How many donations did it cost him?

My stomach churns with concern, then burns at the thoughtfulness of his actions. It means more because of the great sacrifice. I try to tell myself it is the system that puts him in this situation, which angers me more than Marcus himself. Marcus is kind, and thoughtful, and sick, and persistent, and forward. My cheeks blush at the table as I recall his hands on my skin in the dressing room. I hide it quickly, though, and pass the bowl of peas.

I bury my emotions for a low-numbered beggar behind the anticipation of the date with Gannet. Mam is just as ecstatic about the news as I thought she would be. Going on a date with a technician, no matter how low his numbers are, is a sure chance at a secure life. Especially following the news about the Prices, Mam is exceptionally happy for the distraction. She claps and giggles through the dinner and cups my chin every chance she gets. I only get a stiff nod from Mam when I ask if I can go check on Lazuli after dinner.

The streets are quiet tonight, possibly from the scare of officers all over town. Homes have their lights out on their porches to detract guests or unwelcome attention. Any connection to the Price family is bad news right now, especially this close to the auctions. Even a rumor can destroy a Donor's career.

Walking the empty streets of my subdivision, the temperature plummets, and I rub at my arms. A cool fall breeze toys with my hair and tickles my scalp. The eerie silence adds to the chill. I bounce agitatedly on the balls of my feet and soon am jogging. The benefits of being able to feel *are* worth it, but these moments of fear make me question my decision. The incident with the officers today and my worry over Lazuli that pricks my chest makes me pick up my pace as if an officer is on my heels. I look over my shoulder as I round the corner of an abandoned brick home.

When I round the corner, a shadow moves near me, and I jump backwards with a loud yelp.

"We *have* to stop meeting like this," Marcus says. His hands still find a way on my arms, and even in the dim evening light, his smile looks so authentic and beautiful. Or perhaps it is his wonderful gift of art supplies that makes him seem more appealing. His white teeth, right above my face, glow in the darkening light, and I freeze in his grasp. I slowly inhale the scent of his clothes mixed with an almost fruity cologne, but I don't want to think about how he can afford cologne.

It's so dark now I can't see his eyes, just the occasional reflection of light off of them. There's something about being alone on a dark street in the arms of a man who smells nice that makes me lose all sense of where I am and what I was doing. Of course being the only other individual in the world who knows what it means to truly feel has something to do with it, too. I look away from his white smile and down at where my arms disappear in the night as I feel for the first time the muscles of his chest beneath his ribbed knit sweater. I recall the first time I ran into him. He was harder, frailer, skinnier then.

"What are you doing out here anyway?" he asks. "The streets are full of officers tonight."

His words bring me reluctantly back to the reality of our world and my current mission. I gently push off his chest as I back away. His hands loosen on my arms and slide against my forearms, then wrists, then fingertips, touching every inch of my arm he possibly can before dropping his hands altogether. Maybe it's because I can't see the dirt on him that I don't mind the touch so much. Or maybe it is from him seeing more of me in the light of the dressing room that makes me not care.

"Marcus, you almost sound concerned. Your mother did teach you manners then."

I'm smiling in the dark, ready for his retort. When none comes, my smile falters.

His laugh is forced and delayed. "My mother would be appalled to know how I've behaved in a lady's presence."

I smile at his formal words straight out of one of my books. But there's a sadness to his formal teasing.

"My mother died when I was young."

The air feels colder, and I regret my words. The image of a sickly Donor woman dying in her home instead of with a team of doctors at a facility like it should be runs across my mind. It's all too common. Donors whose contracts don't allow maternity leave or account for the hardships of family life.

"I was raised by my father who, I'm sorry to report, is an old grump."

I cross my arms in front of me. I've no clue what to say next. His voice is still lighthearted and trying to joke, but how can I make fun of this? I no longer want to be better than this Donor. I feel foolish and cruel. I've had nothing but disregard for him. Never even given him a chance. From the moment he first bumped into me, I've had my mind made up about who he is without considering any of his trials or hardships.

"I'm sorry," I whisper dumbly.

"Don't be. You didn't know."

The awkward silence rolls on.

"To answer your question, I'm out here because I'm visiting a friend. Actually, I'm a little worried for her."

"Oh, can I..." He hesitates and looks over his shoulder. "Would you want me to..." He rubs at his neck. "Did you want me to escort you there?"

His hesitancy makes me embarrassed. Gannet is too smooth and controlled, drugged even. But Marcus is suddenly so uneasy I get the impression he doesn't want to walk with me at all. The switch from his usual cocky self has me feeling self-conscious about my behavior toward him. I mean, it makes sense. I've only ever insulted him or pushed him down. I wouldn't want to walk with me either. Pleasantries between us are strange.

"No, that's fine—"

"Aston, don't be silly." He steps forward with more confidence now, and I feel the heat radiating off his undrugged body. "There's a reason we are the only ones on this street at eight p.m. I'm walking you there, now lead the way."

The darkness gives me confidence too, and I smile since he can't see. He's right. There is a reason for everything. And I see now that even under all of Marcus's crude behavior he always does what's right. He's, I dare say, a gentleman right from one of my books. I take a few steps before he's grasping for my arm again. It still surprises me that neither of us jump at the interactions anymore.

"Actually, I can't see a scarred thing; give me your hand."

Our fingers interlock, and I like how his burn against my skin.

"Doesn't this town believe in electricity?" Marcus grumbles, with a laugh at the end.

I wish he could see my frown now.

"Hey," I say, "my dad's the town's head electrician, don't bash Livonia's power plant. Plus, our streetlights have never been powered. We've never been given clearance for that amount of electricity. Why would they start now?"

"Because a face like yours deserves a spotlight."

I slap his arm, and his rippling laugh makes my heart feel full, like I could donate a thousand pints and never feel faint. I can't help but smile deeper at the difference from earlier in the day when my heart tried to feel happy about Gannet but stung around the edges with guilt. I don't have to die a little to be with Marcus. I can be one hundred and ten percent myself and never feel guilty about anything. I see now that Marcus does not want my sympathy or charity. He seems to merely want to be around me. And why is that so bad?

As we cross the next street, we hear the feet of the officers and the whirring of their droids in the distance.

"I'm just visiting my friend," I reassure myself.

Marcus doesn't say anything about me talking to myself, and the way he grips my hand makes me wonder if *he* has done something wrong too. I wonder for the first time what he was doing on the streets this late, and what if he came up with the money for the canvas illegally? I know we both have done something wrong regarding the serum. But as far as I know, there hasn't been a test developed to tell if someone is drugged up or not.

A young woman's yelp rings through the chilly night air. It sends ice down my spine like I've been paralyzed. I detach from Marcus and take off running the last block.

"Lazuli!" I shout out of impulse. The light of the upcoming moon highlights the edge of the corner house, and Marcus's feet skip and pound next to mine. I curve, cutting across the lawn of the home, when my arm is jerked, and I'm pulled toward the side of the house.

"Aston!" Marcus whispers fiercely as he cradles me in his arm and then pushes me up against the cool rough brick. He traps me underneath him as he leans an arm against the building. His other arm is around my waist as he hisses, "Officers!"

He leans around the corner, and I twist in his grasp to peek over his arm. A large group of officers move through the night. Their bald heads with the moon shining on them seem to be floating in the air as their black uniforms are lost in the darkness. Lazuli is nowhere in sight, and my chest tightens as I follow the movement of the officers' heads. It's hard to make out what they're doing, but then I hear Lazuli's mother.

"Please don't take that. It wasn't bought, it was handed down from my mother. Oh, please not that vase either."

From the crashing sounds bouncing off the homes down the street towards us, it's clear they are not listening to her. The stress in Mrs. Price's voice increases with every word, "Please! What will become of us? What will you do to us? Where are you taking—"

Shadows blur together in a scuffle, but it doesn't take much imagination when I hear the sound of stick against flesh. I jerk around the corner to run to her, but Marcus holds me back. His arms crisscross around me, and when I lunge to try and run again, I bungee back into his chest.

He doesn't understand. I did this. I made this happen. It's me that stick should have hit, not poor Mrs. Price. The pain and guilt seep up my chest into a sob. As I give up, my weight shifts heavily against him. I slip completely, as if the sound of Mrs. Price falling to the ground is actually me falling into Marcus. I'm no longer supporting myself. I can't tell if my legs are even there anymore. A crisp, harsh voice breaks through the air now.

"D49! Give us some light here."

A droid lights up the area, and I see the lump of a body that's on the uneven street.

"We'll take her on the tram too," the officer orders.

"The tram's closed," I whisper nonsensically, as if the head officer is speaking to me.

"Yes, sir." The obedient invisible worker replies without question. Even their bald heads are lost now that the light is shining away from them and down at Mrs. Price. One of them appears in the spotlight, straddling her body to grab her from behind. When he lifts her by the armpits, her head falls forward. A roll of nausea in me seems to move in time with her hair that dangles and bounces from unconsciousness. The droid light follows them to a trailer loaded with the furniture. Another officer appears in the light, helping lift Mrs. Price onto it. The sounds of breaking furniture, a shattering glass window, shouts, and hard boots against pavement fill the air. The absence of Lazuli makes my stomach twist again. What have they done with her?

The scene of Mrs. Price's helpless body sends blood rushing through me, and I can feel my legs again. I pull free of Marcus's relaxed hands, and soon I am halfway across the lawn. Lazuli's house is only five houses down on the opposite side of the street. I sprint towards the spotlight when something slams me down to the ground. My hands skid across the cold grass as I catch myself. Marcus's body pins me down. I twist and writhe underneath of him.

"I have to help her." I squirm enough to be directly facing him. Pushing with my palms against his chest, I attempt to bring a knee up to wedge space between us.

"What?" his words are winded from the exertion, and he takes several breaths before he continues. I fight against the pity I feel just as much as I fight to free myself from his weight. "What do you have planned, Aston? To march up to a fleet of officers in the dead of night and demand they return everything and apologize to the Prices?" He pauses to catch his breath again. My arms relax against him as his words clear my head. "They're not going to care what numbers you have, or how much you make a week, or where you've been invited. They only have orders. And they'll enforce them on anyone that gets in the way of them."

He's right. He may not have all the specifics since he doesn't know I am the one who they want, but he's still right. Turning myself in won't make them stop. They will only take me *and* the Prices. Maybe I can find a way to get them out.

When my arms and legs give up the fight completely, Marcus lowers slowly on top of me and another sob escapes. I roll my head against the blades of grass and stare through blurry eyes at the now sideways scene on the street. Mrs. Price's body lays in a misshapen heap at the end of the trailer.

"I have to help her," I whimper.

"Shhh." He shifts on top of me to smooth the hair from my face.

"I have to help," I say even weaker this time. Another heave of my chest as the tears come.

"I know." His lips are practically in my ear and my sobs begin in earnest. I don't register those lips kissing my temple or his thumb wiping my tears from the cracks of my squinting eyes. I don't think about how good this boy's clothes smell, only about the girl that I painted a red target on and the soldiers who took her from me.

"They can't feel this," I pull my balled-up fist between our chests pushing against the ache I feel there. "They can't see what they're doing. I have to help." I feel as pathetic inside as my words sound on the outside.

His hand stops in my hair, and he rests his forehead against my temple.

"I know," he says one last time. There is no mistaking the feeling in his words now. He knows and now I know. We can feel. We can see. We know.

I bury my nose in his neck and he engulfs me completely. My hands find the back of his sweater, and I grip it tightly as I continue to cry as quietly as I can. I let the hurt in my chest rage on, spreading through my stomach and into my throat. I try to feel it all for Mrs. Price, for Lazuli, for Gannet, for all the people who cannot. There is a nation of feelings storming inside me. I have to help them escape. Who cares about my contract now? I have to find a way to free these Donors trapped in their own lives.

TWENTY

The knock on my bedroom door the next morning is like brass cymbals in my brain instead of the splintering wood. I clutch my temples and groan.

"What?" I croak and cough, attempting to open my eyelids ballooned from a night of crying. The sounds of clanging furniture haunt me as Mam knocks again.

"Are you ready for your day out with the technician? Can I come in?"

I hear the creak of the door hinges before I can answer.

"Scars galore! Why aren't you ready yet?" Mam whisks my closet open letting the door hit the wall.

How could I think of a date with my technician now, after everything I've seen? After what I've felt? Removing the covers, I sit up then bend over to retrieve my shoes. "I *am* ready."

Her beady eyes look me over before smiling sweetly.

"Yes, you look fine, dear. But you are more than fine, you are the highest Donor in history and need to dress the part." She saunters over to me in her cream linen nightgown, holding a royal blue sweater. Her bare feet hiss along the wood. She whispers next as if there are spies in the walls, "We do not want others to think we made up our numbers as well."

She didn't say *like Lazuli*, but the intention is clear. There is fear in her words, and she means well in her own Mam sort of way. The sound of the stick against flesh is still too fresh in my mind, however, and I rip the sweater from Mam's hands.

"I don't need a shirt to tell people who I am."

Worry crosses her face. Even with all our differences, what would I have done if Mam was the one hauled off on a trailer?

"But," I say softening my voice as much as I can, "maybe you could do my hair?"

My offer is accepted as Mam motions me to the mirror by my closet. As she brushes my hair, which is past my shoulders now, I think about Lazuli. I wish there was a way to go to her today and see how she is. Perhaps Gannett would understand, and we could rearrange plans to go find out where they were taken instead. How would I explain to him the reason I didn't get to talk to her last night or about what I saw? I may be in trouble for witnessing what I had, for knowing what I know. Marcus and I both.

"I brushed your hair every day before basic school. Then in middle grade you started doing it all on your own." Mam rarely shows emotion when it isn't a show for Papa or to get something she wants. "And now you're off to Dearborn with a technician and have the highest numbers in the country."

My hair is split in half, and she finishes pinning back the sides just above my ears letting the rest flow down my back like she always used to do. It makes me look younger and more innocent than I feel. She squeezes my shoulders and peers around me into the mirror. A faint memory of someone saying, "Hair like sunshine through the trees," as they hugged me similarly, floats on the wind. But it feels as mythical as a dream. I cross my arm over my chest and place my hand on hers. Our eyes lock, and hers glisten with concern and pride.

I may not always understand Mam, but in this moment, she's just another frightened Mrs. Price, wondering what the system is going to do with her family.

"Well now." The moment is gone, and Mam wipes at her face.

"You're going to be late if we dawdle any longer." She pauses at the door to look back at me. For a second, I glimpse the loving mother trapped somewhere within the hard, manipulative Mam our division has trained her to be. Will any of us ever make it free?

GANNET IS PACING at the corner of the Merriman tram stop at the end of my street with his hands stuffed down the pockets of his jeans. He flips his head in a nod and smiles when he sees me. Walking towards me, he unstuffs his hands and wrings them.

"Hey," he says.

"Hi."

In this moment, it surprises me that I feel nothing. I'm still numb from feeling so much last night. Right now, Gannet feels like nothing more than my technician. The invisible thread tying me to him was cut in the night, and I find myself not missing him at all.

The ding of the oncoming tram saves us from our awkward greeting. Stepping into the middle car, he offers me the remaining seat while he stands holding the leather handle above him. I am surprised to see this many people on the tram heading the opposite direction from the market. I wonder what takes them east towards the water instead of into town, or how they can even afford it.

A young toddler sits on the lap of the woman next to me. The red shirt he wears is several sizes too small, and the long sleeves barely cover his elbows. His head is shaved, showing off the squareness of his skull. Round cheeks and jowls sit expressionless on either side of his red pouting lips.

I smile at him with no success. I remember the potato candy Mam made for me to share with Gannett and his friends today. Pulling my canvas purse onto my lap, I dig until I feel the pointy, balled foil they are wrapped in.

The boy watches my every move.

"Excuse me?" I say, catching the attention of the boy's mother.

When she pulls the curtain of her brown hair away from her face and looks right at me, her sunken and hollow eyes catch me off guard. I feel my face losing expression as I stare at the young girl, barely older than I, with concave cheeks and brown stringy hair.

"Yes?" Her voice is high-pitched, and her smile seems torturous.

"I was wondering if..." I hesitate as I spy the girl's teeth that are yellow and covered in dark craters of decay. "...if your son could have some potato candy?"

"Oh, how nice. Yes, I'm sure he'd love it."

I hand over the gift. The boy looks at me with weary eyes before he takes it.

"What do you say, Gabe?"

"Tank yu," Gabe answers.

I try a smile at him again. This time the boy offers a weak, grimacing smile that makes his eyes squint as the chewing moves his fat cheeks. The low hum of the tram gets lower and lower as it slows to a stop. The young girl leaves with the boy in her arms. Looking over his mom's shoulder, he waves to me as they exit.

My hand freezes in the wave once he is out of sight. I look up into Gannett's eyes to see them burrowing into me. His face is still warm and inviting, but as always, there are many layers to Gannet.

We are the only ones continuing on, and with a completely different group of people, the tram is again full and on its way. The sun strobes through the trees as we whizz by. Two more stops, and we are alone on the tram. Gannett sits by me, and our shoulders bump against each other. Gannett bounces his knee up and down and occasionally rubs his palms on his jeans.

For once I don't find myself needing to fill the space between Gannet and I with words. No questions or gratitude, and the longing I felt before is gone as well. The silence isn't painful; it somehow feels companionable, as if he also knows that we never could have happened. Perhaps that is the urgent unspoken message in his eyes.

Soon the town disappears, replaced by wild open fields and overgrown bushes. The fields are rimmed with trees that blaze yellow, orange, and red, as if someone splattered the colors with a dripping paintbrush.

The whir of the stopping tram is heard before the town comes into view.

"This is Dearborn Market," Gannett says just as a stonewall passes the window, and then the row of lawyer buildings and market streets almost identical to our own flash by slower and slower.

After walking through the waking Dearborn market, we find the edge of what used to be the original River Rogue. It has morphed into a part of the lakes as Detroit river took over the land meeting River Rogue on its way. Now River Rogue winds its way up through Livonia, separating us from the Recipients. The grass here is greener than any I've ever seen, and it creeps all the way up to the edge of the water. The water is calm, and the orange-tipped leaves are still. Walking side by side, Gannet's knuckles brush mine, and I fold my arms.

"You know, these days were set apart as a day of remembrance once," he says.

It feels weird to have him talk again, like he's breaking some unspoken oath I'd thought our silence formed on the tram. "Remembrance? Of what?"

"Of a day two groups of people sat down together for the first time and found their commonalities instead of their differences."

"Well, I can see why we don't celebrate *that* anymore."

"It became a day of gratitude each year. When one remembered their blessings, they spent the day eating as much as they could."

"Now, instead of once a year, that's forced on us every day."

"What do you mean?" Gannet looks at me expectantly, as if he knows I made a slip and is waiting for me to correct it.

"Nothing, just that...our system makes us appreciate everything already. We have so little that there isn't anything we take for granted. In a way, I pity the Recipients. It must be so hard to find gratitude when everything comes so easily."

He only makes a knowing humming sound as we continue to walk.

"How do you know so much about Old America?" I say.

The wind makes a few dead leaves fall from the trees and race through the sky.

"Before I began donating, I was really fascinated by everything from Old America. I smuggled some books from a closet in middle grade."

I nod at more proof that un-drugged Gannet and myself would have been a match made in heaven.

"Did you know this area used to be a golf course?" He laughs at my incredulous face. "It's a sport that depended on the condition of the land for a small ball to move over the top of easily. Before the wars, they found ways to chemically change the soil to make the grass grow green forever. Now the people of Dearborn Heights keep this park grass tidy, never knowing what makes it grow so different."

"Huh. What a weird day to imagine, having the land built and groomed just for sport. Or a day full of gluttony just because you're grateful for it all."

"You're very different, Aston."

He stops. I step past him and turn to face him. I keep my hands folded and look down at my shoes as my pulse quickens.

"I hope you know that no matter what the catalog brings I'll always think you're number one."

I snort, struggling not to laugh at the cheesy compliment. It's almost as bad as Leonard proposing on my sofa. Why do I have to torture myself with the presence of drugged men? More than ever, I find myself wishing for Marcus. How his eyes sparkle of truth and reality. Sure, his hard, lanky hands are a sad reality of the Donor life, but they are warm, and they are unaltered.

I should say something to end Gannet's modified murmuring, but I can't. That edge of hope in me that wishes Gannet and I could be together returns. If I didn't hate the division so much, perhaps we could be.

"I..." His cold hand slides down my shoulder and stops on my elbow. "From the day I saw you outside the facility I knew...that you were different. That I couldn't just..."

"Gannett—" I try to walk away, but he grabs both my elbows now and pulls me back to face him.

"There's been something I've wanted to tell you. Something I need to tell you. It's why I wanted to come to this place, where we wouldn't be...interrupted."

His eyes are different now, not sunken in like Marcus's, yet not filmy and fake like before. The sun shines through a break in the clouds, and it lights up his hazel eyes, making them look more gold than brown. For a moment, I'm entranced by them, and my eyes flick down, landing on his lips. They are plump and red and parted from his heavy breathing. This glimpse again into the real Gannet makes me dizzy and imagine what we could be. I close my eyes though. It's only a glimpse. I can't live on glimpses. I felt nothing on the tram, but now?

"Especially with you being invited to the ball now, Aston, I need to tell you that—"

"Stop, Gannet." The mention of the ball awakens me from my trance. I pull from his grasp and speed walk back towards the entrance to the park. The breeze that picks up with my pace and the meaning behind his words slap me awake. Of course the recognition from the ambassador would now make me a more tempting match. With Marcus, I'm just Miss Aston Vazeto, me, the girl who feels everything. But with Gannet, I will always be a number, his Donor, his ticket to a secure life. Who would have thought the low-numbered Donor would be the one not to use me.

I can't bear to hear Gannet say how he's found the number he's been looking for all his life, or how perfect we are for each other, because deep down I know in a different world it would be true.

"No, you don't understand you—"

"Gannet." I spin back around, waggling my finger at him. "I don't want to hear what you have to say. I don't think I can bear to hear it. And I do not think I'd be able to...to..." I close my eyes again to erase the view of his pleading eyes. "Just don't, ok?" I whisper.

With my eyes still shut, I am hoping the pause between us is bringing back the system's version of Gannet.

A voice shouts from behind, "Gannet!"

We both turn to see a young redheaded boy running towards us.

"I thought that was you; I saw you headed to the Rogue! Laney has lunch ready, come and have some with us!"

The freckled redhead makes it to our spot on the hill and stops in front of us, catching his breath.

"Mason." Gannet smiles, suddenly at ease, and the two shake hands. "This is Mason, my good friend from harder days. Mason, this is Aston—"

"Aston?" Mason eyes Gannet, raising his golden blond eyebrows. "*The* Aston? Wow, you said you were bringing someone, Gannet, but you didn't say it was Aston." He turns back to me. "I have heard so much about you! Why, you're famous now in—"

"Mason!" Gannet barks as if giving an order. He turns and addresses me now. "I think we all are a little jealous of the ambassador invite, let's just say that."

I look confusedly from one to the other, though I linger on how Gannet's cheeks redden.

The walk to Mason's home is dominated by Mason and Gannet's conversation. I marvel at the birds that swoop over the water and wish my papa could be here to see it. Gannet had refused to let me pay for my tram fare, and once I heard the price, I was glad. Mam would have had a fit, date or no date.

Meeting Laney, Mason's wife, is eye opening. They are both so young, which isn't rare, but the way they maneuver around each other is odd, like they are a couple celebrating fifty years of marriage, not two. They are already acclimated to each other's quirks. They predict each other's moves. She grabs the plate of sandwiches just as he lifts his hand. He leans back and puts his arm around her just as she crosses her legs and leans into him. They are like one living organism sharing the same thoughts. And when he smiles at her, it is like the glimpses that Gannet gives me, only Mason's are returned with the same affection. How can people who don't feel anything look so in love? For a moment, I wonder if they somehow beat the system, too. Maybe they don't take the serum either.

The movie we're watching is full of dialog and references I don't understand, and I shift on the noisy sofa next to Gannet during the romance scenes that show more passion than I have ever seen. That passion, pre-serum period, makes me realize there's no way Mason and Laney could be free from the effects of the system if that's what love was like unaltered. That just must be what marrying your caged-in-soulmate is like. The show seems to make Laney and Mason snuggle closer, but I only chew on my inner lip and avoid Gannet completely. He is probably sorry now that he invited me. I turned a would be romantic proposal into an awkward night we couldn't escape from.

Putting on my jacket by the door, I notice a pot of yellow flowers that give me an odd sense of deja vu. The plant is more bush-like than most potted plants, and the tiny yellow flowers are scattered across it. Where have I seen flowers like this before? I overhear Gannet and Mason talking in the hallway. I lean closer to the flowers to try and hear better.

"Have you asked her?" Mason says.

"No." Gannet's voice is thick with disappointment.

"You saw her on the miniport message when she stood up to those officers."

"Those are supposed to be secret," Gannet hisses, "Only used for—"

"Scars sake, Gannet, what's done is done. Everyone saw her. They have a right to know what's possible. You can't keep her hidden away. You've got to—"

"What? Force her, like the Recipients do?" Gannet's voice grows louder.

"No one is talking about force here, Gannet. Just...Gannet, I told you what happened here when people saw her." Mason's voice takes on a frenzied excitement, making it crackle as he whispers.

I reach out and touch the tips of the spindly yellow stamens that shoot out of the center like fireworks. I lean closer to the hallway. What do Mason's words mean? Am I in trouble? Do they know about everything I've done?

"They know now," Mason hisses. "They all know, and they want it too."

"Pretty aren't they?" Laney says.

Gasping, I spin as I straighten. "Yes." I gesture down to the little bush, unable to concentrate on my eavesdropping any longer. "I feel like I've seen them somewhere. What are they?"

Laney smiles before she answers me, like I'm missing an inside joke. "St John's wort," she says.

Before I can make a joke about the name, Laney wraps me up into a hug.

"Thank you," she says in my ear before I pull away.

I give an uneasy giggle. "Whatever for? I should be thanking you. Lunch was delicious, and you two have a lovely home."

She smiles at me with eyes that say I should know what she's talking about, but I don't. "We are glad Gannet found you. The whole New World is."

The boys step into the entryway, and she cuts her eyes over at Gannet who turns to give her a questioning look. Is it possible her confusing words have anything to do with the strange conversation I just witnessed? When Gannet looks at me with starry eyes and concern on his face, I know it's not possible. Red paints his cheeks, and I feel my lunch of baked potato and sour cream drop in my stomach like we ate stones instead. I have led him on in my indecision. I have led them all to believe he had found the right number.

Sitting on the dark tram home in silence, I think over the events of the last several weeks. I would have given into a day like this with Gannet if it hadn't been for running into Marcus. But I'm learning that emotions have a way of running wild when left untamed, and Marcus is quickly running away with my heart.

Gannet and I are alone on the tram. It is lit up by a row of lights along the ceiling, making the windows more like mirrors.

"Aston, about earlier, I really do need to tell you something."

I sit on my hands and stare at the reflection of my swinging feet. After witnessing Mason and Laney, at first, I had a spark of hope that maybe Gannett and I could make it work. Perhaps I could be happy enough if I got all the glimpses into his true self.

Seeing the way the two moved through the whole night, however, also made me very aware of how Gannett and I seem to shift in opposite directions. My life seems to always be moving towards something else, towards Marcus. Somehow, I always end up in Marcus's arms. He has a way of catching me when I'm falling, saving me when I'm drowning and comforting me before I even know I need him. His arms last night were especially warm and attentive. I never thought a sick boy capable of so much admirable care and affection. Yet I can still feel the way his hands brushed my temple or got lost in my hair or how his chest pinned me in a way that made me feel secure. My face burns at the memory of the way he held me as I cried.

"I wish you wouldn't," I say.

Gannett leans forward, elbows on his knees so he can look over his shoulder, up into my face.

"But Aston—"

"I don't want you to, Gannett. I don't want you to tell me. And I don't ever want you to try again."

"You don't even know what I—"

"I have a good enough idea." My hands are fists. I do, and I don't want him to tell me.

He throws himself back into the hard, blue plastic seat of the tram and folds his arms. The rest of the tram ride is in silence. My head turns away from him, and I see my reflection in the window, betraying the tears I'm trying to hide. I am saying goodbye to Gannett long before my stop. How different the story of Romeo and Juliet may have been if Juliet chose to simply live without Romeo instead of pursuing him into death. If there was a Marcus in the story, I'm sure she would have.

TWENTY-ONE

The next morning, Mam runs up the stairs screaming. My door swings open, and Mam dashes to my bedside.

"Aston." She kisses my forehead. "Oh, you dear sweet girl, the catalog has come! The catalog has come," she sings while dancing along my floor.

"It is an ok score then? Being late didn't matter much?" I start to crawl out of bed, but Papa comes in behind her and his stare has me rooted in place on the cold floor. His hands are stuffed in his navy work pants. I can never please both of them at the same time.

"'Is it an *okay* score'...!" Mam repeats my words mockingly. "Listen to her, Patar." Mam laughs and hits Papa with the red-covered catalog in her hand.

"I heard her, Evelyn, just tell her already." My Papa's harsh voice rolls over the room like the warning of falling rocks before a landslide.

"Number one!" Mam ignores Papa. "Number one, child," she cheers. "Not just in Livonia either. In the whole New World. You are number one!"

Torrin comes in rubbing his eyes.

"Aston did good?"

It's difficult not to feel a small sense of pride, watching Mam dance around the room. Papa just ducks through the door. Torrin's words echo through my mind. Did good? I didn't do anything but bleed.

"Good? Aston is number one, Torri dear. Number one!"

Torrin runs to my side with his sleepy, crusted eyes and hugs me around the middle.

Mam steps forward. "Run to market, Torrin, and tell Mr. Winters to put a beef roast on the tab."

Torrin yawns and scratches his back as he goes.

"Make sure he knows why," she follows him down the hallway yelling. "Make sure he hears the good news that our Aston is number one in the nation."

I sit back on my bed, sinking into the covers, trying to let the news sink in. I knew my numbers were high, but I didn't have the full three months to offer the auctions. Over and over again, I try to tell myself that anything could still happen, no one knows what the auctions may bring after all. Being number one does not automatically guarantee a high contract. Donors have gotten sick before the auction and scared off possible bidders. Ambassadors can find stipulations that disqualify their standing, and most Recipients would want the full three months and might not risk it no matter where I stand on the list. But if I could make enough to appease Mam's spending and feed the family all year, then perhaps it is all worth Papa's disapproval.

Starting down the stairs, I pause when I hear Papa's voice at the desk under the stairs.

"Are you sure?" His crackly low whisper floats up to me. "But the resistance has worked so hard. Are they really willing to—"

The other end of the receiver cuts Papa off, and soon he is agreeing reluctantly to whatever is being said. A resistance? A rebellion? Is this possibly why Papa supported my original decision to never donate so readily? Because there is already a plan in order to free Donors everywhere from contracts and coercion? My heart leaps at the idea. I'm not alone. A part of me wants to run to Papa and tell him everything. Yet Papa doesn't sound supportive of whatever he's listening to. Does he know about a rebellion but not agree with it? If he's not a part of it, would he support me joining them? How do I tell him I'm already devoted to the cause and want to join? Perhaps there's a local leader I can be directed to if I find the right people to ask. But would Papa help or hinder me in finding them and signing up?

"My daughter will be there, you know?" His voice is no longer as quiet, and he sounds worried, outraged. "You better make sure of it."

He's talking about me? Being where? The Ambassador's Ball?

Of course! If there is anywhere for a rebellion to network and spread the word, the ball filled with Donors and lawyers from the entire surrounding area would be the perfect place. If I meet the right people there, perhaps I can find a way to ask them about how to become a part of this resistance.

I descend the stairs as Papa ends his secret conversation. He looks at me with frightened eyes before he steps out the front door without a word. Why wouldn't he just tell me? Is there a reason he doesn't want me to be a part of the rebellion? *"My daughter will be there"*— perhaps I will be carrying out some secret mission without even knowing it. And then Mason and Gannet's conversation floods my mind, and I put a hand out to the wall for support. What if I was wrong about what Gannet was going to tell me? Their heated disagreement makes so much more sense now. They must be part of the resistance. Mason's words fill my ringing ears. *Everyone saw her.* Is the resistance using me without my consent like the conniving Recipients? A pawn in their battle tactics?

A pan clanks in the kitchen, which makes me jump away from the wall. This is silly. They wouldn't use me, and Papa is making sure I'm safe. I spy the red catalog on the dining table and walk towards it as I think. I don't know what to think about Gannet. Wasn't he just a number-sick puppy like the rest of the boys Mam has sent over? For someone free of the serum, I sure feel out of control.

I sigh as I slowly near the table. I wish Papa would just trust me with the truth. My fingers brush the smooth red catalog and freeze in place with guilt. Trust me like I've trusted him with my own little act of rebellion? I keep as much from him as he does from me.

Mam is singing in the kitchen as the smells and sounds of bacon in a pan blends with her melody. I snatch the catalog and rip it open, accidentally tearing a corner. There, at the top in cursive numbers, is "Thirteen Forty-Two." Underneath is "Twelve Ninety-Eight," but it is crossed out with "Disqualified" typed next to it.

"Lazuli," I whisper to the empty room. "What have they done with you? What have *I* done to you?"

TWENTY-TWO

It's the night of the ball, and I haven't seen Marcus since the time I cried in his arms. I wish I could tell him what I have discovered, even though, technically, I haven't unearthed much information yet. All I know is there's a resistance somewhere. After tonight, though, I should have more information, and then I can tell him about how we may not be the only serum-free individuals after all.

I stand in front of my bedroom mirror and swish the beads of my dress back and forth slightly. All of my sisters came to dinner and argued over who would do my hair. In the end, they all had a part in it. Sybil brought her hot iron and framed my face with draping curls. Ari brought a gemstone headband that matched the clear beads of my dress. Shannon twisted parts of my hair into tiny ropes and crisscrossed them over my head, pulling it all into a loose bun at the nape of my neck. The jewels on the headband disappear into the twists and look as if they're embedded into the strands of my golden hair.

With a finger in one of the wispy curls, I stand in awe in my bedroom all alone. I look completely different. I stand out amongst the brown of my room—brown floors, brown walls, brown blankets and curtains. My champagne dress looks pink in comparison. I feel guilty for how good it feels to look pretty, to feel excited.

A knock breaks through my thoughts, and soon I see the worn, warm face of my grandmother peeking around the door behind me.

"Can I come in?" she asks.

"Grandma Bolgi," I say, turning to her with open arms.

Embracing her, she smells of mint candy that I know can be found in her pocket.

"Oh, Little Ash Tree, how you have blossomed."

Her hand is on my cheek, and I softly cover it with my own hand as if I could lock this moment in a locket and keep it forever.

"You didn't come all the way here to see me in a fancy dress. What brings you to Livonia, Grandma Bolgi?"

"What? Why can't an old lady travel across the state to see her granddaughter attend the Ambassador's Ball? It's never been done before, you know. It may never happen again."

Her skin is surprisingly smooth in places like her cheeks as if the surrounding wrinkles have stretched the skin until it's as thin and shiny as silk.

"Plus, I was hoping you could sneak me in for the ride." Her Hungarian is lost, but every now and then I hear a hint of something foreign.

I giggle at her teasing words.

"Ash tree, you look stunning. Give your Grandma Bolgi a twirl."

I do as I'm told and watch the beads flare away from my knees where the dress is fitted.

Grandma hugs me close and slips me a mint from her pocket.

I hear the sound of racing footsteps on the stairs before my door is flung open and Torrin's bright eyes give my jeweled dress a run for its money.

"Aston, there's the coolest tram here to take you to the ball. Come quick and see."

"Tram?" I ask, but he is already gone, thundering down the stairs for another look.

As I descend, I see a man standing at the front door with his hands clasped in front of him. He wears the uniform of an officer but has hair on his head and face and wears a broad smile. He explains he is my tram driver for the evening, and after a blur of goodbyes, I follow him to the so-called tram Torrin told me about. There's really no other way to describe it. It literally looks like a miniature tram without cables overhead, or tracks, or even wheels. It's shaped like a silver bullet and floats in the air. There are no visible lines where a door should be, and I blink as the side of the mini tram disappears, creating an entry. Where metal had been, I now see a u-shape bench. I step in and choose to sit along the back of the vehicle facing forward. The side of the tram reappears silently like a bubbling mirage, and I watch the scene of my family lined up along the porch steps darken through the tinted windows. I only know we are moving when they slide across the window and soon are out of sight.

A black window rolls down in front of me, and I see the driver sitting at a panel of lights and buttons.

"The table in the middle opens up," the chauffeur says over his shoulder. "It's stocked with snacks and drinks if you are hungry or thirsty."

I spot Lazuli walking down the street just as he begins rolling the window between us back up.

"Stop!" I shout. The window stops and so does the mini tram. "It's my friend. Do I have a minute?"

"Sure. I'd want to show off my ride in this too."

I try to match his smile, but showing off is the last thing I want to do right now. The sliding door opens, and I step out carefully with my gold spaghetti strap heels.

"Lazuli," I call out.

She stops then eyes my outfit before making a face. She turns and starts walking away.

"Lazuli," I say again as I cross the cracked road over to her.

She stops and just stands there analyzing my hair and the makeup Mam insisted on.

"What do you want, Aston?"

Her growl makes me stop short, and I feel my face fall. What has happened to her? She's possibly no longer donating and therefore no longer getting the serum. Or perhaps the serum is not strong enough for what they have put her through. What *I* have put her through. I should turn myself in. I should confess to my part in this matter that I am the one who brought the system's attention to the mistake.

"I was worried about you." My voice cracks on *you*, and I ache to tell her I'm sorry for what I did.

We stand several feet apart as if it is a physical representation of what has become of our friendship. I can't help but recall the times we snuck berries from the lawyers' gardens or tried to build a bridge to the ambassador's mansion. An image of Lazuli and I sketching plans of how an artist and a singer would take over the world comes to mind. I feel like I can still hear Mrs. Price clunking around in the kitchen and smell her apple butter cooking down to a delicious brown sauce. My nose burns with the threat of tears.

"Come to gawk at the low-numbered nobody, more like. Well, go ahead, get a good look. You've paraded yourself out here nice and mighty, just take a good look and go away."

Anger dries my tears. "Lazuli, I am not parading myself. We never even wanted to be Donors, remember? How can you call yourself nothing when—"

"Oh come off it, Aston. You were always the one playing rebel, and I was just the quiet sidekick who brought the snacks. Besides, it's easy for you to play the game of 'I don't even want to,' when your numbers are that high. If you had numbers like mine and no other choice than to donate, you wouldn't be saying the same thing."

Her words sink in, clearing my mind: *Numbers like mine?* So it wasn't a mistake?

"What do you mean numbers like yours? I tried to—"

"I'm twenty-nine!" She screams so loud a group of birds stir and fly away.

I'm frozen in place. Twenty-nine? So she did tamper with her numbers. It wasn't *all* my fault? I was doing something illegal to cover up *her crime.* I risked my life and the wellbeing of my family for a treasonous liar. My chest tightens, and I ball my fists. Her eyes flip to my hands. For some reason, my anger seems to make her happy. A deranged grin overtakes her face before she looks at me.

"So now you know the kind of scum you've been hanging around. A twenty-nine. A nothing. So go on and get out of here."

My heart melts against the anger. She wants me to hate her because of her number. The system raises us to hate people like her, but I don't. I look to the ground and open my mouth, but she speaks first.

"Don't you dare try to make this better, little miss know it all." She curls her top lip in a way that makes me step back. "I know you're everyone's blood hero and can't do anything wrong, but there's nothing you can do or say to fix this, Aston. And I won't be the blame for your downfall as well. My family's ruin is enough."

There's a long pause as we stare at each other. I still want to be mad at her, but how can I be? My face softens and relaxes, and I see her sad form deflate as well.

She shrugs and looks down at the pavement. "I'm staying with my aunt Lola two blocks over until a more permanent position can be found."

"Your parents?" I don't tell her what I saw that night or that I know the officers took her mother away. I still hold out hope that Lazuli will say her mom was returned the next day with bruises but a happy countenance.

"They're gone. Everything's gone. My parents hacked the system and changed my numbers saying they did it all for me, but look where it got me. Thanks, Mom!" she shouts up to the sky, laughing like a deranged woman. "Now they will serve the system for payment of their mistakes. And I will be lucky to donate my days and save lives."

"Brandon?"

The frown on her face is deep and soul touching. Like it had years of training digging deep into her pain instead of only a few horrible weeks. Each strained frown line not only ages her but reveals her. The true Lazuli. A Lazuli I may not have ever known existed.

Perhaps the Lazuli I knew in the first place was the real imposter and the drugs only sent her to the verge of brutal honesty.

"He proposed, you know."

"Oh Lazuli, how—"

She shakes her head then stares off into space as if a painful memory plays across her vision. "It's what started all of this. We applied for a match license. My mom bought my dress, the date was set for right after the auctions so we could be wed and contracted and well on our way."

It's clear she can still see that vision of hope. She looks at me now and her eyes gloss over, the antidepressants slowly seeping in. I see it finally kicking in after a long glitch. A creepy forced smile scratches across her face.

"Yes, well, the license application set off a series of questions when the records didn't match up. Officers were at our house a week ago investigating and eventually uncovered my parent's fraud. I am very lucky they let me still donate."

There are my answers. Officers were already aware of something a week before I even noticed anything. And she is still donating and still medicated, yet clearly not a well-balanced dosage for the hell of a life they have made for her. Her parents may be dead for all I know, but she is calling herself lucky to still be pouring her life down a facility machine tube. If only I had been faster, maybe I could have changed the records before it was noticed.

Her smile shifts like she's expecting me to agree with her.

"Yes," I say dumbly. "Lucky."

"Good luck to you too, Aston. I hope you sign a good contract at the auctions. You never know what they may bring." Her words are stiff, and her face fights against the serum.

"Thank you." I wonder momentarily how they will adjust her dosage, or if they will at all. Will they let her roam the New Earth always with a small reminder of what the cost is of disobedience?

I slowly back away from her, and before I turn, I see a glitch again. Underneath the gloss, she hates me. Underneath the serum, she wants revenge. How can the true Lazuli blame me for what has happened to her? Because the facility has taught her to. The system has bred us to compete, with our blood as the weapon.

I return to the tram, numbly taking my seat again. The division tampers with our emotions, then creates the perfect setting to manipulate us. Every one of us are droids, controlled by our own blood.

My stomach flips as we glide over the river, towards the ambassador's mansion. I peer out my window and can see the raging Rogue river directly under us.

"Quite a sight, isn't it?" the chauffeur says.

"Yeah."

"Wait till you see the mansion."

"Oh I've seen the outside before," I say.

The chauffeur laughs and leans back over his shoulder. "I'm not talking about staring over the riverbanks at the guards' station."

My brow pulls together as he speaks.

"I'm talking about the mansion behind it. Now get up here, girl, I've lowered the window so you can have a good look. You may never get to see it again—and most likely one of the last Donors to do so 'cause I doubt they'll invite them every single year."

I navigate up the side bench until I'm leaning against the half wall separating the chauffeur and myself.

"I've only driven lawyers up here for years. It's the first time I've picked up a young, new, regular Donor."

We come up to the tall building I've ogled at my whole life. The mini tram stops at a door on the side of the building that has an open window atop. A bald officer sits inside the window and reaches out with a portable blood scanner. The chauffeur's finger is scanned and then so is mine. After we are given the ok, a grid of green lasers appear in front of the tram like it is stuck in a jail cell. The chauffeur pushes forward on a lever that makes us inch through the lasers, evidently scanning the tram. When we pass through and pick up speed, it first looks like nothing. A never-ending field stretches before us with a forest in the distance.

"Is it in Bloomfield?" I ask as I lean back to roll my tense shoulders. Trepidation squeezes my lungs to imagine going into Recipient territory itself.

"No. Be patient, girl. It will be worth it."

We seem to be headed straight for the forest. The closer we get, the more evident it is that there is a break in the forest for the road to cross through. My prediction is proven correct as we eventually enter through the column of trees. The tram darkens slightly from the coverage, but the light at the end is already visible.

"Wait for it," the chauffeur says. His excitement makes him seem more childlike than the middle-aged man he appears to be. "Almost." He leans forward as we draw nearer to the break in the trees. "There!" He leans back to give me a better look.

I gasp. "It's..." My hand tightens on the half wall, pulling myself forward. All thoughts and worries about the Recipients, about Lazuli, are soon forgotten. As soon as we exit the trees, we curve around a giant pond that sits out front of a white-columned building. I count the six white columns and then the five layers of windows. What could one person possibly do with five floors?

The tram slows as an entourage of other trams come into view and form a line. As we draw closer, I glimpse five crystal chandeliers just inside the columns lighting up the long marble porch. I've never seen such extravagant chandeliers, much less for a porch. The electrical bill here must cost a fortune.

The sun comes out from behind a cloud just then, and my attention is brought to the top of the building. A gold dome peaks out overtop just like the decoy guard house I threw rocks at as a child. For a moment, the reflecting light is too bright, and I shield my eyes. Then we move out of the sun's path. I lean forward more for another look.

The chauffeur starts to laugh. "I knew you'd like it."

"It's beautiful!" I finally say.

The black uniforms of the officers pepper the long porch stairs. Drones swarm over the road and lake as well.

When my door slides open, I'm asked to scan my finger before I even step out of the mini tram. A funny man with red hair and orange eyebrows that curl up onto his forehead helps me out.

"Hello there," he says without looking at me. He consults his handheld blood scanner. "Thirteen forty-two, since tonight's ball will be televised as usual, we will be using your name instead of number for security purposes. We don't want Recipients knowing or recognizing the Donors and choosing favorites. Auctions are purely about the blood." He throws his head back and makes a cackling laugh. "Now, Aston, you are strictly allowed on the first floor only and must be ready to leave by midnight, which is when your maglev cab will be back to pick you up."

I turn to the mini tram as the sliding door is closing. "Maglev?"

"Magnetic levitation." He brushes his hand out flippantly. "Now, here's a bracelet as a gift from the ambassador. Griffin Manny is there on the steps interviewing Donors as they come in. Please stop there before going into the mansion. Here is your name card. Hand that to the other man just inside the door so he can announce you. Look for a similar name card at the dinner table."

He takes a dramatic deep breath from his long-winded explanation and then grins. "And enjoy yourself."

The road leading towards the mansion is perfectly paved, white and smooth like the cement surrounding the tram tracks. I stare at them as I wait my turn for an interview. The stairs beneath me are white shiny marble with streaks of black like webbed veins. The bracelet on my wrist is a simple metal bangle with an unmoving charm that dangles the shape of a droplet onto my palm. In the center of the droplet is a red jewel. Something about it makes me feel uneasy. Maybe receiving a gift from someone so close to the Recipients has me on edge or perhaps the idea of being tagged for all I'm good for: drops of blood. I drop my hand and the charm tickles my palm.

The boy in front of me is up. Climbing the steps, I am soon near enough to hear Griffin Manny interview the Donor. The Donor boy is young but tall and bulky. His jawline is tight and defined like he could break a bone with his teeth. A green droid bobs in front of them, filming the interview live for the whole New World to see.

"So, Eric, are you excited to dance with other high-numbered girls tonight? Plan to do any match searching here, or have you left your heart to someone back in Garden City?"

The boy's silky brown hair is parted down the middle, which he occasionally tosses out of his eyes. "A room full of beautiful high-numbered girls? Scars, yeah. I might be engaged by the end of the night." He flicks his hair back again and gives me a wink in one fluid motion. "There really hasn't been another blood number to match mine back home, at least not high enough to tempt me."

Griffin Manny starts the laughter, and Eric joins in.

"Thank you, Eric, we look forward to watching you on the dance floor tonight and seeing who you pick to tango with."

A lady with headphones and a miniport comes to get me ready. She starts to poke at my curls and smoothes one behind my ear. She wears a black apron around her waist and picks makeup tools from it to paint my face with.

"Oh, I already put makeup on."

"I know, dear." Her tools get to work on my face. "That's what I'm fixing."

At least she shouldn't need to apply any more blush to my cheeks.

Griffin Manny drones on from behind me. "People, it's blood auction week, and I'm on the steps of the New Detroit ambassador's mansion where for the first time ever I am interviewing Donors. Not just any Donors either, but the top numbers from all over the New World."

The apron lady getting me ready grabs a blue bottle and sprays it crisscross over my face then chest then up over my head. It tickles my nose and makes my ears tingle. It smells of honey and vanilla.

"What—" I say, shocked by the surprise spritz.

"Count to three and then walk up the stairs," apron lady says, ignoring me.

Griffin Manny puts out his arm as if he is waiting to embrace me. "My, my, my, you are not going to believe the sight that is approaching me on the stairs right now. A waterfall of diamonds. Come here, love." He grabs my elbow and pulls me closer to him. "Please, rare jewel, tell me your name. Remember, no numbers here tonight, but I dare say if the number of jewels on that dress were any indication, I believe you would be the number one Donor in the country. You look beautiful, Miss..."

The light of the camera is bright in my eyes and the droid and other people disappear behind it.

"Aston Vazeto, and thank you, I feel beautiful tonight." It is strange what the blinding lights, pretty things, and monstrous estate does to my senses. I feel so light and carefree. Everything is suddenly so exciting.

"I'm sure you do. I haven't seen a single dress tonight look quite like yours. Is that a Francesco design?"

"Yes, it is." I rub my hand across the collar and rest my hand on my chest. "My mother found it, and we both just fell in love with it." I feel myself smile and wonder further about the effects of the camera.

"Tell me, Aston, why do you think the ambassadors decided to invite the Donors this year? And only the high-rated Donors, too?"

"I don't know, Griffin." The easy conversation feels odd to me, and for a moment, I wonder what exactly I am saying. "I think this year has produced some of the highest numbers in history, and it is changing the way the auctions are run." I feel like a machine that someone else is controlling.

"Tell me, what did you think when you first opened that invitation?"

My face stretches into a smile against my will, and a sweet giggle escapes before I realize what is happening. "It was pretty surreal. I was ecstatic that someone like me could be invited. I mean, I've spent my whole life staring over the river at the mansion, and tonight, I'm actually stepping through the doors."

Griffin's chuckle makes me question my words. Ecstatic? Why can't I stop smiling? My nose begins to tickle again, and the smell of honey brings me to my senses. My face slowly falls back into my control.

"I'm sure it's a dream come true. Plan on dancing much tonight?"

I stare for the first time truly into the interviewer's face as if seeing it for the first time. His black hair is almost purple and has so much gel it looks like a solid piece of plastic. The black eyeliner rings his eyes like a raccoon. His eyes flip to the camera, wondering about my pause.

"I'm a Donor," I say flatly. "I don't know how to dance."

"Well, what better place to learn than the ambassador's ballroom?" He turns to the camera. "You know, I'm told the ballroom floor is made with nine columns matching these marble ones on the front porch and has nine chandeliers around the edge matching the grand center chandelier. Tonight, for the very purpose Aston brings to our attention, there will be dance instructors. Not only do these lucky Donors get the time of their life, they get free dance lessons as well. What an opportunity." His laugh is precise and artificial. I scratch at where the bandage should be on my arm.

"Now, Aston, it says here"—He glances at his notes on a mini port attached to his wrist like a watch—"that you are from New Livonia, where the new Donor deaths have been occurring. How have these deaths affected you and your donations?"

At first I am shocked he would ask such a question on national news, until I realize we are in a nation of unfeeling Donors. I and Marcus, as far as I know, are the only ones who feel. Of course those who feel so little would take topics as far to the edge of feeling as they possibly could. They crave emotions; they hunger after the appearance of compassion.

I stare into the bright light of the droid camera contemplating what to say. They are, I'm sure, waiting and hoping that one of those deaths was my best friend or true love. The more extreme the answer, the closer they are to feeling something. If I tell too much, though, I could make the wrong people suspicious. The sound of stick against flesh twists my stomach. I start with a smile. Then tone it down to mock sympathy for effect. My words must be very calculated.

"They were so young." I'm not sure if I can keep the pretense. Everyone has their glitches, right? Why not give the world a glimpse of reality. I stare boldly into the camera now and think of brave Mrs. Price trying to make a better life for her daughter, brave Gloria getting chocolate for her brothers, courageous Oliver trying to care for his family, sad Sandy for losing her tail and life to teach a lesson. "So young," I echo. "There was a day they would have been called children. Now we make adults out of children and justify it with good causes. Now the lines of volunteering and coercion are blurred. These children's lives were taken from them just for trying to survive, just for trying to support their families. My heart goes out to their families. Griffin, I *will* dance tonight. I will dance for those that no longer can." I realize I may have gone a bit too far, but what's done is done. I stand, squarely looking into the bright light. I've made the Donors victims, martyrs even. I've made them sound less like test subjects and more like real people. I gave them a story like the Recipients, instead of just another Donor death on the list.

Griffin Manny strains around me, checking for the next Donor. "We are sorry for your town's loss. We hope the allergies are figured out soon." He speeds through the words and frowns for two seconds. "Well, Aston, you look gorgeous, and we are so excited for you tonight. I just know we're going to see more from you."

I am guided back to the shadows of the stairs hidden off screen just as my identity will be on Auction Day this week.

Entering the double door entryway, I'm greeted by more officers, and more scanning. The marble floor is so clean it reflects our movements down the long hallway. At the end of the hallway my breath is taken away by the biggest glass chandelier I've ever seen. The hallway ends at the top of a grand staircase with the chandelier at eye level with me. A tuxedo-clad gentleman approaches me from the top of the banister and holds out his hand.

"Your card, miss?"

I hand over what was given to me when I stepped out of the maglev. I look out over the ballroom as the orchestra starts up a song. It's a spacious, circular area surrounded by a balcony for each level on either side. Opposite me is another staircase. The same mahogany wood gleams back at me. There is laughter and tinkling glasses and the smell of honey again, mixed with flowers this time. The honey gives me a sense of deja vu like I should remember something, but all I can recall is the spray before the show. Thinking on it now, I realize that spray must have been serum to help my nerves before the interview. To guarantee a happy conversation.

"Ready?" He touches my elbow.

I nod.

A few taps at his miniport, and soon his voice is transferred across the room on hidden speakers.

"Miss Aston Vazeto of New Livonia."

I'm descending the stairs slowly, and with each step, my gaze inches upwards. In addition to the balcony, there are four more levels of balconies stacked on top of each other all the way up to the gold dome from which the chandelier is suspended on colossal cables. The second-row balcony has a wall of glass placed around it. I pause on a step and see that there are people behind the glass. Just regular people, yet something seems different about them. Their clothes are the finest I've ever seen, and their mannerisms are sophisticated and confident. It dawns on me finally that these must be Recipients. I am in the same building as the Recipients. A mere glass wall separates us from breathing the same air. The people who will bid on my blood this very week stand under the same roof as me. My knees feel locked and woozy on the step.

I'm baffled by how ordinary they look. Some appear sicker than others. My gaze stops on a familiar face; a man about the age of my papa stands close to the glass. His dark blond hair is thinning, and his hands are behind his back. His eyes are firmly planted on me, and it finally dawns on me who he looks like. He is a younger replica of our leader, Adakin Malloy. The eyes are the same, though the hair is much different.

The room seems to hush as I stare at this face. I wish I could remember his name. If I watched more of the news, I would know. The break between the orchestra's songs makes me fully aware of the silence that has settled over the room. I scan the area to see almost every face looking up at me on the stairs. Even a majority of the Recipients are now staring down at me like Adakin's descendant was. Whispers pick up first, then the orchestra starts up another song. The whine of the violin pushes me along.

"Miss Amber Orville of Dearborn," the announcer rings out again through the building.

Looking over my shoulder, I see a small, orange-headed girl. Her pale skin is washed out by her baby blue dress. Her smile creaks and wobbles as she descends just as crookedly. I slow my pace in case she needs someone to catch her. Even when I reach the ballroom floor, I linger at the bottom just in case. Side stepping out of her way, I hear her sigh as she makes it and gives me a smile

"First time in heels," she says, hefting the blue ruffled skirts of her dress up with a swish and poking out her tiny foot. "Mama insisted I wear these." She twists her toes, showing the long skinny heel of her powder blue shoes. "I'll be lucky to make it through the night alive."

I smile warmly at her, silently grateful Mam fell in love with a low heel.

"I'm Amber." She holds out a dainty hand, bent at the wrist, fingers together.

"I'm Aston."

She gasps and squeezes my hand a little less ladylike.

"Aston?" She moves her eyes over every inch of my face. She moves her hand to her mouth.

"I mean, I know Gannet. I'm best friends with Laney. I heard you visited them."

I only continue to stare. Why would that be news to have me over, unless Amber has a thing for Gannet. That would make the most sense. If Amber and Gannet had something, then of course her best friend would want to tell her when he brought another girl to dinner.

"Oh, yeah. Gannet is a good friend." I feel the need to reassure her of my decision to choose life over Gannet even though I can't help but analyze this imp of a girl and how wrong she is for him.

I see her fiddle with her name card and realize mine is missing.

"My name card," I say, looking up the staircase at the purple-clad announcer.

Amber rests her dainty hand on my arm to calm me. "Oh, don't worry. I don't think we'll make it to dinner."

"What do you mean?"

As someone approaches, she straightens her back and stiffly gathers her skirts. Her face goes white as she tries to smile. She's afraid of something.

"Death by heels, remember?"

She gives me a wink and a smile, but I know that's not what she means. Is she with the rebellion? I should have asked her more direct questions. I need to be more sly yet conspicuous at the same time.

Before I can say anything more to her, the boy I saw interviewed on the steps bows in front of me, and Amber swishes quickly away like a flighty Cinderella.

"I've been taught this is the proper way to approach a lady before asking them to dance." With one hand still behind his half-bent back, he puts a hand out for mine. "May I have your first dance of the evening?"

"I haven't had any dance instructions yet."

"Ah, no worries, it's not that hard. I'll teach you." He reaches and grabs for my hand. His hands are clammy like they can't decide whether to be warm or cold. I can't decide if I like being led out to the floor or not. On one hand, I feel excited to learn for the first time how to move in time to the music with a partner. On the other hand I'm not too wild about the cocky flirt I'm paired with. His hands feel too firm and commanding on me.

"I'm Eric." He flips his hair on schedule as if to allow me a better view of his face. He tips his chin to a corner of the room and beams.

I follow his gaze to a group of boys in the corner giving fist pumps and high-fiving each other as they point at us. I sure hope this guy is not the resistance leader.

"Those are my friends from Garden City. We're all high numbers. I know we're not supposed to talk numbers and all that, but one of us..." He raises his eyebrows like I'm supposed to know it's him. "...almost broke one hundred."

I feel no urge to share my own numbers with him like I had with Marcus. Instead, I pity him—for what our system has done to him, and my sisters, and my best friend, and Gannet. This is no place to weep though.

"So what's my first dance lesson?"

"Uh, yeah. So this hand stays in mine. Your other hand goes around my neck." He gives me a roguish wink. I can't reign in the eye roll. "Then I put my arm around your waist." He pulls me to him; the way I'm pushed up against his chest squeezes the air out of me. His meaningful grin makes a ripple of disgust creep over my arms.

As I examine all the other couples, I push off from him with the hand of mine on his shoulder. "I don't think all the other couples are dancing quite so close."

"It's just because they're not doing it right." His smile seems less playful now and more agitated as he pulls me again up against his chest. My heart fights against my ribs.

"I don't particularly like your way of dancing."

He grips my waist tighter.

I try pushing against him again. "Eric, you're hurting me."

"Come on, don't you want a chance with the highest number here?"

A camera droid whizzes past, and Griffin Manny floats nearby.

"Oh what a cute couple! Smile, you two. Your budding love is being broadcast for the whole New World."

I push against him again, but he pulls me even closer than before, making our cheeks touch for the camera. As soon as the camera is out of sight, he loosens his grip enough for me to wriggle free.

"Ugh. Don't ever ask me to dance again. I don't need your high numbers, or your slimy hands." He takes a step towards me, but I put up a finger. "Don't come near me, or I'll report you for telling everyone your number."

He pauses before throwing his hands out to me. "Not worth it. You probably only made it in because your dad's an officer or something. High numbers can't be *that* good looking."

I, all of a sudden, find humor in the situation and laugh. "Thanks."

I pick at where my bandage should be and make my way to the drink table by the opposite staircase. I pour myself some water, too nervous to try anything else, and head close to the end of the table. I stand by a group of potted plants that are on display by a hallway that runs under the stairs.

A hush falls over the crowd, and I follow their gaze towards the staircase. Descending slowly, hobbling one step at a time with a cane and vice grip on the railing, is Richard Fenway. The oldest of us all. He isn't wearing the traditional Tuxedo but a short sleeve white button up instead. His blood red tie stands out against his white shirt like he is a bleeding Donor in the white facility, perhaps the very effect he was going for. What I can't stop staring at, however, are his arms. As his forearms shift from clenching the railing and cane, white pearly scars take turns catching the light. They line his arm like a ladder climbing up out of sight under his sleeve.

"Scars galore," I whisper. The swear takes on new meaning. It makes my stomach drop, and I wonder how he got those. Are these the war wounds every Donor has to look forward to?

Whispers flutter through the air like butterflies. Bouncing from one group to the next, making its way around the room. I edge toward the plants, wanting nothing to do with the gossip. The orchestra starts up again, and Richard Fenway finally, and surprisingly, makes it to the ballroom without falling or dying. Sipping my water in the shadows, I feel a familiar warm hand on my elbow.

"The one time I *want* you to run into me and you're just standing in the shadows."

"Marcus." I turn and lean into him with a full hug. His embrace is so comforting it soothes the adrenaline and fear left over from the "dance lesson."

"I've changed my mind," he says, laughing. "Being in my arms on purpose is much better than on accident."

My face rejoices at his words, yet I still give him a playful whack on the arm. "I'm glad to see you that's all."

I step back, looking up into his face. He looks so different. So clean. So radiant. No dark circles, his cheeks are fuller and flush. His corn blond hair is smoothed over, shining with hard gel holding every strand in place. My eyes roam from one side of his face to the next, taking in every glorious feature. Yes, Juliet would have chosen him if he were in her story. His eyes seem a lighter blue against his now olive skin. His lips are not the pale pink of his ill self but a bright ruddy color, full and healthy. He isn't the sick, poor Donor I ran into at the market, and this is what makes me realize he is at the Ambassador's Ball.

"Marcus! What are you doing here?" Low numbers would have strong motivation to be in the resistance. Could he already have been a part of the cause all this time and not have told me?

He grins mischievously, pulls me around the plants and deeper into the closet under the stairs. I can't take my eyes off of him. "Aston, has anyone ever told you that you are by far the most gorgeous Donor here tonight?"

I pull my hands from him to hide a laugh, remembering what Eric just said. "Something like that." I turn slowly, examining the closet in order to hide my warm cheeks and smile. It is lit by small can lights in the short, slanted ceiling, and the door-less sides let the music seep into the tunnel. I finish my turn and face him again. "Now, seriously, what are you doing here?"

"I came to dance with you." He steps forward and bows formally.

"Marcus…" I put a hand on my hip for emphasis, though I can't keep the smirk from my face.

"Aston," he copies my tone and posture, which sends me overboard, and I giggle.

He takes my hand in his, and I wonder for a moment about when the change occurred that I now laugh with Marcus instead of growing annoyed by his presence. Perhaps it was the moment he held me in his arms after keeping me from running to my death that night. Perhaps that is what makes my heart flutter more and grumble less.

"Aston, you know we're not supposed to talk about numbers tonight. So stop asking me what I'm doing here. Now, it doesn't look like you received a very good first dance lesson."

My face burns to hear that he saw the disaster of my first dance.

"Your hand rests on my shoulder like so." He lets go of my hand as he places it on his broad shoulder and runs his hand the length of my arm towards my back. I stare at him in awe of how my stomach boils from his hot touch. Perhaps he hasn't changed much at all, perhaps it is me that has changed. His eyes could possibly be just as sunken in, but it is my eyes that have transformed, that have been opened, that make him seem fuller and alive and wonderful. His touch is gentle, yet somehow more commanding than Eric's.

"Now you can let your elbow rest on my arm, and when I push here…" He squeezes his hand against the back of my shoulder blade. "…it means we'll be going this direction." He steps, and I stumble to follow. "When I pull with my hand here…" He grips my hand tighter, and it feels as if he's squeezing my heart as well. I feel numb from the intensity of the moment. "…it means we will move this direction. And when I push against your hand like so and let go of you…" His fingers dig softly into the top of my hand as his other arm releases and pushes off of my side, brushing lightly across my chest. I seem to naturally swirl away with his send off and then follow his lead of stepping out and extending our arms. Our eyes are locked in an intimate dance of their own. Without speaking now, he tugs on my hand that still holds tight to his, and I am twirling back into him. Our connected arms wind against my waist, and soon my back is pressed against his chest. His other hand finds my free one. He is holding me similarly to how he held me back from Mrs. Price that night, but now it feels much more intimate. I turn my head sideways until our chins hit. We are both breathing heavily.

"You're good on your feet, Miss Aston," he whispers. His bottom lip bumps against mine. "When you're not clumsily running into me that is. Where did you learn to dance so well?"

"I have a good teacher." I smile and then turn my head slightly so his lips are now at my ear. His breath is magnified and tickles my hair, sending a wave of chills down my spine. I lower my eyelids, looking down over my shoulder, and struggle to control my own breathing. "When he's not insulting me, invading my dressing room, or pinning me to the ground that is."

His hearty laugh vibrates from his chest, through my back, and I find myself wanting to lean into it more. He releases one of my hands and soon is holding me close again. My chest is pushed against his, and I find myself not minding quite so much as I had with Eric. Marcus knows me. He has slowly become the epitome of safety. The one that makes my heart feel as warm as his hands. Marcus is authentic, and honesty means so much more when it's an option.

His hand wraps around my back and he leads me effortlessly around the room under the stairs. I am so grateful there are no cameras, no other dancers, no one and nothing to interrupt this moment. We are truly the only two people in the New World. The only two that can feel, the only two that know the truth. The music slows to a stop and so do our feet, though our breaths and our eyes are still lost in the moment.

His arms tighten around me, not wanting to let go of the moment any more than I do. I don't pull away from him. His face drops closer to mine.

"Aston," he says. Nothing more, only my name, and I know exactly what he is asking. I lift my chin slightly higher. It is all the encouragement he needs to lower his mouth the last few inches. His lips are warmer than his hands. It lasts only a moment and is over before I want it to be. With my eyes closed, my lips lead my head forward asking for more. Opening my eyes, I see something in his that wasn't there before. Sadness, fear, and hunger. Regret?

"Much better than running into each other." He grins. "Promise me we will do this again. Look around corners and be in my arms on purpose."

I love how safe I feel. "I can't promise anything," I whisper. "Fate has a way of making us collide."

"Fate." He puts both arms around me now, drawing me even closer to him. I clasp my hands behind his neck, and he carefully gives me a soft, slow peck on the lips. "Is that what this is?"

"No," I say realizing the truth. "It's something even more rare in our world. It's choice. It's choosing life."

He seems to be both confused and in agreement when the music starts up again. He pulls away and leans over my hand. "I would choose every day with you..." He kisses the top of my hand and looks up under his caramel brown eyebrows. "...if they were a repeat of this moment."

He stands without releasing my hand. I am frozen. I am free from all serum, all drugs, yet I've never been happier and more controlled. His touch commands me. His eyes rule over me. Thanks to my small act of rebellion, I found love, how it is meant to feel.

"Now that you know how, you can dance the night away."

I tighten my grip on his hand just as he loosens it. "What?"

"I have to go, Aston. I'm not really supposed to be here."

I rip my hand out of his. The fear in his eyes finally makes sense. He's not a high-numbered Donor after all, and when they catch him, they will... I look down at the floor, feeling suddenly dizzy at the thought of what officers might do with him. I place a hand to my head to ward off any oncoming headaches.

"Marcus, after what we saw that night, what the officers did, what they can do, why would you risk—"

"I hadn't planned on coming. But I had to." He gingerly takes my hand, staring at it as if it holds a secret. "I was just going to be in the background, but then I saw you come down the stairs... Everyone saw you walk in the room. Everyone wanted to know about you, and I knew you. I know what can make that *v* in your brow appear." He rubs his thumb over the tightened muscles between my eyes, smoothing it over, and then leaves his fingers wrapped around my cheek. "I know that you love to paint, and hate the facility as much as I do, and can feel so much when others cannot. I know you, and I couldn't just stand in the background and pretend I don't." He steps away abruptly, placing a tense hand on his brow and one on his hip. "And then when I saw that pompous jerk try to dance with you and..." He sighs, analyzing the floor. "Well, I had to see you then and teach you how to dance properly." He stands straight and faces me with his hands grabbing the inside of his tuxedo jacket as if this last bit of information made total sense. As if he's fulfilled his plan, and now that it's over, he needs to return to his other maniac plan, whatever that is.

I cross my arms, trying to process what he is saying. He's practically inviting me, begging me to question him about the resistance, isn't he? How do I ask him? How do we talk about it here in the same building as Recipients and officers?

"Well, thank you. But I would much rather the next time you want to put both our lives in danger you write me a note telling me you know me and stay home. I am sure I would appreciate the sentiment just as much."

His laugh is pure and smooth. "Yes, but you wouldn't know how to dance."

"I hear there are other instructors." I put my arm out towards one of the doorways and take a grandiose step.

He grabs my arm and pulls me to him, his face lighting up with utter amusement. "Just say thank you, Aston."

I heave my chest against his, trying to smile, but fail to free myself from his smile that paralyzes me, that ensnares me with one look. "Thank you, Aston," I mutter.

His deepening smile makes the cheesy response worth it. "You're welcome." He squeezes my arms and kisses me on the cheek. He pulls away, and I kick myself for not at least trying to talk about the resistance with him. Why didn't I? Did I like it better when I believed we were the only two people who could feel? Do I want to find the resistance on my own like he evidently did? Why won't he just tell me about them? Why won't anyone tell me anything?

I watch him duck under the doorway in front of me and stand frozen with my hand touching my cheek. My first kiss was in a coat closet at the Ambassador's Ball. Not with a high-numbered Donor, but with the only other heart that knows mine, that can feel mine. Mam must never find out. No one can.

TWENTY-THREE

I stand by the drink table again, slowly regaining my wits. Being kissed for the first time makes the ballroom look slightly less exquisite, and I will never look at a coat closet in quite the same way. I smile at the memory without noticing the boy that approaches me. I jump when he bows in front of me. He wears a black tuxedo like all the rest, yet he wears a tag that says "Instructor" on it.

"Excuse me, miss, have you had a chance to receive your dance lesson yet?"

I beam at him, remembering my dutiful instructor. "Yes, thank you."

He bows again in retreat just as a familiar voice calls out over my shoulder.

"In that case, may I have this dance?" My mouth drops open when I see Gannet bow before me in a formal tuxedo. I search the floor for officers, remembering how Marcus snuck into the ball.

"Gannet, what are you doing here?" Feeling concern and fear for the second time tonight, remembering again Mrs. Price, I feel sure I will faint. I grab the table for support.

"Don't worry yourself, Aston. Did you not know a few technicians were invited as well?"

I stare at him as strength returns to my legs, and I feel stronger by the minute. "No, I didn't."

"We're working with the officers to make sure no one filters through that shouldn't."

My face feels cold at the mention of Gannet looking for people like Marcus. Looking for the resistance the same as me. "Oh."

"So? May I have this dance?"

I take his cold hand, and he escorts me to the floor. His hold on my back is not quite as firm or close as Marcus's, but still he is a fine dancer. I wonder that he could pick up on the signals of how to lead so quickly.

"You've danced before?" I say.

He shrugs a shoulder. "My mother liked to dance. And you? This does not seem to be your first time."

"Not my first time tonight, no." My cheeks burn, and I look back to the staircase I danced under. "But I received my first lesson tonight."

He raises his eyebrows. "You had a very good instructor then."

I nod and then misjudge his signal, accidently stepping the opposite direction as he intended to. He soon pulls me with him, and my feet skip quickly to catch up. Again the physical analogy of our destinies is unmistakable. We are on two different courses, he and I. Perhaps if things had been different, our paths would have connected.

As we circle around the edge of the dance floor, I spot a straw-like blond head. Marcus is hidden in a doorway against the wall. The only thing moving are his eyes. Shrouded under an angry scowl, he watches our every move. How can I tell him that Gannet and I are like two magnets pushing each other apart? Hopefully he will be able to see that by how poorly we move across the floor together. There's still a part of me that wishes the serum wasn't standing between Gannet and me. That attraction to Gannet's muscular body and tight jawline—that's what I'm hoping Marcus doesn't see.

I'm staring straight at Marcus as we move and so am confused when Gannet stops. He twists his body, looking back over his shoulder at a tall man standing behind him.

"Excuse me, technician, but I believe this is a ball for Donors. May I cut in?" My stomach jumps and cheeks flush when I notice how the room stares. Couples shift their dance around our scene. I study the newcomer with as much distaste as I can muster, yet my chest is already tensing with fear.

Looking longingly into my eyes, Gannet reluctantly steps back and lets this stranger take his place. I open my mouth to say something but am frozen. What if this dancer is like Eric?

I'm soon in the arms of another. Gannett retreats as the stranger twirls me away into the crowd. This partner is not a good leader, but his touch is more respectful than Eric's. I let my hand relax in his.

"I hope you are enjoying your time tonight. It's Aston, right?"

"Yes, how do you—"

"I think everyone here knows your name."

I tilt my head as we stumble in circles along the floor. I am suddenly horrible on the dance floor without a good leader. "Oh?"

Has word leaked about my numbers? I feel slightly smug that Eric could have found out how measly his almost a hundred is in comparison to mine.

"The girl who almost cried about her dying Livonia town?" he says with a smile and so nonchalantly.

"I did *not* almost cry." My heart starts beating, and I search the room. It was only a few sentences said into the camera, but was it too much?

Rounding the room again, I look to see Marcus again hiding in the shadows. He looks just as angry that I am dancing with this stranger. I feel the corner of my mouth lift. He's jealous. Of course, he is the only boy in the room that can truly feel, and he uses those feelings on me. I see it now in the way he scowls at the black-headed boy I dance with, the way he looks at the boy's hands lower on my back than his were. All of a sudden, this dance is so much more fun recognizing all the places Marcus's eyes are on me. My hips, my waist, my face—they all burn each time he notices. My dance partner becomes a tool to feel more as I swirl my way by Marcus. As soon as we pass him, I look over my shoulder and smile. His eyes soften with longing. He wants to be on the floor with me, I can feel it, but it's too dangerous.

A green droid camera moves in place to capture my smile. The boy I dance with joins his face against mine for the camera. We float farther into the crowd of dancers on stumbling Donor feet.

The second round on the floor, Marcus is gone, and the dance with this stranger is no longer as exciting. I search the crowd and every doorway and shadow, but he is gone.

When the dance is over, the stranger and I bow to each other, and before I can take a step away from the floor, there is another tuxedo in front of me. As I take his hand, another tuxedo asks to save a dance for him afterwards. By the time three more dances are done, my feet are throbbing and bulging from the jeweled straps. Not a single one of the dancers shows any signs of being free of the serum, or a part of the rebellion.

I stop another boy before he can even speak by putting my hand out. "Please, no. I need to rest."

I plop down into a white metal fold out chair along the side of the room. While crossing my legs, I bend forward to rub my sore feet. Once I realize there's really nothing my hands can do, I lean back, rest my head against the wall and let my feet recharge, since just sitting alone seems to be rejuvenating them. My gaze lifts upward to the wall of glass. The Recipient spectators seem to be enjoying themselves. Some are tilting their heads back with laughter while sloshing champagne. A few are in scattered groups chatting animatedly with each other, but the majority stand up against the glass, looking down on us as if we are pets at a pet store. Some point and seem to be referencing the catalog. So much for no numbers tonight; they're shopping. My blood curdles at the sight of it. My scrutiny deepens as I stare at the glass like I could break through it with my glare alone.

Just as the next dance is starting up, dancers are in place with hungry Recipients overhead when a trilling fire alarm breaks out through the building. The orchestra stops, and the dance partners break apart one by one. Everyone is looking about the room to see what the matter is.

A faint hissing silences the room, and then, seconds later, it intensifies. I stand and move out from under the balcony, lifting my eyes towards the sound. Level by level, the sprinklers are going off. When the fourth floor balcony goes off and the sound grows louder, sporadic hints of water splash down on me. Seconds later, the third floor goes off. People are panicking, some moving to the side trying to avoid the drops, others looking for the location of our floor's sprinklers, smarter ones searching for a way out.

It's when the muffled sound of the second floor sprinklers go off that chaos breaks loose. Screams behind the glass draw everyone's attention, and then shouts from the ballroom ensue. Donors are dashing for the staircases. I'm frozen in place, confused at what I'm seeing. First, I think there are gunshots ringing through that floor, and people are dying against the glass, their blood spraying against it. And then I remember the sprinklers. Instead of water, bright red blood is shooting forth over the Recipients. The protective glass is soon covered with a dark, opaque waterfall. A body pushes up against the glass and runs their hands over and over on it as if they are trying to doggy-paddle in a sea of blood.

I follow the crowd toward the staircase, but officers are lined across the top, caging in the Donors to let Recipients retreat first. I freeze in place and stare at the glass again. The seconds creep by as no one seems to know exactly what to do. I can only stare at the blood, wondering what it means.

When our floor's sprinklers hiss open, deafening screeches fill the room. Everyone expects the same gruesome fate. They soon die down, however, when they realize our sprinklers spray only water. I see from the tops of the staircases behind the wall of officers that Recipients, drenched and dripping in blood, run toward the door. The scene muddles my mind—blood covers the Recipients, and the Donors are washed clean. I scan the Recipients as they slosh by, and they all seem fine, only covered in red. Water trickles through the jeweled maze of my dress and forms tickling rivers down my skin.

The bath seems to cleanse my thoughts as well. Someone infiltrated the ambassador's mansion and did this. The resistance? Why? As a joke? As a message? Marcus was here unaccounted for, hiding in the shadows of doorways and then gone right before the sprinklers went off. Could he be a part of this? Is he the resistance leader?

The last of the Recipients seem to be out, and yet the officers are still not breaking their human fence. The waterworks are turned off, and an officer's booming voice shushes the shocked crowd.

"We will be double scanning fingers on your way out, and no one is leaving without questioning. Be ready for a long, wet night, Donors."

Gannet's words echo through my mind. He is working with the officers to make sure no one comes in or out that doesn't belong. A chill runs up my arms and then down my back as I hug my dripping self. The stairs begin to empty as people realize they will not be leaving as quickly as they would like.

Wet and shivering, I return to my seat, unable to take my eyes off the glass wall. Rhythmic dots splash across it—the sprinklers are still spraying in waves, yet dousing no one. Precious blood wasted. Perhaps it is only red water, though I can smell the metallic rust of blood from here. Ripples cascade down the length of the glass wall, and soon drips escape through the floor of the balcony. I look to the wet floor in front of me and watch the red dots swirl and then blend in unnoticeably.

My first kiss may be captured tonight. I may never see him again. But Marcus couldn't have acted alone. This was bigger than one low-numbered Donor. What had that imp of a girl said earlier tonight? We won't make it to dinner? Was she a part of the resistance as well, scheming together with Marcus? My chest burns with envy. Why was I being left out of this? I'm the one free of serum. If they only knew how helpful I could be. Was Papa behind this? Recalling his conversation and how angry he was, surely he was not on board with this plan, but why would he not warn me? And Marcus? He is clearly free of the serum as well. It's why we are so attracted to each other, right? What if he isn't feeling what I feel? What if he sees me as a weak Donor, a pawn the rebellion needs ignorant to be effective? I ball my fists again, feeling stupid at how I danced in his arms.

A shiver runs up my back from the cold, and I relax under the water. This is bigger than an elfish redhead and a low-numbered boy that cleans up well. Putting a hand to my forehead, I force my own brow to smooth and recall Marcus's touch. His sincere eyes and soft touch. I refuse to think ill of him like how I used to. There have to be more explanations. There had to be more resistance followers here, but why are they targeting Recipients like that? My mind swirls and is lost like the drops of blood.

"Be safe, Marcus," I say aloud. When my words go unnoticed, I continue to talk to myself like a mad woman. "No mentioning of numbers tonight." I mock the orders given and find myself chuckling as I scan the calming chaos. I really must be mad. Blood numbers always have a way of making it into the room. I just never imagined it raining from the sky.

TWENTY-FOUR

For once, I actually want to see the morning news. Mam is too preoccupied to notice when I grab a sausage from the pan. Everyone is in shock after what happened last night.

Alone in our living room, I tuck my feet up in my brown nightgown and huddle in the corner of our blue sofa. An advertisement for the blood auctions comes on.

Footage of ill Recipients, mothers burying children, and scenes from the last Germ War move across the screen. A small child Torrin's age twinkles her eyes into the camera.

"Thank you, Donors, you saved my life," she chirps.

I swallow wrong when the next image appears. I am choking on my sausage and standing up when my own happy face stares back at me.

"I was ecstatic that someone like me could help."

It was my pre-ball interview, only they had changed my words. I never said all of that. Yet somehow there was never a break in my words, the ones that never entered my mouth never sounded any different. How did they do that, and who are they? Even I recognize my own voice saying foreign words.

"I mean, I've spent my whole life waiting to donate, and now I'm actually a part of this wonderful cause," my fake words say.

I then hear Griffin Manny's familiar words that night in my head, *"I'm sure it's a dream come true."*

The words appear across the screen, "Division of Medical Research: Making Everyone's Dreams Come True."

The introduction to the news show goes by in a blur as I stand in the room feeling violated and used.

"Sit down, Aston. You're in the way, child, move." Mam has her ankles crossed in the rocker, holding her morning tea. Her hair is in a curling bonnet, and her face is washed out with the lack of makeup. "Don't just stare at me, girl, I said sit. Or go set the table for Papa's breakfast. I know you never want to be in with the news."

I sit mechanically back onto the sofa.

"Before we list the Donor deaths, we a have a shocking update about the incident that occurred at the ambassador's mansion last night. As you know, on the first ever invitation of auctioned Donors, the building was somehow hijacked, setting off alarms and sprinklers. What we have just been informed of is that the blood that was pumped into the sprinkler system at the ambassador's mansion was, in fact, this year's auction blood bank."

My mother's teacup tumbles to the floor, and her hot tea splatters against my leg. I don't pay attention to the burn. I can't bear to watch the screen any longer, with Griffin Manny's raccoon eyes smiling back at me and his half-hearted emotions. Instead, I watch my emotions played out on Mam's face as both hands cover her mouth and her eyes string together with worry and fear.

"The ambassador, though under strict lockdown, is consulting with lawyers and Adakin Malloy himself over screen ports to know what action to take next. Rumors are spreading that this was a threat and an act of terrorism directed towards our dear Recipients. Stay tuned throughout the day as we keep you in with the news. You can even receive our miniport updates. As news comes in, it's put live through the system Cloud feed. For now, it looks like the blood auctions will, for the first time in history, be delayed until further notice."

Mam's face never changes. My eyes are still glued to her. A ping on the miniport that sits on the desk under the stairs rings through the room. Mam doesn't even flinch; she's a statue.

I retrieve the miniport and read aloud the words that blink across the screen, "In With the News Update: Donor Arrested on Ambassador Bloodbath Suspicion."

Mam finally breathes. "Well that was fast. See, I'm sure there's nothing to worry about." She stands and gathers her dress around her as she bends to clean up the broken mug. "I always thought the auctions were too close to all the festivities anyway. I think it will be nice to have a break, to just be with family before we go into the auctions."

Her charade of being convinced is believable. My insides churn at the news: "Suspect Caught." My mind first jumps to the friendly yet suspicious Cinderella that I met on the stairs at the ball. But all thoughts of her are washed out with concern for Marcus. He was only there for me, right? What if he was just in the wrong place at the wrong time? I can't help but worry that he's the suspect. Is he safe? How can I contact him? Just go running around all the corners hoping to fall into his arms? The last thought makes a lump form in my throat. His arms, warm and strong. His smell of laundry soap and cologne. I may never bump into him again. I don't care anymore that he was forward and annoying and a scrawny low-numbered Donor.

With miniport in hand, I start my search again. Tapping frantically on the DMR red droplet of blood, I stop when I realize I don't know Marcus's number. Is there any way to do a search by name?

"No matches found" appears across the screen over and over again. I tap on the top of Compass and type in "Donor, Marcus," which doesn't bring up anything helpful either. I drop the miniport onto the desk and rush up to my room to get dressed. Surely someone in town would know something about the scraggly Donor named Marcus.

Except they don't. Martha from the fruit stand is one of the few who knows who I'm talking about. Her lack of teeth makes her lips cave in, and she has a smacking wet lisp as she speaks. "String bean with a yellow mop?"

"That's the one. His name's Marcus."

"I ain't known his name, but he ain't been by my cart for a while. Used to come by almost every day. Hanging around corners always looking for someone."

I wonder if this is where he met his resistance contacts, a busy market street where no one would suspect dirty Donors to orchestrate big rebel plans. It also explains why I ran into him so often. Why would he trust the girl who kept interrupting his secret meetings?

"Can you guess when the last time you saw him was? Do you know where he lives or anything about his family?"

She just shakes her head, making her brown natural dreads hit herself in the face. "Always on 'is own. Ain't seen him since that night he came through just as I was cleaning up. That be almost a week ago now."

The night he saved me from a run in with the officers. Was that really only a week ago?

I thank Martha and buy a bruised pear from her cart. Making my way back home, I review the little information I have. The one person who knows of him hasn't seen him in at least a week. Possibly because he was preparing for the bloodbath at the ball. But what if he isn't around now because he has been caught? Oliver flashes across my memory. I don't know where they took him. Or Mrs. Price. Will I ever know what really happened to Marcus? Or is he gone like all the others?

When I arrive home, I slip around the side of the house, back to the shed where my art supplies are kept. The grass is still cold with frost. It wets the hem of my jeans. I shut the old wooden door behind me and flip the light switch with its exposed wires from the lack of finished walls. I fall back against the door and stare at the white canvas leaning against the wall under the window. My vision blurs with tears. I never got to tell him thank you. Why was I so stubborn and ornery around him? Why couldn't I have just said thank you, or been more sympathetic when I trampled over him so many times, instead of selfishly focused on everything in my own life that felt so much more important?

I move across the room with a mission. I haven't painted since the donations. There have been so many times I have come to this corner and stared at the whiteness and got lost in the thoughts of white facility sheets, floors and technician's coats, and looked at the canvas like it was already complete. Like static on the screens when the programming's off. But now the roller coaster of the kiss and the possible loss is more than I can handle. It needs a way out of me, for one person cannot hold the emotions of the whole New World.

I fold out the easel and lift the canvas onto it. Scrambling around the table next to it, I prepare the colors as the tears start to descend. The first strokes are slow and mournful. I start with the lips. The lines and curves are a feeling, not a description. The soft way they pushed against mine, the ticklish touch of his cheeks bumping mine. The sound of his voice in my ear as he pins me down. It all floods out through my hand, through the brush as if the colors are a direct extension of my memories. Soon I am moving faster than I have time to think. I wipe at my brow, tears now forgotten, and my only goal is to create the replica as a shrine to my first kiss. I open the window in the corner by me and welcome the cool air that rushes in to greet me. Pulling my hair up quickly, I grab a dry paintbrush and jab it through the bun.

Analyzing the painting, I look away from the intense gaze forming in front of me. His hair should be a safe thing to focus on next. Pushing the yellows together, mixing them to create the perfect corn-colored mop of hair, I use browns to create the levels of mess Marcus wears on top of his head. I wipe at my brow again as I examine my work. There is something missing in the eyes. His eyes have more emotion than what I've portrayed. I wash the brush and dab again into the blues. I pause with brush in hand as I realize no matter how realistic I make Marcus this will always be a canvas. A picture of his face as much as Gannett is a picture of who he was when he stands before me. My arms collapse to my sides. I am trying to play recipient, recreating a person to fill a void of the real thing.

"You really do have a secret crush on me, don't you?"

I turn, then blink and blink again. There, leaning into my window, is my painting come to life.

"Marcus," I breathe.

"Although, I think after this painting, it won't be much of a secret anymore."

He is still analyzing my work, and my cheeks burn.

"Oh this? I'm only painting all the boys I kissed at the ball."

His gloating face drops, and he looks at me for the first time. The same scowl appears that he wore while watching me dance. "It better be the only one you're painting then."

I can't help but laugh.

I dash to the window with a skipping heart and light feet. My eyes roam frantically over every inch of him as I draw nearer. Everything is perfect, his messy hair, and gray blue eyes. When I barrel into him, he teeters in place and laughs. Relief washes over me from the sound of it, and I fling my arms around him, burying my face in his neck.

"You're safe," I say.

His embrace tightens. "Of course I am."

We lean apart but keep our hands on each other any way we can. I wish this wall around us was not in the way, yet to part for even a moment feels too long. He lifts his hand and pushes my hair off my face and then wipes at my cheek. Blue paint comes off on his thumb, and I smile. Then I turn serious. I have to know.

"Marcus, did you have anything to do with what happened last night? Did you..."

"What? No. why would I do that to—I would never be a part of something like that."

"But you said so yourself, you weren't supposed to be there, and you were there watching me and then gone and then the sprinklers and then the blood, and the resist—" My voice is cracking and my arms are shaking inside of his.

"Aston, it's ok." He shushes me and rubs my shoulders. "I wasn't supposed to be there, but I wasn't there to make trouble. I only..." His hands stop, and the heat of them on my arms seems to steam dry my tears. "I only wanted to see you. Maybe dance with you." His face brightens with a grin that says he's nothing but trouble. "Kissing you, of course, wasn't part of the plan, but you have a way of getting me tangled in all sorts of messes."

"Me?"

"Yes, you in your see-through dress, sparkling your way through the room. You might as well have been colliding into me with every step you took last night."

"You kissed me, you know, and why is that so much of a problem?" I say playfully and crisscross my arms.

Marcus brings a knee up and places his foot on the windowsill. He is soon crawling through. I step back, making room for him to enter my little hiding place. "Kissing you, Aston..." He hops down in front of me, slowly rising like he did that first day I knocked him to the ground. "...is the worst trouble my heart's ever been in."

He towers over me, and my smile fades as my head tilts backwards. There is a life in his eyes I could never replicate. There is passion that he seems to shower me with every moment we are together. No glimpses. His complete self is here, has always been here. Every place I run to, he is there. No matter the numbers, or our blood, or the auctions, we have been running through life for these moments. Just as Gannet and my life have a way of going in opposite directions, Marcus and myself have been going in the same direction without even seeing each other—until now. I see him and he sees me. He was at the ball for me. He risked so much for me. Because he can feel. Because he is soaring with emotions for me. I like the way his smell of cologne mixes with the smell of my old wooden hideout like two of my favorite things are running into each other for the first time.

When his lips find mine, I cling to them. I want it to last longer and without the fear of anyone walking into the coat closet this time. I melt completely into him. I wrap my arms around his midsection and bind him to me. His arms move frantically over my face then shoulders then my back, and they find their way as easily as we found each other—colliding, bumping, falling into each other's arms in just the way we have perfected. We move together as if we already have each other memorized.

And then an image moves across my mind. Of another Donor and his perfect face. I hate that I think of Gannet in this moment. This perfect moment, full of every intensity and passion, is tainted by the memory of cold, comforting hands. Is this how things could be if Gannet could feel? Is it the serum that points us away from each other? When Marcus moves his mouth down my jawline and drips kisses down my neck, a ripple of joy rolls up my back. Gannet could never give me this much. What Marcus and I have is real.

Our life in the real world crumbles to a halt when I hear Mam calling from the kitchen door. We pant, staring in the direction of Mam's voice, still wrapped in each other's arms.

"See what I mean about you and trouble?" he says through each heavy breath.

"No one invited you in here." I return his smirk.

"Not with words no, but..."

"Aston." Mam sounds closer now.

I jump out of his arms. I place a hand on his chest before I realize what a bad idea it is. His firm, warm body entices my hand to feel more, and I slide it across his pecs before I whip it behind my back to behave.

"Wait here, she will see you go out the window." I rush to the door and poke my head out. "Yes?" I say, winded and pumping with so much blood it rings in my ears.

"Oh, Aston, they released the name of the suspect, and you are never going to believe who it is. I knew she was up to something with her new kitchen set, and when the officers came by, I knew..."

"Who, Mam? Who is it? We know them?"

"Lazuli."

The crisp, cool air falls silent at the name. My ears tingle.

"Your *dearest* friend." She throws her hands up in the air exasperatedly. "And now I'm sure officers will come questioning. We don't need that kind of attention right before the auctions. Oh, dear scars galore, what are we to do?" She holds a handkerchief to her eye for effect. "You didn't know anything of it, did you? Tell me now if you so much as—"

"No, Mam, no. I am just as shocked as you are."

"Good. Well. I guess her family was involved in the tampering with the number system. Did you know she was really only a twenty-nine?"

"I didn't." Stick against flesh, stick against flesh, the blood has drained from my face, and the sounds of ringing is replaced. I wish Mam would just stop, yet I want to know more at the same time. It wasn't my fault after all. The Prices truly were wrapped up in deceit.

"This whole time I had wondered how she was getting all those new things, and we had such a higher number than her Lazuli. I knew this whole time; I knew something like this had to be going on." She waves her handkerchief at me now. "And now, oh." She twists her face as if she may faint. "Well now we know how much higher your number really is than hers, and they have been tended to for their misdeeds."

I feel I may burst when the terms *tended to* escape her wretched mouth. She doesn't know what I saw in the night. She doesn't know how the sound of being *tended to* haunts me. They may have broken the law, but no one deserves to be punished like that.

"Thank you for telling me," I cut her rambling off tersely.

"There, there, Aston dear, I know this is all so difficult. The news says they are opening different holiday hours at the facility for those who are having trouble with the things they saw at the ball last night. I know it is all very traumatic. Alicia Lecky's daughter was so distraught just from seeing it on the screen last night." Mam almost looks as if she may step towards me and hug me before she thinks better of it.

"Good to know. Yes, well, I may go by there when I'm done painting." My hand on the door shoots out with pain at how I grip the wood so hard. I drop my hand to the handle instead, focusing on relaxing as much as possible.

"Yes, painting always was such a good thing for you to do with your rages."

I grip the handle in spite of my attempts. No matter that my *rages*, as she calls them, all stemmed from conversations like these.

"I did think they would calm down when your donations started, however."

My hand instantly relaxes as if I have been caught and need to convince my worst critic.

"But yes, so much has happened lately, I will leave you to it. And...," she hesitates, "...well, if you should need..." Whatever is coming is obviously difficult for her to say. She begins again as if resigning herself to it. "If you should need money for more paints, I suppose if the facility is recognizing this need for something extra, so can I."

I can't unclench my teeth, so I speak through them instead. "Thank you, Mam."

She is gone, and my door is closed. I close my eyes as well, waiting for the red to seep from my vision.

"Are you ok?" Marcus sheepishly whispers. I open my eyes finally to see him standing in the same corner, rocking in his stance every now and then like he is wondering if I am safe to approach.

I walk towards him and sigh. "Yes, and no."

"So you know the person who did this?"

Is it my imagination or is there a hint of disgust in his tone? Why does he care so much? It wasn't like it was his blood that was spilt.

"I can't believe Lazuli would do something like this." I sit down on the windowsill, letting my backside hang out the window as I put my face in my hands and my elbows on my knees. The tampering with numbers was a shock, yes, but I at least understood the motivation. What in the world would possess Lazuli to steal the auction blood and spill it in such a horrible way? "Much less know how." I sit up at my own words, remembering the time a year ago I sat with Lazuli at the miniport.

"What?" Marcus says, noticing my mind working. He steps in front of me until I am staring right into the buttons of his blue and tan plaid shirt.

"Last year I helped Lazuli on her miniport."

"So... So, she didn't know a single thing about how to use it. How to check her family's B-mail. Nothing. There's no way she would know enough about how to hack a facility blood bank when she couldn't open her own family's bank account."

"Maybe she had help."

"Who? The resistance? You think she was with them?" I haven't seen her with anyone since Brandon dumped her, but maybe... My hand jumps to my mouth as I realize how easily I let the news of the resistance slip.

Marcus nods his head. "I've heard rumors about a rebellion, yes."

"But why would they do this?"

This revenge against the Recipients hurts the Donors just as much, if not more. But this is what I wanted, right? To help free a nation of unfeeling people. Why aren't I happier to finally hear a rebellion is accomplishing it? Perhaps I'm feeling let down that Marcus is not a part of it after all. But it feels more personal, like the resistance attacked me as well as the Recipients. "How are enough people caring? I thought everyone was high on happy serum."

He shrugs his shoulders and furrows his brow like he doesn't know exactly what I am talking about.

Does this attack have anything to do with the allergies? Could they be a hoax? Perhaps they're really a secret punishment for those discovered serum-free Donors. The retaliation on Donors they can't control is death, but have enough slipped through to form a rebellion?

"How have you done it?" I say.

"Done what?"

"How have you escaped the happy serum?"

His deep, rich laugh fills the small space, and he rests his hands on my shoulders. "What? Am I not happy enough for you?"

"You are, but—"

"Aston, I don't know how everyone is forming behind the Recipients' backs, but I wish I did." He stares out the window above me.

I lean my head into his shirt. My cheek moves against his stomach as he breathes. He strokes my hair, and I struggle to make sense of any of this. How come Marcus always answers my questions with more questions?

His voice is low and gruff when he speaks next. "I would join them if I found them."

I pull away. I thought I would too, but now...? "Even after what they did last night?"

"No one got hurt," he says. "Whoever did this was just trying to make a statement."

"No one got hurt?" I stand taller, wishing I was tall enough to look right into his eyes. Instead, I have to tilt my chin up, and he looks down at me. "A part of that blood last night was mine, Marcus!"

His eyebrows shift into concern now.

"I may have only contributed two months' worth instead of the required three, but that was still a part of me taken away and flushed down the drain. Wasted! What kind of sloppy rebellion is this? What did that even accomplish?" I step around him now, moving about the room. "If I found the rebellion, I'd have a few choice words for them right now. I never wanted to donate, but I sure as scars didn't want my donations wasted." I stop at my art table and furiously cap the tubes of paint. "I don't know what the system will do now. I doubt they will postpone the auctions long enough for us to donate safely. I may be donating every day now and..." I trail off when I feel the gravel of emotion enter my voice.

He is behind me now. He grabs me again like he is holding me back. From what? Running to my doom, from my words, from donating anymore as if he could have that much control?

"I'm sorry," he whispers into the cool air. His breath smokes out past me in little clouds as the sun shines through the window on this December day.

What will they have us do? How will I donate through the winter months?

"I wasn't thinking. I'm sorry." He kisses the top of my head just as a tear freezes its way down my cheek.

I stare at the palette of paints. The mess of colors mirrors how I feel. Everything is muddled. Just as these colors can create a clear picture, I know that somewhere in this news about Lazuli and a rebellion on the rise there's sense to be made, a way to, one stroke at a time, make a clear picture of what the world is becoming. I can't understand any of it now, but I can feel it. There's a chance we may not be the only ones in this world feeling, and right now, I feel change on the horizon.

Stick against flesh. I close my eyes and squeeze Marcus's hand that is wrapped around my shoulder. I just hope we're all ready for it.

TWENTY-FIVE

I'm donating four times a week now. Sunday and Monday are one after another, and it leaves me feeling as cold as the hard, frozen puddles I avoid on my way to the facility. Winter before the bloodbath was a time of celebrating indoors with family; eating the meats we thought we could enjoy with the new contracts to be signed; friends gathering around fireplaces, bragging about stipulations their lawyer put in their contract; or the candy they got from the lawyer's desk while signing. Now it feels like a never-ending deathtrap as I layer more clothes on my legs and face for the slaughter of the blizzard winds.

The auctions are only delayed for two weeks. Donors are to donate as much as they can before then, and contracts may have different rules applied due to the strange circumstances. I know Marcus isn't in the catalog, but he too must be affected by this demand on donor blood for I haven't seen him since we last argued in my shed about the rebellion. They've stopped reporting the Donor deaths. I know this because a boy died in the facility hallway right in front of my eyes. Walking out from a donation just like me, he led the way and then collapsed. He lay motionless, as frozen and blue as the ice storm outside, and his eyes were glossed over in the happiest expression. I held in my screams because no one else seemed alarmed. No one ran down the hallway to help him or rushed to get a doctor. Droids and nurses scooped him up effortlessly and expressionless, like it was the most normal thing in the world.

"At least he died happy," the nurse had said when she looked at his face.

The truth is he died not knowing what happiness really is.

That night there was nothing on the news. No mention of a boy collapsing in the facility after donating beyond the recommended amount. It made me wonder how many more deaths are slipping by each day unaccounted for. If a Donor falls in a quiet facility, will anyone hear him?

We were informed we would not be paid for these donations either. A sign to the public that even auctioned Donors are not exempt from punishment. A warning paraded around town of what hardship awaits those who rebel. We will donate at our own expense or go to the auctions with nothing to offer, which is bad for business no matter what your number is. Needless to say, Mam was very put out and cursed the Price family further for every inconvenience we've experienced.

It is now the last donation before the auctions, and I lean into the wind on my way home. My fingers are popsicles layered in three pairs of gloves. I read once that the seasons in the Old World were things that crept over the land. A man named Tennyson once wrote, "Now fades the last long streaks of snow." Our seasons now fade less and blow in with abruptness more. This storm blew in the day I last saw Marcus in my shed after painting his face. It killed the remaining leaves on the trees, and the temperature plummeted. No fading sun or cold wind warnings hinting at an oncoming change. I know some day in February this icy air will just stop as suddenly as it came in, and the sun will appear again to save us. The chill in my bones from lack of blood, however, may drag me down long before then. I'm getting a cold, but I don't dare tell anyone. Like winter, it'll pass.

The needles of ice in the wind suddenly cease to pummel my face, though the sound still howls on. I look up to see the storm blocked by a black umbrella.

"This weather is merciless." Gannet's brown eyes peek between a gray woolen hat and a red fuzzy scarf that muffles his words.

I don't try to yell through my own mummification or over the deafening blizzard. We push on behind his umbrella until we are under the tram station shed. The snow drifts are piled around the glass hut making it impossible to see out. We both stand in front of the bench instead of sitting on the frozen metal.

"You left in a hurry today," he says to me.

I shrug. I've resorted to body language as my main source of communication with him. Most days he leaves me alone for my donations after a few shoulder shrugs and nods. I don't know why I stopped talking to him. Maybe because the glimpses of the real him are too taunting. Maybe it is fear of him attempting again to tell me what he wanted to that day in Dearborn. The fear that it is not about the resistance but about what I feared then. That it was about us.

The more I think about Gannet being in the resistance, the sillier it seems. He is so precise. So robotic. Surely, he was going to tell me something much more intimate than the truth about a rebel group of Donors. I think about what would have happened if I let him ask me to marry him. I think about how my kiss with Marcus might never have happened if I was engaged and taken and a slave to the system to be with dead Romeo. Would I have collided with Marcus as easily if I hadn't been repelled from Gannet and his drugged self over and over again?

We don't talk. We only brush off the snow from our layers that seem to be accomplishing nothing. Standing alone with him, waiting for the tram, feels so much more awkward than sitting in the facility together. At least my fleece scarf hides my running nose. My cold is getting worse, but I'm too afraid to mention it to anyone.

He pulls down his scarf and soon his breath is swirling around him. "Are you ready for the auctions this Friday?"

"I meet with my lawyer tomorrow," I say through the fabric.

He nods. Looking down at his feet, he scrapes his black boot against the salt gravel that has melted the snow and ice around the tracks. He looks back at me and then at his feet again. The whistle of the incoming tram harmonizes with the howling wind.

"Good luck." His scarf is winding its way back around his face, and we are boarding the train.

Gannet sits at the front of the tram car. I eye him from the rear. I wish I could bump into Marcus right now. Holding hands with Marcus in front of Gannet would be helpful to help clear the air between Gannet and I, help Gannet see why I don't want him to ask me that question. The idea of the two meeting also has my insides bubbling. If Gannet ever finds out Marcus entered the ball illegally, would he still be required to turn him in?

When the name of my stop flashes across the screen, I stand to ready my hat for the gust that will hit me when the doors slide open. My limbs ache just in the preparation of the onslaught. Gannett looks up at me with a sort of sadness that tugs at my heart. Will I always wish I could be with Gannet? Or will there be a day I can only see Marcus and no one else? No what-ifs or has-beens. The wind blows into the tram car and has me squinting my eyes. I step off without looking back.

The smell of Mam's potato salad burns through the air with cut onions, strong vinegar, and mustard. The sudden heat hurts my fingers and toes, but I know I need to warm them up quickly. Torrin sets the table as I hobble across the room.

"Papa will be late," Mam tells Torrin. "Another pole pulled down by this nasty weather. Amerhein is completely without power, those poor souls." The concern sounds funny on Mam's lips. "They'll miss the auctions if it's not up in time." And there it is. That sounds more like Mam.

I, however, shiver at the thought of being without heat tonight.

Mam sees me and calls out to Torrin. "Torri dear, get some wood from the shed; we'll start a fire. I don't want to turn the heat up anymore, but we can't have Aston catching a cold only days before the auctions."

My heart had warmed at Mam's care until she mentioned the auctions. *Bad for business*, I almost expect her to say.

"It's ok, Tor, I can get it." I rush through the room before Mam can object, pulling my coat back on as I run.

Stepping high in the drifts of snow, I make it to the side of the shed where we keep the wood. Arms loaded with round wedges, I hear a sound float on top of the blizzard breeze. It breaks out again like an animal crying. Looking over the edge of the chest-high fence that encloses our yard, I see a lump of a girl down near the road. The scene before me flashes a memory across my vision, a resemblance of the lump of Mrs. Price's body, and my legs feel funny.

"Lazuli?"

The crying stops, and the red face of what used to be Lazuli is soon looking at me. Her skin is chapped and blistered, whether by wind or something more I can't tell.

"Go away!" Her voice is hoarse, as if she's been screaming for days.

"What happened to you?" I throw the wood into the snow and speed around the fence. She leans against our fence with her legs bundled awkwardly under her like they no longer work. Our fence blocks most of the snow and wind, leaving it quieter and sparse here. I drop in front of her and repeat myself. "Lazuli, what happened to you?"

"What do you think happened? I got blamed for the bloodbath, and they took even more from me."

Took more from her? Is she referring to her missing parents or her glamorous lifestyle she enjoyed on pretense? Lazuli's body convulses, and I can't tell if it's from the cold, an injury, or an unwelcome memory. Why would the system release this mangled, tortured girl back into society? Was prison too luxurious for her? Or was this a message? Advertising. A clear warning meant to have witnesses in order to be effective.

"Let me help you. Come in and get warm. Papa won't be home until late. You can have his mea—"

"I don't need the high-numbered Aston Vazeto handing out her leftovers." She pulls back from my touch.

"Lazuli. I didn't—"

"The worst part is, it was probably you!"

I stare at the cracked, peeling skin around her lips and the dried blood that paints them. "What?"

"You and that technician. I bet you were behind it all, but no one questions the highest blood number. No one—"

"Lazuli, I had nothing to do with it."

"You've always hated the facility. I bet you're this rebel community's leader. Just go away, Aston. I will move on as soon as my legs stop hurting, if you can even call what they left me with legs. Then, you don't have to worry about me or the blame I took for you and your little technician."

"Lazuli—"

"I said *go!*" Her voice wavers with emotion. She grabs at the snow and throws a chunk of it at me. I try to dodge it, but it hits me on my hip. It sends another ache down my already sore leg, but I am hurt more by her words than this snowball. She scrapes for another one, but it just falls apart when she throws it, and it dusts the air.

I suddenly wonder why I should care. She's telling me now that not only did she lie to the facility, she's lied to me. She's not the friend I thought she was. I risked my life and the livelihood of my family to protect her deceit. I longed and mourned over years of laughing and friendship that she now says was only a waiting game she played. Her only regret is not beating me to the auctions. Perhaps the system's punishment is just for criminals like her after all.

Guilt falls in my gut like a heavy piece of coal. I step closer to her, pushing aside my anger. Lazuli pitches another piece of snow, and I don't move fast enough. A chunk of hard ice hits me on the cheek and forces my head to the side. My cheek stings, and blood warms my face. I don't look to see if there is shock or remorse from her. I stare at where the fence disappears in the snow and let betrayal and abandonment flame up into my chest. I let the pain on my face and in my heart blend and weave. How many times will I try to bring back the friend I thought I had? How many times will I try to save something that doesn't want to be saved? I don't want to think about how the system created a villain out of a girl trying to survive. I only focus on the pain and hatred. I'm just as much the victim, and I find myself envying her. What I wouldn't have given to be a number twenty-nine. Bland. Plain. Undesirable. Hidden in the shadows, free to do whatever I please.

"Fine," I yell, looking down toward her. I can barely see through the blurry tears held back by my squinting eyes. "Just remember you're the one who left first. You ran away to your precious facility. You lied! You brought this on yourself." I run back to the house. I stomp off the snow and fling my coat across the heater to dry.

"The wood," Mam says as I run through the living room.

"I'm not cold. And I'm not hungry either." I grab at the railing of the stairs and swing myself around, scrambling up to my room like it could save me. *They took even more from me,* Lazuli's words haunt me through my frustration. My heart softens as the tears fall like ice being melted in my warm home. This isn't her fault. The facility takes anything they feel like. They take our blood, our names, our agency, our emotions. They took my friend, her family, their integrity, their home. Now her legs, too?

I slam my door and pace my floor. From my window, I can see the lump that is Lazuli still huddled over the fence. They sent her out on the streets of Michigan winter to die as a warning to other Donors. They sent her where I would see. I grab at the window and sob heartily now. My throat is sore and burning; my nose immediately clogs; and my head throbs, but I don't stop crying. I'll still help Lazuli any way I can, but right now, I hurt. Right now, I've never felt more alone.

The system did this to me. The Recipients did this to her. I wish it *was* me who had started the bloodbaths. I feel now what Marcus felt when he said if he found the rebel group he would join them. I would join them now too—if I find them. I *have to* find them.

TWENTY-SIX

My brown and black plaid coat drips onto the black marble floor of the lawyer's office waiting room. It hangs with the other Donors' coats, all handed down through trade market sales, in the corner of the large room lined with black leather armchairs. The bell over the door rings, but I don't take my eyes off the puddle on the floor that looks like a black hole I could be sucked into. Not even when the chair next to me bumps against the wall. I stare at the growing dark water mark and wonder about Lazuli. I hung a basket full of breakfast and a brick from the fire to keep it warm over the fence before I left this morning. She wasn't moving and was under a metallic, plastic heat blanket. I hope she wakes. I hope she eats.

"Thirteen forty-two?" two speakers on either side of a door call out. No nurse, no physical contact, just an intercom system. I stare at the speakers without moving.

"They don't bite," the voice says next to me. I don" need to look at him to know it's Gannet. I stare on as the speakers vibrate again. "Thirteen forty-two?"

"I didn't know technicians accompanied their patients to the lawyer's office."

"One of my patients is special. I'm here to make sure their file falls into the right hands and not just any lawyer."

"Gannet." I sigh as I stand. "I don't need you holding my hand." I see him look at my hands, and I grab my elbows. "I can do this myself." I scratch at the bandage he put on me yesterday.

He ignores my words and walks past me through the door between the speakers. With an eye roll, I follow his lead like I did that first donation day.

Behind the door, a row of cubicles form a hallway similar to the one I donate in. They each have a small screen sticking out above them. Gannet walks towards the one flashing thirteen forty-two in red.

"Gannet," I hiss and skip to keep up, "I don't need you." The words make my cheeks warm. It feels weird to say them out loud when my own thoughts have been tortured by the very question. Could I really do without Gannet in my life? Or do I need him? I told myself no over and over again, and yet here he is. He's like bad tasting medicine that also keeps me alive.

"The whole New World needs *you*, Aston." He rounds the corner of my cubicle before I'm even there. When I finally step in, I hear the end of his next sentence spoken to the worker.

"...rare condition that needs someone with knowledge on this matter to represent her." He pulls from his pocket a card and hands it over to the receptionist. "Here is a scan that will show you the facility's orders on what steps should be taken."

I watch the redheaded secretary take the card and scan it under her port screen. She smacks her gums as she taps away.

"This is highly unusual, but everything looks to be in place. Thirteen forty-two, take this up to the third floor." She hands over the card.

When I take it, there is a shiny gold stamp on it with senseless, different-shaped squares.

"Becky can scan that and your finger as well." She taps at her screen, and I see my number disappear and a new one in its place. "Thank you, technician, you may escort the Donor there if you wish. The elevator is at the end of the hallway."

Without another look in our direction, she leans over her port screen while her finger is pressed against it and calls out the next Donor number. These secretaries might as well not have eyebrows with the little emotion they show.

I push the button for the elevator. "What is this about, Gannet?"

"Getting you the best lawyer, of course."

"Come on, I know you're not doing this for every one of your Donors."

The doors open, he steps in, and I follow him.

"Not all my Donors have the condition you have." He presses the button, and the doors shut.

"That's not what's going on, and you know it. Now tell me what this is really about." I feel my eyes raging into him but can't help it.

He meets my eyes with that sadness that plagued him yesterday. "You told me to never tell you."

I look away wishing the doors would open. He's right. Why did I push him into this corner when I already knew? I do and don't want to hear the words on his lips. Hearing that he loves me would ruin everything, but hearing about the rebellion would mean he doesn't love me. Both are risks I'm not willing to face.

"Then why can't you just leave me alone?" I feel childish and lace my fingers together in front of me.

He opens his mouth and stops. He closes his mouth and then tries again, looking defeated. "Because you're rare. Your high numbers need the right lawyer."

The doors open with his lie, and I'm grateful for it.

Becky smiles at us and scans the gold symbol. "We have three lawyers who meet these standards. There's a Mr. Glum, Mr. Johnson, and a Mrs. Laurence."

"Mrs. Laurence shall be fine," answers Gannet as if I'm not even there. Becky taps at the screen. She scans my finger and taps some more.

"Ok, place your finger in the scanner one more time. We are going to tattoo your blood so that every time it's scanned your lawyer and her information will be linked to you. If you are to ever change lawyers, we will need to redo the process. Just leave your finger there, it will only take a moment."

I turn to Gannet, and he nods. The red light shines through my fingernail as usual, but this time it heats up my finger. Just when it feels like I can no longer stand the burn, she says it's done. I nurse my pointer finger as she sends us down the hall.

At the end of a long hallway with shiny reflective floors is a window that stretches from floor to ceiling. Seeing the town three stories below us makes my legs wobble. We enter the door at the end, and the smell of lemons and peppermint flood my senses. A potted plant sits on the floor next to a long, dark wooden desk, and I recognize the bushy yellow flowers: St. John's wort. I spy a box on the desk spitting forth steam and recall a humidifier Grandmother used to speak of. A way of putting oils or other fragrances into the air. The smells feel too overpowering, however, and my nose stings from the peppermint as if it is burning the insides of my nose.

"Aston." A slim woman in a gray dress suit approaches me with her hand outstretched. Her loose brown curls bounce around her shoulders as she walks. She follows my gaze over her shoulder to her desk. "Diffusers. I love the scent of peppermint and lemongrass together." She winks at Gannet who she seems to share a joke with. Gannet chuckles as the woman finally makes contact with my hand. She shakes it vigorously like I'm a movie star.

"Aston, it's so good to finally meet you. I have heard so much about you."

I look at Gannet.

"Not just from your technician. I've been studying your records and interviews as well."

My cheeks burn at the memory of the interview on the steps of the ball when I was intoxicated.

"I do not exaggerate when I say you are every lawyer's dream client right now. I am very honored to be your lawyer and hopefully your friend, too." She gives me a warm smile and then turns toward her desk, motioning to the two chairs that sit in front of it. I am still confused and a little annoyed at why my technician is still with me. No other Donor has a technician holding their hand through the process.

"The main purpose of this first meeting is to pick a lawyer," she says as she sits.

I look to Gannet who seems to have made this decision for me. Do I not get a say in it at all? Mrs. Laurence continues, and I let it go.

"And for basic introductions. I will be keeping track of who the Recipients are that bid on you tomorrow and will negotiate on your behalf with the ambassador for the terms of your agreement. First, we want to ascertain if there are any stipulations on your end, maybe a length of contract you would not like to exceed, number of donations you would prefer in a given month or week, or how you want your payments, in bulk sums or stretched out into monthly salaries. None of this is guaranteed of course. The ambassador will come with the Recipient's own list of stipulations, but it will be my job to fight for what you want. In your case because you—

"Are special," Gannet interrupts. The lawyer gives Gannet a confused look.

I roll my eyes at his interruption.

"Special," the lawyer repeats slowly, looking back at me. "I am sure there will be no problem getting you what you want. Your numbers are highest in the New World right now, and I've heard rumors that there are going to be out-of-state bidders."

"Out-of-state? More than one?"

"You aren't just the highest, you're higher by a good thirty points. That auction room will be the fullest it's ever been. You're making history."

"You mean my blood is."

"Yes, well, they're one and the same, aren't they?"

The next several hours we spend bent over the port screens and mini screens, speaking of months and years. I shrug to most questions and nod to the answers Gannet comes up with. I guess him coming along wasn't so bad. I don't really care about a lot of the particulars.

In fact, many of them make my head feel funny and make it seem like my chair is spinning.

It isn't until she puts the port screen in front of me with an "x" over a blank line that it makes my insides really churn. Three donations a month for six years until a new contract is written up is a really good deal for Donors. Maternity leave, vacations, so many stipulations I should be grateful to get. Yet staring at that black line, all I can think of is how I am signing my life away. I will be owned. Officially. One small signature with the blood under the skin of my forefinger, and I will be bound to this agreement.

I know this hesitancy isn't normal for a Donor. I should be smiling up the wazoo and bouncing in my seat, not glaring at the screen like it is the grim reaper. I pick at the bandage inside my elbow hard, trying to resist the urge to look at Gannet for support. He will just beam at me and gush about what a wonderful contract I have. I don't like how dependent I am on him. He is my dead Romeo, remember? But how would signing this contract be choosing life?

A hand softly squeezes my shoulder. Gannet's cold fingers penetrate through my thin, tan shirt.

"It'll be ok, Aston."

I look at him. He's leaning over me and is giving me a glimpse again into who he really is. No clown faces or drugged expressions. He is leaning over me and staring genuinely into my eyes. He says to me with that hand and those eyes that he cares, that he will be there for me. Just like he is as my technician every step of the way, he will also be there somehow through the auction, through the contracts, through the future donations.

His smile reaches his cheeks, but not his eyes. They are already made of glass.

How? I want to ask out loud. How can he be there for me when he can't even keep this glimpse long enough to take me through the signing? I shrug off his hand and push my finger against the screen. Just like that I sign my blood away.

"Perfect," says the lawyer. She and Gannet share a celebratory grin.

How? I ask myself again. How did I get to this point? I always swore I was going to devote my life to painting, leave the family welfare up to my sisters, hide out in my shed and live off potato soup because as long as I could paint I'd be happy.

Now, I'm sitting in the top lawyer in the state's office, signing a contract to bleed for a living.

I think of how the brush felt in my hands, pushing the red paint, the smooth curves that made Marcus's lips. My hand reaches my own lips, remembering their dance with his mouth. A tear runs unnoticed down my cheek. How did I get to this point? Scars, I wish I could run away with Marcus. Run away to Canada and paint, and feel, and love like no one in the New World ever has.

I'd bleed for Marcus if I had to, but not for them. Not for the Recipients. Not the merciless government that looks over us through glass windows and throws money around, paying anything for our deaths as long as a few of them live. I'd bleed for Marcus. I'd do anything for him; with him. The thought cheers me forward. I know what it's like to love. They think I bleed for them, but I do it for love. Somehow, I will save enough money to buy my way out, paint my way to Canada, love my way to freedom. I will bleed for Marcus, just for a little while.

TWENTY-SEVEN

It's Auction Day, the latest Auction Day in history. The snowstorms blow on our crumbling homes. Screens in every house glitch and dance with static, struggling to send the message from Recipient Upper Detroit, where they are dressed in their finest, painted their brightest, and competing with the wealthiest of their kind.

My sisters squish onto the sofa, and Mam busies herself with the traditional treats like plum pies, carrot dumplings and my favorite: caramel for dipping. Pip toddles on the floor, and I roll a toy ball to her. Ari's boy, Roylance, runs up and snatches the ball from Pip's hands. My sisters are glued to the screen, watching the Recipients stroll down the blood red carpet, sauntering their way in line, waiting to be interviewed by Griffin Manny.

"Pip was playing with the ball, Roy, give it back please," I say.

His four-year-old voice musters as much self-importance as it can. "I'm playing lawyer. Pip isn't contracted to have balls to play with."

How sad that someone so young already understands the unfairness of our society. Pip scampers to my arms, and I stroke her blonde curls from her tear-stained fat cheeks.

"Well then, Lawyer Roylance, I am playing ambassador, and I say I want this little Donor of mine to have her ball back."

His face falters at his own logic being used against him. The little brat throws the ball across the room and runs the opposite direction towards the stairs.

"Roylance sweetie." Ari finally notices him. "Don't go upstairs please. We're going to play down here while we watch the auctions."

He doesn't listen and stomps loudly on the wooden stairs, overpowering the sound of his mom's voice.

"We might get to see daddy on the screen, Roylance, come help us find him."

It's a stretch to think we might see Ari's husband, Derek. The lawyers who represented the Donors are behind the scenes, on the other sides of walls. They are still Donors themselves, after all and must be kept separate from the precious Recipients.

When an upstairs door slams, she slumps back into the sofa in defeat and sighs. "Boys," she says like it excuses her lack of parenting.

With Pip in my arms, I retrieve the rubber purple ball and coax her to play with me again.

"Turn it up, turn it up." Torrin bounces in his seat. "He's my favorite."

I've always gagged at how my friends and sisters worship the Recipients, brainwashed by the screen reports, constantly idolizing the Recipients' lives. To hear Torrin do the same causes a different sort of ache in my chest, like I've failed him like I failed Lazuli.

When Pip climbs into her mother's arms, and just as they are about to interview a blonde-headed Recipient, I retreat toward the kitchen to help Mam. I look over my shoulder at the screen. The back of the Recipient's hair looks plastic and hard like Griffin Manny's purple hair. I roll my eyes as I walk backwards through the swinging kitchen door. My fate is to be determined by plastic heads.

"It's Adakin Malloy's grandson," I hear Torrin say behind me.

"Believe me, we know, Torri," Shannon chides. "I think every girl in the New World knows who he is."

I am glad to leave the excitement from the screen behind me.

"Scars!" Mam sucks on her finger and steam rushes upwards from the sink.

"Need some help?"

"Oh, Aston, you shouldn't be helping in the kitchen on your Auction Day."

"It's ok, Mam, I don't like watching the screen anyway." I reach for the strainer by the sink.

She slaps my hands away. "Who cares what you don't like; I don't want you getting stains on that blouse! Reporters may be lurking near all the top numbers' homes as we speak. They could be at the door the second the auctions are announced."

I stand frozen, feeling stupid for letting myself think again that Mam cares about anything other than the auctions. She uses hot pads to remove the pot and places it on the counter.

"Now shoo, go sit and watch. Or better yet, stand so you don't wrinkle your pants."

"Actually, I left something in the shed," I lie. "I'll only be a minute."

"Well hurry, child. You don't want to miss your own auction. You could be the first number they call, you know."

"I know."

I pull on my winter wool inserts and then my winter boots. My coat falls around the tips of the boots, and the fur lining of my hood makes it hard to see where I'm going. Good thing I have the path to the shed memorized even without the compacted pathway my feet have made.

After stomping my feet inside the shed and removing my hood, I see Papa sitting on my stool by the corner window where Marcus and I kissed. Where is that stupid boy anyway? Not that I expect him here to celebrate with me or give me auction day presents, but a simple good luck would have been nice.

"Couldn't handle the affair either I take it?" His voice sounds gruff, like he's been crying.

"No." I don't move, just make a water spot on the old wooden floor from the snow melting off of me.

"Good."

The wind howls, and the roof creeks threateningly.

"Good?"

"Good. Glad that you're still..." He wipes at the fog on the window from his breathing. "...you."

We both know what each other mean.

He looks over his shoulder at me and smiles with wet cheeks. "Your grandma didn't think you would be. I admit I worried too." He turns back to the window. "She was so mad at me for not doing something."

"What could you have done?" I walk over to him now, wondering if maybe I don't know what we're talking about. We are talking about the serum, right? The one we theorized was behind all the robotic happy soldiers donating their lives away. Oh, how I wish I could talk about it with someone. I know it's risky to speak out in the open about such things, and the sound of stick against flesh reminds me of the threat.

Papa takes my hands. He stares at them and rubs them with his scratchy, chapped thumbs. Looking up at me, he says with glistening eyes, "Well, it all worked out, didn't it?" He pats my cheek. "The rest will work out too, you'll see." He clears his throat and steps towards the door, pulling his coat up over his head. "Now don't be too long. Your Mammy will never forgive you missing your own auction."

I think of something as he reaches for the handle. "What does Grandma Bolgie have to do with it all? Why does she care so much?"

Papa turns and eyes me, like he's calculating the best way to put out an electrical fire. He seems to be examining my face as if searching for something on it that could prove to him I'm trustworthy. "Your Grandmother Bolglarka has always cared about the Donors and donations. And she just wants her family to have what's best for them, that's all." He tries to smile, but I know there is more he is not telling me. Before I can ask any more questions though, he is out the door. The wind blows a pathway of snow across the floor.

I watch the snow turn to water before I head back to the house. Mam has left the kitchen and squeals with my sisters in the living room. The whole house smells of apples and caramel. The auctions used to be my favorite time of the year only because of food like this. There are presents for the whole family on Auction Day.

"Aston," Torrin says with a mouth full of caramel popcorn, "You missed Adakin Malloy! They even had Richard Feneway."

The sound of Griffin Manny's announcing voice blares in the background almost as excited as Torrin sounds. "And here comes Season Holt down the blood walk," Griffin announces as the cameras zoom in on a woman, bone thin and wearing a maroon dress that falls around her to the floor. Her lips match the dark dress and stand out amidst her ghost white skin. "She's new to the auctions this year and hopeful to get her hands on one of the top Donors. Rumors have it she has come with enough money to run out any of the out-of-state bidders. And speaking of the devils themselves, here comes one now."

The cameras scan back to a young man that looks my age yet wears a long white beard, and his black hair has white streaks above his ears. He struts the blood carpet in a metallic blue suit. His black shoes have a trim of bright orange that stand out as he walks.

"This is Shelton Miservy, ladies and gentlemen, and he is here today from New Cleveland to try his hand at our top Donors. He said he will not be even attending Cleveland auctions this year because he is so certain to pluck one of our top Donors right out of our hands. And of course, when we say top Donors..." He laughs a well-planned chuckle. "...we all know we mean our Detroit's own number thirteen forty-two who is at the top of the catalog."

My living room explodes into cheers as the announcer continues.

"Yay, Aston!" Torrin shouts, jumping up and down. Mam shakes my shoulders, and I sway on my knees where I sit on the floor. I try to smile. A corner of my lip even tips up. But Papa's shadow escaping up the stairs makes my head feel empty as it bobs on my jostling shoulders.

I eat to distract myself, and soon, I'm sick from so much caramel, but I don't regret a thing. I am licking my fingers as a fat Recipient sings our anthem. Images of the last Germ War flash across the screen. Rows of cots in war-ravaged hospitals show dying Recipients, the singer's face fades into view. A picture of Mason Cross, the first Donor in history to stand up and help the Recipients, is staring right at me as our red flag with the drop of blood and the hands holding it up, waves behind him interposed. The song makes the hair stand up on my neck; its sharps and flats always seem out of place to me, like it is a death march instead of an inspirational piece. I guess it depends on the listener. A real, undrugged person like myself would hear the irony in the tune.

The last note is belted out as a recorded scan of happy Recipient children is reeling across the screen. My stomach heaves from being full of sweets and angry at the manipulation.

"That. Was. Beautiful," Griffin Manny says as the crowd cheers and the camera shows the Recipients rising to their feet. "Now what we have all been waiting for," Griffin says from his little glass reporter box on the balcony, just to the right of the stage.

Mam bounces in her seat and squeals with her mouth closed.

"But first, a few words from our good leader, Mr. Adakin Malloy."

"Oh come on, no one wants to listen to him," Mam shouts at the screen.

"Mam, careful," Ari warns. Parenting her mother better than her own children. "Don't speak treason."

"Treason? Humph. What's the matter with you, child? I love my leader the same as the next person. I only wish they would get on with it. I have a ham in the oven that won't wait for no one."

The room and the audience hushes as the ancient leader steps up behind the glass podium. His beard is tinted a bright yellow, and his black-striped vest makes him look like a bumble bee. He grips at the podium as if he would fall over without its support. The camera closes in on his face as he takes the time to smile out at the audience.

"My good Recipients. Our faithful Donors. We both keep this wonderful new country alive and thriving. A week ago marked the day the first Donor saved a life and our Division was created. I stand before you as a humble receiver of the life this great system of ours has given me. Donors, we are in your debt. We bid for you this day as a small way to repay you for what you give us." He pauses as the audience claps respectfully. Adakin turns his head to cough, and his shoulders shake in a way that makes him look like paper in the wind instead of a powerful leader.

My stomach churns again, and I grab at it as my eyes are plastered to the screen and how our leader moves like a dying carnivorous dinosaur.

"The recent events at the Detroit ambassador's mansion saddens us all. We are only people like yourselves, trying to survive. We can only do so with the combined help of you Donors. Together, we can keep this great New World alive. Together, we can build a better future for our children." He pauses again. The flaps of skin on his neck under his beard stretch and wag as he nods at the clapping.

"There are those, however, who do not want to work together, that want our children to die, or starve, to suffer. We ask that you please not let this sick way of thinking divide our country again. For I fear we would not survive another war like the one this system has saved us from. Please report those who seek to divide us. Please contact your local officers if someone disgraces our good system. Be our hero, be your children's hero, preserve our system." He leans back, letting the audience clap again. He doesn't wait for them to stop this time, however. "Thank you." The cheering increases as he scuffles away.

"What touching words from our great leader. Thank you, Mr. Adakin Malloy, for your loyal services to this country. And now for the One Hundred and Fifteenth Annual Blood Auctions." As Griffin Manny speaks animatedly, a glass wall descends over the stage like a giant flat curtain. "This year the auctions will be hosted by one of the most famous voices in the New World. We know him from the crazy documentary show *If Blood Could Speak*. He is also the Late Night co-host of *Goodnight, New America.* When he went live with his recent illness from over donating—"

"Oh I saw that on Compass, did you see it?" Shannon asks. "It went viral so fast."

"Yeah," Ari says laughing. "When he threw up on the nurse, I almost peed my pants when I saw her face."

"...We cried, and we laughed as he took us play by play through the recovery of that ridiculously innocent little mistake. All the way here from the great state of New Illinois, please welcome your host and auctioneer for the evening, Mr. Finneous Flagmeyer!"

The Recipient crowd goes wild and stands on their feet as a man in a bright red, sequined suit walks out onto the stage. The glass seals against the floor.

"Hello, New Detroit!"

I recognize neither his face nor his voice. The crowd reaches a higher octave from his encouraging entry.

"You know..." The cheering dies down as he speaks, and people begin sitting at their dinner tables again. "...when I was asked to host this auction, my first question was, could I get a month's break from donating? 'Cause I kinda gave my share last month."

My sisters laugh with the crowd on-screen, and I look at them. I don't think it's funny. Someone almost dying from over donating. If anything, it should be eye-opening to the dangers of our oppression.

"I won't say if they granted my request or not, only that they kindly gifted me this complimentary barf bag before entering the stage." He holds up a little white paper bag, and the audience's laughter is deafening.

Shannon slaps her knee. Ari wipes her eyes. My stomach twists and rumbles.

"But let's get serious for a moment. There are some impatient Donors at home waiting to see what you Recipients have in store for them." He swipes at the top of the clear podium, seeing things on it the rest of us cannot.

"That glass must be a new port screen," Torrin observes. "That's so cool. And look at the way those black beams shine over top. I bet they're completely made of cameras."

I see them for the first time and think he's right. The way the beams above the stage glisten like black flat glass; they do look to be cameras.

Why would they need such precaution, I wonder? Maybe taking extra measures after what happened at the mansion? Or has more happened that we don't know about?

"For one never knows what the auctions may bring." He smiles beautifully into the camera, and the Recipients clap.

"First up is the famous thirteen forty-two—"

"First!" Mam jumps out of her chair and screams. "She is the first one!"

"Shh." My sisters flap their hands at her.

"—with a historical blood number of one hundred and fifty-seven." Murmurs spread across the Recipient floor, and the auctioneer pauses a moment for the number to sink in. "Her contract states she wishes to not go under twenty thousand a year, which is where we will start the bidding."

Sybil has been prestigiously quiet throughout the whole afternoon. She turns to me now, as does the rest of the family.

"Your bid is *starting* at twenty thousand?" she asks snootily. Twenty thousand was Sybil's historic bid price.

I shrug my shoulders. "It's what my lawyer suggested, not me."

"Shh." Mam takes her turn waving her hands, and the attention is back on the screen where my price has already risen.

"Twenty-five from Lord Grenton, I see Malloy junior's twenty-seven."

Sybil cuts her eyes at me again and turns to the screen with her nose in the air.

Recipients bid with light-up wands in a variety of colors. They flash across the dim room like fireflies, as different Recipient houses bid on my blood. The number rises, and the lights blur together. My stomach is under attack by a capsizing storm within.

"Thirty thousand from Lady Holt, matched again by the Royal house of Malloy, Lord Grenton at thirty-five, out-of-state Miservy at forty thousand, Malloy forty-five." Fineous's lips ramble so fast my head can't keep up.

Griffin Manny's voice whispers on the screen. "You're witnessing history, ladies and gentlemen, this is the highest bid war I have ever seen. I hear the Malloy household is bidding for their sick youngest son tonight who I spoke with only moments ago. I'm sure he is on the edge of his seat now, listening to this possibility of having the number one Donor in the New Nation."

"You could be the Malloy Donor, Aston!" Torrin says.

The whole room hisses, even myself. That is not something I want to think about. Recipients aren't supposed to know their Donors, but here we watch our Recipients fight over us. I'd never thought about following the auctions this closely to hear their names. In the past, they always went too fast for me anyway. Today the auctioneer's words speed by, yet my mind is creeping slowly, processing it all at a snail's sickening pace. Time has transformed into the howling storm outside with record breaking wind speeds that freeze and slow the world to a trudging pace.

"Lady Holt fifty-five, Malloy sixty, newcomer Chandeler sixty-five, Grenton is out, Miservy for seventy, Holt Seventy-five, Malloy eighty, Chandeler is out."

Murmurs rumble through the audience, but our living room is so silent you can hear the vibration on the speakers from being turned up so loud.

"Miservy eighty-five, Malloy ninety, do I hear a ninety-five, Holt for ninety-five. Do I hear a hundred? House of Malloy for a hundred thousand dollars, do I hear a hundred and five? Miservy's light is out, Holt's is out," A loud bang rings through the hall and through our tiny living room as the auctioneer bangs the gavel, and the audience goes wild. Fineous shouts over the clamor. "With the highest bid in history, number thirteen forty-two is sold for one hundred thousand dollars a year to the great and royal house of Malloy!" He bangs the gavel again, and our living room explodes.

Mam sounds like she's hyperventilating. Torrin's shaking the house with his jumps and leaps. Ari just yells "Oh my gosh, Malloy," over and over again as Shannon whoops and screams until Pip is crying confusedly.

No one touches me. I'm an ice sculpture on the floor that will shatter if pushed. I look to the stairs and see Papa staring at me. His words come back to me, *It will work out in the end. You will see.* I know he knows more. Why won't he tell me?

I need fresh air. My stomach finally does its last dance, and I run for the front door, wanting to flee, to run and never come back. Instead, I vomit the caramel popcorn onto the front porch. I hear a click and block my face from a flash.

"Are you sick from excitement, or are you coming down with something?"

"How will you handle the contracted donation now that you are coming down with an illness?"

"What will you do with the money?"

"How many days did you contract to donate? Do you think you will get what you asked for?"

"How do you feel about being the Malloy Donor?"

The reporters all speak over top of each other, and they are lost in a sea of flashing lights.

"I..." I throw up again as the clicking cameras drum through the cold air.

TWENTY-EIGHT

"Not only has she made history with her auction, but the footage of her reaction to the news has now hit an all-time high of views. I don't think people are likely to forget thirteen forty-two any time soon."

"Turn that wretched thing off, Torrin," Mam's voice booms through the house. She hasn't let us watch the screen in weeks.

"Don't they have anything else better to talk about?" she murmurs before tears fill her eyes. "And that blouse. Ruined. The whole thing ruined."

Having a whole month and a half off has been wonderful. I stayed in my night dress three days in a row, read two books Papa gave me, and bought more paints and canvases. The auction money was posted into my blood bank that very night. But even with all this rest, the ache that lingers and the occasional tickle in my throat has me worried. I'm getting sick.

At first, I was hesitant to be contracted with the Malloy house, but Mr. Adakin Malloy, and his creepy son who stared at me through the glass that night at the ball, surprisingly met every single one of my terms. The contract was not changed one bit. I will only donate three times a month. I get up to ten days a year to skip without cause or warning, and I will have a physician at my disposal at their expense. Everything my lawyer wrote up was agreed upon, and I signed the final document right away. It was almost too good to be true. With this kind of a contract, surely, I can recover from whatever illness is coming.

I haven't seen Marcus in weeks and grow more worried with each day that passes without him. At first, I was furious at his absence. No note of congratulations. No visit during my holiday. No gift for how well I've done. Even in his absence, he brings out the most selfish parts of me. Now, I fear that perhaps the rapid donations were too much for him. I calm myself only with daydreams of him in my shed again.

This is the last week of my auction vacation. The wind has already ceased its howling these last several days and instead left the New World locked in a silent, empty freezer. Before long, the sun will be close enough to melt our prison only to start a new one.

Dancing around the kitchen in my short night dress, I grab at the tin foil in the drawer and rip a piece off. I fill it with a hardboiled egg and sausage patties I snatch from the pan when Mam isn't looking. I ball up the foil and hide it in my hand.

"Can I take some sausage, Mam? I want to go to the shed and finish a painting."

She turns from the refrigerator after agreeing.

"Hey, just one."

"I only took one," I hold up the patty and the biscuit I put with it, hiding the foil behind my back.

"Torri!"

I slink into my boots and coat before I am found out. In my backyard, there are two compacted pathways. I take them both each morning. The first path is to the fence where I leave food, hoping to help Lazuli in any way I can. A wooden slat in the fence is broken and swings sideways easily. I find ripped pieces of foil and replace them with a new bundle, hoping it is she who is getting the food and not some wild animal. My heart drops with the realization that there isn't much difference between the two any more. Lazuli is wild and unaccounted for.

The second path is to the shed where I spend most of my days hoping to see Marcus instead of truly painting.

When I enter, I flip the switch that now also turns on an electrical heater Papa installed for me. I hang my coat on a nail I hammered into the exposed wood and fall into the giant fluffy chair I purchased for myself. It sits in the corner by the door under the opposite window. It gives me a perfect view of the unfinished painting by the window. I sit here often imagining what I will do when and if I see him at that window again. Fantasizing that I will pull him over to this very chair and share it with him in a way that Mam would never approve of, even if he had high numbers.

When a knock sounds on the window, I jump out of my daydreams and only stare at the messy, corn blond hair behind the dirty glass. He bends down to it, cupping his hand over his eyes as he peers in. He wipes at the winter dirt and tries again. I can't seem to move; my heart beats in every inch of my body and has me weighed down with the strength of it. *I would bleed for Marcus*, my heart seems to remind me. *I would bleed for him*, it says with every throbbing pulse that rocks me in place.

When he sees me in my chair, his face transforms. A rapturous smile lighting up his eyes as he waves. Stuck gazing at his face, I wave back dumbly. He places his palms on the glass and pushes on it. The sound of the wood frame scraping against the metal awakens me from my stupor, and I step over to him nervously.

"Hi," I say stupidly.

He looks up at me under his blond eyebrows as he clambers in, and with heavy breathing says, "Hi."

He turns to shut us into the small room alone, and I can't help but analyze how his back shifts under his plaid shirt. How the end of the shirt waves with his motion over his faded blue jeans or the crease where the jeans hug his backside.

I jump again when he turns, afraid to be caught eyeing his—

"You have really taken this 'not bumping into each other' thing to a new level." He steps closer to me, and my breath catches in my throat full of his soap and fruity cologne scent. "I haven't had you push me to the ground or fall into my arms for exactly thirty-four days!" He wraps me up into his scent.

I allow myself to breathe deeply as I wrap my own arms around his waist and sink into him. "I thought it only fair to let you come to me sometimes too."

"Ahh, the old 'ball in his court' trick."

"Ball?"

"Nevermind, just a saying. I see you haven't done much painting lately. This looks exactly the same." His cheek rests on top of my head as he looks at the canvas. The side of my mouth is pressed against one of the buttons of his shirt. and it shifts as I smile at the painting.

"I think it may be finished already."

"The only part of my face that looks finished are my lips."

I lean back to look at his face. He stares down at me while still holding me to him.

"It's the best part of your face."

He laughs a fluid, single laugh and leans his face into mine.

This isn't how I imagined seeing him again. It is better. I feel his stomach against mine, and his hands run down the sleeve of my nightdress.

I pull away slightly. He leans over and pecks me on the lips then the nose then the forehead as he straightens.

"Uh," I step completely away from him. "Would you like to sit down?" I grab his hand and lead him across the room to the chair.

He tilts his head in question at my sudden formality, but smiles and follows my lead.

"Yes, thank you."

When he sits, he seems to morph the size of my chair with his long legs and tall torso. I grab at the coat on the nail and pull it on.

"I will be right back, if that's ok."

He chuckles. "Aston, what's going on?" He leans over and grabs my hand, pulling me to his lap. I adjust the short nightdress as I sit awkwardly on his legs, and the unzipped coat spreads open. I tug on the hem, pulling it over my knees as best I can as I fidget on his lap. He wraps his arms around my waist like I am a young child sitting on the lap of their father. "Why are you so squirmish?"

"I am not squirmish," I say as I scoot and rock again in his lap because he is not my father, and I am not a child. I can feel the wrinkles of his jeans underneath my bare legs which is why the nightdress will not come down any farther. It is hiked back, creating a draft. "It's just that I am...in my nightgown, and that doesn't seem proper. And I wanted to look nice for this moment anyway." I look down at my hands that are trapped underneath his lock on me.

His laugh is boisterous and fills the room this time.

"Don't laugh," I say. "You shouldn't be here, much less with me in my night clothes."

"Little rich Aston Vazeto, do you forget I have seen you in a lot less than a night dress already?"

"Yes, but I didn't like you then." I cut my eyes over at him at the sound of my honesty.

His face softens, and his eyes squint like he is admiring a fine sunshine. I look back at my hands.

"But I did." He lifts a hand to my chin, gently pulling my face towards his. "And I still do. Even in a nightdress."

As he kisses me again, his hand returns to hold me. He slips it into my coat, wraps it around my waist, then curves it up my back. I pull my arms out from under his and wrap them around his neck. He leans back into the chair, taking me with him as our kissing takes on a new intensity with the change in angles. His tongue slides against my bottom lip. When his hand travels down my back and towards my lifted gown, I pull back breathlessly. I'm held up with my elbows on his chest and our faces are inches apart, euphorically happy.

The cold draft deepens, and something catches my eye. Marcus's face follows mine as we stare at the wild animal in the doorway. Lazuli, my friend turned wild bird, stands there glaring at me, then

Marcus, and then me again. Her skin is cracked, and her once shiny brown hair is matted with grass sticking out of stray clumps.

"I knew it," her voice is as foreign to me as her face. "I knew there had to be a way you did it. You couldn't possibly be as innocent as you pretend to be."

"Lazuli, what are you talking about?"

Her face crinkles as she smiles. The chapped skin protesting the action. "You're just like me," she says.

I sit up on Marcus's lap, and he is frozen beneath me, trapped, caught.

"Only who will feed you when we are both out here, Aston?" With that, she throws the ball of tinfoil on the floor of the shed and shuts the door.

I fall into Marcus's chest, wondering what that was all about. "I hope she doesn't tell Mam," I say.

"Or anyone else." He kisses the top of my head and pushes me off his lap. "I have to go." He walks briskly to the window, and I run after him. When the window is open, he turns back to look at me. There is a fear in his eyes I hadn't seen before.

"What is it?"

"I like you too much." He pulls me in by the waist kissing me with urgency and pulls away forcefully like I am a Band-Aid that must be dealt with quickly so as not to hurt too much.

I shut the window and feel a chill run up under my coat. Why would it hurt to say goodbye to me unless it is forever? Is that why he kissed me differently? With so much urgency? Does Lazuli know something I don't? I haven't watched the screen for weeks, not like I did much before my debut anyway, but was something announced? An image of Marcus dancing with me in the coat closet both makes my face burn and my insides squirm. He was at the ball when he shouldn't have been. Was Marcus found to be the true suspect and turning him in was Lazuli's only way to exoneration? Was that why I haven't seen Marcus for weeks? Because he is on the run and I will now be turned in as his accomplice?

Just like Lazuli? On the streets as a wild animal, was that my fate?

I stare at the canvas with new eyes now. I will never touch this painting with a brush again. I will leave it as a shrine to the first time I kissed the only other feeling person in the New World.

I wish I had known. I would have kissed differently too. I wouldn't have wasted time worrying about my nightdress. I would have told him that I lied to him. I don't like him. I love him.

As I leave the shed wiping at the tears that I can't explain to Mam, to anyone, I pick up the tin foil ball, squeezing it smaller and tighter. I am never leaving food out for that animal again.

TWENTY-NINE

I march through the marketplace with the same long face I wore that first day. The day I became a Donor. The cold wind makes my nose and forehead ache. I haven't been able to breathe through my nose, and my throat burns like fire. I am not getting sick though, and as long as I tell myself this, I believe it.

The snow has closed the street markets. There are no people to weave through. The sun makes the melting top layer of the snow shimmer as I trudge through the empty streets. I pause at the corner I first bumped into Marcus and again at the trade store just barely opening, where he caught me longing for that canvas. My eyes sting at the dress shop where he shared a dressing room with me.

I found no news on the Compass search engine or sneaking onto the screen at night, but what else could Lazuli have meant about Marcus? And wouldn't this be something they would want to keep quiet? The system doesn't like admitting when they're wrong. Can't Lazuli see that they will probably take Marcus and leave her still to run the streets? Does she hate me so much she would sentence my life to her same fate even when she will benefit nothing?

I pause again when I see two officers standing outside in the cold like two sentinels on either side of the facility door. They nod at me with their poor, cold heads as I step through cautiously.

I scan my finger and head for the waiting room like I always have. The same receptionist from that first day power walks over to me with her sweet cheery disposition. "Thirteen forty-two," she sings like we are old friends. "Didn't I tell you you'd do great?" She claps her hands and tilts her head to the sky. "Oh, when I heard your number called first, I just knew you were in for big numbers." She tilts her head down in a pout. "How's your tummy?"

"Uh, fine."

"You're a contracted Donor now, thirteen forty-two. You have your own waiting room."

I follow her back out through the reception area, making the sliding doors hiss open as we go by. On the opposite side of the building, the squat woman opens the door to a waiting room setup for royals.

The chairs are plush and red. A boy across the room has one folded out with his feet propped up and reclining. He is staring at the ceiling and digging into a bag of treats. The white walls match the outside of the facility, and just like Torrin and I predicted, they are screens. There are five of them lighting up across the wall with no seam where one starts or ends; they only blend together. The lighting in the room is soft and pleasant, not the bright sterile lights of the rest of the facility.

"The closet in the corner is for snacks, there's just about any snack you've ever heard of in there. And the fridge is full of drinks. Just help yourself." She pushes me gently in as she retreats backwards out the door. "And congratulations, thirteen forty-two. I knew you were something special when I first helped you."

I turn back to look at her. She gives me a wink, and I recall how that face looked over me with such scrutiny. Sure you did, lady. I smile gratefully at her anyway.

The velvet of the chair is the softest fabric I have ever felt. I run my fingers back and forth on the armrest as I sink into it. My fingers pull then push the fibers of the red seat. I love how they shift and bend at my will.

"The seat is interactive," the boy in the corner says. "No remote, it's voice activated. See the numbers over each screen? Just call out which screen you want, and the speakers are in your headrest." He chomps loudly after filling his mouth with food and then talks through it, "Oh and try the rocket chips, they're amazing. Sweet and salty chips that have flavor bursts on them that explode with each bite." This explains why he chews so loudly.

I muster a thank you and scan the screens. My curiosity to experience an interactive chair is stronger than my desire to see any of these shows. The screen with a glowing number four over the top of it is showing a news report, and I call out to the room feeling ridiculous.

"Four." Do I need to say it louder?

"Oh, say 'screen four.' Too many numbers get said in this room."

Of course, how silly of me. How is the room supposed to know when dealing with electronic machines and human ones?

"Screen four, please."

"Ha, they don't care if you're polite."

I really don't like this other Donor. I hope this is the only other time we share a waiting room.

Voices float from my headrest. I look towards the screen just as it seems to jump from the wall and float down to me. It will smash me if someone doesn't stop it. I put my foot and hand out to stop it when I hear laughing.

Looking over at him, the boy in the room is pointing at me and throwing his head back. "It's a hologram," he says between chuckles. "A 3-D projection of what the screen is showing." He wipes at his eyes as he continues. "Go ahead, put your foot through it."

My foot and hand are frozen in the air. I stretch out my foot towards the screen that has stopped and seems to have stretched and curved all around my chair. My foot disappears right into the reporter's chest. I pull my foot back and then in, seeing it cut off again.

"I think it must be the chair that projects it. I don't really know how they do it and don't really care. Being a Donor is awesome!"

The words of the reporter distract me, and I relax into the chair.

"The suspect in the Detroit bloodbath, a Miss Lazuli Price, has pleaded guilty to the crime this morning."

"Volume," I shout out to the room and the boy, whichever will answer first. "How do I turn up the volume?"

"Just say volume up until it's where you want it."

I repeat it five times until it sounds like this reporter in her orange suit coat is sitting right next to me chatting. "Miss Price turned herself into officers two nights ago where she requested a hearing in front of a whole Recipient audience. It is unclear what her motives are, and with no lawyer or representative, she is arguing for her own plea deal against the Recipients. In other news..." The screen blares on.

I know what Lazuli's motives are. She wants coverage. She wants publicity. She wants to expose the whole world to Marcus and myself. To show them that the highest number is a traitor. How will I defend myself? I danced with almost every Donor at the ball that night and on camera too. I can't come up with a better alibi. But I danced with Marcus also, and how can I prove I didn't smuggle him in? Perhaps Gannet can help. I am sure he'll do anything I ask of him. He will help me prove I had nothing to do with the bloodbath that night. Wouldn't he?

"Screen four..." Talking to the air is not something I will get used to any time soon, I don't think, "...off."

The screen shrinks away as if it is floating its way back to the wall.

I stand up, pacing the floor and scratching at my arm where a bandage will be soon. I almost miss the gluey residue left behind by them. The boy is called back and then only moments later the door opens.

It has been ages since I have seen Gannet, and I spin quickly, needing to talk to him about the ball and the favor I have to ask of him.

"Thirteen forty-two?" My mind is slow to register the voice and the scene before me. My smile falters, and my limbs freeze. It isn't

Gannet that calls my number, but a young woman with coal black hair that falls to her waist. Her smile doesn't move, and she holds her miniport like it is a small puppy instead of a sheet of glass.

"Yes?" I ask, hoping there is something she just needs to tell me or that I must fill out another series of questions like last time.

Her giggle is bubbling like a gentle waterfall, and it sends a torrent of fear down through my toes. "I would think you have been here enough by now, Donor, to know what it means when I call your number." She steps out of the room and looks over her shoulder. "Come with me."

What is happening? Where is Gannet? What will Lazuli's plea deal be?

I follow the black curls of my new technician down new hallways and soon enter a small office very similar to the the test of health rooms.

"We do everything exactly the same, just in different parts of the facility," she says as she snaps red rubber gloves on and lines up the cotton and bandage and gun-like poker.

My breathing echoes in my head, and though I can tell it's going too fast, I can't figure out how to slow it down. Black dots float through my vision, and I close my eyes. My head pounds, and I can't make sense of anything. "My," I breathe through each word, "Technician. From. Before?"

"We don't like to keep the same technician each time. Too much attachment to a person—"

My eyes pop open. "But I have a rare mutation in my blood."

"I saw there were some notes in your chart about that. I will look over them and see how your technician did things."

The large bleeding hole she leaves in my finger does not leave me comforted. Reminds me of another day altogether. Lazuli was right, female technicians are not as gentle. The pain shoots up my arm, and the wet, warm drop that oozes down my finger swamps my brain. The metallic smell that fills the room twists my stomach, and the black dots spread together. The last thing I hear is my new technician asking if I'm alright before I slip into nothing.

A smell of the ammonia cleaner that Mam uses burns my nose as I jump awake. I am on the floor of the test of health room. My new technician leans over me, making her hair tickle my face.

"Took a little spill there, Donor."

I hate how she calls me *Donor*, reminding me over and over again that it's all I am to the system.

"Up we go," she sings cheerily, lifting me awkwardly back to my seat. "Sit there a moment and let yourself recover. I will recheck your file. It does seem you are affected by our process much more than our other patients. Did this happen often with your other technician?"

I think of his cold hands and easy smile, wishing for them as I answer, "No."

She slips out of the room, and while she's gone, I spy the crumpled test results of my health. It isn't hard to guess the meaning behind the red letters and negative symbols. I didn't pass. My pounding head confirms it. My technician returns and my throat stings worse with each swallow. The lights are blinding, and the way they scorch my watering eyes is tortuous. What will they do? Send me home?

"Ok, so I see your technician's notes and that he has been giving you the anti-nausea medicine separately, is that correct?"

I nod, and my throbbing nose swells with pressure. It shoots pain into my ears with each movement.

"Ok, if that's all, we've recently adjusted the formula, and I think it should be just fine to be mixed with the coagulant serum."

She called it serum and she isn't sending me home. Is this possibly the technician of every dead Donor that never left this facility? Her judgment and poor reasoning dramatically reducing the Donor population of our city? Or perhaps our blood is just too precious now to care about a Donor's health.

I follow her again down the hallway, lost in the dark folds of her hair, trying to find a way out of this. If Gannet was right about the serum causing problems with my kind of blood, this donation could cost me my life. Equally bad, however, is the fact that if *my* theories are correct it will be the end of my ability to feel.

Would I remember enough to try and not take it again? Or once a victim of endless happiness and conformity, would I be trapped in a never-ending chain of donations with serum? Never to be freed until the end of my contract or birth of my children.

The prick of the needle stings more than ever before. This technician's hands are not quite as experienced and efficiently gentle as Gannet's. It brings to mind another technician so many months ago who came to my home and fumbled with the needles and devices. My stomach tightens then drops.

I close my eyes, and the burn in them calms. It feels like my eyelids are on fire and my heart is racing to free itself as much as I am. My brain feels foggy and slow. My blood moves through the tube faster than my mind can think. Is it possible I've been subjected to the drugs already? I know I need to run, get away, but how? What do I do?

She leaves the room once I'm hooked up, and the water from my eyes increases whether from tears or the fast approaching cold; I can't tell. My head is full of cloudy pressure making it hard to think. All I want to do is bang it against the wall and pass out again. Think, Aston, think. I shut my eyes, but the pounding explosives in my mind are louder than my thoughts. My eyes sting, and I know they would feel better if I just left them closed.

I can't close them though. Not yet. I glance at the doorway, and it seems to speak to me, bringing me to my feet without thought. I wobble in place. My hand tingles when hanging, and I helplessly call out to Gannet as if he's just picking out a game for us to play. The words sound more strangled than desperate. I call out hopelessly louder this time. "Gannet," I say as I grab at the table for support. It only hurts my head worse from the strain.

My new technician rounds the corner, making her hair fan out around her. "What is it?" she asks with coolness that indicates her extensive training and drugs. Drugs that will soon be in me if I don't act fast.

I step instinctively away from her, which makes me wobble more, and I realize again that I'm not fast. I'm sluggish dark blood moving my way through an endless tube. When I bump into the wall behind me, panic closes my throat completely, and I begin grabbing at the clear bandage that covers the needle in my arm.

Her hands stretch out cautiously. "Donor, wait."

I can't get my fingernail under the edge of the bandage like I habitually do with the tape each day. My breath catches when I see it; my sparkling blood slinks through the clear tube that falls down towards the floor first. "Get it out," I scream and work harder at the bandage. "Get it out of me!"

"It's okay," she soothes as if I'm not a clawing animal in the corner. "Let's just talk—I know there's a lot to take in."

My panic makes me clumsy with the pesky needle. Her cold hands wrap around my wrists and pin me to the wall. I think of Gloria thrashing in old Mr. Winters' grasp, and Oliver squirming in the officers' hands, but I'm weak and sick.

"Assistance needed in cubicle thirteen," the technician shouts, finally sounding flustered.

Two other technicians enter, slowly at first. They rush at us when they see the situation.

"Does she have a record of resistance?" says a tall burly man with hunched shoulders.

"No, she's been perfectly compliant. This is thirteen forty-two, the Malloy donor. She should be celebrating to be here."

"Get her on the bed," says a short girl with dark braids on either side of her round face. I try to move in their grasp, but it's useless. "This exertion isn't good for her." Her words almost sound like she cares about me and not my donation.

I lean away from their hold, letting my weight do what I'm not strong enough to, but my feet slide across the floor. I think of the first conversation Gannet and I had in this facility, and my own words echo back at me. "They don't force us," I had said.

The paper on the table rips and shreds loudly as they force me onto the table. The short technician tries to soothe me while grunting, shushing me like I'm a little child.

"It's okay, Donor," she says then turns to the others. "Up the serum. Maybe her dosage is off. It's no wonder with what these Donors have been through these last few weeks."

My technician nods and pushes buttons on the machine.

With my feet, I push myself off the bed arching my back. "No," I shout, but the hands of the tall technician make me boomerang back onto the bed. The force makes my head sear with pain, and my vision flicker. There's no use. They're healthier. They're stronger. I'm sicker than I realized; I finally admit to myself, which makes me as good as dead anyway.

My head is the only thing free, and I thrash it back and forth against the paper, screaming at the pain it causes. Screaming for Marcus who I will always love and Gannet who gave me the chance to love him. Screaming at my cold blood now entering me as if I could scare it away. Screaming the last scream I can.

It stings as it starts through my skin. Somehow it feels colder than before. My chest heaves with one last sob, and then I am done. I stare at the room as the colors seem to sparkle. This room isn't white like I've always thought. It's not a canvas after all but a prism of sorts, full of rainbows. I see them now where the light hits the wall and where the reflection of the screen shines through, beautiful little rainbows throughout the tiny cubicle. I smile at each one of them. I hate them really, but still I smile. I know they are fake and a side-effect of the serum, yet still I smile.

When the machine beeps, I want to jump in place, but I turn to it happily and wait patiently for my technician to come.

"There," she says as she swings around the corner. "That wasn't so bad, was it? How do you feel?"

I want to strangle her, yet I hear myself coo at her as I tilt my head. Either the throbbing has stopped, or I just don't care about it anymore. I can't tell the difference.

"I feel wonderful," I say and smile so deep it hurts my cheeks. Pain. There, I feel it again. I don't feel wonderful. My nose is throbbing with pain, and my head feels as if it may burst with pressure, yet still I smile.

"That's great. And you shouldn't feel as woozy either. Taking it intravenously is much more effective than orally."

"Thank you so much," I purr at her.

She returns my smiles with more smiles.

A shadow takes over the doorway. "Alli," I recognize the man's voice, yet it sounds more harmonious than it did before, like he is singing. "This is my patient. What have you done?" Gannet charges across the room, opening the doors to the machine and lifting the bags of fluid.

Alli puts her hands on her hips. "Her notes didn't sound that severe, and the serum has been changed anyway. She says she feels fine."

He ignores her as she nicely puts a bandage around my arm and cleans up the tubes.

"How much did you give her?" Gannet almost yells.

"She passed out in the office room of health, so I thought it would be good to help her recover."

Gannet looks at me. My eyes water and blur the image of him, but I don't blink. I smile. I want to ball up in his arms and cry and hit him in the face at the same time for leaving me. How could he let this happen? Is this what it feels like to die? To be screaming and banging against the walls of my own prison while I listen to who I have become prance around for all these people? Perhaps Gannet left me with this technician on purpose so we could now be dead together. I want to slap him and run to him, but all I do is smile demurely like he is my long-lost lover.

Without taking his eyes off me, he says to the other technician, "I will finish up here. You've done enough."

"You know we aren't supposed to get too attached. If you want her to yourself, maybe you should—"

"Enough!" His yell makes my smile leave, and my cheeks are grateful for the rest.

When the other girl is gone, I step in front of him. I feel the tears I would have shed drip down inside my ribs as I cheerily bounce on my toes.

"Hi there," I say.

"Aston." His voice shakes, and I see his eyes fill with emotion. Is my lack of feeling making his seem more real? "Aston, I am so sorry."

"Sorry?" Inside, I know what he means. Inside, I am reaching for him, but my limbs will not obey me. They obey a different order now that runs through my blood and commands my body to recoil from others.

He looks up to the ceiling, then pulls me out into the hallway. Halfway down the hall, he stops and lifts my arm. He rips the bracelet that was a gift from the Ambassador's Ball from my wrist.

"Ouch," I say and then giggle. He throws it in a waste bin on the wall and continues his walk, pulling me with him. "Hey, that was mine."

"It was a way to further connect you to the system; believe me, you don't need it, especially not now."

We walk away from the direction I came in and soon are in a dark emergency exit room. Two sets of doors are covered in red warning signs that say "Alarm Will Sound If Opened."

"Aston, I know this is going to be hard for you, but I need you to push through the fog in your body and try to answer me." He is talking like he knows about the happy juice. Like he knows the prison of my own body I am in right now. If he knows, then he must be fighting against it, too. But how? How do I scream out of my own head to him?

He grabs my shoulders, and I flinch at the touch. "Aston, listen to me. I need to know about Marcus."

Oh no. He knows about Marcus being at the ball. He will turn him in. I knew Gannet would save me, but what about Marcus? Will he help save him as well? And how do I muster enough care to plead with Gannet to please fight for him?

I scream for the words to come. My head hurts, and my nose is dead. And my ears are closing in. My burning eyelids close over my cold eyes. "I don't know what you mean." I smile.

Gannet's head drops in between us. When it comes up, he looks pained and desperate.

"Aston." He pauses and stares deeply into me, like he can pull the real me out through my eyes. "There is nothing wrong with your blood."

My smile drops a little, and I feel somewhat free for a moment. I am allowed to give glimpses too, right? Of the real me inside.

"Your blood is the purest, cleanest blood this world has ever seen. I wrote that in your file so you would be able to be free of this. To be free to move forward. You've given others courage to do the same. And now the cause has stormed across the land as they have watched you. You're their hero. The only drug-free Donor. Everyone in New America knows who you are."

"I don't know what you mean." My mask is lifted again, and I only hope he can see the shock and understanding in my eyes. Not the only drug-free Donor. No one knows of the low-numbered Marcus that stays in the shadows.

"Just." He drops his hands and sighs as he turns full circle. "Just tell me what you were doing with Marcus."

"I danced with him at the ball."

He seems to hyperventilate, but recovers quickly with a hand through his hair, breaking the perfect wave of brown. "You danced with him, ok, and what else? Was that the only time you saw him?"

I feel another glimpse coming up and images flash across my mind again. Revisiting all the places of ours I stopped at on the way.

"No, I bumped into him many times."

"On the street?"

"Yes."

"Ok." He seems to relax slightly.

"And in the dress shop, and at my home."

"Your home? What was he doing at your home?" His face is blazing angry, and I realize there's no way he's just giving me glimpses of himself. I finally see for the first time he has been acting of his own will and not from a funny blue syrup. But why? And how?

"Why do you care?"

"Why do I care? Aston Vazeto, what were you and Marcus doing?"

"We kissed."

He throws his hands in the air and then seems to pull his hair out as he turns again.

"We love each other," I'm able to say. "And I don't care how low his numbers are." I am proud of my glimpse-self relaying what I feel inside, even if it does sound flippant and superficial.

"You kissed?" he growls at me.

It hurts to see the way he looks at me now. But this is hardly the time to be jealous. Poor Gannet and his Romeo love for me.

"Yes, but I hardly see why that is any concern of yours." I can't help the giggle that escapes.

"You don't see—" He lets out an angry grunt. "Aston, just being in the same room as a Recipient means death, making out with one— they may kill your whole family."

"What?" I feel the smile on my face freeze like glue that has finally dried.

"Don't you know who he is? He's not a low-numbered Donor, he's Marcus Malloy! He's your Recipient!"

THIRTY-TWO

My Recipient? Inside I am screaming. I am pounding against the wall of my own body, yelling question after question. On the outside, though, I am smiling.

"Marcus? ...Malloy?" The scene of sick Marcus standing on the street takes a different note, and my insides shout again. He was sick. I saw that on day one in the market street. But he wasn't a sick low-numbered Donor. He was a sick Recipient wanting my blood. But what was he doing in Livonia, the Donor subsection of New Detroit?

Pain seeps through the muscles of my face. My plastered face still out of my control.

Gannet grabs my arms, trying to catch his breath. "Aston, there's an uprising. A small group of Donors and some Recipients have secretly formed to help free the Donors from their contracts. There's something bigger going on in the facilities. Something the system doesn't want anyone finding out about. I'm not from Livonia or Dearborn. In fact, I'm not from New Michigan at all. My family were bee farmers for the system in New Dakota."

"Lazuli buntings," is all I can manage to whisper as his information speeds by me, and I picture the tiny blue birds.

"Yes." He breathes a relieved smile. "That's how I've seen lazuli buntings before. There were many on our farm, before the system took over. The serum is doing more to Donors than just making them happy, Aston. It makes them do things. Things they don't remember.

We think it may even be killing new Donors. The serum is specifically designed for each patient based on their personalities and traits."

I recall how odd I found the personality test on my first day of donating. My cheeks rest for a moment as I struggle to take in what he is saying.

"After years of taking the serum, it attaches to a Donor's genetic makeup somehow. My father learned what the system was doing with his beehives when he caught them testing it on officers and refused to work for them. They slaughtered my whole family!"

His hands are on me again. His breathing is rapid and heavy with grief. I wish I could stop smiling now. I wish I could somehow comfort this technician that has done so much, been through so much, deserves so much more than I have given him.

"I found the resistance and joined as quickly as I could. They sent me here to watch over this facility. I'd worked here for over a year with nothing to report, until I met you." His eyes pucker with a kind of concern I've never noticed on Gannet before.

I wish I could think through this fog. I wish I could ask the questions I know are in me somewhere. All I do is grin as he continues with his sincere eyes.

"You stood in front of the facility like a warrior for battle, wearing everything you felt on your sleeve. I wanted to run to your aid, to tell you everything about the hope that is found in the cause." His hands are on me again, and my body tenses at his words and his touch. "I am sworn to secrecy, and only our captain can give permission to share the whereabouts of our society. But that day you rattled off your proud manifesto of why you were so scared—I never wanted to break a truce more. You were so confident in what you wanted. I wanted to save you from it all." His voice shifts, less frantic and more wistful and caressing. "That's why I was your technician every day. I took you to the same cubicle day after day at the end of the hallway where there were no cameras and the microphones couldn't carry that far. I made my mind up the moment you looked me in the eye and told me it was *your body* and *your blood* and that the serum could never run through it." His head leans against me, foreheads touching, and his arms run up and down mine. "That speech you gave at the Ambassador's Ball brought us more Recipient followers. We have a good amount of help from the inside now because of you. And more and more want to be serum-free like you. The resistance is exploding. It's been hard to keep it organized."

I think of how Marcus heard about the resistance after the ball. Is he a resistance follower from the inside? My heart bobs back and forth, unsure of how to feel about the news. Should I be glad the Recipient who lied to me at least may have betrayed his evil comrades because of me? Nevertheless, Gannet's words stir a real feeling deep within me that stomps out that concern. A small seed of victory is sprouting and pushing against the serum that is trying to suffocate anything real. I did it. I somehow have helped a few see the truth of our injustice, the truth about our imprisonment. I'm so happy my face hurts.

"After that, I got the okay to tell you and initiate you into the cause that day at Dearborn; Mason and Laney are the leaders of the cause for that area. But you wouldn't let me tell you. I thought you knew already and had changed your mind. That you wanted to have a simple, somewhat ignorant life full of luxuries, even if it meant a shortened life. Most Donors change their view even without the serum once they see even a third of your contracted amount of money."

He drops his hands and steps away. His voice is low when he speaks again, like a growling jaguar about to attack. "I didn't know it was because you were dancing away with a Recipient." His sigh sounds heavy with grief and hatred. "I didn't know what to think when I heard the news from headquarters about you. And to think that vile creature's lips were on you." He shivers and scowls at me.

He steps further away as if he can't bear to be near something that touched a Recipient. "I hope he does catch a Donor illness and dies for putting you in this danger."

I smile into the long pause, trying to sort out the behind-the-scene details of my life. "The bloodbath?" My thoughts come out in small staccato sentences that sound disconnected as my true self fights against the serum evident on the outside.

"Not our proudest moment." He shrugs one shoulder. "Some resistance leaders felt we needed to make a statement, to help others know we were out there fighting. So they could search and join, as a way to slow the auction process, too. But really, we would have lost followers from that tantrum if it weren't for your speech. You made others remember what it felt like to have compassion."

My chest flames with rage that these rebels wasted my blood even more than the Recipients did just to prove a point or to advertise their cause. The rage seems to cleanse my mind for a moment, and I am seeing Gannet's face clearly once more. The glossy pearly sheen over his eyes is still there, yet somehow, he has pushed through the drug.

"The serum. Are you...?"

"Trained. Bees hate lemongrass and peppermint, and St. John's wort does the trick."

I stare at him dumbfounded, feeling a smile creeping over me again as he moves effortlessly over to me. St. John's wort? The little yellow flowers growing in Mason and Laney's house? The ones in the lawyer's office? All resistance?

"All of us are trained in ways to overcome the serum's power. But you, you are the first to be completely serum free. You are the most trustworthy of us all. Fighting the effects of the serum isn't enough for Donors now that they know what it is doing to them. They want out. You've proved it's possible. You are free and uncontrollable." He smiles gently as he says this.

I think about how wonderful it felt to be free to love. I thought that was the wonderful consequence of my choices. But now I see the cost of freedom was to make the *wrong* choice. I loved the wrong man. I loved a Recipient.

"Aston." He touches me again, and I turn my clown face to him. "I found out about you and Marcus, which means so have others.

Someone reported you right to the Recipients, and the news is spreading fast. You need to—"

An alarm sounds, and our dark doorway is lit up with red blinking lights.

Gannet's grip on me tightens, and his words rush out. "This door is unmonitored and slips out the back of the building. We are directly over our little cubicle, so just run down the metal staircase."

"But where am I to go? If the officers know, they will be after me."

"Your grandmother," Gannet says as he pushes me towards the door and opens it.

"What?"

"Go home, Aston, and call your grandmother."

"My..." I have a fleeting image of my grandmother snipping away at a wispy yellow bush and realize that is where I've seen the flowers before.

"She's our leader. She will have the answers. Now go!"

With one final shove, I am out onto a metal see-through balcony, and I grab at the railing as I see the ground through it.

After smiling at the ground—like if I am nice enough to it, then it won't crush me when I fall—I take off running down the stairs. The back of the building is empty, with rows of dumpsters and a cinder block wall. When I hit the pavement, I run for the dumpsters, climb on top of them, and jump over the wall into an abandoned park. I don't stop running or smiling all the way home.

When I reach my home, I take the porch stairs two at a time but miss, and my shin scraps against the step. I don't stop to look or think about the pain or register the warm blood dripping down into my sock; I just swing the door open until it slams against the wall.

"Torrin," I hear Mam yell. I dash across the room, pushing the rocker out of the way as I make it to the miniport under the stairs.

"Aston, what are you doing banging the doors open like that?" Mam stands with a wet dish towel in her hand. The smell of fruity dish soap makes tears well in my eyes even though my cheeks are still stiff from smiling. "Just because you make a hundred thousand a year now does not mean you can do whatever you like to this poor house."

I ignore Mam as I press my finger against the glass miniport and call Grams.

Mam drones on angrily. "You will have your own soon enough, I am sure, and you can do what you like with that one, but for now on—"

"I'm sorry, Mam. Grams?" I turn my back on Mam as I hear Gram's wispy hard voice. "Grams, it's Aston."

"Aston, what is it? What has happened?"

I grab at my throbbing head as if I can push the doubled images I'm seeing straight. I teeter in place, and my eyes water, though my smile never fades.

"I talked to Gannet. I know about the—"

"Shut your mouth, child." My inner self recoils at my lovely grandmother talking so harshly to me, yet my face beams on through the phone. I hear ringing in my ears like Grams hasn't yet picked up the phone. Is this conversation my imagination? No, it must be my illness fogging my brain.

"Nowhere is safe to talk about that," she says.

"They're coming for me, Grams," I pant, and it's the first hint that my serum might be wearing off as my voice cracks on the end. Fighting against the serum makes my stomach flip, and I grab for the desk as I feel myself sway. "I didn't know, and now they're coming for me. Who are you, Grams? What's going on, and why didn't you tell me?"

"It'll all be okay, Little Ash Tree." She forces herself to stay calm though I can hear from the inflections in her voice she is shaking as much as I am. "Say nothing when they come for you. Say nothing, you hear?" Her gravelly voice sounds more frightened than mine, and before I can ask her why, the front door clatters to the ground. Dust clouds that will give Mam a heart attack billow up around it. Mam yells and then screams again when she enters the room and notices it isn't another of her children to reprimand, but a team of bald officers.

With their black high-top boots, they step on top of the door they disassembled, aiming their droids right for me.

"Number thirteen forty-two, Aston Vazeto, you are under arrest for fraternizing with a Recipient and possibly tampering with the auctions."

"Aston?" Gram shouts horrifyingly over the earpiece while Mam goes into hysterics, falling to the floor like the door.

The officer speaking stands in place on the door while the others fall in form behind him, forming a circle around me. They inch in closer and closer.

"Aston," Grams shouts in my ear.

"They're here." I wonder if they have already shot a laser through my legs as I can no longer feel them beneath me. I hear my voice echo as if I'm in a tunnel as I say again into the miniport that is falling away from my face, "They're here for me. They're here for me. They're here for me." I hit my head hard before everything goes black.

THIRTY-THREE

The sounds of hell clang against my skull as I awake from my death. Each horrid bang of metal doors and grinding chains on hard floors stabs through my brain, and my eyes are laden with mortar that keeps me shrouded in darkness. The hands under my arms squeeze too hard. It's the first indication I have that I am moving. The sound of scratching must be my own feet, though I still cannot feel them. Is this what the system did to Lazuli, I wonder? Will I be just like her?

A putrid smell of sweat mixed with vomit makes me groan as I become more aware of my new prison. I feel my chin bounce against my chest as my head bobs with each of my captor's steps. More metal drags against the cement floor coupled with more banging and jingling. I twitch my brows together with each sound.

When they toss me into something prickly and noisy with each of my labored motions, I smell the scent of fields and grass before I fall again into a nothing space. To an in-between world, like heaven and hell are both fighting over what to do with me and I must wait here until they decide. Will I be saved because of my ignorance or sentenced for it?

Creaking metal makes me shiver awake. The walls sound like they are dripping with grime. Something scrapes against the floor and hits the scratchy lump I am lying on. The smell of bread wafts up to me wherever I am. Heaven is fighting hard for me. The boom of something closing is like a switch that turns me off to the world again, and I am in between worlds once more.

◆

Tiny scampering feet move over my arm and I can't tell if my eyes are open or closed. Squeaks and chirps come from beside my face where the plate of bread had landed. My throat is on fire and my eyelids burn my eyes. Sweat glues my hair to my head and I shiver at the cold my wetness has brought on.

The creak of metal opening vibrates through the dark space. It moves slower than when the bread plate was thrown in. The sound of boots against rock make the squeaking friends scamper, and I wish I could do the same. Until I feel the warm, faint touch of a familiar hand on my arm.

"Aston," Marcus whispers.

At first, I think heaven has won and has brought me to my love, until I remember what Gannet told me.

I will my arm to move out from under him, though the energy costs me too much. It moves slowly like my arm is a foreign part of my body, and I am shaking uncontrollably at the exertion. A new wave of perspiration flows over me like a sick blanket.

"Thirteen forty-two to you," I am able to scratch out the words to him.

All I hear are his sighs. "I didn't mean to." Another sigh pushes through the stale air. "I only wanted to be able to choose my Donor more specifically. I thought if I could see them at the ball and how they interacted with other Donors, I would be able to make a better choice."

To hear the way he talks of Donors as if we are a pair of shoes he wanted to try on before purchasing makes my blood boil. I realize: my blood is in him.

"I only wanted to see what it was like for Donors—to see them and what they go through."

I see him clearly now for what he is. I see that Marcus is nothing more than a spoiled Recipient prince using us Donors as his pawns and subjects for his own game.

"I only wanted to make a knowledgeable choice instead of a dart thrown at the dartboard blindly. I never imagined I would fall in love with one."

I try to flinch at his touch when his fingers trace my face, but all I do is shiver more.

"Scars galore, you are burning up."

"No, I'm n-n-not, I'm f-f-f-freezing."

"Oh, Aston, how could I have been so stupid? I have brought this on you." He begins to whimper, and I find myself quite enjoying the torture he feels for how he lied to me. "I have put you here. Please forgive me, Aston, please."

I think of Juliet. Wise, fair, old Juliet who knew to choose death, to choose her Romeo, her Gannet, rather than to think there was another. How stupid I was to think there was another option.

"'Oh happy dagger'," I quote my heroin, "'there rust and let me die.' I will forgive you, Marcus, in the life to come."

I feel myself sink deeper into the straw bed that pokes me and hear frantic scuffles around the room. When he speaks again, I realize I had fallen asleep so quickly and deeply.

"I will fix this, Aston." His lips are cold when they press against my wet forehead, and I feel myself already drifting away as he says again, "I love you, and I will make this right." The metal door shuts louder than when it opened, and I think I hear him whisper, "All of it."

THIRTY-FOUR

The passing of time becomes a mythical thing. The sounds of metal doors scraping open blends in with rattling chains or keys and tin plates being thrown against floors. I am once slightly aware of vomiting, though I don't know what since I haven't eaten or drunk anything since I arrived, whenever that was. I lay with my face against my own bile and fall again into a thick, heavy, torturous sleep.

Voices tickle my ears as they have grown accustomed to only the scraping metal. I can't move, though the sour smell of my own filth pulls me to a version of wakefulness. I feel my eyes roll inside my head against my control, and I fight against the waves of illness that wish to take me under, to sleep more, to a better sleep that tempts me. I kick against it to stay afloat a little longer, to hear and understand what these voices are saying. Nothing makes sense, and none of the voices sound familiar.

Soon the sound of metal against cement vibrates the ground beneath me, making me aware that I must not be on the sticky straw bed but on the floor now.

Strong hands move me, and soon fingers are being pressed against my forehead and poking my sides and abdomen. It is worse than being locked under the serum. At least then I had glimpses and could move my limbs. Now I lie trapped in a fog, entombed by my body that will not respond to anything.

"She needs water," an aged man says. His voice sounds angry and caring at the same time.

Feet scuffle, and for a moment, I am asleep again before something cold and wet touches my lips. It feels like the ice storm I marched through to donate is crashing down my throat, and I see Lazuli with her chapped bleeding face in the snow, and Marcus with his warm breath smoking into the cold air, and then Gannet telling me to run home and call Grams.

Somehow the ice waterfall fills me with warmth, and I drift again as I feel hands tuck something around me. My dreams are mixed with the pulling and tugging of cold and warm hands—each of them hold a limb and pull tighter, like I am the rope in a game of tug of war. One hand punches me in the gut, another slaps me on the face. I toss and turn each way over and over, never able to decide which hand to follow, the cold or the warm.

In my dreams, I see Gannett slipping another donation needle into my arm. I feel his cold hands on me, yet the tube is pumping a blue shiny liquid into me as he smiles. It is not cold; however, it is burning hot like he boiled the serum first before giving it to me. Marcus is holding my other hand, and I turn to see his angelic face trying to protest what is happening to me. A hand wrapped in cold, another held by heat, I toss my head to each of their faces.

"She will have all the answers," Gannet says with a smile.

I turn again to Marcus. Beautiful, healthy-because-of-me Marcus.

"I will fix this," he says. They both fade away as I am engulfed in a burning blanket and red flames that calm the seas of darkness.

An argument is jostling my senses awake. A foot stomps against stone floor, and a loud thunderous voice explodes through the air.

"You're stomping your foot like a child and acting like one too with this ridiculous scheme of yours." The voice sounds familiar, like a famous movie star on the screen that I can't quite place. "You cannot throw a fit every time you don't get what you want, Marcus! I'm sorry your fool excuse for parents haven't taught you that by now, but let me make it very clear. This is not a toy you can cry or scream over until we buy it for you. It is a person. A criminal."

"I told you she's no criminal. She didn't even know who I was," I hear the other scoff and a shoe tap against the stone. "I tricked her. *I* should be punished. *I* snuck through town and then sought her out each time. Punish me, Grandfather, not her."

My insides go cold, and I can feel the pain from every bump I've acquired lately. The other voice is Adakin Malloy. He is so close I can hear him breathing deep with thought.

"Fool, I can't just go out there and tell these frightened Donors that one of our Recipients snuck into their land. They will fear everyone, and we will look weak and out of control. Soon, we will have Donors coming to our land! And you think me a simpleton to believe she really had no clue who the grandson of the great ruler of this land is? That she would not know of the great Malloy name?"

"I did not tell her my name—"

"There is no exception for ignorance."

"Look at me, Grandfather! Look how well I am. Her blood is too precious to be wasted. Think of her blood if you have no mercy for her life itself."

"Stupid boy! You think I'm going to kill her?"

The scent of honey fills my nostrils, and I find myself shivering again. The way Malloy senior's voice cracks and slithers like lightning, or a snake, makes my teeth hit together loudly. They don't hear me though and continue with their argument.

"We have ways of dealing with uncooperative high bloods like her. We don't need consent when they are hung in manual comas."

"Is that what she is in now?"

A small chuckle escapes and ripples through the tension.

"This is her own doing. She is sick."

"Then save her. Save her blood at least."

I push through the fog that is taking me under again. I want to hear more about my life sentence. I want to know the outcome of my fate. I hate Marcus now for lying to me, but I still love him for fighting for me. Their words sound like I am listening from underwater, and I am soon drowning in darkness again.

●

Voices blur together, and as I come to again, there are bright lights that shine against my eyelids. A cacophony of voices slap me from every angle. They are gasping and others shouting questions like they are in shock of whatever has just been said. Clicks of cameras, tapping heels, the scent of honey mixed with strong perfume all shoot through my senses. The commanding voice from the last argument amplifies across the room.

"Quiet down. I know that this has come as a shock, but scientists have confirmed this is completely safe for our poor Recipients and everyone involved. We will take every precaution for those helping in this trial. I feel it is a fine and fair ruling for this criminal's sentencing, and I am sure proud of my Grandson Marcus who has come up with it." A slap on the back sounds harsher than pride. "He will be overseeing the program and reporting its results to me each month. This is only a trial run and does not indicate any other changes with other Donors or our facilities."

Reporters and clicking cameras blur together, and I am choking and drowning as the last thing I feel is bile sputtering out of me again.

A KISS ON MY CHEEK. Then a sob and a hug.

"We love you, Aston." Papa's deep, sorrowful voice soothes over me like a magical balm.

It has to be a dream, but I feel if he could only stay a little longer, I am certain I could be healed.

Mam's sobs are pushed on me, and I feel her draped over my chest. "A hundred thousand a year," she shrieks, "gone! How could you?"

The heat and anger from that comment sends me into a raging boiling sea of darkness again. The dream morphs, and I am in a glass container with Recipients from the ball surrounding the outside of it. I circle my little glass cage to see each of them stare at me. One of them lifts an auction wand and then another. Something falls from above, filling the container. It fills fast and knocks me down. I am banging on the glass, screaming at them to help me. Soon the tank is filling, and I am sinking in a quicksand that is pulling me under quickly. They continue to stare at me as emotionless as an officer without eyebrows, lifting their glowing wands one at a time. I am up to my chest when I realize it is money. Small green papers, like the ones I saw in a book once, and silver coins are all falling on me and filling the tank. The coins clink against the glass and weigh heavily on top of me.

Next thing I know, Adakin Malloy is standing right in front of the glass as the last of the money is filling up to my neck. He waves his auction wand, and the money in the tank turns red. I am coughing and swimming and drowning in my own blood.

I feel cold hands on my head, pushing me deeper into the tank of blood, and I hear Gannet whisper to me, "We will be watching you there. Don't worry, Aston, we will make sure you are safe. We will watch them as they watch us."

Cold hands can make me warm. Opposites can attract. Magnets can be turned around. Tanks can be drained. But I am still covered in blood.

THIRTY-SIX

There's a bird singing. Another dream. The blue wings flit from one branch to another. It pauses long enough for me to step closer to it and still doesn't fly away. Instead, it bounces from one direction to another on the same small, scraggly twig. Its red brown bib and white belly make it look like it is wearing a blue hood over its head like a thief. When I am close enough to touch it, I pet its soft lazuli blue feathers. What a tame, sweet animal, I think just before it morphs into the blue of Lazuli's eyes. I step back to see this twig is what holds her up. It sticks out of her chest and has her pinned to the tree. Her cold blue eyes are motionless. They do not flip or move like the bird did on the branch. The sweet animal is dead. She is gone.

I back away, then turn and run through the trees. I swat at the branches and try to wash the image of Lazuli's motionless eyes from my vision. The sound of the trilling bunting's call squeals and bumps through the forest, shooting arrows through my soul like the twig through her heart. I fall into a soft patch of grass and look up into the blue sky, almost as blue as the lazuli flitting on the tree. Songbirds engulf me, louder and louder, as I see wild bird after wild bird accumulate on the branches circling my head.

A warm breeze kisses my cheek as my eyes open.

The songbirds continue, though I am not in the soft grass of a forest. I am lying in a bed softer than any I have ever lain in. My fingers twitch across a blanket like the soft velvet chair in the new facility waiting room. The sheets are silky and as smooth as water. I shift my bare foot against them. My muscles ache from the movement, but the freedom to do so has me pushing through the pain each time.

The birdsong floats through the room, and when I turn my head, I see a large window open with blue sheer curtains twirling out from the wind.

I lean against my elbow and cry out in pain as my muscles protest. With difficulty, and eyes squeezed shut, I inch by inch pull myself up until I am sitting in bed leaned against the headboard. I open my eyes with a sigh and run my hand across the bright cherry wood. It is so shiny I can see my reflection in it. I am ghostly, and my skin sags like an old woman.

My hand falls from exhaustion, and my head does too. The thump against the wood as my neck gives out sends shooting bright pains through my head. When I feel strong enough to lift my eyelids again, I scan the room. It is easily as large as my entire home. By my bed is a night table as big as our desk. It bears a beautiful glass lamp.

On either side of the open window stands two floors of bookshelves that reach the ceiling. Some shelves hold decorative statues and vases instead of books. A gold statue of two hands holding a red ruby droplet stands out. The corner has a desk with a leather seat at it. Another window has a long-cushioned window seat. I look above the four-poster bed to see a matching elaborate glass chandelier like a miniature of the one in the ambassador's mansion.

Nothing about this room evokes fear, yet still something tells me this is not right. How did I go from prison to this?

A bouquet of the most beautiful flowers sits on a circle table directly underneath the chandelier. With the sounds of the birds and the smell of flowers, I feel as though I am lying in a field. Some of the flowers are ones I have never seen before. A blue looking sunflower with an almost opal shimmering center.

A door opens, and I flinch and then gasp at the pain that shoots through my body from it. A young woman in a white button-up dress with a white apron on enters swiftly. She has brown curls and wears a white bandana tied on top of her head. She jumps when she sees me.

"Bloody—I didn't know you were awake." She holds her chest as it heaves.

"Wh—" I try to clear my throat, but it is so dry nothing moves the way I want it to.

"I'm not supposed to talk with you until you've spoken with the head nurse. He will explain everything. Let me get you some water, and some food, too. I bet you're famished."

My stomach grumbles at her mention of food, and she giggles. The way she talks is unlike anything I have heard before. A thick European accent, nothing like Grams' though.

She walks to my bedside and lifts a straw that is atop a clear glass to my mouth. Having exhausted all my energy to sit up, I am at her mercy.

The water slides gloriously down my throat, and my eyes close at the joy of it. An, "Ah," escapes me when the glass is empty.

"I know, that's better," she says. Her smile reminds me of Papa, and I try again to speak.

"Where am I?" My voice stumbles over the forgotten act of speaking.

The nurse clasps her hands in front of her. "Let's have a bath, shall we, before we meet the head nurse? I wasn't able to remove all the..." She looks to my hair as she thinks of what to say, and I suddenly smell myself. "...lingering effects of the cell."

"Cell?" My memory is foggy, and I think back on all the choppy, blurry events, trying to see through the missing pieces to the puzzle.

"Yes, dear. You're a prisoner of the Recipients. You're very lucky though. I don't know of any that have made it here after spending a week in the ambassador's dungeon."

"And where is here?"

After pulling back the covers, she wags a finger at me while clicking her tongue. "Na-ah, missy. You aren't getting me to slip that easily. It is up to the head nurse to decide how much you are told."

She lifts me easily. My face burns, not from fever, but from embarrassment at how this nurse carries me to a bathroom off the massive bedroom.

"Weigh nothing more than a snowflake you do, miss. I will fetch you some lunch after your bath."

"It is afternoon then?"

"Yes, miss. You've been asleep here for three days."

"Three days," I quietly echo.

"Mm-hmm. And tossing in those sheets something fierce. You squawked out something about a bird, so I thought you would enjoy the spring music. And here you are, woke up right away I'd say."

She helps me out of the long, white frilly nightdress. The fabric is nothing like I've ever felt before, and as it passes over my head, I spy the tight stitching. Where am I that can afford such expensive fabric. Recipient prison, she said? Where do the Recipients keep their criminals? I thought they disposed of them rather than shower them with luxury.

The hot water in the large oval bathtub sends chill bumps up my spin, and I feel as though the silky bubbles may tingle the dirt right off of me. My head rests on the back of the tub so naturally as if this is my daily routine. I sigh as my limbs float up under the sheet of bubbles, soaking until every muscle can be moved with less argument. I hadn't noticed when the woman left the room. The warm lavender bath was too distracting. I am glad I cannot hear the birds from here. I do not want to relive any part of the Lazuli dream.

When the woman enters, she carries a blue dress, bright and bold, draped over her arms. It shines like the sheets, cascading over her arms like waterfalls.

"Don't have any jeans, I suppose," I say.

"You will be having dinner with the head nurse tonight. Best to wear this."

She lays it over the long counter, under a giant mirror, and helps me out of the copper tub.

"Am I allowed to ask your name?" I say as she dries my hair.

"You can ask anything you want, miss, but I cannot answer all your questions. Only—"

"The head nurse. Yes, I get that, thank you."

She rubs harder at my matted blond hair and smiles. "Janice, miss. My name is Janice, but they call me Juice."

"What a funny name. Why do they call you that?"

"Another time, miss. This hair will take all my concentration."

My hands hold my neck as she attempts to comb my hair and pulls my head back and forth. My limbs are lotioned, a spray of sweet-smelling perfume showers down on me, and then Janice slips the silky fabric over my head. It looks and feels like wearing water. The fabric ripples with each move I make. It is cold in places and warms up to me in others.

"I like how this feels," I say.

"I'm sure you do. It's Canadian."

"Canada?"

"No one makes silk quite like the Canadians these days."

"Am I in Canada?" My mind reels from the memory of Adakin Malloy's voice speaking at a press conference that seemed right out in front of my cell. Is that how Marcus saved me? Did he trade me to the Canadians? Is that why my family came and kissed me? To say goodbye? *Gone*, Mam's words echo through me.

"He said you would be a tricky one to keep a secret from."

"The head nurse knows me?" I immediately think of Gannet, who traveled across the New World to follow a rebellion. Did he follow me to Canada, too? Or maybe this is where the rebellion headquarters is.

Janice makes a motion like she is zipping her lips together. She leaves the bathroom and calls from the bedroom. "I have ordered you some lunch. It should be here soon, but no one will be offended if you decide to rest some more."

I step out into the massive room watching her clean up the bed and then set out the lunch table.

"Try and get some nourishment before you go to sleep if you

can." She stops and, with the white towel from my bath in her folded arms, looks at me like she is a mother admiring her child all grown up.

"It was a pleasure to meet you, Aston. I will return this evening to help you retire properly to bed."

Before she shuts the door behind her, I try one more time to get answers and call out to her. "Janice, whose room is this?" I am surprised when she pops her head back from behind the door and actually answers.

"Yours, miss. It was made for you."

Made for me? She must mean made up for me. Fluffing the pillows and maybe removing the previous person's things. Looking about the room, I see how new everything looks. It looks like it has never been touched. Not an ounce of dust or scuff marks or handprints.

When the door opens, I smell the food before I see it. I close my eyes to savor the rich, sweet scent.

When I open them, I see Marcus standing in the room with a tray of food. His hair is different, not the messy corn maze but parted neatly and shines like plastic, like all the Recipients wear. He looks so different, except those lips, those eyes. It is him. I bump into the bed behind me and then inch myself around to the other side.

"What are you doing here?" My eyes dart to the window that is open, and I wonder what floor I am on. If I am on the ground floor, perhaps I can just step out. Even the second floor might not be that big of a fall. "We aren't supposed to be together, not in the same room."

He quickly sets down the tray on the round table where Janice set up the chair for lunch. "Aston—"

"Don't call me by my name! Get away! You're not supposed to know me by that name. I'm thirteen forty-two." For once it feels good to hide behind that number.

He steps closer to the bed, and I lunge backwards around the bedpost and towards the window. I feel the cool spring breeze bring in the scents of the season. Pollen and plants and grass. I can't look out to the world just yet, however. My eyes are glued to the Recipient in my room, the enemy, our ruling class, the thief of our bodily goods.

He takes another step, and I find myself lifting my foot onto the windowsill without looking. Death is what comes to those found in a Recipient's presence anyway. To die from flight out a window might be less painful.

He places his hands out in front of him to stop me. "Okay, okay, Thirteen forty-two, will you please just step away from the window?"

"Not until you leave."

"How can you say that? You used to bump into me so easily; now you can't breathe the same air as me?"

"You lied to me!" My yell scratches my throat, and my head starts to pound again. "Besides, I was raised to believe my breath would kill the likes of *you*." I spit the last word with as much hatred as I can muster. Though standing with one foot, teetering over the edge of an unknown depth, takes every bit of my energy at the moment.

"Clearly we proved that theory wrong when we breathed air in much closer quarters. Embraces even."

"Leave!" I yell. How dare he remind me of the very act that almost killed me. That might have killed my family for all I know. I look at the tray on the table and realize they could still be killing me. The tray is filled with food, some towering on top of more food. Perhaps this is the fattening up of the Donor, make her well before you cook her, or drain her in this case. Adakin Malloy's words ring through my ears, *You don't need consent to bleed a Donor in a self-induced coma.* I shiver as the breeze pushes me back in, and I teeter on the windowsill. My head feels separate from my body before it reattaches. Torrin, Papa, are they alright? I don't know how much longer I can balance myself on this window.

"I can't leave," he says. "I'm the head nurse."

My knees give way, and I find the dark dreams that consumed me take over again as I lean out the window. Marcus is there in an instant, gripping my wrist, and against my will I am again in the arms that so often found me through the market and around corners. Marcus lifts me, and I slump against his chest.

A hand brushes the top of my head. Marcus's voice is soft and rich as he whispers close to my face and lays me onto the bed. "I knew you'd find a way into my arms somehow. Though I never considered you the fainting type."

"Get away from me." My voice is more deflated than angry, which makes me angrier. "You're a monster."

"You always did know how to humble me. Oh how I've missed the little *v* in your—"

I cringe as deep into the pillow as I can, away from his touch. His hand stops mid-air.

"You put my whole family's life in danger," I whisper. "Are they alright?"

His face creases now, with a guilt I have never seen on him before. It almost makes me sad for him until I realize he may be sad for the loss of my family. "They're fine. I was not able to save your contracted amount for them, but they're fine for now. Your contract is void. It was part of the deal."

I try to move, and he helps me sit up against the back of the bed. I don't protest him near me this time since there is clearly no way I can move on my own. And he is evidently the mighty head nurse Janice spoke of, the only one that can tell me anything. I scowl at him again.

"There's my Aston. Mad at me for catching you when you fell and helping you to the bed. Furious with me for saving your life from prison and rescuing your family."

"You're the reason we were in danger in the first place. You're a Recipient."

"And you're ungrateful." He answers my scowl with a tired, lowered head and raised eyebrows.

I can't look at those eyes. The ones I painted and never touched-up because I could never make them as perfect as the ones before me. I was right that he was free of the serum like me, but only because of his heritage, not because of his rebel side.

"Yes, I'm a Recipient. But I'm a Recipient that saved your life."

"I've fallen before and lived."

"I'm not talking about the fall." He shivers as if he is imagining a much worse death that had been my fate.

I turn my head away from him, analyzing a cream-colored sofa against the far wall. "Where am I?" I ask, ready to finally get answers. He clears his throat and stands, then walks around the bed and retrieves the tray of food.

"How about you eat..." He comes closer, and the smell of the ham and cheese and the sight of plump grapes taunt me. "...and I'll talk?"

He rests the silver tray on my lap, and I pick from the choices. A hardboiled egg, free of shell, sits in a tiny goblet. It shines divinely, tempting me.

"I take that as a yes."

The cold, soft egg dries my mouth instantly and clogs it up in a mucky mess. I reach for the juice in a larger crystal goblet by the bowl of grapes. It washes down with difficulty, I nod to him to go on and as a way to get the food down.

"You're in Bloomfield."

The lump of egg in my chest inches its way down with the juice as I sputter and cough and gulp. I bend over the tray, trying to swallow and breathe again.

"Bloomfield? You mean—"

"Recipient land, yes. This is my house. This room was built for you."

"Why? How?"

I look at the window I almost dropped out of and realize I would have fallen in Recipient territory. Even if I hadn't died from the fall, I would have died in the hands of the Recipients below.

"We proved the system wrong, you and I. Aston, we were together for weeks, months, closer than any other Recipient and Donor has ever been." He looks at his hands and blushes under his eyelashes at his own words. "And I got healthier and stronger faster than any other Recipient."

I look at his ruddy cheeks and remember he is my Recipient. That it is my blood that runs under his skin. I look away as anger rises up from the thought. This boy has been stealing my kisses and my heart and my blood this whole time.

"I convinced my grandfather and scientists to do a trial experiment. To maybe prove that being integrated with our own Donors actually increases our chances of survival, not weakens our chances."

I look out into the blue sky of the Recipients' town. It looks as blue as our own.

"Of course there are scientists that claim my success is due to your high blood numbers. That your blood is so rich is why I healed quicker. So we have another Donor as well. Your friend, Lazuli, the low-numbered tattletale."

My head whips back to him, realizing the dream of my dead bird friend is possibly not an omen after all. Lazuli? Alive? My head spins from the fast movement or maybe the news.

"She has her own house here as well, as a control."

"Control?"

He points at the tray, and I stuff my face with bread to hear more.

"Yes, every experiment has a control to prove the results. I will receive—" He pauses as he eyes me, suddenly self-conscious to talk with me about this issue. He has been secretly taking my blood for months now, but face to face he can't seem to say it.

"My blood. You will take my blood."

"Yes, and hers too. To make sure my theory is correct. I am certain it is, Aston, and then we can be together. We can start a new system and bring down the walls between our lands. Our own version of a rebellion...just, following the laws as well."

My eyes fall from his face and zone out on his clean, white shirt. Poor Marcus, blinded by this love he thinks he feels for me. He loves what I have done for him without really loving me, a person he knows so little about. What kind of love can exist with such secrets and danger and threats? Doesn't he see we are separated in more ways than one? Geographically, yes, but also mentally, emotionally, in *every way* we are separated. Our Donor deaths were minimized, our life was simplified and coerced. We, the Donors, were made separate because of a disease called indifference, something the Recipient leaders wanted to breed. Can't he see there will never be a "together"? There will always be walls. What kind of rebellion follows rules anyway?

"How'd you do it?" I say, leaning into my pillows, exhausted from the drama. "How did you sneak into Donor territory and never get caught?"

"Donors only see what they're supposed to see." The sigh that escapes him as he stares off into space sounds mournful and experienced. He speaks of us as if we are dummies, puppets on strings, and heat fills my chest with defensive rage until I realize he is right. Hadn't my papa and I noticed the serum long before my donation day?

"Wear dirty clothes, mess up my hair, and suddenly I am a sick Donor no one cares about, instead of the poor Recipient everyone feels sorry for and wants to save. Meeting you was like I was finally alive. You made me better before your blood ever entered me. The day I ran into you I made up the invitations to search you out. The day you didn't rip open the letter I had my first donation from you."

My mind recalls the time I ran into him in front of the trade store when I admired his healing face. I contributed it to cutting back on donations, but he was really filled with my blood. My own blood stood right before me over and over again, lying to my face. My head spins again as I lay limp in the bed.

His voice is changed when he continues, low and gruff as if recalling painful memories. "My family tried two other Donors on me, you know."

His words have a strange effect on my heart, yet I push it away. He is a Recipient. He lied to me. He almost killed me and my family. I will not have pity for him. I will not.

"I wanted to find my Donor on my own since the ambassadors

were doing such a poor job of it. I admit, I quickly became addicted to you. Not your blood or what you had to offer, but you. I arranged more 'chance meetings' than what was probably necessary. Your blood made me healthy, but your presence made me well again." His tone changes, and his face drops. "I knew Donor territory was poorer, but I had no idea..." He looks up at the wall, to the window where I almost fell, and then back to me. "I had no idea how caged in Donors were. I decided eventually I would stop making you run into me, and *choose* me instead."

I look into his eyes and see the compassion that has taken over his form. This is what the system wanted the Recipients to avoid. To care about the blood would mean to care about the person. They are controlled as much as we are it seems, fed a feast of lies, but Marcus found the truth. I picture the night in the coat closet under the stairs, how timid he was, how he mentioned being in his arms on purpose was so much more wonderful.

My heart starts to soar at the memory, and I blink my eyes hard to push it aside. Nothing changes who he is and who I am.

"So it was fate?" I say, avoiding his eyes. "You just decided to go on an excursion into Donor territory and ran into me?"

The crinkling of his face into a grimace draws my attention. Shame? "Not exactly," he says. "I snooped into my grandfather's study to find records of the highest numbers. He had a strange file that held secret testings of several Donors."

"Secret?" My face goes numb as I immediately picture the old technician standing on my doorstep that fateful day.

"Yes. Undocumented test results. For some reason, certain Donors were tested before their test day. Some were from New Ohio or New Minnesota. They were all high, but yours was the highest, so I searched out your file's information." Something crosses his face worse than the grimace. It's as if he can't bear to look at me anymore. When he turns away and steps toward the window with his arms folded, my heart constricts with fear.

"What?" I can't think of anything else to say. My body feels so drained, and my mind is clogged with fatigue, confusing information and memories. "You found me from those test results?" I ask.

"Not at first, no." His voice is barely audible. He doesn't turn around, only stares out the window. The curtains brush against his black slacks. "A ridiculously high antibody rate that was local but not donating. Local would be easier to obtain, and it was such a high number I just knew it would make me better. But I was stuck. How to get the blood if the Donor wasn't donating?"

The way he refers to the Donor confuses me more. I know he's talking about me, but my mind can't follow the conversation fast enough.

He turns around, now with pleading sorrowful eyes. "You have to understand, Aston, I didn't know then what I know now. I was raised to just see the Donor as a means to our existence, not as real people."

My head aches from my confused brow. What is he trying to say? "What else was in my file, Marcus? How did you find me?"

He turns away again when he speaks. His slumped frame is silhouetted by the bright sunshine coming through.

"There was a location. A town. A few more bits of information. About the Donor's source of income. There was enough income to explain why the Donor didn't see the need to donate. All I wanted was to live a little longer."

I think I understand what he is saying before he finishes and long before I react. I first can't breathe. Then my eyes begin to harden as I picture again Greg shouting into the screen. Papa's words on that horrible day scream through my mind, *They knew her blood numbers, and when she didn't donate they...* I suck in a breath and ignore how it stings my ribs as I recall the person I ran into on the street when I ran toward the flames that day.

"It was you!"

He turns around. His face is distorted into pure pain and regret.

"You were who I ran into that day. That tried to keep me from running toward the fire."

He doesn't deny it. He only stares at me mournfully as I make the connection.

"You were on that street because you were the Recipient in the power plant? You were—" I can't finish the thought. It's too much. Tears are streaming down my face now as I realize the truth. I beat myself up for months, blamed myself for what happened at the plant, for the death of Greg and what happened to his family, to Oliver. But here stands before me the whiny brat of a Recipient who didn't think of us as people, who took it in his own hands to force me into the donation facility. "You." I sob softly. "You *are* a monster."

"Aston, I didn't know...I didn't think—"

"You *did* think. You thought of yourself. And all this time I thought I was the selfish one. You killed people, Marcus. You *killed* people. People I knew!"

"My grandfather said it was—"

"I think we can all agree now that he is not someone to be trusted."

Marcus opens his mouth but then closes it and lets his head droop.

"I think I need to rest some more," I say, falling heavily into the pillows, whimpering like a wet, wounded dog.

He steps to remove the tray.

"Leave it," I command without looking at him.

I once said I would bleed for Marcus and not them. Now I will be forced to bleed for him knowing he is the very "them" I hate.

"I'm sorry, Aston..." He hesitates with an outstretched hand as if he is considering a caress along my cheek. I curl up facing the food tray on the nightstand, hoping he doesn't since I'm too tired to pull away.

I close my eyes, squeezing the tears out from the corners. I hear the click of the door, and when I peek through my blurry vision, I spy something hidden under the plate of food.

I stretch forth my aching arm and retrieve a rolled-up piece of paper. Falling back into the bed, I scroll it open. It's rough from repeated recycling, a paper from my Donor town, not the soft smooth paper of the Recipients.

On it is a charcoal sketch of a seabird. Its wings are outstretched and free. I don't know my seabirds well, but I know this bird is a gannet.

I guess he's not the dying Romeo I pegged him to be. He was the one that was real the whole time. He was the life when Marcus meant death. How different things might have been if I let Gannet tell me about the resistance that day.

This well-hidden note gives me strength to step from my bed, and I hobble over the new wooden floor, my legs creaking instead of the floorboards. As I near the window, the sounds and smells of spring increase, and I blink the tears away, facing the bright sun. My eyes soon adjust, and I see below me a beautiful garden, not the functional, humble vegetable garden like my Papa's, but one with flowers of every kind. Some I recognize from the round table in this room. Rows of flowering trees and blossoming vines map against grass like the golf course. It is fenced in by a stone wall covered in ivy, and beyond it the sight is breathtaking. Not a single building looks crumbled or even salvaged from the war. Every one of them looks brand new. With white brick and white sidings and shiny white-tiled roofs that look like screens. Their roads are all the smooth white pavement that run around our tracks and mini trams, like the one that took me to the ball. So many maglevs. I wouldn't be surprised if every person here had their own.

Every home has grass like the golf course and manicured gardens as if for sport instead of necessity. The spectrum of color against the white streets and buildings makes me wonder if I have been drugged from the food after all. There isn't a spec of brown or destruction anywhere. After the wonder dies down, my stomach starts to lurch. Is this the real reason they have kept us so separate after all? To not know what we are missing. To not see how very poor and unimportant we really are.

I look at the sketch on the Donor paper again. It seems to speak to me as if the bird is shaped out of words instead of lines. Hang on, he says to me. Hang on until Gannet comes.

Two magnets will run away from each other until one of them turns around. I know now I'm facing the right direction. I will bide my time waiting for the resistance, and then I will fight with them. I will fight for Gannet, for my family, for Mrs. Price and Lazuli. I will fight for my blood.

ACKNOWLEDGMENTS

Big thank you to my husband, the biologist, who spent countless nights talking with me about viruses. Without his support, encouragement, and time dedicated to helping with the kids so I could write, this never would have been possible. He never once let me minimize my accomplishments yet waved them on a banner and celebrated my milestones. He made me believe in myself. He made me better.

I'd like to thank my children for not killing themselves and letting me write, my parents for supporting me, and my friends who cheered me on.

Big shout out to my critique group and especially Amy Michelle Carpenter who was my very first reader, fan, and advocate for my writing.

I'd like to thank Holli Anderson for getting excited about my book and making this publication happen.

Thanks to all my many beta readers- I loved watching your reactions through the process of reading. Any and all readers are welcome to send me their thoughts and reactions too. I actually love that part more than the writing.

ABOUT THE AUTHOR

C. F. Kreitzer was born in Low Moore, VA next to graffiti that read, "if you ain't from Low Moore, you ain't got a hair," which probably explains her thick curly hair. She now lives in Utah, happily far away from mosquitoes and humidity, with her husband, five kids, two dogs, and a gecko.

This has been an
Immortal Production